PRAISE FOR NATASHA PRESTON'S BESTSELLING THRILLERS

THE LAKE

"An eerie thriller reminiscent of summer horror movies that will keep readers on edge." —*Kirkus Reviews*

THE TWIN

"This fast-paced thriller will be a hit." —*SLJ*

THE LOST

"A fast-paced, plot-driven page-turner for fans of darker mysteries." —*Kirkus Reviews*

"A deeply disturbing tale that explores what can push someone to kill and what people will do to survive." —*PW*

YOU WILL BE MINE

"Another nail-biting thriller . . . heart-stopping suspense." —*RT Book Reviews*

"Keeps readers on edge. . . . Preston's thriller vibe throughout is excellently sustained. A great addition to the thriller shelves. Recommended for fans of Stephen King, Jennifer Barnes, and Ally Carter." —*SLJ*

"An homage to a nostalgic Fear Street novel. . . . An enjoyable blend of mystery and horror." —*Booklist*

"A fresh take on a murder mystery thriller. Rich with plot twists and suspense, readers will not want to put it down." —*VOYA's Teen Perspectives*

BOOKS BY NATASHA PRESTON

The Cellar

Awake

The Cabin

You Will Be Mine

The Lost

The Twin

The Lake

The Fear

THE TWIN

THE LAKE

NATASHA PRESTON

DELACORTE
PRESS

The Twin text copyright © 2020 by Natasha Preston
The Twin cover photograph copyright © 2020 by Marie Carr/Arcangel
The Lake text copyright © 2021 by Natasha Preston
The Lake cover art copyright © 2021 by Kristy Campbell/Arcangel Images

All rights reserved. Published in the United States by Delacorte Press, an imprint of Random House Children's Books, a division of Penguin Random House LLC, New York.

This work contains two previously published works, *The Twin* and *The Lake*. *The Twin* and *The Lake* were originally published separately and in paperback in the United States by Delacorte Press, an imprint of Random House Children's Books, a division of Penguin Random House LLC, in 2020 and 2021 respectively.

Delacorte Press is a registered trademark and the colophon is a trademark of Penguin Random House LLC.

Visit us on the Web! GetUnderlined.com

Educators and librarians, for a variety of teaching tools, visit us at RHTeachersLibrarians.com

Library of Congress Cataloging-in-Publication Data is available upon request.
ISBN 978-0-593-57026-5 (pbk.) — ISBN 978-0-593-57030-2 (ebook)

First Edition

Random House Children's Books supports the First Amendment and celebrates the right to read.

Penguin Random House LLC supports copyright. Copyright fuels creativity, encourages diverse voices, promotes free speech, and creates a vibrant culture. Thank you for buying an authorized edition of this book and for complying with copyright laws by not reproducing, scanning, or distributing any part in any form without permission. You are supporting writers and allowing Penguin Random House to publish books for every reader.

CONTENTS

The Twin   1

The Lake   383

NATASHA PRESTON

NEW YORK TIMES BESTSELLING AUTHOR OF *THE CELLAR*

THE TWIN

DELACORTE
PRESS

For Jon and Rosa.
Thank you for everything.

1

I dig the tips of my yellow-painted fingernails into the firm leather seat as Dad drives us home on the verge of breaking the speed limit. He's anxious to get back, but I would rather he slowed down. My stomach dips, and I hold my breath, squeezing my eyes closed as he takes a sharp corner.

With my muscles locked into place, I raise my eyes to the rearview mirror. Thankfully, Dad's eyes are fixed on the road, but there's a tightness to them that's unsettling. He's a good driver, and I trust him with my life, but I'm not a fan of this speed.

The car, a black Mercedes, is immaculate and still smells brand-new a year on, so I'm surprised that he's driving so fast on dusty country roads.

Everything is going to be different now, and he seems to be in a hurry to start our new life.

It's not right. We need to slow down, savor the ease of what our lives used to be, because the new one waiting for us in just five minutes, I don't want. Things weren't perfect before, but I want my old life back.

The one where Mom was still alive.

It's spring, her favorite season. Flowers have begun to brighten our town, turning the landscape from a dull green to a rainbow of color. It's my favorite time of year, too, when the sun shows itself and the temperature warms enough so you don't need a coat.

I'm always happier in spring. But right now, it might as well be winter again. I don't feel my mood lifting, and I definitely don't care that I'm not wearing a stupid coat.

My twin sister, Iris, is in the front passenger seat. She's staring out the window, occasionally starting a short conversation. It's more than I've done. There's been nothing but silence from me. It's not because I don't care; it's because I don't know what to say. There are no words for what has happened.

Everything I think of seems dumb and insignificant. Nothing is big enough to fill the enormous void left by our mom.

The warm spring sun shines into the car, but it's not strong enough to hurt my eyes. I don't want to close them again anyway. Every time I do, I see her pale face. So pale she didn't look real. Her once rosy cheeks gone forever. It was like staring at a life-size porcelain doll.

I wish I hadn't gone to the funeral home to see her. My last image of her will be her lifeless body.

When I go back to school, I'll be fine. I'll swim and study until it doesn't hurt anymore.

Or I'll want that to work, but I know it's going to take more than a couple of distractions to make the pain disappear.

We turn down our road and my toes curl in my tennis shoes.

I swallow a lump that leaves my throat bone-dry.

Dad slows, pulling into our drive and parking out front. Our house feels like it's in the middle of nowhere, but there are about ten houses nearby and it's a five-minute drive into town. I love the quiet and the peace of my hometown, but I feel like it's going to drive me crazy. Right now I need loud and fast-paced. I need distractions and lots of them.

Iris gets out of the car first, her butt-length, silky blond hair blowing in the warm breeze. She's home with me and Dad forever now.

Our mom died after falling off a bridge while out running two weeks ago. She was by a farm and the land was uneven and hilly. It had been raining and there was mud on the ground. The rail on the steep side of the short bridge was low, there more for guidance than safety, and she slipped off. The bridge wasn't very high, apparently, but she hit her head and died instantly. That's what the police told us.

Mom ran to keep fit and healthy so she could be around for me and Iris longer, but it ended up killing her.

Her death is still impossible to process. I haven't lived with my mom or Iris for six years, since she and Dad divorced, but her permanent absence weighs heavy in my stomach like lead.

When I was ten and our parents sat me and Iris down to explain they were separating, I had been relieved. It had been coming for a long time, and I was sick of hearing arguments while I pretended to sleep upstairs. The atmosphere was cold at best, our parents barely speaking but smiling as if I couldn't see through the crap mask.

Iris and I have never had a conversation about it, but the separation was a surprise to her. She shouted and then she cried while I sat still, silently planning how I would tell them I wanted to live with Dad. It wasn't an easy choice for anyone, but we had to make one. Dad and I had always been close; we share a lot in common, from movies and music to hobbies and food. He's the one to give us clear guidelines, without which I would crumble. Mom was laid back, sometimes too much, and I would never get anything done.

Besides, Mom always wanted to live in the city, and I never liked how densely it's populated.

Mom and Iris moved out; then they moved away to the city. I have spent school holidays flitting between houses, sometimes missing out on time with my twin thanks to conflicting schedules. She would be with Dad while I was with Mom.

None of our family members, friends, or even neighbors could understand it. You don't separate twins. I get it—we're supposed to be able to communicate without speaking and literally feel each other's pain. But Iris and I have never been like that. We're too different.

We're not close, so although she's my sister, it feels more like a distant cousin is moving in.

She still has her bedroom here, which she and Dad redecorated last year when she visited for the summer. But she's brought a *lot* of stuff with her from Mom's. The trunk is full of her things.

I watch her walk to the front door as Dad cuts the engine. She has a key to the house, of course, so she lets herself in.

Dad scratches the dark stubble on his chin. He usually shaves every morning. "Are you okay, Ivy? You've barely said a word the entire time we've been on the road."

"I'm fine," I reply, my voice low and gravelly.

Fine, the modern *I'm not okay* definition of the word, is what I mean here. Everything has changed in the blink of an eye. Two weeks is all it has taken to turn my world upside down. And what about Iris? She was closer to Mom than anyone. What right do I have to fall apart when she has lost even more than me?

"You can talk about it. Whenever you want."

"I know, Dad. Thanks."

His eyes slide to the house. "Let's go inside."

I take a long breath and stare at the front door.

I don't want to go inside. When I go back in there, our new normal starts. I'm not ready to let go of the old just yet. Until I walk through that door, my twin isn't living with us again because our mom has died.

That's all total rubbish, obviously. Not walking through that door changes nothing, but I can pretend. I need longer.

"Ivy?" Dad prompts, watching me in the mirror with caution in his blue eyes, almost afraid to ask me if everything is okay again in case I crumble.

"Can I go to Ty's first? I won't be long."

His brow creases. "We *just* got home. . . ."

"I'll be back soon. I need a little time. It will give you an opportunity to check in with Iris too. She's going to need you a lot, sometimes without me."

He opens his door. "One hour."

I get out, my heart lighter knowing I have an extra sixty minutes, which I can stretch to seventy before he'll call. "Thanks, Dad."

Shutting the car door, I look back at the house.

What?

The hairs on my arms rise. Iris is watching me from the second-floor window.

But she's not in her bedroom.

She's in mine.

2

Tyler lives down the road, so I get there in under a minute and knock on the door.

He opens up and his leaf-green eyes widen. "Ivy." Reaching out, he tugs me into the tightest hug. His arms wrap around my back, and I sink into him. "Hey," he whispers. "You okay?"

"Not really," I mutter against his Ramones T-shirt.

"Come on." His arms loosen but he doesn't let go completely, his fingers sliding between mine as he leads me inside. "When did you get home?"

"A couple of minutes ago. I haven't been in the house yet."

He eyes me curiously as we walk up to his bedroom, his head turning back every second step. Even though his parents are at work, he leaves the bedroom door open. Rule one. If we break it, we'll never be allowed to spend time together without a chaperone.

Neither of us will break it.

I let go of his hand and collapse onto his bed. His pillow is so soft, and it smells like him. It's comforting and everything I need right now.

The bed dips beside me as Ty sits down. Running his hand through his surfer style chestnut hair, he asks, "Do you want to talk?"

I press against the ache in my chest. "I don't know what to say."

"I'm not your dad or sister, Ivy. I'm not looking for comforting words. You don't need to pretend you're okay for me. Tell me how you feel."

I roll from my side to my back so I can see him. "I feel lost, and I feel stupid for being such a wreck."

"Babe, your mom died. Why do you feel stupid?"

Shrugging, I shake my head and swallow so I don't cry. "I don't know. I'm supposed to be more together. Don't I have a reputation for having a cold heart?"

"No, that means you don't cry when whatever boy band breaks up, not that you're made of stone and don't cry for your mom."

I love that he doesn't know the names of any relevant boy bands.

Iris has always been the emotional one. I'm the logical one. Unless something *really* affects my life, I'm not going to cry over it. What I rock at doing, though, is stressing and overthinking.

"Iris hasn't cried once that I know of," I tell him. "And all

I've done is cry. It's like we've reversed roles." Dad and I arrived at their house eleven days ago, the day Mom died. Iris was like a robot. She got up, showered, dressed, and ate. She tidied and watched TV. Iris continued her routine as usual, but it was all in silence as if Dad and I weren't there. She only started talking properly again this morning.

"Everyone handles grief differently."

I look up at his ceiling. Everyone deals with all sorts of things differently; I just didn't realize that Iris and I would walk through this totally out of character. We may look the same, besides her hair being about five inches longer, but we're nothing alike. Now we're swapping parts of our personality?

Sighing, I stare straight into his eyes and whisper, "I don't know how to help her. I barely know her anymore."

"You can't fix it. You only have to be there for her. There's nothing anyone can do to accelerate the grief process; you have to let it happen."

I don't like that at all. I like my control. If there's a problem, I find a solution. I don't handle it well when there's nothing I can do.

He chuckles. "You'll learn how to do that, I promise."

Sighing, I blink rapidly as tears sting the backs of my eyes. "My mom is gone."

"I know, and I'm so sorry."

Get it together.

"Mom asked me to visit for the weekend last month," I tell him.

"Ivy, don't do this."

"I told her I couldn't because I was spending the weekend at the pool to prepare for a swim meet I missed because she died."

"Ivy," he groans. "You had stuff to do, and it's not like that's never happened before."

I sigh into the sinking feeling in my gut. "Logically, I understand that."

"There's no way you could have known what would happen, babe."

I'm not all that good at forgiving myself. Everyone else, sure, but not myself.

Ty shakes his head. "You can't live up to the standards you hold yourself to. No one's perfect."

All right, I'll give him that. But I constantly strive for perfect. The perfect grades, fastest swimmer, solid circle of friends, real relationships. I'm setting myself up to fail, I get that, and I would stop if I could.

"It feels like Iris is only back to visit. We haven't lived together in *six years*."

His fingertips brush my blond hair. "You'll all adjust, I promise."

We will but we shouldn't have to. Mom was too young to die. Iris and I are too young to be without her. "I want things to go back to the way they were."

"You don't want Iris there?" he asks softly.

"No, that's not it. Of course I want her with us. I wish she didn't have to be, you know? So much has changed, and I'm not ready for any of it. Mom is supposed to be here. Who is going to take me prom dress shopping? She was going to scream when I graduate and totally embarrass me. Who will cry first when I try on wedding dresses or when I have a baby? There is so much that she's going to miss. I don't know how to do it all without her."

I have Dad, but all those things won't be the same without Mom.

"Ivy," he says, brushing his fingers across my face and down my cheek. "She will be there for all of that and more."

Yeah, only she won't. Not in the way I need.

"Iris was in my room," I say, changing the subject before I lose the control I've only just regained after yesterday.

"Okay . . ."

"She was watching me from my room when I left to come here."

"Did you tell her you were going out?"

"No."

"Maybe she was curious."

I bite my bottom lip. Maybe, but what was she doing in my room in the first place? Hers is right next to mine, so she could see me outside from her window too.

"Hmm," I reply, not entirely sure where I'm going with this. I've been in her room, so it's not a big deal. "Yeah, maybe. It just seems weird."

Ty lies down beside me. "It's not weird for her to want to be close to you. There's a lot of change for her, and she's the one who's had to move, leaving behind all of her friends."

I wince at his words. "Yeah, I know."

Iris has lost so much, and if being around me and my stuff helps her even a little bit, then it's fine with me. Oh God, and I'm here. She was in my room probably wanting to be close to me, and I left.

I left her!

My heart sinks to my stomach. "I should go."

His hand freezes on my jaw. "Already?"

"I have an hour, but . . ." I've already been a terrible sister, no need to continue that.

He nods. "You need to be home with your dad and Iris."

"Thanks for understanding, Ty."

Well, this was brief, but worth it. We get off the bed and walk downstairs past the line of pictures showing Ty growing up. The last one is of us both, arms around each other smiling at the school Christmas dance.

Ty put things into perspective for me. I've been cooped up in a bubble of me, Dad, Iris, and Mom's side of the family—I haven't gotten enough distance to give myself any clarity.

I follow him out of the house, chewing my lip as I go. I've been so focused on me and how I feel that I haven't really thought about Iris. Maybe we will grow closer, and that can be the one good thing to come out of this tragedy.

"Call me if you need anything," he says, holding on to the edge of the front door.

I lean in and give him a quick kiss. "I will. Thanks." Then I turn and run along the sidewalk all the way back to my house.

My feet hit the asphalt so hard it sends sparks of pain along my shins, but I don't slow down. I pass our neighbors' houses in a blur, their pruned hedges and rosebushes flashing by. Sucking in air that burns, I reach out and almost slam right into the front

door. Bowing my head, I grip the door handle, my lungs screaming for the oxygen I've deprived them of during my sprint.

"Dad? Iris?" I call as I walk into the house.

"In the kitchen," Dad replies.

I swing left and find Dad sitting alone at the table.

"Where's Iris?" I ask, breathless.

"Upstairs. She didn't want to talk."

Oh. It was selfish of me to run off the second we pulled up.
"I'm going to check on her."

Dad nods. "And I'll start dinner. What do you want?"

I shrug. This past eleven days have been nutrient free. We've
grabbed whatever food we could manage, usually sandwiches and
takeout. I feel hungry, but when food is placed in front of me, I
can barely stomach a bite.

"Anything," I reply, heading upstairs.

Iris must feel so lost. I don't know if she's had much contact
with her friends, but I do know I haven't seen her on her phone
at all. She needs them now, probably more than she needs me
and Dad.

I climb the stairs, tying my long wavy hair in a knot on top
of my head, and knock on her door. "Iris, it's me. Can I come in?"

"Sure," she replies.

Okay, I was expecting some resistance.

I open the door and offer a small smile as I head into the
room. She's sitting on the edge of her bed, doing nothing. Her
long hair fans around her body like a cloak.

"Dumb question, but . . . how do you feel?" I ask.

She shrugs one shoulder. "I'm not sure there's a word for it."

Her eyes are sunken, ringed with dark circles that make her look a lot older than she is. I don't think she's sleeping well either.

We have the same shade of dark blond hair and the same pale blue eyes.

"Well, do you need anything?" Besides the obvious.

"I'm good."

Raising my eyebrows, I move deeper into her room. "Are you?"

She meets my gaze. "Are *you?*"

"No, I'm not." I wring my hands. "We can talk . . . if you want?"

We don't talk, not about real, deep stuff, anyway. She has her friends for that, and I have mine. It's actually kind of sad how we've missed out on that close twin bond. It's the only thing I regret about staying with Dad when Iris moved away with Mom.

She tilts her head. "Can we talk?"

"Well, I know that's not usually our thing, but it can be. I mean, I'm willing . . . and we are twins."

"We shared a womb, share a birthday and DNA, but I've never felt like a twin. We never talk."

Okay, ouch. We used to talk when we were little. I remember being five and sneaking into each other's room at night. We didn't share because we were too different—her room candy pink and mine ocean blue. But it didn't matter after dark; we would make a den out of blankets, grab our flashlights, and talk about random fairy-tale things our imaginations would conjure.

Iris was going to marry a British prince and eventually become queen, and I was going to travel the world in an old Mustang like the one our grandad used to own.

Somewhere over time and our parents' separation, our silly dreams died, and we stopped sharing any new ones.

"Do you want to talk, Iris?"

Her haunted eyes look right through me. "I want so much more than that."

3

Neither of us speaks for what feels like hours. The silence stretches, and I pull my bottom lip between my teeth.

This shouldn't be so awkward.

"What do you mean you want so much more than that?"

What more is there to have if we're talking?

She finally moves and shuffles back on the bed until her back hits the wall. Clearing her throat, she says, "Obviously I mean I want to be sisters. *Properly.* We've never stopped being twins, but we stopped being friends."

I blink twice before I reply. "I want that too. I don't enjoy feeling like I only have a sibling during school holidays." Iris and I need to stick together. We might be worlds apart, but we have both lost the same mom.

She gives me a fleeting smile. "Maybe you should sit down then."

"Okay." I let go of my hands and sit on her bed. But that's about as far as I know where to go with this. Words still evade me. Or the right ones do, anyway. I could have a thousand different conversations about shows on Netflix, books, and swimming. I'm not sure any of that is going to help me right now.

"Will you tell me about school and your friends? I assume I'll be enrolling."

"Oh. Yeah, okay." Of course she's going to have to enroll at my high school. I didn't think of that, but she can't go to her old one; it's over an hour away. "So, you've met Haley and Sophie. I trust those girls with my life."

Iris smiles. "I remember Haley and Sophie from last summer. They seemed nice."

"They are." We met when we joined the swim team as freshmen and have been besties ever since.

"Do you think they'll mind me hanging around with you?"

"You're my sister. Of course they won't mind."

"Thanks, Ivy. What about your boyfriend?"

"Ty. You'll get along with him too."

"Don't worry, I won't make myself a third wheel. It would just be nice to spend time with you. I . . . I don't want to be alone right now."

I shake my head. "I'm not worried about that, Iris. You can hang with me whenever you want." Since the first day of high school, Haley, Sophie, and I have been inseparable. I don't mind adding a fourth to our group, and I don't think they would either. Iris will probably make her own friends fast enough anyway; she's a cheerleader, not a swimmer like me and my friends. We have a cheerleading squad that I'm sure Iris can get on. Ty plays football, so he'll be able to introduce her to the team and hopefully make it easier for her to join. That's if she wants to continue cheerleading.

"Is there anyone I need to look out for at school? Like, the mean girls?"

I turn my nose up. "Ellie, cheer captain, so many blond highlights I'm surprised her hair hasn't fallen out, can be a bit snobby, but she's harmless."

Why does she want to talk about people at school and not Mom? I understand that she wants to make the transition as smooth as possible—there is no getting away from this situation—but we've only been home for twenty minutes.

"Iris, you do know that everything will be fine, don't you?"

She presses her lips together and looks away.

"You can tell me how you're feeling. You're not going through this alone."

Iris doesn't move an inch; her body is so still I move closer to see if she's still breathing. Her chest rises.

"I miss her," I say. "I don't see her for weeks, sometimes months, but I already miss her so much, I don't know if I'll ever get past it."

"Ivy," she whispers, her voice calm and cold. "Can we not do this right now, please?"

I take a breath, closing my eyes. "Sure, okay."

"I'm sorry. If you want to talk about her, talk to Dad."

Dad's a good listener. But he can't understand the way Iris can. I open my eyes and give her a smile. "Whenever you're ready."

Her pale eyes watch me closely, like we're playing chess and she's planning her next move. She's pretty unreadable to me. We haven't spent nearly enough time together over the last six years for me to know what all her expressions mean.

"Thank you, Ivy," she replies a little too formally to be sincere. *Back up, she needs time.* "I'll leave you to it, then," I say.

Iris doesn't move or respond, so I get up. *Okay, I'll go.* Turning around, I walk out of her room and pull the door shut.

What just happened there?

"Ivy, Iris," Dad shouts. "Pizza will be here soon."

"Okay, Dad," I reply, running down the stairs.

"I'm worried about her," I tell him.

He looks over his shoulder as he gets plates from the cupboard. "Iris?"

Duh. "Yeah, she's acting strange."

"Ivy . . ."

"No, I get how that sounds, and I know what's going on. But she was more interested in talking about school and my friends. She's talking about fitting in and having a new life here. Don't you think that's too soon?"

He shrugs. "This is new for all of us, Ivy. If that's what helps her at the minute, can it be bad?"

"Yes! Maybe. I can't imagine going back to school yet, let alone a *new* school." Though I don't have much choice. College scouts need to see me at my best. I have to get back in the pool if I want to go to Stanford. Dad can't afford to send me there, so I *need* a scholarship. To be perfect in the pool, I can't afford any more time off.

He tilts his head. "Honey, don't overthink this. We're all doing the best we can. Let her cope in her way."

"By pretending?"

"If that's what she needs, I think we can give her a little more time. Why is this bothering you so much? It's very early days."

I shrug. "I guess I thought we could talk about it, you know? We're going through the same thing." I need to talk about Mom. I need more than the few weeks each year I spent with her.

"You're trying to fix this," he says. "You see everything so black-and-white. I love that you have always been good at solving problems, sometimes before they even become problems, but there is no quick fix here. You can't do anything for Iris until she wants you to, so please focus on what *you* need. Do you want me to arrange grief counseling? I think it would be a good idea for you."

For me. Not for me and Iris. He's worried that I'll try and fix my grief too fast and make things worse. There's a rush with me because I hate when my life is off balance. Iris isn't ready to start at all.

"Yes," I reply. I'm all for talking through your issues, but I don't think a chat with Ty or my friends is going to work here. Therapy with a trained professional is the solution, so I want to do it. The sooner I can stop feeling like I'm treading water, the better.

"There is no fast-track with grief, though, Ivy," Dad says, reading my intention.

That's not true. Anything can be accelerated if done properly. I want to remember Mom without the heavy sadness and bitter anger. It's not fair that she's gone.

"That's not what I'm doing," I lie.

He doesn't believe me, but he doesn't get time to say so because the doorbell rings.

Saved by pizza.

4

In the end, no one ate much of the two large pizzas Dad ordered. I think he had about four slices—nowhere near his record—while Iris and I picked at one each.

I'm disappointed in myself, because I can eat pizza, but my stomach rejected every bite. When Iris and I were younger, we would eat two slices each, then have two for breakfast. We must have been four or so and thought we were cool. We'd eat a whole pizza between us, and the fact that it was over two days didn't take away from our amazement that we were so little and could do it.

Eating seems like such an odd thing to do when your world has been rocked. The same as other mundane things like household chores. It's all so pointless. I want to go to the therapist now, at ten-thirty at night, so I can get this over with and have things resemble some sort of normal again.

I'm in the bathroom, looking at my exhausted reflection in the mirror. Staring back at me are dull blue eyes. I don't remember the last time I got more than five hours of solid sleep, and it's been worse since Mom died. My mind doesn't shut off easily; I'm constantly thinking of things I need to do. I can usually tone it down if I train in the pool a couple extra times in the week or go for a long run.

Swimming is my first love. When I'm in the pool, I'm free. There is nothing but me and the water.

If there was a pool open now, I would go. Actually, going back to school is looking like a good idea, just for the access to the pool. But Dad wants me to take the rest of the week off and return when he enrolls Iris. I wanted that, too, but the thought of spending the next five days indoors, pretending things aren't as bad as they are and talking about friends, is suffocating.

I run my hands over my face. *A few more days . . . you can make it.*

Leaving the bathroom, I cross the hall. Iris must still be awake; I can hear movement from her room. There's no point in trying to talk to her again. Dad is right—she has to be ready to deal with Mom's death.

"Night," I say over my shoulder to Iris as I open my door.

Something in her room falls to the floor with a heavy thud. "Night, Ivy!" she replies.

Frowning, I turn toward her room. "You okay?"

"Just dropped a book."

I grip my door handle. I don't think she's willingly read a book since we were five. Unless that's another change in her.

Does she even have books here? I haven't noticed any, but I don't exactly take inventory of her room.

The noise was loud, though. What are her books made from, stone?

What is she doing in there, and why did it sound like a lie when she told me she dropped a book? I mean, unless she dropped it from the ceiling.

"Okay," I say, and close myself in my room.

Nerves flutter in my stomach. I push my palm into the center of my belly and wince. I don't enjoy feeling like something is majorly off, besides the obvious, and I don't know what it could be.

I don't trust my instincts right now, because I could well be feeling anxious over this being a situation that I have no control over.

Okay, you seriously need to sleep.

Shaking away as many of the swirling thoughts as I can, I climb into bed. This is the part where I lie awake for ages, my mind spinning with a million thoughts, each one of them fighting for time. It's where I make plans to silence the thoughts and worries, one by one.

I curl onto my side and tug my quilt up to my chin.

My eyes flit closed, and Mom's face enters my mind. She's been a prominent thought since she died, but there's nothing I can do about that. I can usually work through a problem in my head until it's solved and then move on to the next. Mom is a sticking point. I would do anything to have her back, but that can never happen. We're not in some fantasy novel.

Every night, I see her and think about her until I want to scream because I miss her so much.

I roll onto my stomach as if a change in position will make everything fall out of my head so I can sleep.

Next door, Iris moves around her room. Her footsteps aren't as light as she's trying to make them. If she's even trying to be quiet. Something scrapes across the carpet. It's almost eleven at night. Who rearranges furniture this late?

Unless she's taken up yoga.

But who does that *after* they've gone to bed? Maybe she does sleep yoga. Okay, I'm ridiculous.

I wish I could get some sleep. My thoughts would be much more rational.

Another thump hits my wall from her side.

For real? I already have countless thoughts that prevent me from falling asleep quickly as it is. I don't need Iris doing . . . whatever it is she's doing keeping me up too.

I don't want to get out of bed because I just got comfortable, so I pick up my phone and text Iris.

> Everything okay?

She takes a minute to reply.

> Fine. Why?

Oh, playing it like that, are we?

The banging?

Sorry, just organizing some things.
I'll be quiet now

Organizing what at this hour? She's not starting school yet; there will be plenty of time to make changes to her room.

Do you need help?

Yeah, I'm being polite. It'll be so annoying if she accepts my offer.

No, thanks. I'm kind of private about
my room and my things.

I relax my muscles and sigh. Good, I'm glad that I don't have to move. My body pulses with the ache of the day and sitting in some awkward position earlier.

Okay. Night.

I love how she's private and her room is off-limits but she has no issue walking into my space. Double standards much?

Putting my phone back on my nightstand, I close my eyes and wait.

Outside, the patter of rain slowly hits my window. It's soothing, the constant yet intermittent taps against the glass. The rain is always the best thing to take my mind off . . . well, my mind. I've tried listening to rain forest noises, but it does nothing for me.

I focus on the rain and breathe deeply until I eventually fall asleep.

5

Stretching my arms above my head, I yawn. It's early—6:05. The rain helped me fall asleep, but I woke up at 3:30 and was drifting in and out for the rest of the night—or morning. Whatever.

I'm tired. Fortunately, I'm used to being tired.

Mom kept popping back in my head in the early hours, consuming every thought. Some of them were facts; some took on a fictional route and ran with it. I know how she died, so why did my mind keep conjuring thoughts and images of her being hit or being drowned? Why did I think about her recovering from the fall and running away? That one was the cruelest, because there is no chance of her coming home. She didn't recover; I've seen her lifeless body. Which, in hindsight, isn't smart for someone with an overactive imagination.

She would never leave us by choice. Nothing could scare her away from her family.

So I tossed and turned for that whole time, worrying that I'll never get Mom out of my head. I don't want to picture her lying on the ground bleeding. Or whatever else I dream up.

The grief process needs to begin now; maybe then I'll get some peace. Or at the very least, I'll stop seeing my mom dead in different scenarios. I'll take that.

My feet hit the carpet as I swing out of bed. I curl my toes, feeling the thick pile under my bare feet.

I practically drag my heavy legs downstairs in search of caffeine.

The house is still and quiet. At this hour it always appears empty, like no one is living here at all. Dad and I don't have much stuff, so the house is a little on the bare side since Mom took all the house "bling," as she called it.

I walk into the kitchen and raise my hand for the light switch.

"Morning," Iris says.

Her chipper voice makes me jump. I flick the light on as my heart races, and Iris smiles. The blinds are shut, so it's still pretty dark.

She laughs. "I didn't mean to scare you."

"What are you doing here?" I ask, taking a breath.

"I live here now, Ivy."

God, my heart is still thumping. "No, I mean, in the kitchen. Sitting in the dark."

"I woke up and couldn't get back to sleep."

"But why are you sitting in the dark?"

"I like it."

She likes sitting alone in the dark in total silence.

"Uh, okay. Do you want coffee?" I ask.

Folding her arms, she rests them on the counter and watches me. "Please. It's nice to have someone make the coffee for me. Mom sometimes did it before she went for a run."

"Ugh, I love running, but I couldn't do it every day."

"Yeah, you and Mom probably had more in common than she and I did. You both like to exercise."

"You cheer," I say, grabbing two mugs from the cupboard as the coffee brews.

"I did. Now I'm not going to be doing anything."

I look over my shoulder. What a bleak view. "Why do you say that?"

"Dad doesn't want me to start school for another two weeks." She rolls her eyes. "Yet you can go back in four days. How is that fair?"

"He's worried about you, Iris. You're not only dealing with Mom's death, but you've also had to move away from everything you've known for the last six years. I'm going back to a school I know. You're going to be the new girl."

"I'm aware, but I'm not made of glass. I can handle a new school. Besides, it's not like this place is all new to me. I did live here once. In this very house."

She has a point. Iris was always the confident one, the kid who played outside. Mom would sit in front and watch her play with a couple of the neighbor's children. Shame that they moved away years ago, because Iris could probably do with seeing a familiar face—one that isn't exactly the same as hers.

"Talk to Dad. He's always been a good listener. If you're ready to start earlier, he'll let you."

At least, I think he will. He's nowhere near as laid back as Mom was, but he's still not great at denying his daughters something they want.

Her pale eyes gloss over like she's no longer listening, or she doesn't believe me. She taps a manicured fingernail on the marble countertop.

The coffeemaker stops and I put a mug down in front of her. I take the next stool, joining her in sitting.

"How are you feeling?" I ask.

Out of the corner of my eye, I see her lips purse. She's uncomfortable when I talk about Mom or ask how she's doing. It's been the same since Mom died. Iris has closed that part of her life completely.

"Fine. You?" she replies in a sharp tone.

She doesn't want to talk, and she doesn't want me to talk. "Yeah, I'm good. I'm going to call a therapist today. Have you thought about talking to someone?"

"Nope. But good for you."

"Okay," I reply, wrapping my hands lightly around the hot mug. "What do you want to do today?"

"I want to go out. No offense, but this house is kind of depressing. Now that I'm living here full-time, we need to decorate."

"Go for it." Iris has good taste; she decorated Mom's house

with her. It doesn't bother me if she wants to hang art or scatter throw cushions on the sofas. Dad is a major minimalist and he loves his gadgets, but I'm sure he wouldn't mind giving the house a little more personality.

"What are you girls doing up so early?"

Iris and I look to the doorway, where Dad is standing. His arms are folded like he's ready to give us the third degree. He's suspicious, but I don't know why.

"We couldn't sleep," I tell him.

"You're huddled together like when you were little and wanted something. Power in numbers?"

Iris laughs and flicks her hair over her shoulder. "We don't want anything, Dad."

"Maybe not right now. What do you want to eat?"

"Do you have Pop-Tarts?" Iris asks. "I haven't had those in years."

I sigh. "I can't go a week without having them."

Iris raises her eyebrows. "You got the better metabolism. I have to eat perfectly for this." She gestures down her body with her hand.

I don't think there's any difference in size. We both keep active, but Iris puts a lot more pressure on herself.

"Neither of you needs to change a thing," Dad says. He's very diplomatic. "I'll get the Pop-Tarts."

"There's coffee in the pot, Dad," I tell him. "So, I'd like to make an appointment with that therapist today. You still have the number, right?"

Dad slowly turns around. "Of course. I'll give Dr. Rajan a call. She comes highly recommended. Iris?"

Iris looks up and blinks slowly. "Yes, Dad?" she asks as if she doesn't know where he's going.

"Would you like me to make you an appointment too? It doesn't have to be the same therapist."

"No, thanks." She smiles tightly, her eyes dropping back to her coffee mug.

6

I don't know what it says about a therapist when they can see you immediately. Or, more to the point, what it says about me when she wants to see me immediately.

Either way, I'm in my bedroom getting dressed because Dr. Rajan managed to squeeze me in this morning.

Does Dad know that I haven't slept as well since Mom died, so he begged her for an emergency appointment? That would be incredibly embarrassing.

It was Dad who answered her questions; he was on his phone with her for ages. In his office, of course, so I don't know what he said. All I know is that he came back after speaking to her at nine and I have an hour to get to my appointment.

I'm overthinking. She probably had a cancellation. I have

taken plenty of appointments for my hair last-minute because someone canceled.

I zip my skinny jeans and tug a dark gray tank top over my head. I have Ty's hoodie in case it gets cooler. Actually, I have a lot of Ty's hoodies here. Also, now *my* hoodies. The sun has scorched away any sign of last night's rain, though, so I think it's going to be hot.

My phone rings and Ty's name flashes on the screen. I texted him about three minutes ago to tell him I'm off to have my head examined.

My session with Dr. Rajan is predominately about bereavement, but I'm not naïve enough to think that's where it's going to end. Not when I have a twin who moved home. I think she's going to say things and ask questions that go way beyond my mom's death. Maybe lots of them are connected. Maybe I'm overthinking. *Again.*

If I could get an off switch for my brain, that would be aces.

"Hey, Ty," I say into the phone.

"Right now? You're going to see someone *right now?*"

His voice is rushed, and he sounds like he's on high alert. He's worried. Ty knows that I find it hard to switch off and that I don't sleep well. But that's nothing new. That's always been me. He's worried this rush-job therapy session is more than the doctor having time to see me so soon.

I think I actually don't want to know. Ignorance can be bliss and all that.

"Like, right now. I'm slipping my shoes on as we speak. What do I say to her?"

"Um . . . I don't know. Let her ask the questions if you're not sure where to start. What happened last night or this morning to make this happen so suddenly?"

"Nothing, really. She has a session free this morning, I guess."

I don't want to worry him. Before me, he didn't worry much about anything. Ty is super laid back, except when it comes to me. It's sweet, but I hate that I cause him stress.

"Okay," he says hesitantly. "You can talk to me, too, you know? I get that you want to speak to a professional, and I'm all for it, but I'm here."

"I know you are, Ty, and I appreciate it."

But I don't want to completely fall apart in front of you. Ty has always been supportive and understanding, but we're teenagers in high school, and we don't need our lives to be dark and heavy.

I can deal with the sleepless nights. During the day it's not so bad. I can still be me and swim and hang with my friends. My chipper attitude begins to fade in the early evening, but by that point I'm usually home. I'll get used to it if I'm to have even less sleep long-term.

"Call me when you're done?"

"I will. Love you," I say.

"Love you, babe."

I hang up, put my phone in my bag, along with my water bottle, and grab my car keys off my dresser. Time to face therapy.

I walk downstairs with my heart thudding and palms sweating. This is something I want, so why do I feel so anxious? If I want to sit in silence for an hour, I can. There's no pressure. At least, I hope there won't be.

My idea of therapy is limited to what I've watched on TV, but the therapists definitely don't force you to talk if you don't want to.

Still, if I'm considering sitting in silence, why am I even going?

I know I'll talk. It's how you heal, how you move on from whatever you're grieving. If there's one thing I like, it's a solution to wrap up a problem in a neat little bow.

"Dad, I'm leaving," I shout as I reach the bottom of the stairs.

His office door opens down the hall and then his footsteps thud on the wooden floor. Dad works in insurance and deals mostly with large companies. Or something like that. He seems to be busy all the time and had to build an office on the house to work from home. It's where he spends most of his time.

"Are you sure you don't want me to take you?"

"No thanks, I'll be fine."

He steps forward and wraps me in a hug. His arms squeeze a touch too hard, and I wince.

"You're crushing me," I squeak.

"Sorry." He lets go and takes a step back. "I'm proud of you, Ivy."

"Thanks, Dad. Hey, where's Iris?"

"She went to her room, so I thought I would get some work done," he says. "You'd better go, or you'll be late."

Maybe I want to be late. So late that I have to reschedule. But that's a dumb idea, because if I keep putting it off, I'll always have this first-session anxiety. Once I'm past that, things will be easier. "Later, Dad."

I turn around and walk out of the house super slowly. Today I don't feel in a hurry to get anywhere.

My thumb slips over the unlock button on my key fob. I shake my hand and press the button again. This time my car clicks, and I get in.

You can do this, Ivy.

Mom would want me to do this. She would be right behind me, spurring me on. She and Dad have always been my biggest cheerleaders, and although I didn't live with her for most of the year, I've always been sure that she has my back.

I feel her with me now. In this car, willing me to start the engine and take the first step to helping myself.

So that's what I do. I turn the key in the ignition and pull off the drive.

Dr. Rajan's office is about thirty minutes away, so I crank the radio and let the music calm my frayed nerves.

Thirty-six minutes later, thanks to traffic, I pull into the parking lot, and the nerves are back with a vengeance.

7

Dr. Rajan is waiting for me inside. I have four minutes until my session starts. My hand is curled tightly around the steering wheel while my stomach buzzes. This is something that I need to do, and I want to do, but that doesn't make going in there and talking about my mom's death any easier.

Above me, the sky clouds over and shines bright gray. It's going to rain hard. I should get in there before it starts, but my body won't move.

Okay, stop being a baby.

I let go of the steering wheel, tug the door handle, and push the door open. The very second my foot touches the ground, I feel the first cold drop of water splat on the tip of my nose.

I get out, slam my door shut, and make a run for the building.

Dr. Rajan looks up as I rush into the foyer.

She smiles, her dark eyes shining with kindness. "You must be Ivy Mason?"

"Yeah." I smooth my hair down. "Hi, Dr. Rajan."

"Please, call me Meera. Before we start, can I offer you a glass of water?" she says, leading me into her office.

I have a feeling I'll need a drink if I'm going to be talking for an hour. "Water would be great, thanks," I reply, threading my fingers together behind my back.

Meera's office is nice. It's large enough for a dark oak desk and two brown leather sofas. The dark is softened with pale blue, pink, and white artwork and accessories. Her credentials are framed on the wall behind one of the sofas.

"Come on in and get comfortable."

"Which one?" I ask, looking between both sofas.

"Whichever one you want."

Stepping slowly, I choose the closer one and sit down. Meera places my water on the coffee table in the middle.

"Thanks."

She smiles again as she sits opposite me. "Would you like a blanket?"

"Ummmm," I say uncertainly. Why would I need a blanket? It's warm today.

She looks at a soft fleece cream blanket on the arm of the chair beside me. "Feel free to use the blanket. I want you to be as relaxed and comfortable as possible. A lot of my clients choose to cover themselves during our sessions."

"Lots of people have used this?"

Meera laughs. "I have ten blankets and they're washed after every use. It's up to you, but it's there should you want it."

I press my lips together. Was I making a face at her blanket? It's a nice touch, I suppose. But I don't want it.

"This session is all about you, Ivy. We'll go at your pace. You can talk about whatever you want. I won't push. If I ask a question that you don't feel safe answering, please let me know, and we'll move on."

I nod and clench my trembling hands. "I . . . I don't know where to start."

"May I start?"

"Yeah," I whisper.

"Your dad said that you recently lost your mom. Can we talk about her?"

A smile touches my lips as tears sting my eyes. "She was awesome. I remember laughing every day with her. When I was ten, she and my dad divorced. I felt like I should go with her—you know, moms often get custody and all that—but I couldn't leave my dad."

"Do you regret that decision?"

"No, but I wish I had spent more time with her. My twin sister, Iris, lived with Mom, and as we got older, we both spent less time with our other parent."

"Teenagers have lives of their own, friends and activities. It's rare that a person spends as much time with their parents when they reach teenage years. You did nothing abnormal, and I'm sure your mom understood."

"Oh, she definitely understood, but *I* feel bad."

She nods. "What was your relationship with her like?"

"It was good. We spoke often, but I went to my dad with any problems I had. I guess living away from her shifted our relationship." I frown. "I think we became a little more like friends."

"How did you feel about that?"

I shrug. "I never really thought about it. Besides missing her being at home, I didn't feel like I was missing a mom, if that makes sense. She would discipline and all that, but only when she absolutely needed to."

"How is your relationship with Iris? Did it change like the relationship with your mom did?"

"Despite everyone assuming twins are joined at the hip, we weren't particularly close," I say. "Iris is very . . . people-y."

Meera chuckles under her breath. "And you're not?"

"I like my group of friends. I prefer a small circle of people I trust."

"Wise."

I think so too.

"Iris doesn't have anyone now. She was popular and always hanging around with a massive crew, but she doesn't talk to anyone from her old school anymore. It's crazy how someone who was always surrounded by people doesn't have a single friend left."

"She has you."

"Yeah, but she doesn't know me."

"Well, only you and Iris can change that. Is it something you want?"

"Mom would have loved it if we were closer."

"But is it what *you* want?"

"It is."

She lifts an eyebrow. "I'm sensing a 'but,' Ivy."

"Intuitive."

Smiling, she says, "I would hope so."

"Things have changed a lot. I'm still getting my head around losing Mom, and now my sister has moved home. I want her with me and Dad, but I'm not used to her being there." Lowering my head, I add, "And I feel awful for feeling like that."

"I don't know, I think most people would feel the same, to a certain degree. You can want your sister with you while wishing the circumstances were different. If she wasn't living with you, that would mean your mom was still here. No one can deny that would be the best scenario."

"Yeah, I suppose." I still feel bad, though. "She hasn't cried yet."

"That's not uncommon. Some people need more time. What about you, Ivy? How do you feel?"

Suddenly, the blanket seems like a great idea. It's not to keep you warm; it's an emotional blanket, and I want to wrap it around me and curl into a ball.

Meera waits a second before saying, "Ivy, that's there for you. I got it out of the closet before you arrived."

I chew on my bottom lip like it's steak. Meera is silent, waiting to see if I go for it.

This is stupid. I shouldn't need a damn blanket to talk about my mom's death. But I do. Gripping the blanket, I tug it over my lap and keep my eyes low.

That was ridiculous.

I raise my eyes because there's silence.

Meera doesn't react. She watches me with the same expression as before.

"I miss her," I whisper. "This summer she was going to take me and Iris to Europe for two weeks. She had been to London, Berlin, and Paris and wanted to show us. I was so excited to share that experience with her. I wanted that time together." I take a deep breath. "I want that *so* much."

Meera's smile is full of sympathy. "Do you think that maybe you could take a trip to Europe with your sister one day?"

I shrug. "I'm not sure if Iris would want to. She's not really up for anything to do with Mom right now."

"Well, it doesn't have to be a now thing."

"No, I suppose we could do it in the future. Maybe."

"Why do you not sound convinced that it's a possibility?"

Frowning, I search for an answer to her question. We won't always be strangers; she's here to stay now. "There's just . . . something there. I feel a total disconnect with her, and it's only gotten worse since Mom died. She doesn't seem real with me."

"If Iris and her friends have cut ties so easily, do you think she knows how to be real with her peers?"

Oh. I squirm on the sofa. "No, maybe she doesn't."

That's really sad. How lonely it must be to not have someone you can confide in. I don't know what I would do without Sophie, Haley, and Ty. I love my family, but my friends are the people I talk to about important things. I need them.

Iris doesn't have anyone.

What is she keeping to herself that she wants to share? I think I would go crazy if I kept *all* my secrets to myself.

"I don't like to think of her with no one to talk to."

"Are you able to let her know that she can talk to you?"

"Yeah, I told her she can talk to me anytime. Didn't go so well. . . . She turned me down."

"She's not used to sharing her thoughts and feelings. If working on your relationship with your sister is something you want, take it slow. There has to be a level of trust with a person before you open up."

I smile. "It took me, Sophie, and Haley about six months before we spoke about real stuff. The day we did, though, it was like opening a dam. They definitely know me better than anyone else. Even Ty."

"Ty is your boyfriend?"

"Yeah."

"Have you been able to talk to him or your friends about your mom?"

"A little. I haven't seen them much since the day she died. Dad and I left, and we were there a week and a half. I'm not going back to school until Monday. Dad didn't want anyone to come over just yet."

"He wants to give Iris time to settle in first?"

"That's what he said."

"You don't believe him?"

"I believe him, but I think he doesn't want to see anyone just yet either. He's been quiet and withdrawn. And he has stubble now."

"He was with your mother for a long time."

"Did he tell you that?" I ask.

"He answered a few basic questions when he booked your appointment."

"I feel like things are falling apart. I know it's been no time at all, but I hate waiting for it to get better. Dad and Iris don't think they need to talk to anyone. How are they going to heal without it? I don't want to walk around with this . . . fear forever."

"Is the heaviness because you haven't healed or because you're worried they won't?"

I pull the blanket up a little. "Both. I feel a tiny bit better that I've taken the first step, but I won't ever be totally comfortable at home if they're not happy."

She smiles. "Does it affect you when there's something you can't fix?"

I take a breath. "Like you wouldn't believe. It's a horrible feeling that's always there. I can forget it for a little while, but there's this, I don't know . . . tugging feeling in my chest that keeps reminding me something is wrong."

"We can work on that. Give you some tools to help ease the feeling. There will be a lot of things in your life that are out of your control."

Yeah, that's what scares me the most.

"Shouldn't we be talking about my mom?"

Meera tilts her head. "It's all relevant, Ivy, I promise you."

It doesn't feel very relevant anymore. Her words feel like an itchy sweater I can't take off. There is so much more I need to work on than just my grief.

I swallow. "I need to take a break."

Meera nods. "All right. I'm sorry I pushed too hard. Take your time."

I reach out and grab my glass of water.

Everything is off.

8

By the time I arrive home after therapy, I'm questioning whether it worked. I'm not sure I feel any better than I did before I went. Dad was right. Therapy really isn't a quick fix. Not that I was naïve enough to believe that one session would solve all my problems, but, you know, it would have been nice.

If I could jump into a pool right now and swim my problems away, I wouldn't hesitate.

Dad is waiting for me when I walk into the living room. He's sitting on the sofa, watching the door. The gray hairs near his temples have increased, but Dad has always taken care of himself. Although he could easily pass as ten years younger, he's definitely aged over these last two weeks. The stubble is still there, which isn't helping.

"Hey, Dad. Where's Iris?"

He looks over his shoulder and clears his throat. "Locked in her room."

That doesn't sound good. Like, actually locked or she just doesn't want to see anyone?

Sitting up straighter, he asks, "How was therapy?"

That's a pretty loaded question. One I'm not entirely sure how to answer.

"Well, it was interesting."

He nods. "Interesting? Ivy, you have always been good at expressing your emotions. Is *interesting* a good thing?"

I drop down next to him. "I think it will be good, but right now it feels exhausting. Kind of like I ran a marathon, turned around, and ran back. My whole body just wants to be horizontal."

"I think that's therapy. Talking about your life and your problems can be tiring."

How would you know? My dad has many talents, but admitting he has any weaknesses is not one of them. I don't think he has ever spoken to anyone about any of his problems. It was certainly a point of contention with Mom. It was one of the things I often heard them arguing about, right up until they split.

"So . . . do you think you'll go too, Dad? Meera was surprisingly easy to talk to." When she wasn't pressing too hard.

"I won't pretend that everything is okay, but I don't need therapy."

Yes, you do.

"You really believe that?" I ask, curling my fingers into my palms. "Because I know Mom's death has affected you more than you let us see."

"Ivy, I loved your mom because she gave me you and Iris. I'm sad that she's gone and that you will grow up without her, but I am okay. This is about you two. I want to help *you*."

Classic Dad move. Nice to see that not everything around here has changed.

"Fine," I reply, conceding, because Dad can be stubborn when he wants to be. I don't think I'll be able to convince him to talk to anyone.

"Do you want to discuss your session?"

"Not really," I reply.

He holds his hands up. "Fair enough. Promise you'll let me know if you change your mind. I'm always here for you."

"Yeah, I promise."

"Good."

Dad hands me the remote, and for the rest of the morning and into the afternoon, we watch movies. Iris doesn't come downstairs once.

When our second movie finishes, Dad stretches. "All right, it's almost five. What do you want for dinner?"

"Burgers and lots of fries." Today calls for carbs.

"Your comfort meal."

I shrug. "Seems like a good day for it."

"I'll place the order soon. Will you see what Iris wants?"

Standing, I raise an eyebrow "And by that you mean find out if she's okay."

He laughs and scratches his stubble-covered jaw. If he wants me to believe he's fine, he's going to have to take better care of himself again.

"I'll admit, I'm not very good at talking to your sister."

I give him a sympathetic smile. "You'll get better at it. I'm kind of hoping I will too."

"You at least have the whole teen thing working in your favor."

"The *whole teen thing*? You really need to stop trying to be down with the kids, Dad."

"Noted," he says with a smirk. "Now go talk to her."

I want to help Iris, but I feel the responsibility pressing down on my shoulders like I'm giving someone a freakin' piggyback. Holding on to the bannister as I walk upstairs, I purse my lips, trying to think of what to say to her.

Iris is in her room listening to music. I hover outside her closed door with my hand raised. I need to find out what she wants to eat, but for some reason, I can't convince myself to knock.

Besides sitting in the kitchen before sunrise, she has barely left her bedroom. Meera's words pop back into my head. *Do you think she knows how to be real?*

Is that why she hides in her room? We're twin strangers and she hasn't made friends here yet, so she doesn't even have anyone to pretend with. She's all alone, and that thought makes me queasy.

With a deep breath, I swing my hand forward and let my knuckles rap on her door. "Iris, can I come in?"

The music cuts off. I lean closer to the door. She can't pretend to not be in there.

"Sure," she replies.

I open the door and step inside. "Wow, things look different in here." Her bed, chair, and drawers are in different places, and all the posters on her walls are gone. "Ah, you finally caved and moved the bed to the right place," I joke.

Our bedrooms are the same size, with the closet and window in the same place. My bed is on the far wall near the window, and hers used to be on the opposite side. We used to argue about it. She thought it was stupid to be near a window in case someone came in, and I thought it was stupid to not be in case you need to quickly get out.

Her jaw tightens. "I wanted a change, Ivy, that's all."

"Okay," I reply cautiously. She did not take that as a joke. "Dad is ordering dinner. It's a burger, salads, pizza place. I personally recommend the guacamole cheese burger."

"I can't eat burgers."

"You *can't?*" Is that a thing?

"Do they have grilled chicken salad?"

"Probably. I didn't know you don't like burgers anymore."

Now that she's said it, I don't remember the last time I saw her eat one. Certainly not since we started high school.

"I like burgers. I don't eat them."

"Right. I'll tell Dad you want the salad." Man, I have a lot of respect for people who can completely cut certain foods out of their diet. I still need to have the junk food sometimes. "So . . .

what have you been doing in here?" Besides rearranging the furniture.

Her blue eyes stare at me. "I've been on my laptop and listening to music."

"Oh, yeah? You been catching up with your friends?"

I'm treading on thin ice here. She hasn't been doing that; she hasn't mentioned anyone, and I haven't seen her use her cell once. But I want her to say that. I want something from her, something real.

"Not really."

"I'm sure they miss you."

Stop pushing.

"Do you think?" she snips, her voice curt. She is totally over my questions.

Well, now I don't think they miss her. Snappy.

She had this one friend she would always go meet whenever I was there. They seemed close, not that I actually met her or can remember her name.

"Is everything okay, Iris? You seem stressed."

She twists her whole body toward me. "I'm fine. I'm bored, that's all."

"We probably have about an hour before food arrives. Do you want to go for a walk?" I ask. "It might make you feel better."

Iris smiles but it doesn't touch her eyes. "Okay. Can I borrow a jacket? I'm not really feeling mine right now."

"Sure."

I give her my denim jacket and we tell Dad what we want to

order. I still want the burger, but I decide to swap out the fries for a salad to be slightly healthier. I'll be back in the pool next week.

"Where do you want to go?" I ask her as we walk across the road toward the field.

"Let's go through town. It's so pretty with all the trees, flowers, and shops."

As we walk through the fields and the few trees separating us from town, Iris says, "So . . . convince me therapy isn't a waste of time."

I'm sorry, what now?

Iris wants me to convince her that therapy isn't pointless.

My skin prickles with heat. She may not believe that therapy works, but that was a pretty crappy thing to say to a person who does.

"I think you have to be open to it for it to be helpful."

She purses her glittery pink lips. "Hmm. Maybe."

My shoulders rise. "Why do you think it's a waste of time? Have you ever been?"

She scoffs. "Of course not. I have no reason to sit on a couch and get my head examined."

Her words and her ignorance are a blow to the gut. She's my sister; she should be supportive. "It's not only for that, Iris."

"Whatever. Talking to a stranger isn't going to fix anything."

"Perhaps not for you!" I snap, frowning.

Why is she being so hostile? There's no need to be ... and she brought it up first. If she doesn't think it helps, why bring it up at all? Other than to provoke me.

"Are you over her death?" Iris asks.

My eyebrows rise. Her cold, emotionless tone chills my blood.

Her.

Her death.

Mom's death.

"Will I ever be?" I ask.

"That's rhetorical, right?"

I stop in the middle of the field just before the smattering of trees. "What's gotten into you?"

Her shoulders hunch. "Ivy, I'm sorry." She sighs and shakes her head and her hair swishes side to side. "I'm not having a great day. I apologize for being grouchy."

Huh?

I shift from one foot to the other. "Do you want to discuss it?"

Laughing, she replies, "Wow, you really are an advocate for talking it out, aren't you?"

"Believe it or not, it does help. You just have to find someone you're comfortable speaking to."

Her eyebrows draw together.

She doesn't have anyone anymore.

"That person can be me," I rush out, making it very clear that I want her to be able to speak to me.

"I don't mean to be rude here, but I don't feel comfortable with you yet."

"No, I get that." Honestly I don't feel comfortable with her either. I don't trust her with my secrets. "We can work on it. I mean, we agreed to try and be proper sisters, right?"

We start walking again, her carefully in heels and me comfortably in Toms.

"I want to go out more," she tells me.

"You could go to the library."

Laughing, she looks up to the sky. "Not a chance. I don't like sitting in silence."

Unless it's dark and first thing in the morning . . .

"Well, after school a lot of us hang around at Dex's Diner. They have good fries and even better shakes."

"That sounds like a lot of sugar."

"Oh, it is. You definitely shouldn't have too many. It's good, though."

We hit the edge of town and look down along the row of stores and restaurants. The town is super small, stores on the outside of the square, with a big patch of grass in the middle. It's where the town throws all different kinds of events. Most of the residential areas are set in a square surrounding it.

It's all very cute, but it wasn't big enough for Mom or Iris.

"Can we go to the diner? Do you think your friends will be there?" she asks.

"We can go, yeah. I'll text them, but we can go anyway."

I turn left and we head down one side of the square as I message Ty. Dex's is on the corner.

A few people from school are on the green in the middle, hanging out on the benches. It's warm today, and it makes town so much nicer.

Ty's reply comes through, letting me know that he's at the diner with some of the team just as we walk up.

"They're here," I tell Iris, pushing the diner door open.

She fluffs her hair.

I raise my hand as they wave, no doubt talking about us. Iris knows some of my friends, but she never bothered coming into town when she stayed here, not unless we were going out for dinner, which was rare.

I kind of wish that I had taken her out more; then maybe she would already have some friends here. All the people we used to play with as young kids have moved away or Iris has lost contact with. She's having to start from scratch.

"People are looking at us," she says, standing taller.

"Small town and all that. Most people mean well."

She shrugs. "It's fine with me."

Okay, then.

I recognize everyone in here. There are about twenty tables, and most are full of people from school. The diner is painted white and pale yellow on the inside and it always smells like fries.

"Ivy, hey," Ty says, sliding out of a booth.

God, it is good to see him.

"Hey," I say, wrapping my arms around him. This is normal. Being here with Ty, even if it won't be for long or on our own, makes me breathe easier.

"How are you?" he asks, releasing me.

"Ugh, okay." I turn to Iris. "Ty, Iris."

"Hey," he says, smiling at my twin.

She returns the smile, but it doesn't reach her eyes. "Hi."

He looks back at me. "Are you two joining us?"

"Probably not."

"Ivy, it's fine. If we wanted to sit alone, we could have stayed at the house."

Oh, we definitely could not have stayed at the house.

"Great," Ty says, taking my hand and pulling me over to the table he's sharing with three guys from the football team.

I wish Sophie and Haley were here too.

The guys greet me and then look to my sister.

"Iris, this is Todd, Alec, and Leo. Guys, this is my sister." I don't need to tell her they're on the football team; their clothes are doing that.

"You want anything?" Ty asks as we sit down.

"I'm good, thanks. Dad is ordering food. We just needed to get out for a while."

"Iris?" Ty asks.

"No, thanks." She looks around the table like she's trying to figure out some super-complicated math equation, focusing on each person as she goes.

What is wrong with her this afternoon? She's sweet one minute and sour the next.

Now she's observing my friends. Why? Is she planning who to take under her wing? Plotting who will be good to own as minions? I don't know.

10

"How did it go today?" Ty whispers when everyone else strikes up a conversation about football. Iris is laughing at Todd. He's the joker of the group, the one to pull pranks in class and leave whoopee cushions on teachers' chairs.

I've only told him about therapy and we haven't had a chance to speak since I got home because, frankly, it was nice to have Dad to myself for a while, and I didn't want to bail to call Ty.

"It was all right. I'm going back next week."

"Did you lie on a sofa?"

He's trying to lighten the mood and it's working.

"Really, Ty?" I can't fight the smile stretching on my face. "She gave me a blanket. Apparently, most of her clients like to be under it."

He turns his nose up. "You used a communal blanket?"

"Not until she assured me that she has a clean one for every person."

With an adorable smirk, he says, "It's cute you believe that."

"Don't be gross."

"I can't wait until next week," he says. "I've barely seen you."

Smiling half-heartedly, I reply, "I'm looking forward to seeing more of you and getting back in the pool, but not going back to classes."

Ty's eyes flick up to Iris, who's deep in conversation with Todd, Alec, and Leo about the best excuse for cutting class. He runs a hand through his messy chestnut hair. "Are you both coming on Monday?"

I shrug. "She wants to."

"You cool with it, though?"

Ty is the only person who has asked if I'm okay with Iris coming to live with me and Dad. Obviously, I am, but it's nice to have someone ask.

"Kind of. I think she's using school to ignore everything else that's going on."

"While you're actively trying to work through it as fast as you can. You know neither way is the best way."

I roll my eyes. "I'm doing fine, Ty." He's always telling me to slow down when I try to fast-track a solution. It's not easy for me to sit back and wait. He's right, though—I've come unstuck a few times when I've reacted too fast because I haven't given myself enough time to think something through.

Therapy is clearly the way to go with this, though, so I don't feel like it's going to come back and bite me on the ass.

"I'm glad to hear that. Make sure you keep talking to me, too, okay?"

I bump his arm with mine. "You got it. Tell me about the game I missed this week."

"We won."

I take a sip of his chocolate milkshake. "Ah, very informative."

"Ivy, are you getting something of your own to drink?" Iris asks. Her jaw is tight and her gaze just brushes above my forehead rather than my eyes.

We said no before, but . . . "I'm good, but you can if you want. We have time."

She turns back to Todd, Alec, and Leo, who are hanging on her every word.

Ty chucks his arm over the back of the booth and drops his hand in my hair. "How has Iris been since she got back with you guys?" Ty asks as Iris heads to the counter to place an order. Leo follows her. Leo is probably Ty's closest friend; he confides in him a lot more than he does with Alec and Todd.

"Honestly, it's been like any other visit. I know it's permanent, but it doesn't feel like it. The house seems fragile, though. Like we're all walking around scared to say too much. I hate living like that."

"Yeah, you're not good at keeping what you want to say inside."

My mouth falls open. "What are you trying to say, Ty?"

Todd laughs as he brushes his hand through his shoulder-length chestnut hair. "Ivy, last month you told me my haircut made me look like an inmate."

"Your orange T-shirt didn't help."

Ty chuckles beside me. "See, babe?"

"Whatever. It's best to be honest."

"There's honest, then there's you," Todd replies with a smirk.

"Can we move on, please? I only have forty minutes, and I want to hear any new gossip."

The guys fill me in on what I've missed, which, besides a few breakups, is nothing much. But it is so good to hear about something normal and, frankly, mundane. This is the stuff that I would usually talk about because I was lucky enough to have nothing bigger going on in my life.

I miss how easy and safe my life was, how small and insignificant my old problems were. A month ago, I was wondering if the head cheerleader, Ellie, would finally realize that Jake is also seeing a girl from another school.

She did, and now she's dating Logan, another guy on the football team.

I used to care about stuff like that. It seems so crazy now.

I'd do anything to go back there.

My sister returns with a large glass of lemonade. She places it on the table, and I watch tiny bubbles rise to the surface and pop.

Iris smiles at Leo from across the table. She raises the glass to her lips and takes a delicate sip. "So, Leo, what position do you play?"

Ty nudges my arm, his eyes flitting between me and my sister. "All good?"

"Yeah. Being here again, it's good. For sure." Ty and his friends are my people. My world might have changed but they haven't. The old Ivy can still exist here.

Iris and I stay until she finishes her lemonade; then we head back home.

We walk in silence across the field, through the trees, and across the final field before home. I look up to the sky and feel the late sun warming my face.

"I'm going to talk to Dad about school," Iris says as our footsteps crunch on the rocky driveway. "Your friends are nice, and I want to be there."

"Okay," I reply. Maybe I shouldn't have taken her out yet. Just because we had one positive hour with Ty and his friends doesn't mean that school will go the same way if she's not ready.

Iris walks ahead of me, her chin tipped up, ready for war.

It's a tad dramatic. If she feels ready for school, Dad will be fine with it. She doesn't need to try to convince him of anything.

He's a lot more reasonable than she gives him credit for.

I follow her into the house.

"You girls have a good time?" Dad asks. He's unloading the dishwasher.

"Yeah," Iris replies for us both. "I have something to talk to you about."

His eyebrows rise. "Oh?"

"I want to go to school on Monday with Ivy."

He puts down the plates he's holding. "Are you sure that's a good idea?"

"I'm sure. Can you call tomorrow and tell them, please?"

Dad looks at me like he's asking for help. I shrug. No one but Iris can decide when she's ready. I understand her need to jump into normality. I want things to be settled too.

"Iris, do you think you might need some more time? Perhaps you should see a therapist before you start."

Her body visibly stiffens. I watch her fingers curl into her palms. I bite my lip.

She narrows her eyes. "No, I don't need that. I just want to go back to school."

"Dad, maybe it's best that Iris goes to school now. It beats hanging around the house, overthinking. Besides, I'll be there."

Iris turns to me and smiles. "Thanks, Ivy." She faces him again. "See, Dad, we've got this figured out."

I wouldn't go that far. For the first time, I don't feel like I have anything figured out. Even when Mom and Dad split up, I had it together. I had a plan and it really was for the best. Mom dying wasn't best in any reality.

"Well, if you think you'll be okay," he says. It was never going to take him long to cave. He's powerless when it comes to something Iris or I want. Though it seems he has a little more power with me.

"I'll be fine. I promise. Like Ivy said, we'll be together. It's not like I'm doing any of this on my own."

Then why do I feel like I'm doing this on my own? Iris won't even say Mom's name. She won't talk about her old house, school, or friends. Dad, too, is refusing to accept that he needs to speak about Mom's death and how it's affecting him.

So who am I doing all this with?

At least I have Meera now. It was so nice to have someone listen. I don't have to tread on eggshells around her, too afraid to mention my own mom. Meera welcomes it. She knows, as do I, that I have to speak about Mom. I have to keep her alive in my life somehow.

"Okay," he tells her.

"Yay." Iris claps her hands together. "Thanks, Dad."

He smiles, but he looks worried.

This is new territory for all of us, but he is going to need to be the strict but fair dad to her as well. How much grace is he going to give her before he goes full-on dad? If he didn't want me to start back at school yet, I wouldn't be starting. There are some things he won't compromise on, and if thinks he's doing the best thing for me, that's it; there is no changing his mind.

The doorbell rings.

"I'll get it," Iris says, grabbing the cash off the counter.

I turn to him. "You know it's ultimately up to you when she starts back at school, right?"

Tilting his head, he says, "Don't complicate things."

"How am I doing that?"

Sighing, he says, "We need to have a level of understanding with her, Ivy. I can count on you for that, too, can't I?"

"Yeah," I reply with a frown. "You can count on me."

That didn't really answer my question, but I don't think he actually has an answer. By "level of understanding," he means let her get her own way so we don't upset her.

That sounds like a fantastic idea. . . .

11

The weekends have a bad habit of flying by too fast. Thursday and Friday dragged, but then I blinked and it was Monday again.

My session with Meera on Friday was good, though. Exhausting and emotional to talk about Mom so much, but good. She asked about some of my favorite memories of Mom, and I found it so comforting to remember how much fun we had.

Meera still thinks that Iris doesn't know how to have genuine friends, the ones who actually care about you and want the best for you. I still find it super sad.

Haley and Sophie are incredibly supportive, cheering me on and helping me train because they know how much I want a swimming scholarship to Stanford. They don't want it for themselves, though they love to swim.

It's a future to me but a hobby to them.

So now I'm determined to be that person to Iris, the one to back her no matter what, to celebrate her achievements even when I fail.

Dad, Iris, and I are on campus, standing outside my car as the morning sun prickles my face. I drove with Iris this morning and Dad took his car.

I take a deep breath and squeeze my clammy hands into fists. Once we climb the three steps, we'll be in school. I've had two days off and it still doesn't feel like enough, but I have to get back to normal. I want to move forward. My pulsing heart is trying to tell me otherwise.

Iris is doing much better than me. Much better than anyone would have predicted. I loved my mom and it's hell without her, but I don't know what I would do without Dad. He's been the one constant in my life.

Iris is acting like being here is just one of her weeks with us—not a permanent move because our mom died unexpectedly.

There still have been no tears, and I'm awake a lot at night, so I would have heard her.

"Are you two ready?" Dad asks.

Iris gives him a bright, toothy smile that lights her face. "A little nervous, but I'm ready."

She doesn't look nervous.

"Let's go," I say. I walk ahead of them and we catch the attention of almost everyone standing around.

Walking through the open double doors, I take a breath as

what feels like a hundred pairs of eyes snap to us, heads turning as we walk past.

Iris and I are identical in body only. Our faces are the same, but her hair almost touches her butt, and she likes skirts and heels and often wears pink. I'm more of a jeans-and-T-shirt kind of girl. If the T-shirt has a band or dumb slogan, even better.

The two girls who look the same but dress worlds apart. The twins who were split up but forced back together by tragedy.

"Hey, Ivy," a couple guys from Ty's football team call over, and I wave. Trent and Michael aren't that close to Ty, so I only know them in passing and don't feel like I need to stop and chat. I just want to get this over with and have a normal school day.

Inside the main office, Dad has to check over some paperwork with one of the secretaries. I stay with Iris as Mrs. Lewis, the assistant principal, hands her a schedule. I don't think she usually deals with admissions, but I guess we're a special case.

Iris glances around as if she's surveying her property. Mrs. Lewis watches her, like she's assessing where Iris will fit in. Her leathery face gives nothing away, but I think she knows my sister is destined for the popular circle. She looks perfect, clearly pays attention to her appearance, and doesn't care much for authority.

Turning to me, Iris asks, "Do you have any of these classes, Ivy?"

I scan her schedule. As much as I want to be there for her, I'm glad that we don't have all of the same classes. She's my twin, but I still need my own time. I'll be sharing so much more now, and I want some space.

I shake my head. "Only the first one, but I can show you where the other classrooms are."

Iris sinks, her body visibly shrinking. "Oh." She takes a shaky breath. "I . . . I don't think I can do this."

She can't do this? Three seconds ago, she was standing like she owned the place already. I wrap my hand around her arm. "Iris, what's wrong?"

She turns to me, eyes wide like she's seen a ghost. "Ivy, I can't." She looks like she wants to run back to Dad's car.

"Okay, calm down." I grip both of her upper arms. "It's fine if you don't want to do this yet."

Mrs. Lewis waves Dad over.

Iris's eyes flit to Dad and then back to me. "I want to, but I can't do it alone."

"You're not alone. I'm here too."

"But I won't see you. I'll be alone for almost the entire time."

I let go of her. "I'll find you at lunch."

She takes another ragged breath that sounds like she's breathing through a blanket. "I'll have three classes before that. I don't know anyone. I can't."

Seriously, what is going on? I look to Dad for help, but he's as thrown by her reaction as me. She's always been outgoing, making friends in seconds. Why so scared about not knowing anyone?

"I think I should take you home and we'll try again next week," Dad says.

Iris shakes her head. "It'll only get worse if I put it off. We all know that, right? The longer you leave something, the harder it is."

What? I'm confused as hell. This yoyo thing she's got going on is giving me a headache. I didn't have nearly enough sleep last night for this.

The school psychologist comes over. "Iris, would you feel better if we changed your schedule to match Ivy's?"

What! My head snaps in her direction.

Iris's mouth falls open. "Really? Can you do that? I would feel a lot better with Ivy with me."

Am I dreaming? Have I been sucked into some sort of alternate reality? Iris doesn't need anyone to hold her hand. All through our life she's been the fearless one. She rolled, crawled, climbed, and walked first.

"Are you sure you want to do this, Iris?" Dad asks her.

She peels her eyes away from me and smiles up at Dad. "I'm sure. If Ivy is with me, I'll be fine. I don't want to miss any more school and fall behind, not with everything else that's going on. It would be too much."

"Then we'd love it if you could change Iris's schedule," Dad says.

Iris looks thrilled. "Thank you so much."

My ears ring.

I walk out of the office in a bit of a daze five minutes later.

Iris makes a joke with Mrs. Lewis. She's smiling and laughing. The anxious moment has passed. Sayonara, moment. The girl is now fine.

I'm trying to process what just happened. One minute, everything is cool—Iris is desperate to get to school and start her new life—and the next she's breaking down and we have *all* the same classes. Like, every single time I sit at a desk, she will be there.

I'm pretty sure that no one else would be allowed to change classes on the spot—our school is notorious for refusing to budge once a schedule is made. What does that tell you? We're a special case because our mom is dead. And Iris really can get whatever she wants.

Iris takes a deep breath. "Time for our first class!" She turns to Dad. "Thanks for letting me start early."

He gives her a hug and kisses the top of her head. "If you need anything, call me. That goes for you too, Ivy. The school psychologist is aware of the situation, so you can go to her any time if you want."

Iris shrugs. "I'll be fine. Ready, Ivy?"

"Yeah, let's go. Later, Dad."

Laughing, he replies, "Later."

I guide Iris through the corridors toward our first class. We have a little time since we got to school super early, so I'm hoping I'll spot Ty.

"This school is tiny," Iris says.

"Yep." It's about half the size of Iris's school in the city. I love it, though. I'm not a city girl. I love forests and fields too much to be in a place that's super built up. And I love that I know, or know of, pretty much everyone in this school. It makes it harder to keep a secret, but if you're into gossip, this school is for you.

Iris is most definitely into gossip. I always heard her on the phone with her friends talking about everyone else at her school.

It's still driving me crazy that I can't remember her old bestie's name. She hasn't mentioned her either. Or anyone else.

As we walk, Iris makes clicking sounds with her shoes, while my Converse are silent. Her heels put her about two inches taller than me. There is no way I could wear shoes like that all day.

I only have good coordination when I'm in the pool.

"Will you introduce me to more people?"

"Of course. If you want to take up cheerleading here, too, I can introduce you to Ellie."

"She's head, right?"

"Yep."

"Hmm," Iris murmurs, and it almost sounded like she said, "For now." Well, if anyone could take the throne from Ellie, it's my sister. Iris has this ability to wrap people around her little finger. Growing up, she rarely got into trouble, easily talking her way out of situations that I couldn't get away with. People seem to be drawn to her, to the way she owns everything she looks at. Case in point with the schedule thing.

"Do you think you want to join the squad?"

"Maybe. I enjoyed it before." Then she shrugs. "But you never know what the team's going to be like . . . how you'll fit in."

I look at her black skirt, yellow top, and yellow heels. She looks like Ellie and her team. That was her inner circle in the city. She'll slot right into their group like she created it.

"Oh, you'll fit in," I assure her.

"What are the boys like here? I need to know who's a snake so I can avoid them."

"I don't really have a lot to do with many of them. Ty's friends are cool. You seemed to get along well with Leo, Alec, and Todd."

"Yeah, they seem nice. What positions do they play?"

"Err . . . they play on the field. I don't know. Ty is the quarterback."

She laughs. "Wow, Ivy. You should really pay more attention to Tyler's team."

"He doesn't want me to pay more attention to his team. I know where he plays, and I sit through *hours* of his games, but that doesn't mean I need to know the game."

"You know you're not really American if you don't like football, right?"

I bump her arm with mine and laugh. "That's okay, I'd love to live in Europe anyway."

"Who is that?" she asks.

Following her line of sight, I spot Logan standing tall with his footballer's body and short, sandy hair. "Don't go there. Logan is the running back and Ellie's boyfriend."

"Okay, I'm going to ask a question now, and I don't want you to take it the wrong way."

Oh, that does not sound like I'm going to take it the right way. "Go on . . . ," I say.

Iris stops in the middle of the hall. "You're not a cheerleader, you're not friends with Ellie, but you're dating the star of the football team."

"You're wondering why he's interested in me."

She smirks. "Babe, you look like me, so of course I'm not."

"I never really knew him; then one day we were both at Leo's house. I was Leo's lab partner and found out he's actually really cool. So we were in Leo's living room watching *Texas Chainsaw Massacre,* and Ty and I talked through the whole movie. Then he asked me out."

"Did anyone say anything about you two?"

"Why, because I'm not in the super-popular inner circle?" I shrug. "Probably, but neither of us cares. Ty might be the quarterback, but he's perfectly happy to be himself. He doesn't try to fit in and neither do I. Everyone is really nice and inviting me to parties now, though." Well, everyone but Ellie.

Iris nods. "I don't think we've ever spoken so much about what's going on in your life before."

"We haven't. Maybe you can tell me more about your life soon."

"My life starts now, so you'll know it all anyway." She looks up and raises her arm. "Leo, hey."

"Hey, Iris." His almost black eyes are warm and sympathetic. "Ty's behind me somewhere."

I look over his shoulder and sure enough, Ty walks around the corner.

"I'm glad you're back," Ty says, grabbing my hand and tugging me to him.

"Me too," I whisper, pressing against his chest. It feels like such a long time since I was here. I've missed Ty and my friends. I've even missed school. "Do you have practice tonight?"

He smiles as he brushes a strand of hair from my face. "Yeah.

Why don't you come and watch? I've missed looking up and seeing you. Or do you need to get home with Iris?"

"I can stay," I tell him before I think about it. It's Iris's first day, so I probably should go straight home with her, but I need to be here. I need something normal, something that hasn't changed beyond recognition since Mom died.

I'll even watch football practice for that feeling.

"You sure?"

"Definitely. I've missed watching you running around a patch of grass, throwing a bag of air."

Ty chuckles and flicks the end of my nose. "I'll make a football fan of you eventually."

"I like the snacks."

Ty's family go all out for big games. Dad and I have been to their tailgates a couple of times. Ty's mom makes football-themed food and everything. It's kind of ridiculous to me, but everything she makes tastes amazing, so go team.

He glances above my head. "How's it going with the sister?"

"Okay. She has the same schedule as me."

"That's good. It'll help her settle in faster, right?" He tilts his head. "Not that she's going to need any help."

Twisting my head, I look over my shoulder. "No, I guess not."

Ellie and Logan have joined Leo and Iris. My sister is charismatic, laughing, flicking her super-long hair over her shoulder and waving her hands as she talks to them.

"Have you heard when the scout is coming?" Ty asks.

I take a breath and lay my head on his shoulder. "Nope. I just want it over because it's stressing me out, but I need more time to practice."

His arm snakes around my back. "Babe, you're in. There is no way Stanford wouldn't want you."

"There are tons of amazing swimmers."

"It's not just about that. You can do it all; you're passionate and focused. Don't stress, swim."

He's right about all of that. But the boyfriend or girlfriend of every other teen desperate for a scholarship is just as sure as Ty.

"Stanford won't be as fun if you're not there too."

He shrugs. "Doesn't matter where we are, Ivy. I got you."

"Long distance is stupid."

Laughing, he nods. "It'll suck not seeing you every day but there are these things called phones—"

"Ha ha," I mutter dryly. "For that I'm making you FaceTime me every night so it's like we're living together even if you turn traitorous and pick a different college."

The bell pierces through the school, signaling the start of classes. "Go to class, Ivy," he says with a smirk and humor in his green eyes. "I'll see you at lunch?"

"Definitely."

I kiss him before he heads in the opposite direction.

"Ready, Iris?"

"Uh-huh. Later, guys," she says to Ellie, Logan, and Leo.

"Looks like you don't need me to introduce you to anyone. Did you speak to Ellie about joining the team?"

"I figured high school is high school no matter where you are.

And no, I didn't mention it. I don't even know if I want to do it yet. One step at a time."

Okay, I'm kind of glad that she's taking her time with this one. Iris seems to want to jump headfirst into her new life. At least she's not filling her schedule to the max before she's comfortable here.

There is a reason why Iris left with Mom. Even at the age of ten, she wanted more. She wanted the city life. The pace is different here.

We walk into class and Iris introduces herself to the teacher. I take my seat.

Why did she need to be on the same schedule as me again?

The only thing she's needed me for so far is to show her where to go. I could have done that and gone to my next class. There is always going to be someone around who will tell you where a room is.

She doesn't need me. Her reaction to her original schedule was an act. Iris wants to be in my classes for some other reason.

Why?

12

Iris and I are meeting up with Ty and Leo at lunch. They're waiting for us in the cafeteria because Iris wanted to touch up her makeup before we join them. So I've spent the last five minutes in the bathroom watching my sister apply mascara. I'm hungry and cranky.

"Okay," Iris says, pressing her lips together after applying a layer of pink gloss right *before* she eats. Where's the sense there?

My stomach rumbles. "You're done now?" I ask her, my tone not quite as light as I intended.

She slips the gloss in her bag. "I am. Let's go to lunch. Is there much of a selection?"

"It's not too bad. There was a lot of campaigning for healthier meals a year ago, which helped. I'm sure you'll find something."

Iris opens the bathroom door and we walk out. "Good. I hate it when cafeteria food looks like cafeteria food."

"When did I say it doesn't look like cafeteria food?"

She laughs. "Do you usually sit with Ty?"

"Most of the time, yeah. Sophie and Haley too."

"Do you think they'll mind me joining you?"

I lead Iris to the cafeteria. "They definitely won't mind."

She smiles. "I'm glad I'm here. It's kind of cool to chill with you again, so thanks for letting me in your crew."

"Of course."

As weird as it is, I am enjoying having Iris back. I did miss her when we lived apart, despite not really hanging out together. If we share friends, we'll get to spend more time together. Maybe we can pull some twin switches on the teachers and our friends. We both missed out on that one. That's got to be a perk of being an identical twin, right?

Ellie steps in front of us, flicking her heavily highlighted hair. "Iris, sit with us?" she asks. "You too, Ivy."

I would rather eat in the bathroom.

Maybe that's a bit harsh.

But not really.

"Oh, we're meeting Tyler and Leo," Iris replies. "Why don't you join us?"

I side-eye my sister. Come on!

"Do you mind, Ivy?" Ellie says. "I know how you like Ty all to yourself."

"What's that supposed to mean?"

Ellie shrugs. "He just used to sit with us more often before you."

"Oh, you mean the way Logan used to hang at Ty's until he started dating you?"

Iris laughs, nudging my arm.

Nope. I'm not being nice to Ellie when she's being a bitch. I don't care if she is Queen Bee.

Ellie just laughs. "Touché, Ivy. Is it okay that we sit with you?"

I force a smile. "It's fine."

Sometimes I think that Ellie likes me. Or at least likes that I fight back. It must get old having people agree with you all the time.

Hey, we're all just trying to survive high school, right?

I head to grab some food. I pick up a bottle of water and a plate of fries. Yes, I'm having a plate of carbs. They're comforting, and I need that right now.

Iris and I are the talk of the school. It'll blow over fast, I know that, but I hate being the center of attention. All I want is to get through the day with no drama so I can chill with Ty and my friends, or swim.

Ty raises his eyebrows as he sees us approach.

I shake my head. *Don't ask.*

He knows that Ellie and I aren't close. He sees through her fake nice-girl act. She works so hard being popular that she probably doesn't show one honest trait.

Is that what life was like for Iris too? Faking it to make it? What's the point of being popular if you're never yourself?

Placing my food next to Ty's, I sit down.

"Fries, Ivy?" he asks, smirking at my pitiful lunch.

"One of those days," I reply. There have been a lot of them recently. I should have picked something sweet up too, because now I have to deal with Ellie while I eat.

I push the scout to the back of my mind. Fries won't ruin my chances. I'm back in the pool soon and will train harder than before.

"How is Ivy so thin, right?" Iris says, leaning across me.

I move back and pray her long hair doesn't touch my food.

Ty frowns at her, but before anyone can say another word, she's gone, turned to the side and chatting to Ellie.

I run and swim and don't usually binge on carbs, that's how. There is no way I could cut out fries and chocolate permanently. I'd be walking around growling and punching people.

"How's it going?" Ty asks.

"Not too bad. People keep looking at me and Iris, though." Like right now. I can see at least three people at nearby tables glancing over.

He shrugs. "They'll move on soon."

"I wish they would move on now." I pop a fry into my mouth. "Clara in my PE class actually stammered when she said hi."

"It's not always easy to find the right words. I've been there. When it first happened, I felt like I was saying everything wrong," he admits.

"You weren't at all. You were perfect."

His mouth curves in a smile. "Clara wasn't being rude."

"Yeah, I know. It's just hard." I take a breath as the void in my heart grows. It's bad enough that I'm missing my mom so much, but I have to hear whispers about it at school too.

"Do you want to get out of here?" he asks.

"No, I'm fine," I reply, picking up a fry even though my stomach rolls at the thought of food now. Iris seems to be doing much better than me, but I still can't leave her on her own.

"You're not," he whispers.

No, I'm not. I need to get through the day, though, so I'm going to pretend. When school is out, I can sit on the field and watch Ty play for a while. That time on my own in silence calls to me.

I haven't seen Haley or Sophie yet, not since I passed them in the hall, but they said they'd meet me here.

The distance between me and Ty is about three inches, but it feels a lot wider. He wants me to leave with him, to put myself first and take some time away from a situation that's making me uncomfortable.

Ty thinks only of me, and I don't have that luxury anymore. I have to think like a twin now. At least until Iris makes her own friends. Which looks like it will take all of three minutes to do.

Juggling the grief, all of the changes, and trying to get back to some kind of normality is exhausting. I feel like I could sleep for a whole day.

"Ivy," Haley calls. I look over my shoulder as my two best friends bound toward me.

Sophie, a step behind Haley, smiles and it lights up her dark brown eyes. Her hair is so light it's almost white. I love the contrast between her hair and eyes, but she doesn't, so she always wears her hair in a ponytail.

Haley gives me a hug from behind. "How are you?" she asks, taking a seat next to Ty while Sophie sits opposite me.

"I'm fine," I tell them.

Sophie's dark eyes glare. We don't lie to each other, and I totally just did. They know, but they also know that I'll talk about it when we're not in a room full of people who breathe gossip.

Sophie and Haley introduce themselves to Iris and spark random small talk with her.

Haley scoops her tight black ringlets into her hands and pushes them behind her ears. It's useless, though, because her hair falls straight back down. I love Haley's hair. Her whole family has the curls, her older brother opting for a full Afro. She once asked me to straighten it for her, and I almost cried while doing it.

We both insisted that night that Haley should fully embrace her African American hair, and she's never straightened it again.

Iris laughs at something Sophie said but I didn't hear. My sister is much better at holding conversations while the world falls apart than I am. I can get through, I can go to class and do the work, but I can't fool people.

Nothing is okay right now, and I'm scared it never will be again.

13

My shoulders sag as the relief to leave the day behind washes over me. Ty is out on the field with his team. So far no one has moved much—there has been a lot of talking.

Like, just run.

It doesn't bother me that I'm watching him stand still, though. I'm glad for some peace, no matter how I get it.

I stretch my legs out in front of me on the bench. There's a book in my bag and a packet of M&M's. All I need to keep myself occupied for the next hour. I've been looking forward to this moment since this morning.

Iris is watching Ellie and the girls at cheer practice. She heads straight for the spotlight. I don't know if she's there with the aim of getting on the team or not, but I don't particularly care. As long as she's happy.

I open the candy and dig my hand in.

The sun above beats down on my face. If I lie down, I could probably fall asleep right now.

I don't trust Ty and his friends to not draw on my face, though. I would totally do it to them. So I'm staying awake and enjoying the silence while it lasts.

But it doesn't last long because I hear my name being called.

"Hey," Iris says, sitting down beside me.

"Hi. I thought you were watching cheerleading practice," I say with a frown.

She shrugs. "I was, but I've seen it all before."

"Right. So do you understand what's going on in this game, then?"

"Of course I do. I love football."

I love Ty, and I don't mind watching it when he's playing, but I can never quite follow what's happening.

"Good, then help me out!"

She laughs. "Don't worry, sis, you'll soon learn every rule."

"Dad and Ty have tried explaining before too, but I just don't really like it."

Iris rolls her eyes. "Your boyfriend is the quarterback and you don't even like football."

"Ty doesn't like to swim."

We like the same films and music. We're both horrible at bowling but go anyway. We love Halloween but he thinks couples' costumes and even matching costumes are lame, though I definitely would have gone as Pennywise and Georgie last year.

He couldn't be convinced, though, so he was Michael Myers and I was Sally from *The Nightmare Before Christmas.*

We can't like *all* of the same things, but we like enough for us to work.

She shakes her head. "Ivy, Ivy, Ivy."

"What? I'm not going to pretend to like something."

"Why not?"

"Because I'm not a deceitful shrew!"

Rolling her eyes, she digs around in her bag. "It's not deceitful."

"You've pretended to like things you don't for a guy before?"

"Sure."

"Weren't you bored?"

"Ugh. Totally. But he was so cute."

Yeah, I couldn't do it. I'd go crazy sitting down having a conversation about something I don't like for date after date. My face would give me away too. I'm crap at lying.

"And how did that end?"

She laughs and slides her lip gloss wand across her bottom lip. "I ditched him after a month. His friend was hotter."

Lovely.

"Did you have more in common with the friend?"

"Not really. He liked *The Walking Dead,* which helped."

"One show. That's all you talked about?"

"At least this one topic was one we mutually enjoyed."

That's awesome. No wonder her relationships haven't worked out. She's picking guys based purely on looks and pretending she likes what they like.

Is that how she picks friends too? Because she sure has found it easy to leave ... ugh, no, her name still isn't coming to me, but Iris left her behind.

"So ... who on the team is single?"

"Leo and Todd for sure. Ty and Logan are not. I have no idea about the rest of them."

"You know the relationship status of only four people?"

"This might shock you, but I don't take a tally."

"Oh, girl, you have got to high-school better."

Frowning, I put my book down. "I'm sorry, what? Do it better?"

"This is your life for four years, Ivy. You still have one and a half left. To survive high school, you need to own high school."

"No offense, Iris, but you sound insane right now."

She puts her lip gloss away and twists her body. The football field is forgotten. Hunting down her next squeeze has taken a backseat, because she's about to school me.

Not that I want or need it.

"It's not insane to want to make the best of your time here. We have to do it, so why not do it right? You can coast through under the radar or you can have a freakin' party."

"But what do you get in the end? Because you'll leave school with a diploma and a bunch of empty memories."

"Stop living in the future, Ivy. We're here now. If you want something, take it. That's exactly what I plan on doing."

"You're taking the school?"

"It took me all of five seconds to get Ellie to want to be my bestie. That is the circle that will give you the best experience. Who cares if you leave with nothing but a diploma? Everyone knows you meet your lifelong friends in college."

Not to be naïve or anything, but I plan on being friends with Sophie and Haley beyond senior year.

"So is that why you've ditched everyone in the city?" My eyes widen at my words. I did not mean for that to come out. Especially in the way it came out.

I raise my palms. "Iris, I didn't mean it."

She looks away and takes a breath. "It's not like that."

"I know. Of course, there is more to it."

"This is my life now. I have to make this work. It's that simple."

"Yeah, I get that. Dad would let you have your friends over and go there anytime you want."

"Not sure I want to go back there."

"Understandable. It's going to be hard when we have to pack up Mom's stuff."

Iris freezes. "I don't want to do that. Mom's friends have offered to do it."

I glance at her, half keeping an eye on what Ty is doing. Which is standing still talking. They take forever to get into practice. "I don't like the idea of someone else going through her things. Besides, you still have some stuff there too."

"I'll do my room. You can do hers if you want. Her friends won't mind either way."

My stomach dips.

"Okay," I reply. "Maybe we can go together one weekend. It should be us. You can fill your room here with more of your pink stuff and makeup."

A smile stretches across her face. "I do miss all of my stuff."

I flinch. Her stuff is what she misses from that house.

Stop reading into it.

"They're playing," she says, shifting to get more comfortable on the bench.

I watch her vacant eyes for a second before turning my head to Ty and swallowing a lump in my throat.

14

Iris and I wait for Ty while he changes after practice, standing outside the front doors in silence. She's scrolling through Instagram like she's looking for something specific.

"Do you want to take the car?" I ask her.

Her thumb jams into her screen and her eyes flick to mine. "Take your car?"

"Yeah, so you can go home. I'm going to dinner with Ty."

"Oh." She shakes her head. "I didn't realize you were going on a date with him after. I'm sorry, I didn't mean to be a third wheel."

"You're not a third wheel. I was going to take you home first, but if you take the car, it saves you waiting around now. Ty will drive me home after."

"Right. Sure, I can do that . . . and you can go on your date."

Her voice is low, barely above a whisper. She licks her lips and drops her phone into her bag.

"Okay," I say. "I won't be late home."

She tilts her head. "Do you ever miss curfew?"

"Not much." I happen to like being able to leave the house, and the chances of that happening decrease dramatically if I break curfew. "Do you?" I ask her.

A tight smile curls her lips. "Of course I don't."

Yep, she definitely sneaks out. But to where? Surely she hasn't snuck out here? She must mean at Mom's.

"Spill, Iris!"

"Sorry, I need to leave." She holds her hand out, palm up, and raises her eyebrow.

Sighing, I drop the keys into her hand. She curls her fingers around them. "Thanks. Have fun."

I watch her as she walks down the steps toward the parking lot. She has a skip in her step, which is a stark contrast to her hunched posture when I told her to go home because I'm going out with Ty.

What changed?

No matter how hard I try, I can't quite figure her out.

"Hey, where's Iris going?" Ty asks, throwing his arm around my waist.

Jumping at his sudden appearance, I look up at him. "Home. You can give me a ride back to mine after dinner, right?"

Lifting his eyebrow, he replies, "You need to ask?"

I don't, but you know, it's polite. "Take me to dinner, then. I'm starving."

"Diner or somewhere you don't get served fries in a plastic basket?"

"Don't hate on the baskets. They've served us well for years."

Ty shakes his head. "You're so easy."

We start walking, falling into the same pace since he's not letting go of me. "I'm not sure if that's an insult or not."

"You know what I mean, Ivy. But I can rephrase. You're so laid back." He snorts. "Most of the time."

Ah, he fixed it. I was beginning to think that he doesn't know me. I might be laid back about where we eat or where we go on dates—basically I don't care what we do—but with just about everything else in my life, I'm going out of my mind.

"Yeah, yeah. Ivy overthinks," I mutter.

"You overthink and stress when there's never any reason to. There's nothing you don't get done. School, swim team, whatever you want."

That's right. But it's because I stress and overthink that it all gets done. I don't remember the last time I didn't worry about something I was doing. Whether that's at school or stressing over an argument with one of my friends.

Logically, I know things will work out one way or another. But I've never been fantastic with logic when I'm in the middle of anything remotely important.

Maybe I should put Meera on speed dial.

"What the . . ." I crane my neck, watching Iris drive out of the parking lot.

"You want to clue me in?" Ty asks, following where I'm looking.

"Iris turned left out of the lot, not right."

"Maybe she had something to do first? She might be picking up some dinner."

I stare up at him. She's been here a week, and this is her first day at school. What could she be doing?

"Okay, maybe not," he adds.

"She's secretive and she's doing weird things at night."

We reach his car and get in. I wait until Ty starts the engine.

"What things?"

Something she said a minute ago has me frowning. "I think she's sneaking out."

"You think that's weird?" he asks. "I don't think I know one person who hasn't. Besides you."

"I've never had to. Besides, I would *definitely* get caught."

Laughing, he tears out of the parking lot and heads right, toward the diner. "You know what, I think you would too. You're a horrible liar. Your dad would never believe whatever excuse you thought up."

I don't think the inability to lie is a bad thing, but it certainly doesn't help when Dad asks if I've ever had a drink or if I've cut classes at school. He's never punished me, so he must believe me.

"But if she's sneaking out here, where is she going?"

Ty shrugs like I'm overreacting.

"Tyler! She doesn't know anyone."

His eyebrows rise. "You *Tylered* me."

"Because you're not taking this seriously. Do you think we should turn around and follow her?" I ask, biting my lip.

"No. Why would you want to?"

"Because I'm nosy."

"Really, Ivy," Ty says, chuckling. He makes a left at the light and the square isn't too far away. I'm so hungry; it better not be busy tonight.

"Sorry. I'll forget my sister for a while. I enjoyed watching you practice tonight."

"You mean you tolerated it?"

"I tolerated it in a very enjoyable manner. It was warm out but not too hot. I had a book and you ran a lot more than the last time I watched."

Laughing, he shakes his head. "So you really want to follow Iris? Because we could get the burger and fries to go."

"You want to spend our date hunting down my twin sister?"

He shrugs. "It's something different."

"It's different, sure."

Pulling into a parking space outside the diner, he smirks. "We've never stalked anyone together before."

I frown. "Have you stalked anyone on your own before?"

"Only you."

My eyebrows shoot up. "What?"

"'Stalked' is a stretch. I've followed you at school. It was before we got together, back when I wanted to ask you out but was too chicken."

"Where did you follow me to, you creep?" I ask, playfully slapping his arm as my jaw drops.

"To the pool."

Why did I not know this?

"Wait, is that the day I literally bumped into you outside the changing rooms?"

His grin widens, which answers my question for me. "I needed a reason to talk to you."

"We had two of the same classes together, Ty. You needed me to whack my head against yours to start a conversation?"

"I hadn't planned for your lack of concentration."

We get out of the car and head inside. As much as I want to know what Iris is up to, I'd rather just chill with Ty. My sister is taking up so much of my mind lately. There is something wrong, that I'm sure of, but I doubt I'll figure it out by following her once.

"I wasn't expecting someone to be standing right outside the door."

Ty opens the door for me, and we head inside to find a table. "I wasn't *right* outside. Besides, you were at Leo's party that weekend and the rest is history."

He definitely was standing right outside the door. I remember it very clearly because I slammed into him and wanted the whole world to swallow me. Ty had been on my radar for months prior to our bump. He was the only guy in school that I thought was hot; he was fit and didn't exclude anyone based on who they hung out with. He still doesn't, and I love that about him most.

We came from different circles and made one that works for us both.

Okay, so he's dragged me into his circle a little more than I originally hoped, but not all of his friends are intolerable. I actually like quite a few of them, and I don't really like anyone.

As we walk to a booth, Ellie passes us with a group of her friends. "I'm meeting Iris, girls. I'll see you all later."

I turn and narrow my eyes. What? She's meeting Iris where? They only met today.

"Come on," Ty says, grabbing my hand. "We can borderline break some laws another time. None of our crew are here, and I kind of like the idea of having you all to myself tonight."

"Yeah, I'm in," I tell him, taking one last glance back at Ellie leaving to meet Iris . . . at some secret place for some secret reason. They're strangers. This is weird. Why doesn't Ty think it's weird?

What are they doing, and why didn't she tell me they were meeting up?

15

When I get home from dinner with Ty, Dad is shut away in his office and Iris must be upstairs since my car is in the driveway. I can hear music coming from her room.

I want to run straight up there and grill her on where she's been with Ellie, but I don't think I'm supposed to know. The more time I spend with my sister, the less I think I know her. She has secrets. They're probably not even good ones—part of me thinks she tries really hard to appear deep and mysterious. She probably just hung out with Ellie at her house for an hour.

Still . . . what are they doing?

In my room, I grab my pajamas and take a towel from the linen closet on the way to the bathroom.

Iris is playing Katy Perry as I walk past. I wish I could spy on her. I'm not going to—that would be creepy and weird. But she's so protective of her room. I haven't been invited inside since she moved back in.

I shower, dry off, and get into my pajamas before hanging up the towel and heading out of the bathroom. I tiptoe past Iris's room and hover by the door.

The music is still playing, Lady Gaga this time. But every ten seconds or so, the music cuts out for a beep.

She's messaging someone. Ellie? One of her old friends?

It didn't take Iris long to not need me. Which we all knew would happen, so I'm still unsure why she had to have the same schedule. But whatever.

I debate knocking and seeing if she will let me in, but I don't really have a reason. She hasn't said good night to me before unless we passed each other, so it would be weird to start that.

Ah, screw it. I'm going to knock anyway.

I raise my hand at the same time the door swings open.

"Ivy, you almost punched me!" Iris squeals.

I let out a nervous laugh. "I didn't hear you walking over your music."

"Well, I'm sorry if I disturbed you."

"That's not why I'm knocking," I tell her. "I wanted to check in."

She shrugs. "I saw you a few hours ago, Ivy. Nothing's changed."

Yeah, and I saw you drive off in the opposite direction of our house.

"Have you been in here all night?"

"Mmm-hmmm. I like my room." She steps forward, forcing me back, and pulls her door closed. "It's my safe space."

Safe from what?

"I kind of hope the whole house is that for you."

She looks toward the stairs. "This house is still yours and Dad's."

"Iris," I say, the shock in my voice crystal clear. "It's yours too. Even when you weren't living here. You said that you want to decorate. Why don't you do that?"

Scoffing, she replies, "I need to use the bathroom. Don't worry about it, *Ivy*, I'm fine."

She pushes past me and disappears into the bathroom.

I blink and turn to watch her close the door.

What the hell was that about?

Her bedroom door isn't closed all the way. I could stick my head through the gap and take a peek.

I look back. She'll be in there at least a few minutes if she's brushing her teeth and washing her face . . . and maybe she'll even take a shower. With no clue of what I'm even looking for, though, is it worth it? She probably doesn't have a voodoo doll of me. For whatever reason, I'm the source of her anger this evening. I can live with that for a while.

It's not like I don't have anger too. Mine is more spread across the entire situation. Why did Mom have to run so close to the edge of the bridge? Why did it have to be raining the night before when the weather had been dry for weeks? Why us?

There is so much I miss about her, and it seems like each day something else comes up. We usually send a voice message every week to fully catch up if we haven't managed to talk. I haven't had a voice message in one month, to the day.

Thinking of my mom gives me courage, and slowly I stick my head through the gap and peer into my sister's room. Everything seems the same. Her light is off, which means the only light in there is what is pouring in from outside.

Then I spot something different. An old, retro-style leather suitcase sitting on her bed. I haven't seen that before. It could have been in one of her boxes she brought from Mom's. Iris didn't want any help packing or unpacking her things. Dad and I only helped to carry big cardboard boxes.

What could she have in there?

Down the hall, the toilet flushes.

Gasping, I leap back and dash into my room and quietly close my door almost all the way. My heart pounds against my rib cage.

No more snooping unless she's out of the house.

I tiptoe backward and get into bed. I hear the water running in the shower. Tapping my fingers on my stomach, I lie still. I could go back to her room, but my pulse is racing.

I want Iris to trust me. That's unlikely to happen if she catches me looking through her things. Despite her helping herself to my clothes whenever she likes.

So I wait. My phone is charging and I can't see the time, but it feels like she has been in the shower for hours.

Finally, the water cuts off.

She takes her time drying off and getting changed. A few

minutes later, the bathroom door opens. I bite my lip and turn my head toward the wall.

I hear Iris's soft footsteps on the carpet. She walks along the hall past my door. Is she going downstairs? It would be nice for Dad if she went to see him. He constantly looks worried about her.

I hear her door close.

16

I didn't sleep well, and I have my twin to thank for that. At least I didn't spend the first hour of lying in bed thinking about how much I miss Mom. Instead I was trying to figure out why Iris was so angry at me last night. And I keep coming up blank.

New day, new mood. All morning, she's been chipper. We're at school and her irritation toward me yesterday seems to be forgotten.

Iris walks a step ahead of me down the hall toward the lockers.

"Sophie!" Iris calls. She turns and lifts her hand, her ponytail swinging from side to side. "See you later, Ivy."

Wait. Was I just dismissed?

Charming.

"Bye," I say, watching Iris skip off to one of *my* best friends and frowning.

All right.

Sophie gives me a little wave, but as soon as Iris reaches her, their heads are together and they're in deep conversation.

I shake my head and hang a right down the hall that leads to the pool. Getting in the water will help.

Pushing the door to the changing room, I walk inside and spot Haley with a towel around her.

"Hey," I say.

Her head whips around and she grips the towel in her fist. "God, Ivy, you made me jump." Her hair is tamed in a tight bun.

"Sorry," I say, laughing. "You okay?"

"Yeah, I just need to get my time up."

"I'd recommend working on getting it down."

She rolls her eyes and pulls her jeans on under her towel. "I'm not getting any faster. I haven't been improving."

"Plateaus are normal. We've all been there."

"Yours lasted weeks and since then you've been swimming like a fish."

It was more like months and it felt like years. Everyone tried giving me pep talks and I know how much it didn't actually help. It felt more like *Hey, you might suck now, but you won't always*. Yeah, thanks for that, champ. No help at all. "Haley, you're an awesome swimmer. Don't be too hard on yourself."

"Hmm. I'll figure it out. Coach said I can practice a couple of mornings too."

I hate that she's struggling with this.

"You want to head to the community pool this weekend? Or I can come in early and swim with you next week."

Her dark eyes fly to me. "Ivy, you don't need to fix this."

"That's not what I'm trying to do. You helped me and I just want to help you."

Dropping her towel, she puts on her bra at lightning speed and tugs a T-shirt over her head. I watch her with a frown as she stuffs her towel in her locker and grabs her bag from the bench.

Taking a breath, she says, "Ignore me, I'm having an off day. You all right?"

She's having more and more off days recently.

"Yeah, I'm good. Sure you're okay?"

She nods. "Yeah, I'll see you later."

Okay. She's frustrated. That wasn't about me. It's so hard when you're doing everything you can but you're not improving. You have to push through.

I shove the changing room door open and walk around the lockers to Coach's office. I can see her through the glass, sitting at her desk and chewing her lip. She does that when she's worrying about something.

Is she worried about having this chat with me? Whatever the chat is going to be about. I don't think I've done anything wrong. In fact, I'm swimming more and getting faster.

Raising my hand, I rap on the door.

She swivels on her seat and makes a sharp gesture with her head for me to come in.

Here goes nothing.

"Hi, Coach. You wanted to see me?"

"Come and sit down, Ivy."

"All right." I step toward the seat opposite her desk and sit down. "Is everything okay?"

Coach smiles as she lets her shoulder-length brown hair out of a hair tie. "Yes, relax, Ivy. I can hear your mind freaking out."

My shoulders slump on a long exhale. "So, what do you need to see me about?"

"I just wanted to check in. You've just got back, and your first practice is coming up."

"Oh. I'm fine, ready to jump in. I *need* to get in the pool."

"I'm glad you're finding the outlet you need when you get in that water, but are you getting help outside of it?"

We're all encouraged to leave whatever issues we have at the side of the pool when we get in. I wasn't aware that it's suddenly the wrong thing to do. Frowning, I shift in my seat and clear my throat. "Yeah. Are you okay for me to come back?"

She shakes her head and places her palms on her desk. "I think the question is, are you okay with it, Ivy. You know that if you need some time, that's all right."

"I have a therapist," I tell her. "Look, I'm not going to pretend that I'm okay because I'm not. I miss my mom, and I'm not sure this hole in my chest is ever going to heal, but I'm dealing with it. When I come to school, I want to focus on everything I need to do, not just in the pool."

"That makes sense," Coach says with a warm smile. "I want you to know that this is coming purely from a place of concern. You've had a lot to deal with."

"Yeah, well, I still do. Iris is home, and everything is different.

But I know when I'm swimming, nothing will be difficult for a little while."

"Does your sister swim?"

I shrug. "A little." Where is this going?

She holds her palms up and presses her thin lips together. "Okay, I get it. This is your thing."

Yeah, it is.

I dip my head.

"The panic in your eyes tells me a lot, Ivy."

"I like that I have something for myself. We're sharing a lot these days. But you know if she was a strong swimmer, I would recommend her."

She picks up a full mug of black coffee. "That's exactly why you're where you are right now."

"Nothing to do with all the practice, then?"

Laughing, she shakes her head. "You better get to class."

"Okay, see you this afternoon." I pause. "Since I've missed a couple of weeks, I thought maybe I should come in today for an extra practice."

She lifts her eyes to mine. "Of course. I'll see you in the pool in the morning as well, Ivy."

● ● ●

I put my tray down on the table at lunch. Iris, Haley, and Sophie look up. They all have the same grilled chicken salad and water in front of them. Sophie eats healthily most of the time, but I've never seen her eat a salad.

"Hey," I say, unscrewing my water bottle cap.

Haley gives me a tight smile, her full lips flattening with the effort.

She's still annoyed from earlier then. I wasn't suggesting that I have all the answers or I'm the best swimmer out there. Jeez, I just want to help.

"Did you get whatever you need from Coach this morning?" Sophie asks me.

"Yeah. She was just checking in and seeing how I'm doing. We spoke a little about me wanting to get back in the pool, and I'm going to have an extra swim tomorrow morning."

Haley arches her eyebrow almost to her hairline.

What is her deal?

"If you want to swim alone, Haley, I can do alternate mornings." I take a sip of water, trying not to take her attitude personally.

"Is Coach watching you?" she asks.

"Yes, why?"

What else would she do during practice? It's one thing to swim in the mornings just for myself, we've all done that occasionally, but if we're practicing, Coach is poolside with her stopwatch. Besides, it's not like she can let us swim without a member of trained staff there.

She shrugs. "Nothing. I'm being stupid."

"What's wrong?" I ask her. "Is it something I've done?"

"It's not all about you, Ivy," Iris teases.

At least, I think she's joking.

I turn to my sister. "I never said it was."

Iris raises her hands and then goes back to her salad.

Stabbing a tomato with venom, Haley lifts her eyes. "You haven't done anything, Ivy. It's awesome to see you going so fast and kicking butt in the water. But it's hard at the same time because I feel like I'm failing."

"But you're not failing," I tell her. "Take the pressure off. Trust me, you'll be surprised what that does for you."

Early last year when I hit my plateau, I was super stressed. The more I worried that I couldn't improve, the worse it got. I had to reset and forget about times before I got better.

"Yeah," Sophie says. "But that's harder to do when we have a million meets coming up."

Slight exaggeration.

"You're worried too, Soph?"

"Not everyone is the star, Ivy," Sophie replies. There is no jealousy or malice in her tone, but I didn't realize they felt this way. Have they been discussing it?

I take a bite of my chicken salad wrap. What do I say to that? I'm not going to apologize for working my ass off to get where I am. Nothing was handed to me. I've put the hard work in, and I deserve to be the anchor.

"Well," Iris says breezily. "This is uncomfortable." She turns to Haley and Sophie. "You guys are just as good as Ivy. Believe you can beat her, push yourself, and you can."

"Yeah, right," Haley says. "I can't move any faster right now. I'd never beat her."

"Guys, we're not competing against each other," I say, trying to remind them what really matters here. Neither Sophie nor Haley wants to take swimming further than high school. They both want it as a fallback in case they need it for college, but they have never been too worried about being the fastest before.

Why now?

"Come on, Ivy," Sophie says. "We all want to be the best."

"Damn straight!" Iris exclaims. "You want it, babe, you take it."

It's all I can do not to kick her. Why is she rooting for someone else?

My heart sinks as I realize that my twin wants me to lose.

17

Two weeks have passed very slowly. We're almost at the end of another school week. Iris has been a nightmare through every class the last three days. If she's not whispering to me, she's tapping her pen on her books or humming to herself.

She didn't do it the first week, so I don't know what is going on with her.

It feels intentional—like she knows I only work my best with very few distractions and she's trying to mess me up. But why? Not to mention that she barely does any work, so now I'm stressing about *her* passing her classes. What's going to happen if she fails?

I have a session with Meera straight after school, and then I'm free. I have a full weekend planned, though, so there won't be much relaxing. Tomorrow I'm spending the morning in the pool with Haley and Sophie; then in the evening I'm going out with Ty. On Sunday, Nan and Grandad are visiting.

It will be the first time we've seen them since Mom's funeral, and I know Dad is nervous about having his ex-in-laws over. We were going to spend the day at their house, but Iris doesn't want to go back into the city.

She doesn't seem to want to go anywhere near memories of Mom.

Dad must be a little frustrated with her, but he never says a word. I think she could do pretty much anything right now and he would let her off. But it's only a matter of time before he goes full dad-mode on her. She's not going to like all the rules she's about to have imposed. I can't wait for that day, because then at least we'll be on the normal track, out of this tiptoeing around her limbo stage.

Mom didn't have a curfew, though I think if it was past midnight on a school day she might have called. I remember so many times when I'd visit, Iris would come home around one in the morning.

As long as Mom knew where we were, she didn't mind how long we were out. Though I can't imagine Iris stayed at her friends' houses all night. Over the past two years, Iris had started visiting us for shorter periods. Her three weeks turned into two. She would give the excuse of events happening back home, but in reality, it was probably because she didn't have the freedom or the friends here.

She doesn't seem to have that problem here now, though. She's latched very well on to my friends and they seem to be annoyed at me. I don't even know what to do with that, but I'm sure it'll blow over.

Haley and I are researching in the library. I don't know where Iris is, but she was walking with Ellie, so I assume they're together in here somewhere.

It's nice to have Haley to myself for a while.

"What time are we meeting at the pool tomorrow?" I ask.

"Around nine?"

"Cool. Do you need a ride?"

"No, I'll walk. I could use the exercise to loosen me up."

I glance at her out of the corner of my eye. "Are you and Soph really worried about swimming?"

"It's just hard this year, Ivy. I feel like you and a couple others have progressed so much, and I haven't. I don't know how long Coach will let that slide. At what point does she have other girls try out?"

"I don't think that will happen. Besides, if it does, you and Soph still aren't even close to being the weakest swimmers."

She rolls her eyes. "Not yet, but give it another year."

"Look, if you're that worried, why don't you add another practice? Join me on Wednesdays too."

"See, that's the thing. When do I get time to chill? Time to do schoolwork?"

You make time. I have to be strict with myself because I lose three afternoons a week to swimming, plus now a Friday with

Meera. "Study and do homework first. I don't swim on a Saturday or Sunday unless I want to."

She chews on her bottom lip. "I want to get better, but I don't want to lose my social life."

"Well, you only really hang out with me and Sophie anyway, and we'll be at practice with you."

"How do you fit Ty in too?"

I shrug. "Mostly Saturdays and Sundays. You have to make a decision, Haley. It's either worth it to you or it's not."

She slumps in her seat. "What do you think I should do?"

"I don't want you to leave the team, but I don't want you to be unhappy either."

"None of this would have happened if Iris hadn't mentioned our times."

I put down the pen I'm holding. "What?"

Haley sighs. "Oh, she didn't mean anything by it. We were talking about who's the fastest and all that. I realized that you had improved so much, and I hadn't. Before that, I never really thought about it. I just swam."

"I'm sorry she did that," I say, frowning.

"Forget I said anything," Haley tells me. "I mean, she wasn't prying or calling anyone out."

"Still a crappy thing to do."

Haley shakes her head, her mass of hair bouncing back and forth. "She didn't realize you've flown past us."

I rub the back of my neck. This is so awkward. Iris has royally put her foot in it.

I'm all for healthy competition, but we never worried about our times before, not between each other. Other girls on the team, sure, but we're best friends and it doesn't matter. Or it shouldn't.

Iris must have known it would cause problems between us. She's a cheerleader and knows all about competition. She would have known they would feel like I'm racing ahead and they're getting left behind.

Iris did that on purpose. She wants to cause a rift.

18

I get home from therapy and Iris is watching *The Bachelor*. She has her feet kicked up on the coffee table and is holding a Diet Pepsi in her hand.

"Hey," I say. "I'd ask what you're up to but it's obvious."

She looks up and smiles. "There is so much drama on this show. I love it."

I'd never guess.

"There's always so much fakeness, bitching, and backstabbing. They might pretend to be nice to each other, but you can see they just want to rip each other's hair extensions out," I say, crossing my arms.

"You need to be able to switch off, Ivy. It's just a show."

"Sure. A dumb one."

"Are you going to watch it with me or not?"

"Of course I am."

Iris laughs and turns her attention back to the TV. Well, hallelujah. That went well. We had a tiny little conversation, but it was a nice one. There was no sarcasm. I didn't feel like she's secretly laughing behind my back or eye rolling in her head.

I should mention what happened today. Iris definitely would have known that bringing up our swim times could cause a rift.

"Sophie and Haley seemed a little annoyed with me today," I tell her, keeping my eyes on the screen so I appear more casual than I feel.

"Why?"

"They mentioned you spoke about our times."

Her back straightens. "And why did that make them annoyed with you?"

"They mentioned how far I've come in comparison. I think it made them feel like they're not good enough."

"Well, how was I supposed to know talking about the thing you're all passionate about would be bad?"

"I'm not saying you did anything wrong. I know you wouldn't intentionally try to cause issues between them and me." Or I want to think that, anyway.

"Of course I wouldn't," she replies. Her voice is thick with emotion like she's trying not to cry. Her identical pale eyes are calm, though. "Are you guys okay now?"

"Yeah, we're good."

Her smile is tight. "Well, no harm done, then."

There was harm done. Sophie, Haley, and I have the best

friendship and Iris is creating little fractures in it. She might not be doing big things to hurt us, but even tiny fractures cause breaks if you inflict too many.

"Ah, I bet she ditches this guy for the new one," Iris says, pointing to the TV and leaning forward.

She's done with me for now, over the conversation, and doesn't care about Haley and Sophie. Yet, she's quick to join us for lunch and meet up with them when she's not with Ellie. What exactly does she want from my friends?

"I can't wait to see Nan and Grandad on Sunday," I tell her.

"Huh?" She looks over, doing a double take before returning to *The Bachelor*. "Oh, right. Yeah, me too."

"Do you speak to them much? I only really text. Does Nan try to use emojis with you too?"

"Ivy, really!" she snaps.

Whoa, and there it is. Her frustration over a dumb conversation about emojis. Anything to do with Mom and her side of the family ultimately leads to her snapping or going quiet.

"What? I was only asking you a question."

"During my TV show."

"Hey, you were just talking too." I tap my thumb and index finger together and run them across my lips, telling her I'll be quiet.

Iris sinks back against the cushion behind her and crosses her arms.

Whatever is going on with my twin, it needs to improve.

The tension radiating off Iris is suffocating. My stomach is heavy, and I'm sitting so still. Although I like watching the drama unfold on reality TV shows like this one, I can't stand to be sitting next to my sister feeling like I've done something wrong.

When I'm stressing or have anxiety over a situation, I feel it physically, from the twist in my stomach to the ache between my eyes. When I was eight, my mom went on anxiety meds. She never told me or Iris but I heard her discussing it with Dad. I knew something was up because she was acting different, sleeping a lot and snapping. They were the wrong meds, I understand that now, but back then all I knew was that Mom started taking medication and she and Dad argued more.

Iris is definitely covering up her pain . . . but what can I do about it until she's ready to talk?

Absolutely nothing. So I'll wait patiently.

Well. I'll wait.

. . .

When I get up in the morning, I freeze. The drawer on my desk is open. Not even just a little but, like, several inches open. It was closed last night. I remember putting my pencil case away after completing homework.

Was Iris in my room last night? How late did she wait up? Did she keep peeking through my door to see when I'd drifted off? What was she looking for, anyway? I didn't fall asleep until sometime after two, so she must have stayed up past that.

I tiptoe toward the desk and peek through the gap as if something is going to jump out at me. My poster of the Killers stares down at me. Shame I can't ask them what they saw last night.

There isn't much in the drawer besides some photos and other random crap I've collected over the years. Nothing of value to anyone but me.

Iris doesn't need money. Can she really be that interested in notes from Ty or pictures of me, Haley, and Sophie? She wants to get closer to my friends but surely sneaking peeks at letters between us isn't the way to go.

Reaching out, I pull the handle and the drawer slides open. I rifle through but there was a lot in here, and I don't think I'd even notice something missing.

Slamming the drawer shut, I sigh. What am I even supposed to do?

If I tell Dad, Iris will deny it. She'll tell me I obviously didn't close it properly because that is more believable than her going through my things at two in the morning. Or whenever she was being a sneak.

Maybe she needed to borrow something. But at that hour?

I get changed, brush my teeth, and grab my swimming bag before heading downstairs. I'll need to eat if I'm going to be in and out of the pool all morning.

Dad is in the kitchen making pancakes and washing berries when I get downstairs.

"Morning," I say, leaning against the counter.

He looks over his shoulder. "Morning, Ivy."

"You're cooking breakfast."

"I do that occasionally. You want pancakes?"

"Please. What are your plans for this morning?"

"I'm meeting up with Ken to watch soccer."

"Cool. You need to get out more . . . and not go to the office."

"Noted, Ivy. Is your sister up yet?"

No, she's probably too tired after her snooping session last night.

"I haven't seen her," I tell him.

"I'm up," Iris says as she walks into the room. "Ooh, those smell nice, Dad."

I turn around. "Hey. How did you sleep?"

Her eyes have the faint tell of dark circles. Not enough to be obvious, but if you're looking like I am, you can see that she didn't sleep well last night.

"Great," she replies with a toothy smile. "You?"

I nod, staring into her eyes and willing myself to switch on that twin telepathic thing we're supposed to have. "You hungry? Because Dad has made about a thousand pancakes."

"There's an extra mouth to feed now," he mutters.

"Yes, one. You've made enough for ten."

There is a big stack and he's adding more batter to the pan.

"Hmm. You can snack on them later."

I'm supposed to maintain a relatively healthy diet, but sure, I'll eat pancakes all day.

Cheat days are still a thing, right?

I devour four pancakes and a handful of strawberries, raspberries, and blueberries. I'm going to burn it off in an hour.

Iris and I sit at the table with a cup of coffee as Dad finishes up with breakfast.

"What time are you home?" she asks.

"Probably around midday. Ty and I are going out around seven. Why, did you want to do something?"

She shakes her head. "I was just wondering. I'm meeting Ellie and we're going out for the afternoon."

"Oh, cool."

Dad looks over, the spatula still in his hand. "What are you doing with Ellie?"

She shrugs. "Hanging out. I think we're having lunch at the diner."

"Okay," he replies.

Are you serious? If I'd said that, he would have asked me where I was going. He would need locations and the names of everyone I planned to meet up with.

Why does Iris get off with an "okay" to her vague reply?

It's totally unfair.

"I need to head out," I say flatly, putting my dishes in the dishwasher. Dad and Iris mutter a quick bye, and I leave as fast as I can so I don't snap and say something that's going to make this situation harder.

I drive to the pool and arrive five minutes later because traffic was light. It's not actually open yet, so I wait in the car and watch the road for Haley and Sophie.

It only takes a couple of seconds for Haley to pull up in her silver Beetle complete with pink fluffy dice. It's a much cooler car than my "safe" Volvo but it is like Edward Cullen's one in *Twilight*. I thought she and Sophie would come together since they live close, but Sophie isn't with her.

Opening the door, I get out and she does too.

"Morning. Ready to swim your ass off?" she says.

"Definitely. Is Sophie coming?"

"Yeah, she's going out with Sam after, so we came separately. I think she's walking."

"Okay."

Sam and Sophie have been dating for three months and he seems cool. He's not into sports or anything, so I rarely see him around school. He's more into computer games.

"Ivy . . . do you really think I can get, like, considerably better? I feel like I'm wasting my time."

I shake my head. "You're not wasting your time. We'll get you there. You just have to be prepared to work harder."

"I am."

"You've got this."

With a small smile, she nods. "Hey, how are you doing?"

"I'm okay."

"You miss her."

I lower my gaze. "All the time."

Haley wraps her arm around my shoulder. "It's going to be okay."

I lift my eyes to her. "Thank you."

Sophie pulls into the parking lot and Haley drops her arm.

We look over and she has a big grin for us. Getting out of her car, she says, "Morning, losers! Let's do this."

"You drove."

"Yeah. I figure I'll need the energy for swimming," she says.

"Damn straight. Ready to win?" I ask.

"We both are," Haley says.

Good. Things are back to normal with them. I bite my lip as I feel ten pounds lighter.

"I'm going to need a massive lunch after this," Sophie tells us, wrapping her arm around my and Haley's shoulder as we head to the pool.

"Don't eat too much—we're out with Iris tonight," Haley replies.

My head snaps in Haley's direction.

What? They're doing what with Iris?

"Oh? Iris didn't mention anything to me this morning."

Haley looks over her shoulder; my shock has set me back a step or two.

"You'd probably already left your house. She only sent us a new group message about ten minutes ago."

A what now? I'm not in this new group.

Why does Iris need a group chat with *my* friends?

19

Iris is going out with Haley and Sophie without me. That's all I could think about during our swim. Sure, I managed to get it together long enough to give them some pointers, things they couldn't see themselves, and they left feeling more positive, but my head wasn't in it.

Coaching is one of my favorite things to do, but today Iris ruined that.

Why is *she* going out with *my* friends? Iris definitely invited them out tonight because she knew I couldn't go. I don't get why she would do that.

When I get home, she's in my room, borrowing one of my T-shirts since we haven't packed up Mom's house yet. Still, she brought almost her whole wardrobe with her.

"What about this?" she asks, spinning around in my favorite Maroon 5 T-shirt.

"Do you even like them? You know it's only okay to wear band T-shirts if you listen to them, right?"

Her shoulder lifts in a lazy shrug as she pulls the T-shirt over her head. "I like the lead singer."

There is no point in arguing this.

"Looks good on you," I tell her, opting for maturity.

"That's because I look like you."

"You were born first, so technically *I* look like *you*."

That makes her laugh. The first proper laugh that has her body shaking. "Well, yeah. I'm the original and you're the imposter."

Not sure I would go that far, but I like the teasing. It's so . . . normal.

"Or you weren't quite perfect, so Mother Nature had to try again."

Her grin widens. "No, I don't think that's it."

She looks like a perfect mixture between the two of us, like she's trying to bridge the gap. Her yellow pencil skirt and my band tee. It's cool but doesn't look like the top half is her.

"Where are you guys going?" I ask.

"Movies. What about you and Tyler?"

"I have no idea. He won't tell me."

Her eyes widen. "Really? I would hate that. How do you know what to wear?"

"Jeans and a T-shirt."

"Ivy! You should make an effort."

"I put more curls in my hair, didn't I?"

"He's your boyfriend."

"And we've been together long enough that neither of us feels the need to impress the other anymore. It's a good place to be." Ty wouldn't care if he saw me before I put makeup on. He doesn't care when I've just got out of the pool with no makeup on! He won't care if I'm wearing jeans or a dress, or if my hair is tied up or curled all pretty.

Iris bites her lip, staring off into the distance. "That must be nice."

"Yeah, it is. We've never really talked about boys before. Is there anyone back at your old school?"

She shakes her head slowly. "No, I dated a little, but nothing went anywhere."

"Well, there are a couple of cute *and* nice guys at our school. Besides, we're only sixteen. Plenty of time to play the field."

"Yep. Plenty of time for me to nab the one I want." She purses her pink-tinted lips. "No one has caught my eye yet, though."

"Well, when someone does, he'd be crazy not to want you."

"We could double-date."

I hate formal double dates. It would have to be something casual we would do with a group. The only time I've felt awkward with Ty is when we went to dinner with one of his teammates and his girlfriend.

"Sounds good. What time are you meeting Sophie and Haley?"

"I need to leave soon. Can I take your car?"

"Um, okay. Ty is picking me up, so I won't need it."

"He's the perfect boyfriend," she says quietly, almost to herself, as she's not looking at me anymore. Grabbing my leather jacket off my chair, Iris wiggles her fingers in a *Mean Girls*–style wave. "See you later."

That's fine, sis, I didn't want to wear that jacket anyway.

I finish getting ready in my room, hearing Iris start my car and drive away. It's weird. I don't mind sharing friends, but we're so different, and she has nothing in common with Haley and Sophie, other than that they're best friends with her twin.

She should be out with Ellie and her gang of merry cheerleaders.

And, no, I'm not jealous. This whole sharing everything with my sister is very new to me. I haven't had to do it in six years.

It bothers me that she's suddenly wanting to hang out with me and my friends when she never has before. She spent four weeks here every summer and didn't once want to come out with us.

Maybe it is genuine. Mom's death could have changed what she wants in friends. I'm not saying Ellie and her friends are faking it, but they all look and behave in the same way. Iris might not want to have to change who she is to fit in anymore.

That or she's totally trying to wedge herself between me and my friends.

Biting my lip, I glance toward her room as if I'll be able to see through the wall. She left already. I could be in and out in minutes. Tiptoeing out of my room, I tilt my head to the stairs.

The house is silent. Dad will be in his office, doing whatever it is people working in insurance do.

• • •

I hear the roar of an engine as Ty rolls up on the gravel outside. A date with him is the distraction I need, especially after an hour of math homework. He is very good at putting things into perspective when my mind runs away.

"See you later," I call to Dad as I rush downstairs and out of the house.

"Back by ten!" he shouts as if I've suddenly forgotten the weekend curfew he set a whole year ago.

I close the front door and jog to Ty's car.

"Eager," he teases as I get in and buckle the seat belt. He leans over and gives me a kiss. Ty looks amazing in a plain white tee and dark jeans. His messy hair has been tamed against its will. Thankfully his surfer style is breaking through; he looks like he's only arrived at the beach rather than his usual coming-home-from-it mess.

I love both.

"Where are we going?"

He sits back in his seat. "Movies."

Oh great.

Seeing my face, he frowns. "You don't want to?"

"Iris is there with Haley and Sophie."

Raising an eyebrow, he questions, "And that means we need to boycott the place?"

"Don't you think it's weird that she's going out with them on her own?"

"Not really . . . ," he replies.

"Tyler!"

He holds his hands up. "Babe, I'm not sure what you want me to say. I don't think it's weird. She's friends with them too and you're out with me tonight. Are you saying you don't want them to be friends?"

I bite my lip. Damn, I'm in the wrong here.

"Ivy, what's going on?" he asks. "You've been acting weird about Iris since she got here."

Wow. Looking to my right, I scowl at him. Shouldn't he be on my side?

"Don't give me the death stare. You're too cute and it doesn't work. I'm trying to understand why you're so hostile toward her."

"I'm not," I defend. How am I the hostile one?

"Do you not want her here?"

Sighing, I reply, "Of course I do."

"You don't want to share anything with her?"

"I don't mind sharing."

He rubs his hand over his face. "You need to help me out, here."

"I'm being unreasonable."

"Yes, you are, but why?" he presses.

Throwing my hands up, I reply, "I don't have an answer, Ty, okay?"

I hate feeling like this, like my own sister is playing a game. But I do.

He looks away. "Movies or somewhere else?"

"Do you already have tickets?"

Shaking his head, he puts the car in drive.

Although he's denied having the tickets, his lack of a verbal no tells me he has.

"A movie sounds good. As long as you don't refuse M&M's and then try to eat mine."

His lips tug into a grin, and I know I've won him back. The earlier frustration with our conversation is gone. "That's tradition."

Ty drives down the winding country lanes toward the movie theater with a casual smile on his face. He holds the steering wheel with one hand and the other is curled around mine.

"Do you think you'll make the gala next month?" I ask him.

"Haven't missed one yet."

"I know, but training is going to get crazy for you soon. You have way too many games coming up."

With a small shake of his head, he says, "I'll be there, Ivy."

He likes swimming about as much as I like football.

"Well maybe I'll share my M&M's with you tonight then."

Ty laughs as we pull up at the theater.

I sit straighter as I immediately spot Iris, Haley, and Sophie outside. They're huddled together and laugh in unison. Sophie and Haley are a little more dressed up than usual. Haley is wearing skinny jeans and a blue and white striped shirt. Sophie has an orange summer dress, hair still tied high on her head.

They look like they belong with Iris and Ellie.

Ty side-eyes me but he doesn't mention them.

He thinks I'm being unreasonable, and I hate that. I wish it didn't bother me, but I'm not usually wrong when my gut tells me something is off. Though, clearly, I'm the only one who thinks that.

He parks the car and we get out. I slam the door with slightly too much force, but he doesn't say anything. I wince. It's not his car's fault.

Ty walks around the car and wraps his arm around my waist. "We are going to have a good night."

It's almost like he's pleading with me.

I bump him with my hip. "Obviously. Maybe after we can go to the lake and jump in fully clothed."

"One time, Ivy, and it was so cold I almost lost my toes."

That time was last October; the lake is considerably warmer now. But I didn't bring a change of clothes with me.

Ty leads me to the snacks, and I assume he's bought tickets online. "Popcorn and M&M's?"

I lift my eyebrow, and he chuckles.

We get the same snacks and drinks every time, so there's no need for him to ask.

"Ivy, you're here too," Iris says.

My body recoils, and I look to my side. Where did she come from?

"I am, yep."

"That's so funny."

Amazing what she finds amusing.

I smile. "Where are Sophie and Haley?"

"They went ahead with our popcorn. I came back to use the bathroom and saw you. Are you watching *Buried* too?"

"That's what you're watching?" Iris and Sophie hate scary movies.

She shrugs. "The trailer didn't look that bad. Hey, do you two want to sit with us?"

"They prebook the seats, so we might not be able to," I tell her.

Shaking her head, her smile widens. "I'm such an idiot. You're on a date. I'll see you after." Turning on her heel like she's auditioning for ballet, she jogs in the direction of the screens, not the bathrooms.

"If looks could kill, your sister would be dead," Ty says, handing me a box of popcorn and my Coke.

I blink away the narrow eyes I was giving Iris. "Thanks for this."

"Everything okay?"

"Sure."

Not really. Why did she come back if she didn't need the toilet?

Ty shows his ticket receipt on his phone and we head to Screen 8. "We're near the back, the double seats on their own," he tells me as we navigate walking in the dark. Behind us the screen is already playing trailers. We never get here too early; I hate finishing my popcorn before the movie has even started.

Ty caught on pretty quickly to arrive ten minutes late when coming with me.

We find our seats, and I try to ignore the urge to look around. We're right near the wall, out of the way. I should focus on Ty and not worry about where Iris is.

So why can't I?

The tips of my fingers pad against my leg.

"What's wrong?" Ty whispers in my ear.

I keep my head straight, looking at the screen. "Nothing," I reply, and take his hand with my other. Ty squeezes, and I feel my shoulders relax.

That doesn't last long, though. As soon as the movie starts and Ty is engrossed, my eyes wander. I scan the darkness, looking for her.

My gaze halts and my grip on Ty tightens as I find her across the other side of the darkened theater . . . staring back at me.

20

In the morning, I wake at six and get straight up. Nan and Grandad won't be here until ten, but I want to be ready. It's going to be weird having them here, but I'm also excited about it. It's been just me, Dad, and Iris for three weeks now. She's seen our grandparents a lot more than she's seen me and Dad since our parents split, so hopefully they will be able to get through to her.

I take a quick shower, get dressed, blow-dry my hair, making my blond waves more pronounced, and put on a light layer of neutral makeup. Nan always goes on about how Iris and I are naturally pretty and don't need anything, but I don't feel very confident without a little on.

When I get downstairs, Dad is in the kitchen, scrubbing the countertop.

"Morning, Dad. That looks clean to me."

He looks over his shoulder and smiles. "Right. It's not like your nan and grandad have never been here before."

His stubble is gone and he's wearing a new shirt. He looks like the dad I know.

"Nope, so chill."

"What do you want for breakfast?"

"I'll just grab some cereal in a minute. Is Iris up?"

"I haven't seen her yet. I'll wake her in an hour if she's not."

I turn my nose up. "You think she's asleep? She's been getting up earlier than me."

"She has? I didn't know that was possible."

For the next two hours, I watch Dad clean and rearrange things. I have never seen him so nervous before. Iris came down about thirty minutes after me, her hair and makeup looking runway ready.

When the doorbell rings, Iris doesn't even look up from her phone.

"Ivy!" Nan coos, wrapping me in a tight hug that stops me breathing while simultaneously making me feel safe. "How are you, darling?"

"I'm doing okay," I tell her, and give Grandad a hug too.

They both look a little older and their eyes a little duller. That's not surprising, though; they lost a daughter.

"How are you two?"

"Oh, darling, we're hanging in there," Nan replies. Dad shakes Grandad's hand and hugs Nan. They all seem kind of stiff, like they're strangers. Iris hugs them but then hangs back, like she doesn't want to get too close.

"Time to start lunch," Nan says, picking up some grocery bags.

"You know it's ten in the morning, right?" I ask.

"Yes," Dad says. "And I thought I would take us all out to eat."

Nan waves her hand. "Nonsense. I'm making pasta and sauce from scratch. My granddaughters can help me."

Oh, I have missed cooking with Nan. She's a bit much in the kitchen—food is her passion—but I love it. Besides, I'm not going to learn how to cook from Dad, and I can already dial for takeout.

I follow Nan into the kitchen. I get the feeling that she is separating us, taking on the girls while Grandad talks to Dad.

They're probably worried about how we're coping. All of her texts are geared toward finding out as much information as possible without actually pushing. She asks a lot about what we're doing, if we're spending time together, if we need to talk to a female adult in the family. All of the embarrassing conversations already happened with Mom, so I don't know what we would specifically need a female for.

I look back over and see Iris hovering by the door.

"Ivy, grab the canned tomatoes and the herbs. Iris, you can get a bowl and start mixing the ingredients for the pasta."

I put the bags on the counter and take out what we need.

"I'll put on a pot of coffee and we can have some girl time in here."

Girl time is code for her grilling us and finding out if we're okay.

Iris hasn't moved from the doorway. "The bowls are in that drawer," I say, pointing to a cabinet.

She gives a small shake of her head. "I don't like cooking."

Nan turns to her. "It's not about the cooking. It's about us spending time together. That's even more important now your mom is gone."

I lower my head as my heart tears a little bit. God, I would love to cook with Mom just one more time.

Iris folds her arms. "We've never done this, or not since we were little, anyway. Why do we need to do it now just because Mom is gone? I'm not pretending. You two are on your own."

Turning on her heel, she stalks out of the room.

Sighing, Nan begins measuring out coffee grounds. "She's hurt and angry."

"She won't talk about Mom," I tell Nan.

"She will, Ivy. Give her time." Nan wraps her arm around my waist. "Why don't we make lunch and Iris can join in or not when she's ready."

Nan mixes the dough while I begin chopping fresh oregano and basil.

"I'm worried about her," I say to Nan, keeping my voice low so Dad won't hear. He and Grandad are talking about sports.

"I know," she says. "Your sister has never been very good at dealing with major events. She either shouts and cries or ignores it entirely."

"I've been struggling to find some way to help her." I pause. "I guess I was kind of hoping you might have some good advice."

Nan sighs. "I'll continue to reach out to her, but I can't force her to listen. Your mom was having issues with her too."

I put the knife down. "She was? What kind of issues?"

"Iris was acting out, and your mom wasn't sure why."

"Nothing had happened?"

"Not that I or your mom was aware of. She spoke to a few of her teachers and no one had noticed anything off at school besides some shifting in friendships, but that was nothing out of the ordinary."

Frowning, I pop my hip against the counter. "When Iris first got here and we were talking about my friends, I told her that I have a small friendship group and prefer that. She said she *had* that too. I didn't think much about it because she'd just moved away, but she hasn't mentioned anyone back in the city," I say. "Plus, my therapist said something interesting."

"Oh?"

"Yeah, she said that Iris might not know how to be real around people because her friendships at school were based on hanging around with the people who would keep her popular."

Nan puts the fresh dough through her chrome pasta maker and turns the wheel. "You think something happened with her friends?"

I shrug. "Maybe she was cast out or something. It's kind of weird that she's cut them all out of her life since moving here. Even if you eventually grew apart, you would be in contact to begin with."

"I'll talk to her," Nan says. "I don't want you to worry yourself with this, Ivy. You need to look after yourself too."

I smile, but I don't agree with her. It's so much easier to help someone else rather than myself, and I want nothing more than to make sure my sister is okay.

When lunch is ready, we all eat in the dining room. Iris joins us for twenty minutes and then escapes back to her room. No one but me seems to mind. Iris needs time and all that. I think it's kind of rude and crappy on her part, but apparently I'm wrong.

21

Mondays have never been my favorite, but after the weekend, I was happy to go to school. I'm drained from being the one to hold conversations with Nan and Grandad. Not to mention that I still can't quite figure out what was going on between Iris and Mom before she died.

Iris follows me to the pool after classes let out. "Are you sure you don't mind me tagging along?"

"Nope," I tell her.

"Really? Because I don't want you to think I'm wedging myself into your crew."

I take her wrist and stop walking. Iris stops too. *Be the bigger person here.* "We're sisters and we have to stick together. Mom would want that. Listen, I should get in there. Coach will be ready to start and I'm already cutting it close."

Iris bites her lip, her eyes watering.

"What?" I ask. *Oh, please don't cry.* I don't do well with crying, never knowing what to say to make it better.

"It's just . . ." She averts her eyes and takes a breath. "Gosh, ignore me!" She glances back.

"No, what's wrong? Do you want to go and see the guidance counselor?"

"Not at all. It's dumb and unimportant."

"It's not. Tell me, Iris."

She shrugs. "It just hit me that I don't have much going on. You're the star of the swim team."

"And you've been here two minutes, and everyone loves you." She laughs.

"Mom would be proud of how you're trying at school, Iris," I tell her.

Her eyes flicker with annoyance. Every time I've mentioned anything to do with Mom, she's built a wall around herself. I won't ever stop talking about her, but I also won't expect Iris to be okay with it. Dad is right, she'll get there when she's ready.

"Thanks, Ivy. Now, show me how awesome you are at swimming."

Iris follows me inside the changing room.

My teammates are all ready before I even put my bag down.

"Ivy," Coach says. "Nice of you to join us."

I wince. "Sorry. I'll be quick," I reply, heading for my locker. I could tell her I was talking to my sister—we've been offered all sorts of leniency short-term—but I don't want to use my mom's death as an excuse for letting myself down. I'm not late to classes or swim practice. I hand homework in on time. Okay, so I do that mostly because my dad would ground me if my grades slip and I won't be allowed to swim, but still.

Besides, the last detention I got for talking in class was *so* boring.

I strip my clothes, my hands shaking slightly from being late. I need to be out there now. Everyone has left; it's only me and Iris in the changing room. Late to me is loss of control.

I open my locker to grab my towel. Instantly my nose stings from the putrid smell that slams into my face.

"Oh my God," I mumble through my hand as I step back.

Iris steps around the open door of my locker. "What's that?"

I drop my hand and glance at her out of the corner of my eye. "Something dead? I think it's under my towel."

We sometimes get mice in the school but it's been a long time since one made it into the building. Is that what's under my towel?

Slowly, because I don't actually want to do this, I reach my arm out and my fingers brush the towel.

"Don't touch it, Ivy."

"I wasn't planning on touching it!" I hiss.

Iris grips her hair in her fist at the side of her head as if the dead animal is going to leap up and bury itself in her shiny curls.

Breathing lightly through my nose, I pull the towel. Iris squeals and I jump back, slamming into the row of lockers behind me as the mouse thuds to the floor.

"Oh my God, so gross," I exclaim, shuddering as I think about how I need to burn my towel now.

"Ivy, what's taking so long?" Coach says, popping her head back into the changing room.

Iris holds her hands up. "Mouse in Ivy's locker."

"Dead," I add.

Coach walks over to us with a frown. "Poor guy must have gotten himself trapped. I'll take it out. Iris, you can go through and take a seat."

"Okay."

Iris looks back as she heads toward the pool. "Do you have a spare towel?"

"No, but Coach does."

"See you out there."

Shuddering, I slip my swimsuit on, tie my hair up, and tug my goggles onto my head. My heart is thankfully slowing down after almost having the dead mouse fall on my feet.

How did it manage to get in there? And what did it die of? It could have starved over the weekend maybe.

Poor mouse.

The team is at the edge of the pool when I get out there. I power-walk toward them, looking for Iris out of the corner of my eye. She's sitting alone. There aren't usually people watching practice.

"Ivy, you're up," Coach says as she returns to us. I don't know where she put the mouse, I'm just glad it's gone.

"Okay," I reply. So I'm not going to get a recap of what she was saying, but they were only here for a couple of minutes, so it was probably a pep talk. I don't need one of those; I just need to get in the water.

I step onto the block and pull the goggles over my eyes.

Bending my knees, I launch forward and dive in. The second my head is under, I'm free. I push hard, lap after lap, challenging myself to beat my times.

There are so many great swimmers on the team, but I couldn't care less about beating them. Dad has always told me to swim for me, even when I'm swimming competitively.

I swim, gliding through the water like I was made to do this. Every stroke of my arms brings me a sense of peace I long for every day. I could do this forever.

Coach calls it when practice is over, and I climb out of the pool.

Now back to a reality where my mom is gone.

"Ivy, that was amazing!" Iris gushes as I meet up with her outside the pool.

I rushed getting dressed, so my hair is still damp, but I can shower when I'm back home. I didn't want to leave Iris waiting around for me longer than necessary.

It's been cool to have her here watching. My conversation with Nan still plays in my mind. Iris might have lost something before she lost Mom. That has to make the breathtaking sting of losing Mom even worse.

I grin at her. "Thanks."

"I would love to be able to swim like that."

"You can swim."

"Yeah, but not like *that*."

"Maybe we should head to the community pool one weekend, and I'll give you some pointers."

"You would do that?"

"Sure."

She links arms with me as we head out of school. "Want to get grab some dinner out? Dad's cooking isn't bad but . . ."

I laugh. "Yeah, he tries. There's a new restaurant called the Cove we could try."

"I've heard it's nice."

"You're into seafood, right?"

She nods. "I love seafood."

Seafood was Mom's favorite too. I press my lips together before I voice that thought. Iris doesn't take well to talk about Mom.

"Dad gave me a fifty this morning, so dinner is on him," she says.

Okay, where's my fifty? I won't be voicing that thought either or I'll sound like a brat. Dad has given me way more money than he's given Iris over the years because, obviously, Mom and Dad didn't pay each other child support.

"Perfect," I say, trying to keep my voice light. We reach my car and get in.

"Did you have to try out for the swim team?" she asks after we've been driving in silence for a mile.

"Uh-huh."

"Hmm." She's staring out the window. "I spoke to Ellie about cheerleading at lunch today. Well, she actually spoke to me about joining."

"Really?" I knew Rosemary Anderson left last month and they hadn't replaced her yet.

"Ellie and her friends are exactly like my friends back home. Fitting in with them is so easy."

It doesn't sound like she wants to fit in with them.

"You want to make friends, right? I mean, you have with Ellie." She shrugs. "Sure."

"But I mean, if you don't want to cheer, you shouldn't do it," I tell her.

Her eyes glaze over like she's repeating my words in her mind and trying to make sense of them.

She blinks and smiles. "No, I want to."

As much as I love it when a person doesn't need someone else, we all want friends. I don't know why Iris is being so blasé about it. She had friends in the city. They might not have been as real as what I've got with Haley and Sophie, but she knows what it's like to have friends.

No one wants to be alone. Not really.

22

Tuesdays are usually pretty quiet, only today I've thrown in another session in the pool after school. But I don't care that I've lost one of my free evenings because last night was kind of cool. At least nothing dead dropped out of my locker again.

Iris and I enjoyed dinner at the Cove, and we talked. Not about Mom or anything heavy, but it was still nice. When she's being the rational version of herself, I like her. She has been shying away from giving me any credit for swimming, even going as far as making me feel bad about it, but after watching my practice yesterday, she's practically been waving her pom-poms.

Speaking of which, she was meeting up with Ellie today to tell her she does want to be on the team.

I'm happy about that too. Iris will have a hobby, something

that's all hers to focus on. She won't worry about my friends or what I have.

Kicking like my life depends on it, I reach the edge and pull myself out of the pool. My legs shake and my arms feel like jelly. I've overdone it. Stumbling into the changing room, I lean against the tile in the first shower cubicle and wait for my heart rate to return to normal. I pushed it too hard, but I beat my personal best time.

I got my personal best!

It's worth every second of the muscle burn.

The elation of swimming faster has a goofy smile stretching across my face. This feeling is addictive, knowing I'm strong enough to push my body and achieve my goals.

I shut the water off, the last of the chlorine spiraling down the drain.

Closing my eyes, I slide down the wall as the muscles in my thighs throb and my breath rasps from my lungs.

I'm going to ache tomorrow, but I don't care. It has been a long time since I've pushed this hard. If Coach could see me right now, she would say I've gone too far. After swimming I should still be able to walk, so it's a good thing I kept it together until I got into the changing room.

The harder I pushed, the more everything else fell away. There was no dead Mom in the background, no sister pushing boundaries, no dad pretending he's unaffected by it all.

I would spend my life swimming like that if I felt the same complete freedom.

Flicking my eyes open, I wiggle my toes. I have to get up and leave. Coach will be going home soon. The showers and changing room are eerily silent. I've had the longest shower of my life, so it won't be surprising if the rest of the team have left.

I place my palms on the floor and push myself up. Bracing against the wall, I give my legs a minute to support my weight. I need to get home and eat.

Iris picked a great day to need the car. The walk isn't far, but I'm exhausted. I step out of the shower and grab my towel from the peg. Wrapping it around me, I lean against the wall again.

Maybe I need to do some sort of weight training to improve my strength.

Or maybe I need to work up to swimming like an actual fish.

I stand still with my towel around me as if I've frozen on the spot. I don't have the energy to dry myself. Damn, I need some food.

Pushing myself, I walk out of the cubicle and head to my locker.

"Coach?" I call out, only to be met by silence. She doesn't leave before us. "Coach, are you here?"

On unsteady legs, I walk to the next row of lockers and peer into her office through the window. It's empty and her computer screen is black.

Great. She probably thought everyone was gone while I was sitting in the shower with the water turned off.

Well, it's not a big deal. The doors is locked into the pool but not into school, so I'm not trapped in the changing room. I dash back to my locker, drop my towel, and tug my clothes on.

Dad is out, so he's not expecting me home. Which is good

because I'm going to be later than usual tonight. He calls about ten minutes after five if I'm not home on practice days. It's thirteen minutes past now.

The fatigue is really slowing me down. I need to start running regularly again. I don't class myself as unfit in the slightest, but I need to be able to swim as hard as I did today without feeling like I'm going to die.

I grab my bag, sling it over my shoulder, and leave the changing room. My hair sits damp against my back. The corridor is empty. The janitor will be around here somewhere and there are usually teachers who stay later than this, but I don't see any now.

My heart beats faster as my footsteps echo through the air. I keep my head down and head to the door.

The sky is dark, and thick gray clouds hover above, waiting to rupture and soak me. I could call Iris, but I heard her talking about going out with Ellie. Ty is having dinner with his grandparents, Sophie has extra tutoring in Spanish, and Haley is shopping with her mom.

I'm going to get wet. Good thing I have a great rapport with water.

I jog across the street at the crossing and head for the fields.

Above me, the sky rumbles. I knew a storm was close. *Fantastic.*

Leaning forward, I up my pace despite my burning thighs screaming in protest. It's so dark with the sun hidden away as if it's lost the fight to the storm.

Once I'm across one field, trees lining the second one make it so much darker out. I usually walk through the middle since it's a more direct route and the forest isn't too thick, but I'm not stupid. It's dark, I'm alone, and I've seen plenty of horror movies.

Curling my arms around my stomach, I walk faster. Above me, in the trees, a flock of birds flee from the branches. The flapping of their wings makes me jump. I step back, head shooting up to see about fifty of them flying toward town.

My eyes flit shut, and I press my palm to my racing heart.

The sky lights up with a bright silver fork overhead, followed by another crackling rumble. The storm is almost on top of me.

Screw it, I need to get home. I turn to my side and stomp into the trees. I'll be out the other side in less than a minute. We don't have a lot of forest in town, only a few patches of trees here and there. It just happens that the widest one separates my house from school. During winter, you can pretty much see straight through them.

I tread carefully, placing my feet between broken branches and rocks. There is kind of a man-made path, but I missed it because I tried to be smart and go around.

Drops of water patter down on the leaves above me. As of now, I'm protected by the trees, but I can already see the clearing and then it's wide-open fields.

Thunder booms, making me gasp. The trees cast shadows on the ground as lightning makes the sky glow.

Behind me, a branch cracks like it's succumbed to the weight of a person. I whip my head around. My eyes dart back and forth but all I can see is more trees. The rain falls harder, dripping through the trees and onto my head.

You're paranoid. Keep moving.

With trembling hands, I step close to the edge of the tree line and push my hands behind me in case I bump into a tree.

I should have called Iris.

Now I'm in a field, getting wet and hearing noises because the second it gets dark, my mind starts playing games. The rain pours harder, pelting my skin, but I don't turn around and run because something is in the trees.

This is ridiculous!

You're being ridiculous.

Just go home, Ivy.

Another crunch cuts through the sound of water hitting the ground. I swing my head to my left. I slow my breathing as I try to eliminate every noise I can so I can hear better.

There is no one there.

There is no one there!

I'm drenched. Water cascades down my face, making it difficult to see. I wipe my eyes with the back of my hand. I want to run but fear burns through my body, rooting me to the spot and preventing me from moving.

I would have seen someone by now if I wasn't alone. The forest is eerily dark, but the trees aren't particularly thick. Though the storm makes it ten times harder to see.

God, I need to get home.

Turning around, I scan the area again, taking everything in so fast I'm sure I'm not really seeing anything at all. My heart races so fast my head feels light.

Go. You're alone and paranoid.

Leaping forward, I get a good boost and sprint out of the field and into the forest. My lungs scream for oxygen, but I can't slow down to allow it. I pelt between trees, raising my arms and keeping them in front of me in case I fall.

I whimper as I see the clearing ahead. My house is so close.

Behind me, a branch crunches, sending a chill through my spine.

No.

Keep going.

I push myself faster, force my fatigued legs to move quicker than ever before. The rain hits my body with such force it hurts, but I don't care. The weather is getting worse, rain pelting my face through the trees.

Wiping my eyes, I stumble. I shove my hands out and hiss as my palms dig into broken twigs. Lifting my head, I look over my shoulder.

Get up, Ivy!

I push myself to my feet and wipe my hands against my trousers.

My heart beats wildly as I whip my head around, turning in a circle.

Something is here.

My breath catches as a shadow darts between the trees.

What was that?

I back up and hit a tree as my eyes search everywhere.

It's probably a deer.

Where is it?

In front of me, somewhere between the rolling thunder, I hear the snap of wood and I jump.

Oh God. Go!

Shoving off the tree, I sprint again.

Pain shoots the length of my shins with each frantic step.

Reaching the edge of the forest, I pant. *Come on, you're almost there.*

The muscles in my thighs scream in protest of my speed, but I push harder, faster until my lungs burn, and I see red spots around bullets of rain.

With the trees now behind me, I whimper. I made it, but I can't breathe easy. I still have to get across the field and find my house key in my bag. I want to look back but I can't afford to slow down and be caught.

With one final push, I leap over the stream, my knee jarring as I hit the ground on the other side. Pain slices through my leg.

Crying out, I grip the strap of my bag tighter and push on. My house is in view.

I run faster, cutting through the second field and down the side of my house. Slamming my hands down, I leap over the low-level wall in the back garden.

Collapsing in a heap on the soggy grass, I burst. Fat tears fall from my eyes as I pant.

I turn my head and look up but there's nothing there.

Pushing myself to my feet, I stumble to the back door and dig around in my bag for my key.

I'm such an idiot. There was no one out there. The noise probably was just a deer.

But a tall one?

Letting myself into the house, I lean back against the door and bury my head in my hands, gasping for air.

23

It took me longer than I'd like to admit to pull myself to-gether, but I did it.

I feel like a fool, freaking out over nothing. I'm so glad no one saw me fall to pieces like that. I would never live it down.

After another shower, I feel much better.

Dad sent us a text in our group chat. He's going to be home late—after eleven. And he expects us to believe it's a business dinner. So I put on my most comfortable pajamas and ate dinner, and now I'm curled up on the sofa alone with a blanket watching TV. My heart rate has returned to normal and my tears washed away in the shower.

Could it have been a person following me? But who would want to scare me like that?

It's eight. Iris should be home—but since she knows Dad's

out, I doubt she'll be back for a couple hours yet. She has no regard for his rules, and he's not strong enough to risk upsetting her.

Tomorrow, when Dad asks, Iris will say she was home at eight and expect me to cover for her. I will because the last thing I need is more tension in the house. Meera told me to allow Iris some adjustment time and warned me she could be difficult as she comes to terms with how things are now. There's a lot to settle for my sister. If I react to her, it could make things worse long-term.

I don't want that. All I want is my nice little life back, so I'll let things slide for now to keep the peace I'm so desperate for.

Closing my eyes, I snuggle into a scatter cushion Iris picked up last week and in seconds, I drift straight to sleep.

And then, suddenly, I'm startled awake. I grip the blanket and scramble to sit up.

Iris laughs, her hands on her hips. "Sorry, I shut the door too hard. I didn't realize you were asleep there."

She doesn't look sorry, with a slight grin and amusement in her eyes.

I tap my cell and the time lights up: 10:48.

"Get lots of studying done?" I ask.

Smirking, she drops down on the sofa next to mine. "Yep. And then we hung out at the diner. How was practice?"

"It was great. I beat my best time."

"That's awesome, Ivy! What did you do after? Please tell me you haven't been here watching *Riverdale* all night."

"Er, I have."

Iris shakes her head. "You should have come out with us."

"That's okay. I was kind of beat after practice. I still am," I say, pressing the back of my hand to my mouth as I yawn.

"Did you get wet walking home? I didn't realize the time until it was six, and I figured you'd be home by then."

"I got drenched but it was okay. What did you do after the diner closed?" Nine is when they close the doors on weeknights. Iris has been out almost an extra two hours.

"We just hung around the square."

In the rain? Where did she really go?

"When do you think Dad will be back?" she asks.

I shrug and grab my bottle of water from the coffee table. "No idea."

Iris sinks back into the sofa. "He'd tell us if he was on a date, wouldn't he?"

I shrug. "Over the last couple of years, he's been open about when he dates. Before that I knew nothing. I would have thought he would say, but he hasn't." It's definitely odd since we tell each other everything. Maybe he's not dating. His workload has increased recently, so it could be that. Maybe.

"Ivy, do you think he should be dating now?"

"Yeah. Why shouldn't he?"

"Well . . . because of Mom," she deadpans, as if I'm the one who's said something ridiculous.

I can understand how she feels uncomfortable, but our parents were long divorced. "They've been apart for six years, Iris."

"I know that. But there has been a lot of change, and is

bringing someone else into the equation right now really a good idea? I know I've had enough change to last me at least another ten years. Don't you feel the same?"

"I . . ." How do I feel about it? I haven't really given it much thought. "Maybe."

"Think about how weird it would be to get to know this woman when we're still grieving and all getting used to living together again. I can't imagine setting another place at the table until we're more settled." Her eyes fill with tears. "Does that make me a totally selfish bitch?"

My stomach rolls with nausea, shocking me because I'm always happy for whatever Dad has going on in his private life if it makes him happy.

This time I'm not. Iris is right . . . the thought of him bringing someone home makes my head feel like exploding.

"It doesn't make you a bitch," I say, my voice raspy like I'm recovering from a sore throat. "I don't like the thought of someone new yet either."

I barely have my head above water as it is. I miss Mom, everything is unsettled at home, and I can't shake the feeling that something else is coming. I'm not emotionally ready for anything else. I need a pause button on life because I've reached my limit for now.

"Do you think we should talk to him together?" Iris asks. "We could explain how we feel, tell him that we're not opposed to him dating but we're not ready for it just yet."

My stomach knots. "Can we ask that of him?"

She frowns. "We're not asking anything. We're telling him

how we feel, being honest like he demands from us, and he can decide what he does from there."

"The decision he will make is to not see anyone until we're settled." I know that for sure. Dad puts being a father first, he always has, so if he knows me and Iris aren't okay with more change, he won't do anything to change our lives.

"Good. That's how it needs to be right now."

"I don't know, Iris . . ."

"No. Look, I'm not trying to be unreasonable. We're not saying he has to die alone; we just want him to hold off bringing someone new into our lives." She speaks so powerfully, like she's a professional public speaker. Her voice is clear, and every word is said with absolute conviction.

No wonder she has people eating out of her hand.

I inhale long and deep. *In for four. Out for four.*

I'm not sure about this. I do agree that we need time. At the moment, I don't want to get to know a woman my dad is seeing. He's been separated from Mom for a long time, so it's not that, but I don't want the change yet.

"Okay," I concede. "We'll talk to him when he gets home."

"You're with me? Really? I don't want to start this conversation with Dad and have you back down. We do this together or not at all."

"I've got you, Iris. I agree that it's too soon to have someone else coming around the house." I'm fine with him dating; I'm not fine with him introducing anyone new to my life yet.

Her shoulders slump. "Good. How should we tell him?"

"We just say it. He values honesty. Besides, I've never been that good at skirting around an issue."

Until now, when I don't tell Dad about some of the weird stuff Iris has done. I can talk to my dad about anything. He's always very open, even when I don't want him to be, so why can't I bring myself to tell him that Iris is inserting herself into my life a little too much?

He would listen. But I'm scared he would tell me I'm over-reacting.

Meera says it's natural for her to hold on to someone so tightly after losing Mom. I just have to ride it out until she's confident enough to let go.

"Sounds good. I like to be straight up too." She grins. "I guess I get that from Dad."

The front door swings open. Dad looks up at us and smiles, and my heart sinks. "Hey, girls. How was your day?"

Iris looks at me.

"Good," I say. "I beat my time in the pool, but now I'm ex-hausted."

"Ivy, that's great. I'm proud of you."

I beam, my chest filling with warmth. "Thanks, Dad."

"How about you, Iris?" he asks, setting his laptop bag down and kicking off his shoes.

She shrugs. "I didn't beat my time in the pool."

Grinning, Dad shakes his head. "School was okay?"

"It was fine. Nothing much happened. Actually, can Ivy and I talk to you?" Iris asks as she ties her long hair into a bun on the top of her head.

Showtime, then.

I pull my bottom lip between my teeth. All Dad has done recently is work and make sure Iris and I are okay. He's having a hard time with Mom's death, despite what he says, and we're about to tell him we don't want him to date. What if he is dating and he likes her? If she's helping him adjust to his ex-wife dying, his other daughter moving in, and supporting us both, should we really take that away?

I can't talk to Iris, but if Dad's happiness is at stake, I will deal with another person coming here.

It's not just about Dad, though. If I tell him I will be okay with him dating, I'm telling Iris her feelings don't matter.

I'm going to give myself a headache.

Choosing between people I love makes me nauseous.

"Well," Iris says. "Ivy and I have noticed a few things about you recently, and we're worried that you're seeing someone."

Why would you go straight in by saying we're worried about it? I mean, we are, but let's not put him on the defensive right from the start.

"I see," he says, his eyes flicking from her to me. "Ivy?"

"We want you to be happy, Dad." Iris nods along, agreeing with me. "We . . . we just aren't ready for more change. If things are getting serious with this woman, we'll eventually have to meet her, right?"

Dad slaps his chest as he clears his throat. "I am seeing someone," he confirms. "And things are going well. She is in agreement with me that we shouldn't introduce you all until our lives have settled down."

So he does have a girlfriend.

I push my hair behind my shoulder. "Can I ask her name?"

"Rachel."

Iris turns her head. "You're serious with her?"

He nods. "It is going that way. She's a wonderful woman, and I think you will both like her, but I'm not pushing anything. When you're ready, you can meet her."

"I'm not ready," Iris says, her eyes narrowing. "I'm not even close to being ready." She looks at me, her eyes wide like she's petrified he's going to move her in.

"It's okay," I tell her. "No one expects you to be ready yet."

"Iris," Dad says. "There is no rush, I promise you. We'll follow your lead. Yours and Ivy's. Rachel and I would never force you two to do anything you're uncomfortable with."

"When do you even have time to date, anyway? You're either at the office or here with us. We need you way more than she does." Her face reddens, and I don't know if it's because she's upset or angry.

"Iris, you and Ivy are my priority and you always will be. Rachel understands that I need to be here as much as I can right now."

"That's good, because we do need you. We don't need another mom."

Dad holds his hands up. "No one is trying to replace your mom. That will never happen, okay?"

Obviously, and Iris must know that too. Emotions are a little high right now and she's letting hers take over.

"Damn right it won't."

This is the first time I've heard Iris mention Mom. It's not a particularly positive conversation, which is a shame, but she is saying that she doesn't want anyone to replace our mom.

"I care about Rachel a lot, but nothing compares to you two. You will always be my two number ones."

"We know that, Dad," I tell him.

"Speak for yourself, Ivy. You've lived with Dad your entire life; you know him much better than I do. How do I believe what he says until I see it?"

Frowning, I reply, "Just because you haven't lived here doesn't mean Dad's not been in your life. He's never gone back on his word with you either."

What has gotten into her? Hello, hostility.

"Okay, girls," Dad says, sitting forward. "We're not going to argue. I'm telling you that I will put you first, Iris. I know you believe that because you believe me. We are going to continue to be honest with each other, and Rachel and I will give this some time before we start seeing each other again."

So he's really telling us he won't see her at all until we're okay with it. That seems a bit much. I don't mind if he still goes out with her; I just don't want to have a new person insert themselves into our lives. We're not ready to add someone else, especially since that person could eventually take on a mother-type role. There's no way to get away with it, really; if she stays with Dad and eventually moves in, she'll have to play a part in the family. It wouldn't work any other way.

"It's late. I suggest we all get some sleep," Dad says.

Iris clenches her jaw. She doesn't like being told what to do.

She likes free rein and making her own decisions about when she gets home and when she goes to bed.

Me? Well, I can't be bothered to argue anymore. I'm still tired, I still feel stupid from earlier, and my body hurts.

"Night," I say to them both, and leave them to it, whatever Iris is about to do.

When I get into bed, my muscles unlock, and I sink into the mattress. My eyelids are heavy, and they close as soon as I pull the quilt up to my chin.

My mind is working overtime. Does Dad love Rachel? How long will he be able to stay away from her? It's not fair that we ask him to put his life on hold indefinitely. I want to wait a few months before I meet her, but I don't know how long Iris is thinking. It didn't sound like she wants him to date at all.

She was angry.

Her face, her tense posture, the sharp tone in her voice. It was as if she thinks Dad is dating to spite her or something. I squeeze my eyes tighter together.

I want to support Iris and make sure she's comfortable here, but I don't want that to be at the expense of Dad's happiness.

How do we manage this? And what about Rachel? If she wants to be with my dad, she's going to want to meet us. I hope she doesn't think we don't like her already just because we're not ready to meet her.

My door creaks. It does that when you very first open it, only for the first inch.

I don't know if it's Dad or Iris, but I don't want to talk, so I keep still.

With my eyes closed, my hearing is heightened. The pad of quiet footsteps and shallow breathing sounds like it's right in my ear. It's Iris.

I lay still but curl my hands into fists under my cover. What does she want?

My heart beats faster, and I have to slow my breathing, so I don't give myself away.

Why is she watching me?

Another minute later, I hear her retreat and my door creaks again as she closes it. The sliver of light let in my room from outside disappears and I see nothing but darkness through my eyelids.

24

The next morning, I'm exhausted. I barely slept at all.

Getting out of bed, I grab my phone and Ty's hoodie from the back of my chair. The house is silent and dark. I walk down the corridor and downstairs.

Creepy Iris isn't down here, so she's still sleeping rather than people watching. I don't think I can face her before I've had a coffee. I'll never get through school without a little caffeine.

I make a pot of coffee and think back to yesterday. It's like she's fixated on me—sliding in with my group of friends, watching my practice, needing to be in the same classes.

Was she like this with her old friends? It doesn't seem like her. Iris was always a leader. She even has Ellie waiting for her and calling her first.

I sip my coffee. I think it's time I check her social media.

Maybe I'll find her old bestie. Kate? Cara? I'm sure her name started with a *K* or a *C*.

Unlocking my cell, I pull up Instagram. Back when I had time to spend hours on my phone, I noticed how much Iris posts on there compared to Facebook. That's the best place to start.

Iris's profile pops up, and I scroll through the people she's following. There are a lot of celebrities, a lot of people from school, none who I recognize from visiting Mom's. I don't really remember all her friends, but I think I could recognize faces.

Wait. I scroll through her friends list with a frown. Most of these are people I know. Relatives and distant relatives we both added at family weddings, though we knew it was unlikely we'd see them again. A few friends of the family.

Where are her friends?

I scroll faster, my eyes quickly scanning the name and picture of each one as my heart beats harder.

Then my mouth drops and the hairs on my forearms rise as I realize.

She's unfollowed all her friends from her old school.

I personally know everyone on her list. The only people she has kept are family.

She has erased her past and the life she and Mom built with the click of a button.

Why doesn't she want to stay friends with the people she spent years with?

I get needing to have a fresh start. Sometimes, when my anxiety is running wild, I would love to run away to someplace new. But you can't outrun who you are. There is only so long that

Iris can put off grieving for Mom and missing her old home and friends.

I go to her Facebook profile. She hasn't posted much at all. A lot of people have posted on her page. Lots of sympathy over our mom's death.

She hasn't replied to any of them.

I scroll back up. There must be someone from her old school who she was close to. I click on her photos but most of them are gone. All that is left is a picture of her and Dad she has as her profile picture from years ago, a couple random photos of shoes she'd bought, and a lot of selfies.

Where are the pictures of us? I remember being tagged. I remember reading her friends' comments about how crazy it is that we look so alike and laughing.

Identical twins looking alike. Crazy stuff there.

I'm not a part of her old life, her old circle of friends. I'm family. Why am I gone too? She's left me on her friends list, at least.

Did she delete me because of her friends' comments on our pictures or did she not want *me*?

So she has been on here to remove people and pictures. Not recently, though—she hasn't deleted the posts from her classmates.

Ugh, I don't know what I'm doing. What am I even looking for?

Social media isn't going to give me any answers. I flick the TV on. I could really use a distraction, so an early-morning *Gilmore Girls* marathon sounds perfect.

At least my relationship with my sister isn't as messy as Lorelai's is with her mom.

I'm on the second episode and my second coffee when I hear light footsteps thudding downstairs.

My body tenses and I look over. Iris wears a frown as she approaches.

"What are you doing, Ivy?"

"I couldn't sleep," I reply. "Coffee is still hot if you want one."

She tilts her head. "How long have you been down here?"

"Since about five-thirty. Why?"

"Why did you wake up?" she presses.

Because I couldn't sleep after you spent a whole minute watching me.

I don't go with that, though. I'm a chicken and I don't want to cause a fuss. She would go on the defensive, and Dad would tell me I'm being unreasonable and need to cut her some more slack. So I go with "I'm not sure, just one of those nights."

She sits down. "You seem to have a lot of those nights."

"I've never slept well. You know that."

"Yeah, the parents used to talk about the good sleeper and the bad one."

I nod. "I'm the bad one."

"Do you need a refill?" she asks, glancing at my mug.

"No, thanks, already on my second cup."

"Okay, be back in a minute. I love *Gilmore Girls.*"

I look over my shoulder as she bounds into the kitchen. I'm envious of her energy.

We manage to watch an entire episode before we need to leave for school. In the parking lot we bump into Ellie and Logan.

"Morning," Ellie says, letting go of Logan and linking arms with Iris.

"Morning, Ellie," Iris replies.

Logan and I kind of fall into step with each other as Ellie and Iris move to the side.

I give him a tight smile. "Logan."

Wringing my hands, I force my eyes ahead. It's always awkward seeing him again after what happened last year. The party, his drunk lips. Nope. I didn't even want him to kiss me and now I have to keep our secret.

He nods. "Hey, Ivy. How's swimming?"

"Fine. Football? Ty says you're scoring more. That's good."

He scratches the back of his neck. "Yeah, it's awesome."

This feels really uncomfortable. I wish the steps to school would move closer.

Logan slaps his forehead. "Just remembered that I need to check in with Coach this morning," he says. "See you later."

I look away quickly.

He leans over and pecks Ellie on the lips before jogging off ahead of us.

"Got the smell of death out of your locker yet?" Ellie asks.

Now, if she was asking that to make general conversation, she wouldn't have asked like such a bitch. Nor would she have a smirk on her glossy lips. She blinks her hazel eyes.

"Yes, thanks."

"Terrible how it got in and died."

My eyes narrow. It might be terrible, but it might not be an accident. No, Ellie would never touch a mouse. No way. She refused to dissect the frog in class and won't play any sport outside in case her manicure gets ruined.

Iris nudges her arm. "You two would get along if you spent any time together."

Ellie folds her arms over her chest.

I smile, but I'm sure my expression is saying much more. Ellie and I don't get along.

"I'm going to head in and find Ty," I tell Iris and Ellie.

I rush through the large double doors. Ty's not usually at school before me unless he needs to come in early for something football related, but I'm still looking for him in case. He's not by his locker. Mine is a little farther away, but I can see it and there's no Ty in front of it.

Damn it. I could really do with him being here. I need to know we're okay. I'm tired and he will make things better. He's so good at that, even without trying.

Walking up to his locker, I lean back against it and wait.

Sophie and Haley walk toward me, but I see Sophie looking at her phone and suddenly they turn around. I look over Haley's shoulder. Iris and Ellie are heading toward them.

They talk for a second and I watch, wondering what they're laughing about.

My heart drops as they all walk off. They definitely saw me, but they acted like I'm not here. Sophie and Haley don't even like Ellie. They've spent hours gossiping over how she thinks she's better than everyone else. Why do they suddenly want to be friends with her?

What kind of influence does Iris have?

25

Iris is already sitting at her desk when I get to Geography. I slide in next to her and open my book.

Mrs. Lynden starts class, and Iris silently listens. I flick my eyes to my sister. She usually chats through most classes and causes me to lose focus.

Shaking my head, I turn my attention back to my book and try to follow what we're being taught. Which is geography, so it might as well be a foreign language.

Iris taps her fingertips on the desk, one slightly after the other and all so lightly I can barely hear it.

So she doesn't want to talk to me, but she also doesn't want to let me focus. Excellent.

Squeezing my eyes shut, I try to block out the constant

tapping. It sounds like a mouse scuttling across the floor. I dig my fingers into the wooden desktop and take a deep breath.

My heart skips.

She needs to stop.

I want to slam my hand down on hers.

Focus on reading. I know what page we're on in the textbook, but I'm not following, so I start at the top.

Why doesn't it make sense?

Tap, tap, tap.

My eye twitches.

Focus on the book.

I press my lips together.

Out of the corner of my eye, I see Iris smiling.

Tap, tap, tap, tap, tap.

She's doing this on purpose.

Tap, tap, tap.

"Iris, stop!" I snap, shouting so loud my body jolts at the volume.

Gasping, I turn my head to my sister. She's staring back at me wide-eyed. As is the rest of the class.

"Ivy, is there a problem?" Mrs. Lynden asks.

Burning with humiliation, I lower my gaze. "No, sorry."

"Iris?"

"I have no idea what's going on. I don't know why she shouted at me." Iris looks back at me. "Are you feeling okay?"

As if she's trying to make out that I'm the one with the problem. "I'm fine," I say, swallowing.

"If you need to go to the nurse, please do," Mrs. Lynden tells me.

"I'm fine," I repeat, sinking in my seat as my classmates whisper about me.

I shouted out in the middle of class while the teacher was talking. Iris was looking ahead. The taps on the table so slight and quiet that no one else noticed.

They must think I'm crazy.

"You haven't been sleeping," Iris says. "Maybe you should go to the nurse or go home."

Mrs. Lynden walks down the aisle and stops by my desk. "Ivy," she says softly, lowering her voice so the whole classroom can't hear. "Would you like to be excused?"

No, I don't want to be excused. I want my sister to stop messing with me.

I rub my eyes and say, "I'm fine."

"Well, I trust there will be no more outbursts, then."

Looking down at my book, I nod. Iris got the better of me there, but I won't let it happen again.

Class obviously passes slowly. Iris doesn't mention anything as we walk to English. Not that I expected her to—that would be admitting she's done something wrong.

But I can't walk into English and have her do the same thing. I can't snap again.

"Hey," I say, grabbing her wrist as we get closer to the door. "What was that back there?"

She pulls her arm out of my grasp and frowns. "What was what?"

"The tapping. It's usually constant chatter, now you're tapping."

"Huh?"

Scoffing, I say, "Don't play dumb. You were tapping on the desk and that's why I shouted. You made me look like a total idiot."

"I didn't even know I was doing it. Why would that make you all crazy, anyway? Honestly, Ivy, I can't believe you're blaming me for this when you're the one who freaked out in class."

My lips part. Is she for real? "You knew what you were doing."

She holds her palms up. "Okay, you're being ridiculous, and I can't talk to you when you're like this."

When *I'm* like this? Is she for real?

I watch her walk into class with her head in the air.

Bitch.

"Ivy, what happened?"

I look to my side as Ty jogs toward me.

"Ty, what are you doing here?"

"I got a text saying you screamed at Iris in class."

Rolling my eyes, I mumble, "Great. First, I didn't scream. Second, she was constantly tapping her fingers on the desk, so I snapped at her."

His head tilts to the side, looking at me with concern brimming in his forest-green eyes. "Babe . . ."

"Don't. I shouldn't have done that. But I'm struggling in Geography enough as it is."

He frowns at me. "You're getting As in Geography."

"Yes, but I'm struggling." Looking up to the ceiling, I take a long breath. "Ty, I don't know what's going on with her."

"Iris?"

"Yeah. But listen, we're both late. I'll talk to you at lunch, okay?"

She's so back and forth. Now she's getting to my friends first thing in the morning when they would usually look for me.

And where is her old friend? Why hasn't she got in touch?

He grabs my hand. "Uh-uh, not happening. Something is going on with you and we're not going anywhere until I'm convinced that you're okay."

I raise my eyebrows. "Oh really?"

"Yeah. Let's go."

"Ty, come on. Iris will definitely tell if I cut class."

He shrugs. "I think the teachers will understand given the circumstances."

Yeah, they will, but I don't want to use Mom's death as an excuse. I don't want *understanding* because I lost someone I love. That doesn't feel right to me.

He looks around the hallway. It's completely clear, but it won't be in a minute, because Iris will tell the teacher I'm out here. He takes my hand. "Come on."

I let him lead me away because although I don't want to crumble and let Mom's death affect school, it clearly is. Before she died, I had more patience. I would have been able to ignore Iris back there. Now I'm unsure if my lack of patience is due to grief or my sister being super frustrating.

We leave the school building and go to his car. He's parked far enough away that we won't be seen. If we go back when the bell rings, we should be able to blend in with the crowd.

Not that it'll matter because our teachers will know we're absent from this class and they'll ask questions.

I'm too tired to care.

I lie back against the passenger seat and close my eyes.

"Any time you want to start talking, babe . . ."

"I don't know what to say."

"I'm worried about you," he confesses. "Losing it in class is . . ."

"Yeah, I know." Out of character. Embarrassing. "And everyone is talking about it. Do you think Mrs. Lynden will call my dad?"

"Probably not. Unless you do it again." He winks at me. "I'm sure Mrs. Lynden has forgotten it already."

God, I hope so.

"She was watching me sleep."

His head rolls to the side, facing me. "What?"

"I've heard her by my door. I pretend to be asleep."

A frown pulls his eyebrows together. "You're sure she's watching you sleep?"

"Well, I hear her breathing outside my door. Clearly I don't see her because I'm pretending to be asleep."

He says nothing for the longest time. Silence stretches into minutes. I sink lower in the seat. He thinks I'm insane. I sound like it, so why wouldn't he think that? Maybe I should have picked a better time to tell him, not straight after a classroom meltdown.

"Ty, say something," I whisper.

"I'm not sure what to say. Is Iris looking to talk?"

"While I'm asleep?"

He lifts one shoulder in another shrug. "Who knows? I'm not really worried about Iris, though."

I am.

"I think I should take you home."

My eyes widen. "What? No! Dad will freak out."

"When has your dad ever freaked out?"

"You know what I mean. If I skipped class he would, and you know it."

My phone buzzes in my pocket.

Oh great, it's starting. Ty looks at my pocket and lifts his eyebrow. Nope, I don't really want to look at the message.

But he keeps looking at me.

> Where are you? Should I go to the office?

> No! I'll be in the next class.
> Don't go to anyone!

"Who is it?" Ty asks.

"My twin. She's asking where I am."

Someone taps on the glass.

"Ivy, I need you to come with me," the school psychologist, Ms. Hart, says.

My mouth drops open. Did she tell? Did my sister actually

tell someone that I skipped class? Who asked the psychologist to come and get me? Shouldn't it be a teacher ready to chuck a punishment my way?

Or because my mom died that means every time I screw up I need to *talk*? Ms. Hart briefly explains what's going to happen.

Ty walks in the opposite direction to us. He gets to go back to class. I get to have a meeting. Oh, and my dad will be invited to a meeting after school too.

Wonderful.

I'm so over school, and I'm so over my sister. I don't care what she's going through; there is no reason for her to make my life difficult.

"I needed a minute before returning to class. Ty was only trying to help," I tell Ms. Hart as we walk through the double doors and make a right into her office.

"Take a seat, Ivy."

I do as I'm told because although I want to get shouty again, that's not going to go down well in here.

"Please tell me Ty isn't in trouble."

"Tyler is fine, Ivy. You are the one I'm worried about."

"Look, I know I should have gone to class but—"

She shakes her head. "This isn't about class. Ivy, your dad has informed me you are seeing a therapist, which is fantastic, but I think it's become clear that you need more help at school. We've been observing you."

Who is *we*?

"Why do you need my dad here to tell me that?"

"We've been aware that you have been struggling for a while."

"What?"

"Your teachers have reported that you're distracted in class."

That's because Iris always hums or taps or whispers, and she is in every one of my classes. "My grades haven't slipped."

She sits down opposite me and threads her fingers together. "And that is great, but we can't ignore this because it eventually could affect your grades. Your outburst in class only shows me that I'm right. We need to get your father involved so we can put in place the help you need now."

I fold my arms. "Transfer Iris out of my classes and you will see a vast improvement."

Her eyebrows rise.

"Or transfer me out. I don't really care which one of us goes at this point."

Calm down. You're doing a crap job of convincing her you're okay.

The worst part is if my mom hadn't just died, no one would question me having one crappy moment. Now suddenly everything I do is because I'm grieving. I can't just have a bad day anymore.

I break eye contact with Ms. Hart because it's pointless talking to her. She's made up her mind. I can only imagine what Iris said to her.

Dad will know the truth when I tell him what actually happened. He's always believed me.

I spend the next two class periods with her, doing work on my own because I can only assume that I'm now not trusted to be silent in class.

Dad has taken time off work to come here. He's dropping

everything to attend this meeting, so that's going to have him in a bad mood coming through the door.

"What's going on?" he asks as Ms. Hart lets him into the room.

"Please, take a seat," she says.

I close my book for English Lit. It doesn't feel much like a Shakespeare day anyway.

Dad sits beside me on the uncomfortable brown leather chair. His blue eyes are pinned on me. "Ivy?"

I shake my head. "Iris has been irritating me in class since, like, the third day here. Today I snapped because I couldn't concentrate. Now it's all my fault."

That about sums it up.

Ms. Hart takes over. "Ivy's outburst in class today prompted her teacher to have a word with me. I found her in the car lot with Tyler West."

Dad raises his sandy eyebrows at me.

"I needed a minute to calm down and Ty knew that. We weren't going to go anywhere."

"That's not why we're here, Ivy. We're worried about you."

"You don't need to be, Ms. Hart, but I do think I should be moved out of Iris's classes."

"What?" Dad's voice is laced with shock. "Why do you want that? Ivy, what is going on? I wasn't even aware you two are having issues."

I place my hands on the desk. "I think it's better if we have different schedules. She doesn't need me anymore; she's settled in and made friends just fine."

Dad watches me like he thinks I've been abducted and

someone else was left in my place. "That seems very hasty. You didn't sleep well; you haven't for a while."

"Ivy, we can give you more emotional support at school if you're finding it difficult."

Right now, I'm finding Iris difficult.

I shake my head. "No, I don't need that."

"I would like to suggest that you come and see me on a regular basis for now. I'm here for you, whenever you need."

Dad pipes up. "I think that would be a good idea. I know Meera is helping you, but if you're getting stressed at school, it'll be good for you to talk to someone here too."

Taking a deep breath, I force a smile. "Okay."

Ugh, agreeing with them is like swallowing salt. But we're not getting anywhere. Dad is siding with Ms. Hart and Iris. No one is seeing what she's been doing wrong because I'm the one who reacted to her.

Well, fine. I'll deal with it on my own.

26

All of last night, Dad and Iris kept their distance. I can barely look at her, the little liar. She wanted a reaction in the classroom, she got one, and now she's very smug. I want to scream, but I have to be smart about this.

She is clever, but I'm not going to be sucked into her games. I don't care if she taps on every table in school. I'm going to keep my cool and be civil. I refuse to react to her again. I'm cutting off the oxygen.

It's been the longest week in history, thanks to Iris and her mind games, but it's Friday. I'm watched constantly at school now, the teachers waiting for another outburst and Ms. Hart dropping by classes to see how I'm doing. Even Coach keeps her eyes on me more than usual.

I'm trying not to be too hostile to everyone, though I feel it.

My teachers think that I'm struggling and they're looking out for me. No one has seen the games that Iris is playing, but that's fine, because she can't continue them forever.

I keep my eyes on the floor as I walk. I can feel people staring, eyes burning into me hoping to catch my next show. I don't know what Iris has said, but no one is as chatty to me anymore. All I've done is snap at my sister in a class. How that suddenly makes me an outcast, I don't know. But whatever.

I don't need these people anyway. Ty, Haley, and Sophie know me. Whatever Iris is saying about me, and I can only imagine how she's making me look, it doesn't matter.

One of the first thing that Mom and Dad taught us is that someone's opinion about you only matters if you care about them. At this moment I don't care much for Iris.

"Ivy!" Ty shouts.

I twist because his voice is deep, intense and snappy.

"What's up?" I ask as he reaches me.

"What is this?" He holds up his phone.

Frowning, I take the cell. No.

Oh my God. It's a picture of me and Logan. It was taken about a year ago at a party. At the party where Logan kissed me.

I shake my head, the blood draining from my face, making me dizzy. "Ty, I can explain."

He takes a deep breath. "You kissed Logan."

I stare him in the eyes. "No, I didn't."

"I have the picture, Ivy!"

I glance around as people walking past start to pay attention to us. Ty shoves his phone in his pocket and folds his arms.

The way he's looking at me, eyes narrowed and jaw tight, has my stomach churning. His nose is scrunched like he's disgusted.

"I can see how it looks, Ty, but I didn't kiss him." I take a step closer and his body tenses. "Please. Logan was drunk at Ellie's party and he kissed me. I pushed him away and he realized what he'd done. It was all over in a second."

"If that's what happened, why didn't you tell me?"

"Can we go somewhere else and talk?" I plead. People have stopped to watch.

Looks like my next show is right now.

"We'll miss class."

"I don't care!" I exclaim. "Please take a walk with me. I won't be able to focus until we sort this out."

His chest expands as he takes a long breath. I hate what he's thinking right now. He's so mad at me his face is red. But the worst part is the pain in his eyes.

"Fine," he growls.

Ty turns and stalks off away from me. I follow, my heart dropping at the possibility he won't believe me.

"Ivy, where are you going?" Iris asks.

I barely hear her as I rush past, trying to catch up with Ty.

"Ivy?"

Looking over my shoulder, I snap, "Later!"

I don't hear a reply because I run to catch the door. My palms slam into the wood as it swings back from Ty practically kicking it open. I push and slip outside.

"Tyler, will you wait up?"

He doesn't slow at all.

"Tyler!" Gripping hold of the strap of my bag over my shoulder, I break into a sprint and follow.

Ty runs around the corner and we're by the side of the building, just visible from the front doors.

"What?" he snaps.

"Stop running from me."

"I have." He runs his hands through his hair. "God, Ivy, you kissed someone else."

"No, I said I didn't, and I was telling the truth. When I pushed Logan away, he was shocked. Neither of us planned it and neither of us is attracted to the other. He was so apologetic and scared that you would find out."

"So you chose him over me?"

"No! I didn't want to ruin your friendship with him because of one dumb mistake."

"Did you kiss him back?"

"Of course I didn't. It was instant, Ty. I shoved him so hard he almost fell over. I need you to believe me. I would *never* cheat on you."

He looks away, his green eyes frosting over.

I'm petrified that he won't forgive me. Not for the kiss but because I kept it secret.

"Ty, please," I say, taking a step closer to him. My vision blurs with tears. "Don't turn away from me like we're over. I'm sorry I didn't tell you."

How did this happen?

"Did he ask you not to tell me or was that your idea?"

"We both kind of decided."

"While he was drunk?"

Closing my eyes, I breathe, "We spoke the following day."

He laughs without humor. "Of course you did."

When I open my eyes again, he's watching me, but I might as well be made of glass. "Ty, you're not listening to me."

"Yeah, I am."

"You might hear the words but you're not listening. I'm sorry I didn't tell you before."

"You already said that."

"And I'll keep saying it until you believe me."

He shakes his head, eyes downcast. "I can't believe this."

"Where did you get that picture?"

"It was sent to me."

"By who?"

"I don't know. It was a blocked number."

I didn't see anyone else in the basement when Logan kissed me. But I was distracted, pushing him off and yelling at him.

A blocked number?

Whoever took it waited five months to share it with Ty. So why now?

"You know, at first I thought it was Photoshopped. There is no way you or Logan would have done that."

"I didn't."

"No, he did, and you lied about it."

"What would you have done if I'd gone straight to you at that party?"

Ty's eyes narrow. He would have started something with Logan.

"Exactly. I'm not excusing his behavior because he never

should have done that, but he'd had too much to drink and he made a massive mistake. He was so worried that you would hate him."

"Ivy, he would have been worried that I would have him kicked off the team. He couldn't care less about me."

"You guys are friends."

He glares. "Not good friends. I wouldn't tell him any real stuff, and I wouldn't trust him with my girlfriend."

"I didn't know that. But having him kicked off the team for some stupid mistake would have been wrong."

"You're defending him?"

"You know I'm not. Don't be dramatic."

His eyes meet mine again and he whispers, "You lied to me."

"Ty," I say, swiping tears as they drop. "Please, we can fix this."

"You thought I would never find out."

That's exactly what I thought because too much time had passed. We grew closer, things were working out, and I couldn't say it.

"I hoped you wouldn't because I didn't want to hurt you."

He shakes his head again. "Keeping something from me is what hurts, Ivy. You pushing some dude away who tried to kiss you wouldn't."

"Well, I didn't know that. We had only been together three months and you never said you didn't really like Logan. I was trying to protect your friendship."

"What else are you keeping from me?"

I ball my hands. "Don't. Maybe I used bad judgment; you do not get to act like I'm some stranger. You know me, Ty, even if you want to pretend that you don't right now."

Above us, the sky clouds over dark gray.

He looks away and inhales sharply. "You have to tell me things like that."

"I know. I'm sorry."

"I need to talk to Logan."

"This doesn't need to be a big deal. He was drunk and super apologetic when he realized what he'd done."

Tucking his phone back in his pocket, he replies, "I need to talk to him."

Ty walks away from me, and I press my palm against the wall.

My eyes lift as the hairs on my forearms rise.

With my breath catching in my throat, I dig my nails into the brick. Iris is by the front door of the hall, watching with a faint smile on her devil lips.

She sent the picture. How? And why is she doing this to me?

I spend the rest of the day walking around with the heaviest unsettled feeling in my heart. Nausea rolls in the pit of my stomach.

Iris was watching like she was waiting for this. But I can't get my head around it. Sure, we've had a few arguments and snapped at each other, but I thought we were doing okay. There has been more good than bad between us.

Why is she trying to irritate me in class and cause a rift between me and Ty? And where the hell did she get that picture? She didn't even know my friends until she moved here, so there is no way she took it.

Who else is behind this? No one else has a problem with me. That I know of.

No, it has to be Iris. There are too many things happening for it not to be.

I wince as my head throbs with an intense ache. I backed her up with Dad not introducing Rachel to our lives. I'm trying to be a good sister.

Why is she trying to get back at me?

27

After my session with Meera on Friday, I head to Ellie's pool party with Ty. A very quiet and still sulking Ty. It's been four days since the entirely different kind of photo bomb was dropped on us, and although he says he's okay, he's not.

All I can do is wait for him to get over it and assure him that I won't doubt us again. Things are so much different now compared to when we first started dating.

If I'm honest, I thought he would get bored with me and find someone in his circle. That led to me making a mistake.

Logan hasn't been at school the last couple of days. Apparently, he's out of town with his family, but it seems a bit coincidental. He usually has a house party when his family goes away. This time, right after Ty finds out he tried to kiss me, he goes with them.

Iris is laughing with Ellie by the pool. They're wearing the same color bikini—hot pink. They seem to be getting closer, though Iris barely ever mentions her at home. She's all about me, Sophie, and Haley when Ellie isn't around. So I have no idea if their friendship is genuine or if she would sever the cord as easily as she did with her old friends.

"Here," Ty says, handing me a Dr Pepper.

"Thanks."

The corner of his mouth curls in a half-smile. And that's about as friendly as he's being with me. He's distant while standing right beside me.

Every part of my being is screaming at me to fix it, to talk to him, to do something so we will really be okay again. But I'm scared to push in case he decides he's done.

Meera said he might need time to think it through. If he's thinking rationally, he would see that moment for what it was, but because emotions are involved, they're clouding his judgment.

So I basically have to wait an indefinite amount of time for the clouds to shift.

Which sucks because I hate it when we're in a fight.

"Are you going to swim?" I ask him.

We used to go to the local public pool a lot but since Iris arrived, we haven't been once.

"I'll never beat you," he replies.

"We don't have to race." We've never raced. He just doesn't want to do anything with me. I glance over at my sister. "Iris and Ellie look like the twins here."

They even have the same white high-heeled sandals.

"They don't have the same face," he replies.

"You didn't used to think Iris and I had the same face."

He looks at me. "I can tell the difference. It would get awkward if I couldn't." There is no humor to the words; he sounds like he's making small talk with a stranger.

I sigh. "Okay, what the hell is going on? You said you forgave me for not telling you about Logan, but you've given me nothing but attitude. It's not okay, Ty. If you need to talk, that's fine. If you want to yell at me, go ahead. But stop shutting me out because that's not how we do things."

Yeah, I'm not good at waiting.

"People are looking, Ivy."

"Well, then, it's my turn to not care who's watching." I cross my arms, which would send a message of defiance a lot more successfully if I didn't have to be careful not to spill my soda.

I don't need to look to know that Iris is watching. She's everywhere.

He flexes his jaw. "I'm still angry."

"I've noticed. What is it going to take to get through this?"

Meera would be tutting at me right now. I don't care.

"I don't know, Ivy. Let's forget it now and enjoy the party."

That's not going to work for me. My chest aches at the distance. I can't be around him when he's like this with me; it's not us.

"Yeah, well, I won't be enjoying it when you can barely look at me. I'll see you on Monday, Ty."

I can't stay here and pretend. Doing that, added to the feeling of something being wrong, is making me nauseous. Ty doesn't stop me as I walk past him and around the side of the house. Although I came with Ty, my house is within walking distance.

He doesn't call out to me or follow. So that tells me everything I need to know. I was right the first time; I need to give him time and space.

The sun has only just begun to set. I sip my Dr Pepper as I walk. There is no actual sidewalk, just a wide grassy path that people use.

My phone buzzes in my pocket.

It's Iris.

Rolling my eyes, I answer the call. "What?"

"Ivy, where are you? Ty said you left."

You watched me leave!

"Yeah, I'm not feeling it."

"Well, hold up, I'll come with you."

"No, stay," I reply a little too quickly to be polite. "I mean, you were having fun, and to be honest, I would rather be alone right now."

"Did you and Tyler fight?"

"Not really. I just don't feel like partying. Me and Ty will be fine."

"Sure you're okay?" she asks.

"Yep, I'm all good. Enjoy the party, and let Sophie and Haley know what's happened. Tell them I'll call them tomorrow."

"I will when they arrive. See you at home."

"Bye," I reply, and hang up.

Dad is out when I get home. He said he's meeting his friends at a bar to have a couple beers and play darts. I think he's meeting Rachel.

I lock the front door behind me and head to the kitchen to fix a snack. Something super unhealthy, like a massive bar of chocolate or chips. Or both.

I'm wallowing.

I take my food into the living room and flick on the TV. Under different circumstances, I would enjoy being home alone. But everything being still tonight means there aren't enough distractions to stop my mind spinning. Ty is showing no signs of forgiving me anytime soon. I think maybe he wants me to sweat a little first.

I suppose I can understand that. I'm the one who made the mistake of not telling him about Logan kissing me. I should have known that his issue would be with me lying about it. Though, in my defense, back then, I didn't know him as well as I do now. How was I supposed to know Logan wasn't a real friend? I thought I was saving their relationship and ours, keeping secret a silly moment that meant nothing to me or Logan.

I don't even remember everyone who was at the party, so I don't know who took the picture. Or who would have given it to Iris. When Logan kissed me, I thought we were in the basement alone. The other guys down there had gone up first.

This is such a mess.

I pop a square of chocolate in my mouth as my phone buzzes.

It's my group chat with Haley and Sophie.

SOPHIE: Why did you leave?

HALEY: Did you argue with Ty again?

SOPHIE: He's still mad but you shouldn't leave. Come back and show him you're fighting for him.

Fantastic. Now my best friends think that I'm in the wrong for leaving.

My skin prickles. They have no idea what I'm doing. Haley is single and Sophie has been seeing Sam for, like, three months. So for them to judge me over this is seriously irritating.

We're always honest with each other, even if we don't want to hear it, but I'm not in the wrong here. Giving Ty space is clearly what he needs; getting in his face right now isn't going to make things better.

Besides, Logan is due back today. I overheard Ellie talking about him coming back at school.

I don't think he's going to Ellie's party because apparently his family doesn't get back to town until late, but the fact that he's coming back is probably adding to Ty's bad mood. Take me and Logan out of the equation and maybe he'll calm down.

I do hate that I'm not there with him, though.

Not that he would ever do anything.

Laying my head back on the sofa, I close my eyes. Not only is Ty angry, but it sounds like Sophie and Haley are too. Why can no one see this from my point of view? I curl my blanket around my body, feeling insecure and hating it.

Closing my eyes, I feel a tear trickle down my cheek.

28

"How are you feeling about seeing Ty today?" Iris asks, checking her face in the mirror as I drive to school. She flips the sun shade up and looks at me.

I press my lips together as my eye twitches. I don't want her in my car, but I have no choice. I've had to let the tapping thing in the classroom go, as it only makes me look bad. I can't accuse her of sending Ty that picture, as I have no proof—which would make me in the wrong again.

So I'm stuck . . . for now.

Iris asking about Ty is the first thing she's said to me this morning, and she's straight into it. No small talk and asking each other how we slept.

"Fine," I reply, fire burning in my chest. "We spoke last night."

Her eyebrow lifts. "All is forgiven, then?"

My heart beats a little faster. I tighten my grip around the steering wheel. "You say that like he shouldn't forgive me."

"He can do what he wants."

"But you don't think he should."

She hums. "You lied to him. All I'm saying is I think I would be angry for longer than two minutes."

"I didn't lie to hurt him, Iris. I did it for the exact opposite reason." God, it's too early for this conversation. I don't have nearly enough coffee in my body to discuss whether my sister thinks my boyfriend should be cool with me now. Especially with her.

"Ellie is angry too."

"Ellie has no reason to be angry. She wasn't with Logan then. It's not like she was a nun until he came along."

Iris folds her arms. "You're starting to make enemies. I'm worried."

"Enemies? That's a tad dramatic, don't you think?"

"Whatever. People aren't happy that you've been lying. People aren't happy that Ty is hurting."

I glance at her briefly. "Who are these people specifically?"

"I'm not a rat."

Are you sure about that?

"Sounds like you're annoyed with me too."

"Please, you're my sister, Ivy. I'm just worried that things might start falling apart for you. Sophie and Haley didn't have the best things to say about you last night."

My smile drops. "What?"

"Look, I don't like talking about people behind their back, so

I'm not giving you a list, but those two are your best friends and that's unacceptable."

"What were they saying?" I ask, my voice as low as I feel.

No, she's lying.

She looks away. "That you shouldn't have left Tyler at the party."

That's what they said to me too.

"They said you're in the wrong for the secret about Logan as well."

Sure, I know all of this is true, but it kind of stings hearing that my best friends are discussing it with other people too.

"Right," I reply.

"Don't worry, they won't stay mad."

Well, that's great, but I'm not entirely sure I'm not mad at them now. Since when do we judge each other's mistakes?

Since now, apparently. Kind of crappy, since I didn't judge Haley when she ditched her ex by text. Or Sophie when she copied an essay from the internet to pass a class she was stressed over.

"Yay, we're here," Iris says as I pull into the parking lot and stop the car.

I take a quick look in the side mirror when I get out. Iris's morning routine takes about an hour. She's as polished as Ellie. I go to school much the same as when I woke up—a mess.

I did have the good sense to brush my wavy hair, but it still looks awful, so I've tied it up. I have on a small amount of mascara and that's it. I can't bring myself to care much about my appearance today.

Iris looks like a model. No one will get us mixed up today.

She's wearing one of my T-shirts, though.

I don't care about that today either.

We head inside together. I'm surprised Iris doesn't want to go in separately so her image isn't hurt by being with me.

"There's Tyler," she says as we walk the corridor. He's standing by his locker talking to a couple of his friends. Sophie and Haley are with them.

"I have eyes," I say, annoyed that she's pointing him out to me.

She puts her hands on her hips. "Ellie wants to meet me outside the library. Do you want me to hang around with you?"

"No thanks."

Not ever.

"Message if you need anything," Iris says. "And remember you're better than all of them."

Huh? I watch her leave and shake my head. I'm what, now? Is she trying to tell me that I'm better than my friends? So I'll ditch them and be alone?

Ty spots me first. He slaps Leo on the back and walks away from his teammates.

My heart races as he heads toward me. I bite my lip. His face is straight, emotionless. I don't know what kind of reception I'm going to get.

"Hey," he says.

I swallow. "Hey, Ty."

"Ivy." He opens his arms and tugs me to him. "Damn it, I'm sorry."

I hug him back tightly, sure I'm about to crack a rib, but he doesn't complain. "You have nothing to be sorry about."

"I do. I shut you out when I should have spoken to you. I get it, okay. I understand why you didn't tell me, and I should have thought it through before reacting."

I look up at him and smile. "I promise I won't keep anything from you again."

"That sounds good to me."

"Want to walk me to class?" I ask.

"You know I love walking you to your first class and having to run at the speed of light to make it to mine on time."

He's back. The tension around his eyes has disappeared and the leafy green is crystal clear again. His smile is easy and just for me.

"I thought so." I let go and he takes my hand. "Are we meeting after swim and football practice tonight?"

"Yeah, let's go to dinner. Will Iris—"

"She's going to Ellie's."

His smile grows. "Good."

We pass Haley and Sophie. They both raise their hand in greeting. I'm not sure if they know that I've been told what they said but it's not unusual for us to give a quick wave if one of us is busy or talking to someone else.

Sophie has her hair down today. Glossy white hair sits on her shoulders. I like it, but I wonder what changed?

"You guys okay?" Ty asks when we're out of earshot.

"Yeah, why?"

"You tensed when we walked past. Has something happened?"

"I just heard that they're annoyed with me."

Ty rolls his eyes. "You guys have had fights before. They never last long, so don't worry."

"I'm not worried," I reply. I'm hurt. Even when we're not on the best terms, which is rare, I never talk behind their backs. I don't know if they got swept up in the moment because Ty was clearly unhappy but it's not cool.

Ty walks me to class, kisses me, then turns and runs down the hall.

"See you later, babe," he calls over his shoulder.

I laugh to myself and head inside the classroom.

Iris and Ellie are already there. I sit by the window next to Iris.

"Ty walked you. So sweet," Ellie says. Her voice is as fake as her Louis Vuitton bag.

I don't let it pass when someone takes a dig at me, but I can't exactly talk about her boyfriend not bothering to walk her any-where. Her boyfriend is Logan.

Ignoring her, I give Iris a look as the bell rings. *See what you're friends with?* Ellie isn't usually that bitchy. Not to me, anyway, but she'll be boiling inside because her boyfriend made a pass at me first.

That won't go over well.

The classroom fills up quickly and a second after Mrs. Harris walks in, Logan ducks inside and takes his seat behind me.

I feel his gaze burning the back of my head. Ty hadn't mentioned confronting Logan, though that's no surprise, but I'm sure Logan would have been told by multiple people that Ty knows.

If Logan is mad at me, he can get lost. The person who sent the message is to blame for it coming out now.

"Ivy," Logan whispers as Mrs. Harris gets started with the class.

I keep my eyes ahead and curl my hand around my pen. He is going to make this class a misery.

Iris and Ellie are looking at me; I can just about see two pairs of eyes staring. One set eerily like mine look mildly bored and the other look ready to attack.

Can I get a do-over today?

"Ivy?" Logan whispers again.

I turn my head to the side, the window side, of course, as I don't want to see Ellie. "What?" I hiss.

"I need to talk to you."

"Not now."

"I haven't seen Ty yet."

Really, we're doing this now, in the middle of class?

I shrug because I don't care. They're going to have it out whatever I say or do. It's best that Ty yells at Logan a bit and then everyone moves on.

"Who sent it?"

Yeah, good question, Logan. I have no idea.

I shrug again.

"Well, what number did it come from?"

Mrs. Harris looks over. Her eyes move along the row, unable to figure out who's talking.

The second she goes back to explaining . . . whatever she's explaining, Logan starts again. "We need to figure out who it was. I'm going to kill them."

I turn up my nose. That's a big threat for a sixteen-year-old who almost cried when another player kicked his shin on the field last month.

There are lots of rumors that go around school, lots of gossip about people's mistakes and decisions. I've always been very happy to stay out of it. I'm front and center of this one, and it royally sucks.

Before Ty, I was pretty much in a bubble with Haley and Sophie. We have a few peripheral friends, but it was mostly us, hanging out, going to movies, swimming, and shopping. Now Ty has dragged me into his circle of friends and it's finally creating drama that I don't want.

I couldn't care less about being popular, so if the cheerleaders hate me now because Ellie's boyfriend kissed me for half a second before they got together, then so be it.

They don't want to be friends with me. Most of them aren't even friends with each other.

29

At lunch I sit down at a table with Sophie and Haley. Iris is nowhere to be seen, but I think I overheard something about the cheerleaders meeting, so she probably has other lunch plans. Good.

Sophie eats quietly, popping a pasta twist in her mouth every ten seconds. Her hair is pushed behind her ears like she's unsure if she wants it down. I want to say something but she's self-conscious, and I don't want to make it worse.

I squirm in my seat. "Are you two practicing after school today? Coach is letting me use the pool."

"You get an extra session in the pool *again* this week?" Sophie presses her thin lips together like she spoke before she could stop herself.

I drop my chicken salad wrap back on my plate. "Not to

myself, Sophie. Anyone on the team can use it as long as you let Coach know, and I'm asking if you want to come too!"

Haley raises her dark eyebrows. "Sophie knows that. It's just that you seem to be in the pool a lot."

"What, is that a problem? I'm not stopping anyone else from using it."

"You kind of are, Ivy. Some of the girls . . ." Sophie looks away, rubbing her lips.

I tilt my head toward Haley. "Some of the girls what?"

"Nothing."

"Nothing? Come on, Haley, what's going on?"

She sighs harshly. "People are concerned. You've changed a lot, and it's making them feel uncomfortable."

That's not right at all. "I haven't changed."

"You don't usually shout out in class."

"So I do *one* thing because I was provoked, and you all think there's something wrong with me? Why is no one asking *why* I snapped at Iris?"

"Because she tapped the table," Sophie says, her voice monotone and bored. "Then there's the Ty thing."

I shake my head. "You don't get it. She is always disturbing me in class, and she knows that geography is my weakest subject. Can you not see that she was trying to irritate me? And what happened with Ty is no one else's business!"

"Why would Iris do that?"

I throw my hands up. "Why would I make it up?"

"I don't think you're making it up. We just think that you're overreacting," Haley says.

Nice to know my two best friends have been discussing me again.

Ty sits down at the table. He looks at me and then at them. "Everything okay?"

Nope. The tension around the table is so thick I feel it choking me. I press the ache in my stomach.

"Fine," Sophie says.

"I heard you were speaking to Logan this morning," Ty says.

God, can we not do this right now?

Sighing, I look over at him. His jaw is tight, eyes narrowed. "He wanted to know who sent you the picture, and I told him I don't know. That's all."

But I have a pretty good idea. I would love to know how Iris found it and who took it.

"Does it matter who sent it?"

"Yeah, it does. Why did they take that photo and why send it now?"

Ty shrugs. "Someone wants to cause trouble for us."

Yeah. Iris!

"Who do you think that could be?"

Haley and Sophie are listening to our conversation. I hope they read between the lines here too.

It. Was. Iris.

He exhales and shakes his head. "I don't know. Look, I've got to go. I need to speak to Coach."

"Ty . . ."

Standing, he leaves without looking back at me. He doesn't need to speak to his coach.

I slump back in my seat. Iris has succeeded in causing a rift between me and Ty. He might believe that I didn't cheat, and I pushed Logan away, but he certainly hasn't forgiven me for not telling him.

What can I do about it besides wait for him to cool down? Oh right, nothing.

Doing nothing sucks.

"I'm not hungry anymore." Rising to my feet, I pick up my half-eaten lunch and head out.

• • •

I wrap a towel around myself and sit down on the bench. Today has been rough, so I'm more than happy to have extra time in the pool. But I had to get out because Coach needs to leave to go to her nan's birthday dinner.

"You okay, Ivy?" Coach asks, gripping the strap of the handbag hanging over her shoulder.

"Yeah, I'll let myself out when I'm dressed," I tell her. "No need to wait."

"Are you sure?"

Nodding, I stand up so she doesn't worry that I'll stay there forever. I don't want her to know that anything is wrong because I don't want to talk about it.

"Okay, see you tomorrow."

The janitor doesn't lock up until much later in the evening, knowing there are extracurriculars going on most days after school. I have plenty of time to get out.

Keeping my eyes on her, I watch as she leaves and the door closes. I'm alone. I close my eyes and inhale. My happy place is the pool, so I picture myself a few minutes ago, flying through the water like I was made to swim.

A loud metal thud echoes through the changing room.

Gasping, I grip the towel in my fist and swing my head in the direction of the noise. *What was that?*

"Hello?" I call. "Coach?"

My heart races, thudding in my chest so hard I can hear the whoosh of my pulse in my ears.

Someone is in here. I'm not alone.

"Coach, is that you?"

She would have answered. She knew where I was getting changed. If it was her, she would have come straight to me and told me she was back because she forgot something.

So if it's not her . . . who is it?

Oh God, I'm naked under this towel too.

Okay, calm down, you're not going to have to fight.

It's probably someone on the team grabbing something from their locker.

I tiptoe toward the end of the first row of lockers and peer around the side.

A light tap comes from the other side of the room, like fingertips hitting a locker. The sound is barely audible over the pounding in my chest.

I didn't hear wrong the first time; there definitely is someone in here, and whoever it is wants me to be scared.

"Who's there?" I demand, forcing my voice to be loud and strong.

I make my way back in the other direction, sticking close to the lockers. My palms clam and I tighten the grip around the towel. This isn't funny.

"Iris? I-is that you?"

She's supposed to be home; Ellie was giving her a lift. But I never saw her leave school after class because I came straight here. There is no reason for her to play a prank on me, though. I thought we cleared the air earlier. Why would she be in here trying to scare me now?

"Iris!" I snap.

I freeze. The sound of light footsteps tapping on the floor steals my breath.

What if it's not Iris?

I need to get out of here. I glance over my shoulder to the door. There are two rows of lockers between me and the exit. I can make that.

Metal clinks across the room, echoing loudly. I press my back to the locker and wince.

Who is in here?

It has to be my sister. No one else would want to scare me.

Unless . . .

No. Haley and Sophie are angry with me, but they wouldn't do this. No way.

Iris wouldn't actually hurt me. I could walk toward the noise and find out who it is.

That's what I should do. But what if it's not Iris? Ellie? She didn't like me before, so I dread to think how much she hates me after finding out that Logan tried to kiss me.

I can take Ellie, though. She's not a threat.

I take a ragged breath.

Suddenly, someone hammers on a locker over and over. The deafening tinny thud of fists pummeling metal pierces my eardrums. Whimpering, I shove myself off the locker and sprint toward the door.

I hold my arm out and slam into the door as I shove it open. I run straight into something hard. A person. A scream rips from my throat and I leap back.

"Jeez, Ivy, what's wrong?"

Ty.

My eyes widen, and I sob.

"What happened?" he asks, stepping toward me.

I fall forward, my legs giving way. Ty catches me, his face twisted with worry. My breathing is rough. I grip Ty and look back behind me.

"Ivy, talk to me," he orders.

"There was someone in there with me," I rasp.

"Who?"

I take a breath, trying to get it under control, but my heart is thumping, adrenaline coursing through my veins. "I don't know. I was alone and then I kept hearing noises."

"Coach?"

"No, I watched her leave and she didn't come back. Besides, she wouldn't keep making noises and she would answer me. Someone else is in there."

Ty steadies me and holds me at arm's length. "Wait right here."

My mouth falls open as he goes into the changing room. I'm still only in a towel. If a teacher comes past now . . .

I bite my lip while I wait but the changing room is silent. Using my free hand, I wipe the damp tears under my eyes.

The door flies open and Ty smiles. "There's no one in there, babe."

"There was. I heard them multiple times. They were banging on the lockers. You didn't hear?"

He shrugs. "I heard a bang and then you ran out. Whoever it was, they're gone now. It was probably someone from the team playing a prank."

"Who would do that?" I don't want to be all dramatic and look super weak in front of Ty, but I was scared. I can't imagine anyone on the team taking it that far. They would have laughed or said something after a minute.

"I don't know, but don't worry. If we find out, we'll think of some revenge prank, okay?"

Looking into his eyes, I search for any sign that he's taking this seriously. He's not.

My heart plummets. He thinks I'm overreacting.

Maybe I am.

I do have a track record of it.

Forcing a smile, I reply, "It better be a good prank."

"It'll be the best. Do you want me to come in with you while you get dressed?"

Smirking, I walk past him and shut the door, keeping him safely on the outside.

I can tell immediately that no one is here anymore. It feels empty and silent.

My hands tremble as I drop my towel and tug on my clothes as fast as I can. I catch my foot inside the leg of my jeans and pull hard at the waistband to get it through. Once I'm dressed, I pick up my bag and scuttle out of the changing room fast. I never want to be in there after hours without Coach again.

Ty is still waiting for me. Our fight is paused for the minute.

"All right?" he asks, staring into my eyes.

"Yeah, I'm fine."

We walk back to my car. My hands twitch to get in Iris's room. If people are going to believe me about her, I need to find evidence that she sent the photo to Ty.

And I'm pretty sure it's in there somewhere.

30

I'm so doing this. Biting my lip. I tiptoe past my door and toward Iris's room like I'm escaping prison.

Dad is downstairs watching football, but I don't think he would question me even if he caught me in Iris's room.

Yeah, I'm snooping.

She's out and I'm tired of being one step behind her. My last snoop was cut short and I finally have another opportunity.

Reaching out, I push her door with the tips of my fingers and step inside. Her room is decorated with light, neutral colors and she has about nine throw pillows on her bed. That would drive me crazy.

Her closet door is full of clothes and I don't think I've seen her wear even half of them. Why buy them all, load your closet to bursting point, then borrow your sister's stuff? Her stuff is trendy and bright, while I'm much more . . . boring.

What is she up to?

I stay close to the wall, as far away from the window as I can get in case she comes home and sees from outside. I'm paranoid like that.

As I cross her room, I notice a drawer open a centimeter. For someone who has nine scatter cushions and a bed runner perfectly placed like it's in a show home, she sure has left the closet and her drawer out of place.

Iris doesn't leave things lying around or forget to close something. She makes every move and speaks every sentence with careful planning.

Did she have to leave in a hurry? Looking over my shoulder, I sidestep to her desk and reach my hand out. I run my finger along the lip of the drawer and then tug.

There is no noise outside the room, and I can still hear football downstairs. Dad would have paused it if he'd gotten up.

My eyes drop to the drawer. She has a collection of makeup brushes, a small flashlight, and an old black flip phone. I didn't even know you could still buy them. I remember Nan had one and used to let me play with it.

My fingers curl around the phone. Maybe she's a hoarder. She has a lot of things at Mom's still. The house was left to me and Iris. I don't know what we're going to do with it yet because Iris won't talk about it.

I dig my thumb between the screen and keypad and flip the

phone open. It's turned off. I hold down the ON button, but nothing happens. No battery and I can't see a charger. Like the great meddler she is, she keeps the two separate. I could buy my own for it; there are probably some on eBay.

Placing the phone back in her drawer in the exact same place, between the puffy pink makeup brush and a stack of Post-it Notes, I push it almost closed.

"Ivy?" Dad calls.

Jumping, I tiptoe very quickly out of Iris's room and clear my throat. "Yeah, Dad?"

We're still not great, but I don't want to be in a fight with him too.

"I'm going out with Ken. There's cash on the side table for pizza. Have you done your homework?"

"Yeah, all done. Have a good night," I reply.

I wait for him to leave the house because I'm pretty sure I look guilty. When I hear the front door open and close, then hear his car start, I head down.

As I reach the bottom, the doorbell rings.

I'm not expecting anyone. I pad over to the door quietly and peek through the hole. Ty.

Opening up, I say, "Hey, everything okay?"

"I didn't want to leave you alone after what happened today."

I step to the side and let him in. "Thanks, but I really am okay."

"Does that mean you don't want me to stay?"

I wasn't done being sneaky, but I need to make things right with Ty more. Plus, if Iris is going out more often, I'll have plenty of opportunities.

"No, stay," I reply a little too quickly to be cool. I'm not cool when it comes to Ty, though, especially not at the minute when things are a little tense between us.

Chuckling, Ty kicks off his shoes and heads up to my room. I follow.

"Have you eaten yet?" he asks as he lies down on my bed.

I pull the door half closed. "Nope, but Dad left cash for pizza. You want our usual?"

He throws his arms over his head and smiles. "Sure."

I sit down next to him. "Are we okay, Ty? I hate it when we're fighting."

"We're not fighting."

"Maybe not right now, but things are off."

With a sigh, he sits up and replies, "We're okay. I'm trying."

Trying to do what? Believe me?

"I need you to trust me, Ty. I would never do anything to intentionally hurt you."

"I do trust you. That's not what I'm struggling with. I wish you had told me."

I dip my head. "I was scared to. Neither of us wanted to hurt you, so we agreed to put it down to a dumb mistake and move on. I don't know why someone took a picture of it, and I don't know why they waited until now to send it."

"You have a theory."

"I don't know who originally took it, but I do think that Iris found it on their phone."

He bites his lip. "Can we forget about this for a while?"

"Yeah. Movie and pizza?"

Smiling, he throws his arm around my shoulders and replies, "Sounds good."

Ty and I watch *Iron Man* and eat a stuffed-crust BBQ chicken pizza. Halfway through *Iron Man 2*, Ty wraps his arm around me and pulls me onto his lap. I sink into his embrace, feeling safe for the first time in a while. Right now, there is no sister or distance between me and Ty, and I love it.

Ty kisses me and I curl my fingers into his hair. My heart is racing for the second time today but this time I like it. I pull away from his lips and grin. "My dad will be home soon."

"We're not doing anything wrong."

"You want him to catch me lying half on you?"

He narrows his eyes. "My hearing is good. I'll chuck you off when I hear a car."

Giggling, I press my lips against his again.

"Oh my God!" Iris's shrill voice makes my heart stop. Ty leaps off me, and I look up at the doorway. Where she is.

Great, she's home.

"What the hell is wrong with you?" I snap, scowling at her.

"What are you two doing?"

"Kissing," I reply like it's the most obvious thing in the world. I mean, she could see that.

Ty sits up and sighs. "What do you want, Iris?"

"I want you to get your grubby hands off my sister!"

"Hey!" I shout. "Back off and calm down!" I say, folding my arms. "You're overreacting."

"No, I'm not."

I turn to Ty. "You should go while I deal with this."

He rolls his eyes at Iris and kisses the top of my head before leaving my room.

"What would have happened if I hadn't come home, Ivy? You and Tyler were clearly not thinking straight."

What is wrong with her? I get off the bed, push past her, and walk downstairs.

She follows.

"Come on, Ivy, what would have happened if I hadn't come home?" she repeats. "He was all over you. Literally."

I hear Ty's car pull out of the drive.

"Our clothes were still on."

"Yeah, but for how long?"

"Ugh, seriously!" I love Ty and we've been together for a long time now, but I'm still not ready. I'm not about to lose my virginity ten minutes before my dad gets home. I'm kind of hoping it will be a little more special than that.

"I'm deadly serious. Are you even on contraception?"

"We're not having sex!"

"You were about to have sex, and if you're not taking precautions, you'll get pregnant!"

"What?" Dad roars.

My eyes widen, stomach bottoming out. I turn slowly.

Dad is standing in the doorway, arms folded and face red as a tomato. If we were in a cartoon, steam would be billowing from his ears. "Where is Tyler?"

"Dad, calm down. Nothing happened."

I look back at Iris and she looks between me and Dad, totally emotionless.

"Tell me what happened right now, Iris."

"Um . . ." She bites her lip.

Tears pool in my eyes. "Dad, please, I can explain."

"I'm asking Iris," he replies tightly. "The truth. Now."

"I came home and saw Ivy and Ty in her room."

Dad takes a deep breath. "You know the rules, Ivy."

"My door wasn't closed all the way," I tell him. "We were watching a movie. I swear to you nothing happened."

"What did you see, Iris?" Dad asks as if I'm no longer in the room.

"They were kissing."

"Just kissing? Why would you two argue if they were just kissing? Why would you worry about Ivy going on contraception or getting pregnant if they were just kissing? I asked for the truth, and I want it now."

I close my eyes and want to curl inside myself.

"Tyler was on top of her."

Oh God, I want to run away.

Dad's teeth grind together. "You are sixteen, Ivy."

"It wasn't as bad as it sounds. We were lying on the bed. He was *on the bed*, not directly on me." This is a conversation I never wanted to have.

"Go to your room, please."

My jaw drops. "What?"

"Go to your room."

"This is ridiculous! Iris, tell him the truth!"

"I did, Ivy."

"You're lying!" I shout. "Why are you doing this? What have I ever done to you?"

"Stop trying to make me out to be the bad one here! It was you in bed with a boy."

Oh my God, I want to shake her!

"Enough, Ivy!" Dad snaps. "Go upstairs. Now."

I throw my hands up. "This is unbelievable, Dad. Well done, Iris, you got what you want."

Storming past them both, I stomp upstairs and slam my bedroom door.

They can both go to hell.

31

When I wake up the next morning, I am still raging that Dad believed Iris over me. Haley and Sophie listen silently, leaning forward as I dish the details at lunchtime.

Not that she would, but Iris doesn't care that she totally dropped me in it with Dad. It was clearly her plan. I didn't hear her come in, but I bet that's what she wanted. It's easier to snoop and be generally super creepy when no one knows you're there. She hit the jackpot, though, when she saw me and Ty kissing.

She probably knew when Dad was due home, watched from her window as he pulled onto the drive, and then everything fell perfectly into place for her.

I'm grounded, Ty probably won't be welcome in my house until he's thirty, and Dad can barely look at me. All because our kiss looked "too heated" to Iris. We weren't getting carried away or doing anything out of the ordinary for us.

In fact, her kiss with Todd at Alec's party last weekend was way more heated than me and Ty last night, from what I was told, anyway. I don't know when lying down watching a film and having the occasional lazy kiss began to look like sex.

Iris is crazy.

She hasn't even apologized.

Haley and Sophie give me a sympathetic look, though Sophie doesn't meet my eye. She's been off with me for days now. "It's not even like anything was happening! That's the part I'm most mad at. He believed Iris over me. She's totally blown it up, and now he doesn't trust *me*!" I rant. "I have never given him a reason to not trust me. Ever!"

"Your dad is protective, Ivy. He's going to imagine the worst," Sophie says quietly. Her hair is back up today.

"Uncool of Iris to make it sound worse, though," Haley adds.

"So uncool," I agree. "She's supposed to have my back."

Haley purses her lips. "Wait. Do you think she's worried about you? I mean, she was talking about contraception, right? She's probably scared that you'll get pregnant."

"Yeah, Haley's right," Sophie says. Her gaze is on Haley and not me as she speaks. "Iris has always had your back. With the Logan thing she was telling people to back off when she overheard someone talking about you."

What about when she heard you talking about me? Or when she was the one spreading the details?

"That's beside the point. Of all the things she decides to be honest to Dad about. Hell, she wasn't even honest—she made it seem worse!"

"Okay, you need to calm down," Sophie mutters, holding her hands up. "We get it."

Haley wraps her arm around my shoulders, her wild hair tickling my cheek. "Forget about if for now. You can make up with Iris later."

"Why should I? She keeps defending her decision to tell Dad the embellished version of what she saw."

"Well, she probably did that because she was scared," Haley repeats. "Why else would she do it? If you're grounded, it's much harder for her to get around since it's your car and you don't like her taking it."

"What? I've never said I don't like her taking my car."

The bell rings. "Come on, let's go," Haley says.

Sophie waves us off as she heads to her class. Haley and I have first class next door to each other.

Iris told them I don't like her using my car? The sneaky bitch. I've never been so relieved to have a session with Meera scheduled.

I get through school in kind of a blur. The teachers are still watching, so I force myself to ignore Iris and focus on the work. I'm pretty sure that although I have tons of notes, I won't be able to understand any of them. Not that it really matters, since I'll need to read the material again anyway.

As soon as I arrive at Meera's office, my shoulders loosen and the knot in my stomach unravels.

I go straight for the blanket.

"How have you been this week, Ivy?" Meera asks.

I blow out a long breath and tug the blanket higher over my lap.

"Ah," Meera says. "Start wherever you like."

"Iris has done something, and I think you can help me get some clarity. I don't think I'm overreacting, but I could be."

"Go ahead. I'm listening."

I don't want to talk about the locker room thing because I have no proof.

"So . . . Iris comes home early and finds me and Ty lying on my bed, watching a movie. We were kissing and she freaked out."

Meera cocks her head to the left. "Freaked out how?"

"She starts shouting that he shouldn't be in my room when we're home alone and he shouldn't be on top of me."

She raises her eyes from her notepad.

"However, Ty wasn't actually on top of me. Like, his chest was half on me and the rest of him was completely on the bed next to me. Anyway, Ty leaves and we argue for a minute—me and Iris, not me and him. She follows me downstairs when he's gone, going on about me not taking birth control and she thinks I'm going to get pregnant. That's when my dad walks into the room."

Meera's mouth pops open. "Oh dear."

"Right. Ty and I were fully dressed, my hands were on his back and his were in my hair. Like, how did she even jump there? She told my dad he was on top of me and of course he believes her. Now Ty can't even come in the house, I'm not allowed at his, and the only time I can leave is for school, swim practice, or to come here. It's so unfair."

"Okay, there has been a lot going on. Did you speak with Iris and clear the air? Perhaps from her perspective your position didn't look as innocent as it was."

"I told her that, but she keeps saying she's worried. She's not worried!"

"What makes you think she's not?"

"Because she's not. She's dated. She's seen me sitting on Ty's lap before."

Meera nods. "Do you think the fact that you two were alone in your house is why she was uncomfortable?"

I frown. "No."

Laughing, Meera says, "I'm only trying to work through Iris's reasons to see if we can get some clarity."

Sinking into the cushion behind me, I reply, "Okay. Sorry, I'm still worked up over it."

"You feel that she's let you down."

"I feel like she's thrown me under a bus. Only I have no idea why."

"If she doesn't have a motive, could you consider her reaction genuine? Again, just questions."

"I don't know." I look up. "The timing was convenient too."

"You think she was aware your dad was almost home?"

"Perhaps. There's not much I'm sure of anymore."

"You're questioning your friends a lot more than usual."

"Yeah, well after I found out Sophie and Haley have been talking behind my back, I've been suspicious. If my best friends can do that, anyone can."

"How do you feel about Iris living with you now?"

"You mean, like, right now or now in general?"

She smiles. "In general."

"Honestly, it's fine. I think I've mostly adjusted. The only thing that's hard is not having much time to myself. But she's started hanging out with her friends more and more, so it's all right." I raise my eyebrow. "I'm not jealous."

"I wasn't going to suggest you are. Is there a reason you felt you need to specify that?"

"Because I know that's how it looks."

Meera nods.

"I just don't understand why she would want to mess with me like that. She knew we weren't doing anything. She did *know* that."

Meera jots something down, and I don't know if her note makes Iris look bad or me.

"Am I being unreasonable?"

She raises her head. "I don't think you are, Ivy. We feel how we feel, and you are fully entitled to that."

Okay, that wasn't a "Yes, I agree with you, Ivy," so I'm not sure what to do with it.

"How is your relationship with your dad recently? Before last night, of course."

"Same. He still has as much time for me as before. Though I

think he'll be watching a lot more closely now. How do I make him trust me?"

"You can't make someone trust you. All you can do is use your actions to prove that you're not lying."

"I've done nothing but that and it's not working."

"What are the rules regarding boys? You said you and Tyler were in your room home alone."

"Oh, right. I don't think he's ever specifically said no to that. There's a no-closed-door rule . . . which we didn't break. I mean, come on, if we were going to have sex, we would have at least shut the door!" I throw my hands up.

"Would you like some water?" Meera asks.

I press my hands together in my lap. "No, thanks. I'm calm."

"You're angry."

"Yeah, that too."

"What do you think you can do to improve your relationship with your sister and your father?"

I shrug. "Iris is still a bit of a mystery. Sometimes I just plain don't understand her. Dad I think will take time. Like you said, I have to show him that he can trust me."

"Do you think you can have an open conversation with him? I'm sure the subject matter is what has blown this situation out of proportion."

I'm sure my face has just set on fire. I feel the heat tickle the top of my head and the tips of my fingers. "Talk to my dad about sex?" I exclaim.

She stifles a laugh. "I think it's a good way of showing him your maturity. Are you ready for that step with Ty?"

"No."

"I'm sure your dad will be happy to hear that."

"Show him I'm not an immature kid and he might believe I'm not?"

"Something like that."

That's only going to work if Iris stays out of my business.

32

I'm bored out of my mind. Not literally. Being out of my mind would rock right now. Today, I get to have a conversation with my dad about sex. I would rather slice off my own face.

First, I have to wait for Iris to go to the mall with Ellie and her band of cheerful bitches. They all think it's hilarious that Dad busted me and Ty. I've heard her talking to her friends on the phone.

Ty hasn't texted me yet today. I usually wake up to a message.

Iris is upstairs. I can hear her footsteps dancing on the floorboards above me. Her music is obnoxiously loud. I don't know if she's dancing around while she gets ready to leave or if she's dancing around because she's plotting. Either way, I can't wait for her to go out.

Dad crashes around the kitchen, tidying up very loudly, making it crystal clear that he's still angry too.

This house is toxic at the minute.

There is not enough swimming in the world right now.

I don't even think I'll be getting much snooping done today since Dad hasn't been near his office. It's like he's scared to close a door in case I sneak Ty into the house.

I curl up tighter on the sofa and jab my finger into the volume button, turning *Riverdale* up. Today is a Netflix binge day for sure. It's not like I can go out and have a life since I'm grounded until the end of time.

Iris's music suddenly shuts off. I turn to the stairs and sure enough, she bounds down seconds later.

"I'm going, Dad," she calls, ignoring me totally.

I look back at my phone and narrow my eyes. I click purchase on the cell phone charger in my eBay cart. Iris either doesn't use it—unlikely—or she runs it down, keeping just enough charge to do her evil.

Whichever it is, I'm going to find out soon enough.

"Have fun, Iris. Home by eleven, remember."

"Sure thing," she replies, and skips to grab her shoes.

At least today she's wearing her own clothes: a denim skirt, purple tank, and silver heeled sandals. Without a glance in my direction, she slams the front door behind her and gets into *my* car.

"Ivy, would you like something to eat?" Dad asks. His voice tight and controlled.

I twist my body and look over the back of the sofa. "No, thanks. Can I talk to you for a minute?"

He clears his throat. "All right."

"Will you come and sit?" I ask.

He takes a second, but then he walks slowly to the sofa and sits opposite me. We usually sit next to each other when we talk. Though the subject I'm about to raise makes me kind of glad that he's not closer.

"Okay," I say, rubbing my hands together. "So . . ." My face sets on fire, skin prickling.

"Ivy, what is it?"

I can't meet his eye.

Floor, please open up.

"About the other day," I say quickly, pressing my nails into my palms.

"Yes?"

"I know what you think, and I know that you're worried. But, Dad . . . I . . ." Oh my God, this is awful. "I'm not even thinking about doing that," I blurt out, looking up at the ceiling.

Meera did say that I should be mature about this. But how do you have this conversation without feeling the full force of embarrassment? Look up *embarrassment* in the dictionary and you'll find this conversation.

"When I told you that nothing is happening between me and Ty, I wasn't lying. I'm not trying to get out of trouble here. I'm not ready, and Ty is fine with that. We've spoken about it."

Dad clears his throat again. "I see."

"So please don't worry about . . . anything. Ty would never

pressure me, and I'm not ready." I feel like I should repeat that part about not being ready, really drive it home so he hears me.

He takes a deep breath and scrubs his jaw with his fist. "I'm glad you told me this. However, I once was sixteen. All the greatest intentions in the world don't mean . . . things won't happen."

"What can I say to make you trust me? I'm not stupid. I won't be doing anything until I want to."

"That's reassuring, but it doesn't change my stance on this."

"You like Ty. Nothing has changed."

"Everything has changed, Ivy."

"No, it hasn't! You have what Iris thought she saw. I get that she was worried I'd do something stupid, but this has been blown way out of proportion," I say. "Dad, please. You know me and you know Ty."

He looks away for a long time and exhales. "It's difficult to not think of you as a child, Ivy. I understand you're growing up and you have a long-term boyfriend."

"That doesn't mean we're having sex!"

My eyes pop. *I can't believe I said the S word.*

Move past it. Move past it.

"Dad, I really need you to trust me. We've always been honest with each other, and I would hate if that changed. What do I have to do to get us back to that?"

Dad blinks and shuffles in his seat. "Ivy," he whispers. "Honey, okay, I believe you."

My body sinks, and I manage a small smile. "You do?"

He makes eye contact for the first time since we started talking. "Yes, of course I do. I'm sorry it's taken me so long. But listen, although I believe that you're not going to do something stupid, there will be new rules in this house."

"Rules?"

He nods. "You will not be alone in this house or any other house with Tyler. You will not ride in a car alone together. You will not be in your room even with someone else in the house. In fact, there is no reason why he needs to be upstairs at all. Same goes for you at his. I will be speaking to his parents about this too. You will not go to a party until I'm happy that you're both follow-ing the rules. Is that clear?"

My mouth drops open. "That's clear . . . and crazy. Dad!"

"Ivy, I'm doing this to protect you. If you're unhappy with it, you can always wait until you're eighteen to date."

Is he actually suggesting I break up with Ty for a year and a half?

Pick your battles, Ivy.

I wave my hand. "Whatever. Fine. I agree to your terms."

"Rules," he says, and then he cracks a small smile that I haven't seen in days.

"You know, I actually am hungry."

He stands up. "I knew you would crack when your stomach started making those noises."

I press my hand to my tummy as a low growl rolls through my abdomen. "Pancakes?"

"You want them in shapes?"

"You just said that you understand that I'm growing up. . . ."

He lifts his eyebrows. "All right, normal pancakes it is."

"No, I want little hearts."

Dad stops and looks back at me. "I knew you were still in there."

"Always."

I watch him go back into the kitchen. My face still feels hot. I press my fingers to my cheek and close my eyes. That was awful . . . right up until we cleared the air. My only hope is that he believes me because I do not ever want to have that conversation with him again.

As soon as I hear him cracking eggs, I text Ty to let him know what's happened.

> Are you serious????

>> For real. You're banned from being upstairs. At least he knows we're not having sex though.

> What a bitch

>> I'm not disagreeing. Are you going to Ellie's party tonight?

> Yeah, going with Leo. Think you can sneak out for a bit?

>> Would you if you were me?

> Hell no! Your dad is scary

Smiling, I put my phone down and go into the kitchen. I don't want to sneak around, and I won't do that, not since we're trying to be open with each other again. But I really do want to go tonight. So it's worth asking, right?

Sure, I'm officially crazy since, like, three minutes ago he told me no parties. But it's worth a shot.

"Dad," I say.

He stops mid-whisk and looks over his shoulder. "What do you want?"

"Ellie is having a party."

Laughing out loud, he places the bowl on the counter and turns around. "Are you joking?"

"Well, I knew it was a long shot, but I figured that since I'm still working on having you trust me fully again, you might give me the opportunity to."

"Oh, did you?" His smirk widens.

"Please?"

"I'm not going back on my decision, Ivy. You'll have to miss this one."

My shoulders slump. "Okay."

I was hoping I could turn up without Iris knowing and observe her. When I'm not around, she might give something away. I'm not sure what since I don't understand her crazy . . . but I need to know her plan.

33

There is definitely something wrong with Iris. The more I watch her, the more I see a stranger. My sister is gone, and I want to find out what has replaced her.

I need to reach out to her old friends. Particularly the C or K one. Cassie? Kay?

Haley and Sophie thought what Iris did with the Ty thing was crappy, but they've hardly shunned her.

Iris tilts her head back as she laughs. She has the whole package. She's pretty, dressed the same as the rest of them, leads with conviction. Not to mention the fact that she is convincing.

She has everything it takes to be a successful psychopath.

Is this what happened before? Why Mom was worried about her?

A couple girls from the team walk past. They glance at me out of the corner of their eye and move faster.

Really?

I roll my eyes.

Iris has done a fantastic job of convincing everyone that I'm the one with the problem. Granted, I haven't helped by reacting to her.

Keep walking, nothing to see here.

Ty is chatting to the guys on the team and Iris is hanging around them with Ellie and the cheerleaders.

"Hey," Sophie says, nudging my arm and taking my attention off my sister.

"Hey, Soph. Where's Haley?"

She shrugs. "I don't think she's here yet. Why are you standing on your own?"

"I've been standing on my own since I was nine months old."

Sophie rolls her dark eyes. "Why aren't you with Ty?"

Because my creepy sister is over there. Sophie and Haley believe Iris's façade too, and although they seem cool with me now, I'm not convinced they're not having secret discussions about how I've changed.

"I'll go over there in a minute. There's only so much makeup talk a girl can handle," I tell her.

Sophie laughs as she looks over at Ellie and her friends. They're actually pretty nice to my face, but I've overheard a lot of shallow conversations that have made me want to whack my head against a wall.

"You okay?"

I dip my head. "Yeah, I'm fine."

"Are you sure?" Sophie asks. But I barely hear her because Iris takes out her ponytail and her hair is shorter. It no longer sits just below her butt; it's just below her shoulder blades. The same as mine.

"Ivy?" Sophie prompts.

"Hmm?" I mumble.

"What are you looking at?" Sophie asks, almost to herself. "What is it?"

I clear my throat and it burns. "Iris cut her hair."

When did she do that?

"Okay . . ."

"Look." I turn to my friend, a silent plea in my eyes for her to get what's going on. "Sophie, what do you see?"

With a prominent frown on her forehead, Sophie turns toward Iris.

"What do you see?" I ask again.

"I see your sister talking to her friends and the football team."

My shoulders sink.

No, you see me.

"Forget it." I sigh.

No one is getting this.

"No, tell me what I'm supposed to see."

So I can look insane? No, thanks.

"What's going on with you? You've been frosty with Iris for weeks."

"I haven't."

"Everyone has noticed that something is off with you."

With me!

"What?" I splutter, my heart racing a touch faster. "You honestly think something is off with me?"

"I don't want to upset you, but you've been different. You say you're okay with Iris being here but you're not. I can tell when you're lying."

"Don't. I'm not unhappy that she's here. She's my twin sister."

She raises her blond eyebrows. "Then what is going on?"

Is there any benefit to me telling Sophie my fears? I want someone else to understand, to tell me it's not all in my head, but I can't risk being told I'm insane. I think Iris is trying to imitate me. Trying to *be* me.

She wears my clothes though she has her own. She hangs with my friends though she has her own. And now she's cut her super-long hair that she's been so precious about since she was six years old.

I shake my head. "Nothing. I guess it's just taking longer than I thought to adjust to all the change."

"Hey, that's fine, but it really isn't Iris's fault. I bet she's finding it equally difficult, if not more. She's the one who's had to move and totally start again."

And there it is, the reason why no one will see it. Iris lost more than me, so I'll always be the jealous, overreacting sister. She has everything she needs to take over my life and no one will believe me when I tell them what she's doing.

They'll see it eventually, right? About the time she asks them to call her Ivy.

Well, two can play your game, Iris.

She wants to get buddy-buddy with my friends: I can reach out to hers. She hasn't seen them since we brought her home: I could invite them for the weekend.

All I need to do is find them. She's deleted everyone on Facebook and unfollowed them on Instagram.

"I get all of that, Sophie, and I'm not trying to be hostile. I miss my mom, and I'm trying to figure out how this new dynamic works. Iris doesn't want to talk about Mom at all, and I don't know who else to talk to. Iris understands the most what it's like to lose her."

I'm drowning here, and I need my sister to be herself and not try to be me.

"Oh, Ivy. Why didn't you say something sooner? You know Haley and I are here for you."

"I appreciate that, but I kind of need Iris." Or I did.

"Why don't you tell her how important talking about your mom is to you?"

"I've tried. She shuts down and then changes the subject or asks to borrow another one of my T-shirts."

"Why don't you suggest a shopping trip and see if she's open to talking then?"

"She has clothes, Soph. She just wants all of mine."

I glance back over and she's talking to Ty. My eyes narrow. She can borrow a shirt, but she's not having him.

"Do you want to get out of here?" Sophie asks. "I'm sure Ty wouldn't mind."

Yeah, I'm not leaving him alone with her.

"That's okay. I feel better getting that off my chest. I know I need to try harder with her."

"Or maybe let her settle in before you try harder? She might need time to get her head around your mom's death. You're a great sister, Ivy. You just need to allow you both some time before you can heal."

I'm not good at waiting.

I give her a smile. "Yeah. Thanks."

"And you know you can talk to me anytime you want."

I thought I could but not now. She's not listening. She's not even willing to keep an open mind when it comes to Iris. Everyone assumes the best because she lost her mom and had to relocate her life.

Why do people automatically assume the worst in me because I'm getting some sketchy vibes from my twin?

Double standards. I've lost too.

"Ivy," Ty shouts, and waves his hand, calling me over.

I don't want to go over there but Iris is still standing by him with Ellie.

"Come on," Sophie says, linking my arm. "Let's go and pretend we care about different brands of makeup."

I'm not sure my acting skills are that good.

Sophie lets go of my arm when we reach Ty.

"What's up?" I ask him.

He gives me a tight smile. "Missed you, that's all."

Oh, that is a lie. He's seen me all day. This was a rescue mission.

The whole world might be completely gaga about my sister, but Ty isn't.

He's my one hope of getting someone to believe me, but I have to be careful, as he's blown me off over this before. The more he's around her, the more he's getting uncomfortable. I can bide my time until he sees what's going on here.

"Oh, really?" I tease, sinking into his outstretched arm.

His body relaxes as I lean against him. I feel his shoulders lower and the arm around me holds me close.

I think he's starting to see through her too.

34

I sit in my usual spot on Meera's sofa. The blanket is tucked tightly around me, pushed down around my legs. It's the first thing I do now. Who would have thought a blanket could hold so much protection?

She's making us coffee because I've had a long week, and I requested a little caffeine. Meera has started to blink a lot more during our sessions, so I think she needs the coffee too.

I can't blame her really. These were supposed to be straight-forward bereavement sessions; instead I've offloaded a whole heap of my teenage drama onto her. Dad has said he will keep paying as long as I want to come here.

Meera places two white cups and saucers down on the coffee table. She gives me a warm smile that makes thin lines pop at the corners of her eyes.

"Thanks," I say.

"You're welcome." She sits down and picks up her notepad that seems to always rest on the arm of the sofa. "Okay. How have things with Iris been this week?"

"Quiet. I don't know what's wrong with her or why she feels the need to mess things up for me. She's my twin sister."

"Iris has lost an awful lot, Ivy. I appreciate that you have too, but on top of losing your mom, Iris has moved home and left behind her friends. That's a lot of adjusting, especially when you see your sister having it all. Can you understand why she would be jealous?"

"Yeah, I can."

"Then can you understand why things going wrong for you would make her feel less like the one whose whole life is crumbling?"

"I wish she would want to make her life less crumbly, not make mine more."

"Humans are a little more complicated than that."

"Being human sucks."

Meera cracks a full, toothy smile. "It's not always easy."

"Iris seems to enjoy it, though. Like, it's more than just feeling a bit better because her twin's life isn't as perfect as she thinks. It's the only time her body doesn't seem tense." I shake my head. "Maybe I'm reading too much into this—we both know how awesome I am at that—but I think she wants me to be unhappy."

"You said this week has been quieter. Do you think she has realized she's gone too far?"

"I don't know. She's kind of kept out of my way, just been

watching how things settle after the storm she created. I haven't seen any form of remorse from her about stirring things with Ty and my dad . . . but she's hardly been doing victory dances around the kitchen either."

Meera nods. "And did you have that open conversation with your dad?"

My body shudders involuntarily and it makes Meera laugh. "I did. Not something I ever want to repeat."

"That's great, Ivy. I think it was important. Will you tell me how it went?"

"Imagine the most awkward moment in your whole life, then multiply it by about a million. That's what it was like. He listened and I think he believes that nothing was about to happen with Ty. But he's still not letting up on the new laws about boys."

The corner of Meera's mouth curves. "Laws, huh."

Oh, they're not just rules anymore.

"He's allowing Ty back in the house, but he can only be on the ground floor. So basically, I know he heard me, but I don't think he really trusts me."

"Why do you say that?"

"Because of the no going upstairs thing. I've told him I'm not ready to have sex, but he still wants us as far apart as possible. We're talking, sitting on different sofas, and riding in separate cars. I don't know when I'll be allowed to go to a party again." I shake my head. "It's so frustrating because I've been completely honest. Iris's words have scared him. He's petrified I'll get pregnant."

"That's not an unreasonable fear for a parent of teenagers."

Okay, I like her a whole lot less when she's not on my side.

"I'll give him that, but it would be an immaculate conception if I got pregnant."

Meera laughs. "Give him some time, Ivy."

"Yeah, sure." I turn my nose up. "I hate time."

"I know it's hard for you to wait, but I'm afraid you're going to have to. People go through all manner of situations in life, and not one of them reacts the same way or gets past issues at the same time. Your dad trusting you will take time. Maybe you can focus on something else to pass the time."

"I need to study more. My head isn't in it."

"We can work on some anxiety techniques, something to help you focus. Your mind works overtime, and we need to get you to slow down."

"What kind of techniques?"

"We'll train your mind to hold off on the things you need to fix. Kind of like telling your mind that you'll deal with something later so it's okay to ignore it."

"Does that work? Because I've never been able to switch off, not until I fall asleep."

"If it doesn't, we'll try something else until we find what does work for you. Okay?"

I nod. That sounds perfect. I'm willing to try anything.

• • •

When I arrive home, Dad is in his office and Iris is sitting on the sofa, her fingers moving a million miles an hour, tapping furiously on her phone.

"Hey, Iris," I say.

She jerks, startled. "You're early," she says flatly.

"Traffic wasn't too bad. Did Dad cook? I'm starving."

"He made pasta. Yours is in the microwave."

"Thanks." I tilt my chin at her phone. "Everything okay?"

Iris rolls her eyes. "Yep."

I decide to try a different approach. "So I was thinking we could go to the house sometime and go through more of Mom's things. Maybe even see some of your old friends," I tell her. "I'm sure they miss you."

"Yeah, maybe." She starts typing again.

Another closed door. "Or you can stay here while I go to Mom's if you'd prefer."

Iris just keeps typing.

Yep, I'm going on my own.

It's so weird that she won't talk about anything to do with Mom at all. Mom's place in the city was her home too. It's almost as if she's scared to say something in case she lets the cat out of the bag. Whatever that cat is.

Oh my God. Kat! My mouth drops. That's the name of her old friend.

I back out of the living room with my heart racing. Iris doesn't look up again.

While I eat my pasta, I check my phone. There's a message from Ty, asking how therapy went. He sends the same text every Friday. I love it.

Sophie and Haley have been talking in our group chat, trying to set up a movie night. I message them back first because it will be quicker. Once I've done that, I'm finding Kat.

"Hey, Ivy," Dad says, walking into the kitchen with an empty glass.

I put my fork down. "Hey, Dad. How was work?"

"Busy. I had to respond to a few emails tonight, but I'm done now. How was your session with Meera?"

"It was good. I'm tired now. I don't have any homework, so do you want to watch a movie?"

"I would, kid, but Iris has asked if I would spend some time with her tonight. We're going to the movies. Want me to book something for us too?"

Okay. He's her dad as well. There is no need for this to be odd.

But it is, and I want to scratch her eyes out.

"Sounds good, Dad."

"You're okay with this? Iris has made me see the importance of working on our individual relationships. You both need one-on-one time with me."

Oh, I'm sure she has.

"It's a great idea. I'll have a think for something we can do."

He smiles. "Great. I'll see you later. We'll be late, so don't wait up if you're tired."

I nod, watching him leave the room and call for Iris.

Oh, it's so on, bitch.

35

All right. So I don't know exactly how I feel about this. Iris might be trying to take over my life, but that doesn't mean I have to lower myself to her level.

Yet here I am, with my finger hovering above a button that will send a message to Iris's friend from her old school. Kat.

I can take the high road and ignore what my sister is doing, or I can press SEND and find out what's going on with her. As far as I'm aware, she still hasn't had contact with her other friends. She's never mentioned them other than to say she fell out with Kat a while ago, and I haven't seen or heard her on the phone to anyone other than *my* friends and her cheer squad.

It all seems weird. Straight-up weirdness that I'm over.

Taking a deep breath, I slam my index finger into my laptop key and the message pings through the air.

The high road is forgotten.

Over the last few days, Ty has put visible distance between himself and Iris. He sticks closer to me at school and when we're all out. He hasn't mentioned anything, but I get the impression that Iris has been flirting and it's making him uncomfortable.

Back off, Twin A. He knows which one he loves.

After I send the message, I click on Kat's photos. She, Iris, and a couple other girls I don't know pose in a few of the traditional positions. Duck lips, fake surprise, kissing the air, hands covering their mouth, and hands on hips. All what I'd expect, and I don't think there's a single one without a filter.

Kat has super-long auburn hair and round blue eyes. She's pretty. Every photo is of her looking like she spends a huge chunk of her morning on her appearance.

I could be looking at Ellie and her friends' pictures.

Iris looks happy; she's in almost all of the images. It seems like she had a very active social life, much more than now. Dad doesn't let us go out every night, but Iris hasn't complained, so it can't bother her that much.

Mom was a lot more relaxed with the rules. I'd be allowed out when I stayed there, and I barely knew anyone. Iris never hung around with me or invited me out with her.

There are pictures of Iris in her cheerleading uniform with boys on the football team. I don't know if she dated much, but there are multiple photos of her with two different boys spaced about eight months apart.

One of them looks kind of similar to Ty. Chestnut hair and deep green eyes.

I'm not going to look too much into it. Although I totally am. Is that what she's trying to do? Does she want to re-create some sort of romance she had with him? I mean, she looks like me and that guy looks like Ty.

My back shudders with a bolt down my spine.

Okay, that makes the copying me thing even creepier.

I click back because looking at Kat's photos is giving me a nasty taste in my mouth. *What does Iris want?*

Is she trying to re-create her old life?

But why does she need me and Ty for that?

A message pops up along the bottom of my screen. Kat.

> Ivy. I haven't spoken to Iris for months. I can't help.

What's my next move?

Kat's message is abrupt. For someone who has hundreds of photos with my sister, you would think she wouldn't cut her out of her life so quickly.

Out of sight, out of mind? Or is there a reason why Kat doesn't want anything to do with Iris?

The more I learn, or think I'm learning, the more confused I get. There are too many questions, and each answer only adds more.

Well, I've gone down this rabbit hole, so I might as well plow on. I write out a reply to Kat.

> Did something happen? I think she needs her friends.
> Is there anyone else I can get in contact with?

I chose Kat because she has the most photos with Iris; the rest of the cheer squad are in the background. It looks like they were the closest.

Her reply comes almost instantly.

Sorry, can't help.

Can't or won't?

Iris is sketchy and so is Kat. I'm not buying any of it. I will find out what's going on.

Her location is all over Facebook. She checks in everywhere she goes. The only issue I have with following her—besides the creepy obvious—is that I have the same face as Iris. She'll notice me immediately. Kat has spent a solid four years with Iris—she'll notice.

I can't bring anyone else in on this because no one believes me. It's too early to have the conversation with Ty again, and I'm not comfortable with getting him this involved.

God, I sound crazy.

This paranoid version of myself is going to make me prematurely gray.

I could try another one of the girls in the photos with Iris, but they probably all talk. Kat will tell them, or they'll tell her, and I'll get nowhere.

The only way I can make Kat listen and talk is if I go and find her. Not that it will be easy. I don't know how or when I'll have enough time to be gone for at least four hours without anyone noticing. Dad practically has tracking devices on us.

I could be back by curfew without Dad knowing where I am, but Ty and my friends will question where I am, and if I tell them I'm staying home, Iris will know.

So I need to think of a plan. A date with Ty out of town? But then he will be with me.

Shopping! Iris's town has the best shopping, lots of cute independent stores. I could go with Haley and Sophie when Iris has cheer practice, so she won't want to tag along.

Okay. I'm not sure if I'm proud of my new sneaky nature. But I kind of am.

At least I'm doing something proactive. This is where I excel. There's a problem, I find the solution and do it.

I'm going to figure out what happened between Iris and her friends.

I have to.

36

On Monday morning, I slam through the double doors and power walk into the girls' changing room. I want to get a few laps in before my first class. We have thirty minutes before class.

It's been a while since I've crammed a fifteen-minute swim into my morning, but I need the distraction. I need to glide through water and let the irritation of Iris and the uncertainty of her intentions wash away.

"Ivy, you okay?" a girl on my team named Lexi asks.

"Yep. Just need to swim."

I need my scholarship so I can get away from Iris.

She gives me a sympathetic look. "Yeah, me too."

"Are you okay?" I ask. Wow, I was so wrapped up in myself that I didn't think to ask why she's here thirty minutes before class too.

"Home stuff. Coach is poolside, so we can go straight in. Want me to wait?"

"No, go ahead. I'll see you in a few."

Lexi walks off toward the pool, and I strip down.

I'm addicted to swimming. It's like a drug to me. I'm the fastest on the team, but I need them much more than they need me. There are much worse things I could rely on, I suppose.

Once I'm changed and have chucked my things in my locker, I pad through the changing room and tie my hair up on the way. I'm not practicing, so I don't bother with a swim cap. We have hairdryers in the changing room. The smell of chlorine hits the back of my throat, and I breathe.

"Morning, Ivy," Coach says, looking up from her poolside desk. I swear she lives in here; she uses her desk here much more than the one in her office.

"Morning."

Coach is cool. She understands that we're not always here to better our time. She's big on mental health and knows the more mentally stable we are, the better we perform. In and out of the water. So she's here every day, forty-five minutes before she needs to be in case we need her.

"You have twenty-five minutes before the bell goes."

"I'm on it," I tell her, and step up on a diving block.

Lexi is already doing lengths.

I pull on my goggles, raise my arms, and close my eyes. I don't need to see to dive. It's second nature. I know how many strokes it takes to reach the other side.

My legs bend and then I'm flying. My face hits the water and I sink down. I don't even care that it's momentarily cold because I know in a few seconds, I'll be warm again.

I kick my legs and swim away from all of my problems.

When I get to the end of the pool, I turn and kick off the wall, catapulting myself back.

I take three strokes and raise my head, about to take a breath. As I do, I see Iris standing in the corner of the room, staring with her lip curled like she's snarling.

At the same time, I take my breath, but startled at her presence, I take it too soon.

Water rushes into my mouth and down my throat.

My lungs seem to flatten. I'm too deep to stand so I kick my legs and my head breaks water. Choking, I pound my chest with my fist as I gasp for breath.

"Ivy!" Coach shouts.

My torso bends as I choke, and I crane my neck to keep my head out of the water. My legs burn with the effort it takes to tread water in this moment. Gasping again, I feel my head float.

Oh God.

I kick my legs harder and harder.

My blood chills as I try to keep my head above water while my throat closes up around each punching cough.

Both Lexi and Coach reach me a second later.

"Oh gosh, Ivy," Coach says, grabbing my arms and pulling me up. Lexi helps by pushing my legs. As soon as they have me, I stop kicking, allowing them to keep me up while I choke.

They swim me to the edge and roll me out onto my side on the floor. I push myself onto my hands and knees and retch. My eyes water and my hands shake on the tile.

I gasp and air hits my lungs. Relief washes over me, and I sink to the floor.

"Are you okay?" Coach's eyes are wide with worry when I look to my side.

I nod. My stomach muscles burn.

"What happened?" Lexi asks.

"I . . . I don't know. I was distracted." Coughing, I rasp, "Did you see Iris?"

Coach frowns. "In here? No."

I take another ragged breath. "She was at the side of the pool."

"I don't think so."

Lexi shrugs. "I didn't see her, but I was in the water."

"Look at me, Ivy," Coach says. "How do you feel?"

Like an idiot. "I'm fine. I mostly feel stupid."

"Don't feel stupid. Accidents happen. Let's get you to the changing room. I want you to see the school nurse before class."

"I really don't need to do that."

Coach lifts her dark eyebrow. "That's non-optional."

I figured it would be.

Lexi and Coach hold an arm each as I stand.

"Okay, I'll go to the nurse, but I promise I don't need help to get up and get changed. I'm all right."

Neither of them listens to me as they walk me into the changing room.

I look back just as the door on the other side of the room

shuts. Iris? If she's just left, she would have seen me choke. Why didn't she come over and make sure I was okay? That's the twin thing to do. That's the *human* thing to do.

My legs, although shaky, carry me safely into the changing room while Lexi and Coach continue to act like I need to be carried.

"I'm fine," I tell them again. This time they let go of me, but both stay close.

Coach stops by my locker and grabs my towel from the bench. "I'll give you a few minutes to change and I'll call the nurse's office to let them know what's happened. Lexi will stay with you."

Lexi nods, wrapping her towel around herself.

"Thanks," I mutter. I'm sure my face is bright red. I can't believe I choked in the middle of the pool. I'm also pretty sure I've torn my stomach muscles.

The door through to the pool thuds shut as Coach leaves.

"What happened out there?" Lexi asks.

"I got distracted, that's really all."

"You thought you saw Iris poolside?"

I rub the towel over my legs. "I turned my head and she was there, but I wasn't out of the water enough. She surprised me, I guess."

"Maybe what you saw was that swim poster of the girl on the wall? That's near the door."

Could that have been it?

I didn't have time to take her in, so I don't know if she was wearing clothes. Perhaps it could have been the giant poster of a swimmer. But why would I have thought that was Iris?

"Yeah, could have been. I feel so stupid. This is humiliating."

"Please, we've all been distracted before. I trip over almost everything. Besides, it was only me and Coach, and neither of us is laughing."

"Thanks, Lexi. Sorry I ruined your swim."

"Nah, that's okay."

We both get dressed quickly and dry our hair. Coach walks into the changing room as we finish up.

"How are you feeling?"

"I have a headache and my stomach hurts, but I'm all right."

"I've called the nurse and she's expecting us."

Great. Let's tell more people about my humiliating fail. The pool is where I come to leave my distractions behind. Iris is taking that away from me too.

No, she won't. I won't allow it.

I follow Coach and Lexi walks beside me.

"You sure you're okay?" Lexi whispers.

"Yeah, I promise."

No one but the three of us knows what happened back there, but I feel everyone's eyes on me as if they all know. They obviously don't.

My eyes prickle with unshed tears. This is a one-off. I won't make a mistake like that in the pool again. Next time I'm not going to look up. I never usually look up.

As we walk to the nurse's office, I spot Ty leaning against his locker talking to Iris. His arms are folded over his chest, guarded. Iris is a safe distance from him, but he still looks like he wants to run away. Ellie and a few guys from the football team are nearby too.

It would be so easy for one of them to spot me, and usually I would want that. But I don't want them to ask where I'm going. Then I would have to explain.

"There's Ty," Lexi says.

I look down, letting my hair cover the side of my face. "This is embarrassing enough; I don't want them asking questions."

Lexi rolls her eyes. "I told you there is no reason to be embarrassed."

Well, I am. How can I be the strongest member on the team, yet I couldn't move my head out of the water to breathe? No one can know about this. I hope Lexi won't tell anyone.

My heart thuds in my chest. I'm losing control of my own mind.

Iris is still with her friends, the same ones she left me to meet as we walked into school. Could she have got away from her friends, into the pool from the back entrance, and then met up with them all again?

Coach opens the door to the nurse's room.

"You better get to your first class, Lexi. The bell will ring soon."

Lexi looks at me. "Er . . ."

"I'm fine. Thanks for making sure I was okay."

She nods and heads off toward her first class.

"Come on, Ivy. I know you think this is an overreaction, but we need to get you checked."

Groaning, I open the door and Coach follows me in. Okay, she does not trust me to follow through with this on my own. I hadn't planned on running as soon as she left. I want to swim after school, so I need to get cleared.

"Hi, Ivy," Nurse Kelly says. "I heard you had an accident in the pool. You swallowed water."

"Yeah, but I'm fine now."

"Come and sit down and let me worry about whether you're fine."

I almost roll my eyes, but I hop up on the bed and wait.

"Do you think you swallowed a lot?"

"Yep," I reply. "I feel fine now. Besides the muscle aches and headache."

She smiles. "That will subside. I want to check your lungs are clear."

"Okay."

I sit still and breathe normally and deeply as she listens to my lungs. I'm being Punk'd surely.

"Right," she says, removing the stethoscope from my back. "Your lungs sound clear, so I don't think there is any water in them, thankfully."

I glance up but I can't see her face, as my head is bowed.

"Great."

"I don't see why you can't return to classes."

She steps back, and I hop down off the table. "Cool. Thanks."

"Before you go," she adds as I'm halfway to the door.

Stopping, I twist on the spot. "Yeah?"

"Even though your lungs are clear, if you feel sick, I want you to come straight back. If you feel unwell tonight, have your dad take you to the ER."

"Okay," I reply.

I leave her office with a late slip and head to math. Iris is going to ask why I'm late, since she is in every one of my classes.

If I say that I fell or felt ill and that was her by the pool, she will know I'm lying. I'm not very good at knowing when she's telling a lie. She used to wince when we were kids, but I guess she grew out of that.

I veer right along the corridor and open the door to my math class. Mr. Grady looks up and takes the slip from my hand. He nods, so I take my seat next to Iris and wait.

"Where were you?" she asks.

"Nurse's office, but I'm fine."

She tilts her head to the side. Her eyes stare into mine and with a soft and steady voice, she asks, "What happened?"

I think you know what happened.

"I was swimming, took in some water, and choked. It's no big deal."

"Ivy! I guess that will teach you to exercise so early in the morning."

I look away at the clear board at the front of the class as if it's the most interesting thing.

I'm not sure how to take that. God, my sister is an excellent liar.

Where did she learn that? Mom was always too laid back to

lie. She never really minded if we were out late, if we didn't complete homework, or if we ate chocolate for breakfast. We never had to lie to her, and Dad always demands honesty.

What happened to Iris?

Between scribbling answers to sums on my page, I glance to the side. Iris has her head down but she's mouthing something. Her lips move silently, too fast to be talking so it must be a song.

My eye twitches.

Nope, not going there. Ignore her.

I still don't know if it was Iris by the pool. I've been in class for ten minutes and she hasn't stopped taking glances at me when she thinks I'm concentrating on math. I can't concentrate on anything but her watching me.

What is she thinking?

I'm not going to react to her again. If that's what she's trying to make me do.

Even though there is a lot going on between us right now, I would never imagine she would want to hurt me—in any way.

My sister isn't stupid; she must understand that trying to wedge herself into every aspect of my life isn't right. It's not normal to leave your whole life behind, ignore your friends, and befriend the people your sister hangs around with. People you have nothing in common with.

What she's doing is a conscious choice. She wants me in the background.

Ever since we were kids, she's loved being the center of

attention, always the outgoing one who would put on perfor-
mances for our family and dress up constantly. It's different
now—she's not cute and five anymore.

I don't want to think badly of her, but I have no idea how far
she will take this or what she's capable of.

Iris smiles as I turn my head toward her, catching her watching. Her eyes are big; they look as genuine as her smile. "You sure
you're okay?" she whispers.

I nod.

I have to get Kat to talk.

The shrill ringing of the bell signals the end of class. Everyone
moves quickly to grab their books and get out. I always hang back
to avoid the rush. I'm not running for anything.

"How are you feeling now?" Iris asks.

That's one too many times. She's asked if I'm okay three times
in the space of thirty minutes. It was her by the pool.

"I'm fine," I reply, picking up my book and holding it against
my chest.

Iris follows me as we walk to English. "What happened?"

"I thought I saw something, a figure where there wasn't one
before. I didn't have my head fully turned before I took a breath
because I wasn't concentrating on swimming."

"I didn't think you had to concentrate in the pool? Isn't it
second nature now? You could do it in your sleep."

I could do it in my sleep. But I can't do it with my sister creeping around watching.

I shrug. "Accidents can happen to anyone."

"Yeah."

Why is the English classroom so far away from math?

"Is it a good idea to stay at school? You choked so hard you had to see the nurse."

"Iris, I'm fine!"

"Wow, grouchy. Maybe you've got water on your lungs."

Maybe I've got an evil twin.

"I don't. The nurse made sure. Can we drop it?"

"I'm worried about you, Ivy. You don't seem yourself."

A few people around us stop and watch our exchange.

How would you know what "myself" is?

I scrunch my nose and lower my voice. "What? Why do you think that?"

Her mouth pops open. I've surprised her. She wasn't expecting me to question that. Iris wants me to agree; she wants me to doubt myself . . . because she doesn't want me to swim after school. Why? We agreed that she can come and watch, so it's not like she'll be twiddling her thumbs, waiting for me to finish.

"Iris? What am I doing that makes you assume I have water in my lungs?"

Did you get a medical degree you forgot to mention?

She shakes her head and the mask drops securely back on her face. "Silly, Ivy. You're hostile when I ask if you're okay. You spent the entire math lesson staring at your page and you only completed, like, five minutes' worth of work. Loss of concentration is a symptom of concussion, you know? I should take you back to the nurse."

"No, you shouldn't." I stop walking, which forces her to as

well. People walk either side of us, ducking into their classrooms. We're going to be late, but I can't bring myself to care. "I'm not stupid, Iris. My health is important, and I know that if I don't look after myself, I can't swim. My head is not an issue, so please don't try to make it one."

Iris's light, professionally plucked eyebrow arches. A silent challenge passes through us. Is she realizing that I will fight back if she tries to take me down?

If she wants to be genuine, to share our lives and be proper sisters, I could work on that for the future. If she just wants to take what I have and keep it for herself, it's on.

"I'm not making it an issue." She takes a deep breath, her eyes welling with tears. "I've lost my mom, and I'm scared of something happening to someone else I love. If I'm worried, it's because I care. Don't take it the wrong way."

Oh, she is good. The girl can cry on cue.

One point for big sis.

Actually, she might be a little too good. I'm not sure what I can say to that, so she knows I'm not playing here. If I carry on the offense, she is going to play the victim.

"Glad we got that cleared up. No need for you to worry about me. I can handle myself," I tell her.

The hidden meaning here: I can handle you.

With a deep sigh, she steps forward. "Air cleared. Let's get to English before Mr. Tenner gets any more grays. We've already been late twice in the last two weeks."

Iris turns and walks away from me, her heels clicking on the floor.

I watch a stranger with a hidden agenda walk. She's so confident. The art of a good lie is confidence. If people think you're sure of what you're saying, they will believe you. Iris says everything with such conviction, I think she believes her lies.

The girl is good.

I'm going to be better.

• • •

After school, Iris and I go home together because I can't deal with another argument about me swimming this afternoon. That's never a good day, but what can I do? The little devil lives with me.

I pull into our drive and we head into the house. Dad is home; his car is in the drive. Why is he back so early? He's been better about spending more time at home, but not usually until around six.

"How was school, girls?" he asks as we walk into the kitchen.

I dump my bag on the counter. "Fine."

"You have to tell him, Ivy."

Freezing, I narrow my eyes.

"Tell me what? Ivy?" Dad's voice is drowning in concern.

Very slowly, I turn around and face him. "I was swimming and choked on water. I'm fine."

He looks over to Iris, then back to me. He's questioning. I can practically see the gears in his head turning as he tries to figure out why that's news.

"Is there more to that?" he asks.

"Not really. Coach sent me to the nurse to get checked out. Lungs are clear."

He stands. "You don't have to go to the nurse every time you choke on water. Why did your coach feel you needed medical help?"

"I choked a lot." I had felt light-headed, like I was fading. "Finally got my breath back, but Coach wanted to be safe. Honestly, Dad, it's nothing."

I don't know why I'm playing this down so much. Coach will probably contact Dad, and I have a form in my bag from the nurse that I'm supposed to pass on.

There is no need for anyone to be dramatic about this. Everyone already thinks I'm attention seeking.

"Where's the form? You did get an incident form, right?"

Groaning, I reach behind my back and grab my bag.

Dad holds out his hand while I find the letter and hand it over. I glance at Iris over his shoulder and glare.

She shrugs, popping a grape in her mouth.

Dad reads the letter about a thousand times. I might be exaggerating, but his eyes flick back to the top of the page a lot.

"You're definitely okay? Maybe we should go to the ER to be on the safe side."

"I've been checked by a *nurse*. I'm fine."

"She listened to your lungs? Secondary drowning is—"

"Not something that's going to happen to me," I say, cutting him off.

"All right." He holds his hand up. "But I'm going to call the school and see if I can speak to the nurse."

The very second Dad is out of the door, I turn to Iris. "Why did you do that?"

"You had to be pulled out of the pool because you were choking so much. Lexi said you looked deathly pale when you were choking. I think that's something our dad needs to know."

"Right, because you're so concerned about my well-being."

"What makes you think I'm not?"

"Literally everything you've done since you got here," I reply.

She folds her hands, popping her hip. "Ivy, you're taking everything the wrong way. You're so emotional at the minute that you're not seeing clearly. Everything I've done, you would have done the same if our roles were reversed. It's not my fault that your grief is clouding your judgment. I mean, you weren't even going to tell Dad that you could have died today."

"I could die any day, Iris. Tomorrow is never a guarantee."

"Okay, there is no need to be like that. I'm trying, here."

"Yeah, but what are you trying, Iris? Since you moved in, all you've done is make things harder for me. I'm unsure why you seem to hate me so much."

"Dramatic much? I don't hate you. I get frustrated with you."

"Look, all I want is for you to do your own thing and for me to do mine."

At this point, I would find it super hard to be any friendlier than we are. We probably won't be close ever, but especially not while we're living under the same roof. Maybe when she's older and not so spiteful, things can be different.

But, yeah, right now she shouldn't hold her breath for a reconciliation. Especially when she's trying to steal my breath.

37

It's been a long week. The kind where you're sure it must be Friday by Tuesday. I slide into the booth next to Sophie with my Oreo crazy shake that looks straight out of an Instagram feed. It's loaded with sugar, but it's Saturday. Sugar on a Saturday doesn't count.

"Do you have any idea how many calories are in that?" Iris asks, twirling her red and white striped straw in her fingers. She has a strawberry shake, no fun extras.

"Nope," I reply. "We always get a freak shake when we're here on the weekend."

Iris lifts her eyebrow. "I only see one."

I glance across at Haley's chocolate shake and Sophie's vanilla.

Why aren't they having a freak shake? They always have one. "Okay. We usually do."

Haley shrugs. "I need to watch what I'm eating and drinking. We have a competition coming up, Ivy."

Frowning, I reply, "We're still allowed to have a treat. If I go sugar free, I get stabby. It's not worth it."

Haley and Sophie look at each other, their heads tilting like they're having a secret conversation. Unfortunately for them, I understand what they say when they say nothing. There's something going on. They think I'm wrong for drinking a ton of sugar when two months ago they were joining me. We've never gone on any kind of excessive diet even when a competition was imminent.

"You guys okay?" I prompt. When one of us has an issue, we talk it through. Right now, they seem to be ignoring whatever is going on. They were fine this morning.

"Yes, why do you say that?" Sophie asks.

"Well, both of you seem . . . distant. Have I done something?" I mean specifically done something to them.

Iris purses her lips around the straw and looks up at Sophie. Whatever is going on, Iris knows about it. What is it? Things have been absolutely fine this week. Better than fine actually. I've been sleeping better, and Iris and I have been getting along. Now there's a weird tension that's fraying my nerves.

What have I done?

Haley sighs. "Ivy, we're just stressed about swimming. Not all of us are naturals."

This *again*? Why do we keep coming back here? I look at my sister. She keeps opening the wound.

Haley's words scrape against my skin like sandpaper. It's not like I just rock up on competition days and win. I train hard. A duck floats gracefully on the water but no one sees its legs working a million miles an hour underwater. I am the duck. Everyone only sees the success, not the sacrifice and effort.

"You're both amazing swimmers," I tell them. "I hate it when you doubt yourselves. Whether you have a freak shake or not, you're still going to be some of our best swimmers."

"Ivy, don't patronize them," Iris snaps, shaking her head.

Her tone makes my stomach roll. She sounds like she's irritated with me, the way she was before we bonded over swimming.

No, we can't go back to that.

"Iris, I'm not patronizing anyone!"

Haley shakes her head and looks away.

Oh, come on!

"Haley," I plead. "I mean what I said."

Sophie rolls her head in my direction. "We know you do, Ivy, and we love you for that."

"But," I say, prompting her to finish what she clearly wants to say. There's more to that than what she's voiced.

Sighing sharply, she says, "Okay, please don't take offense, but when you say things like that, it kind of makes us feel worse. You're the best swimmer and we can't get near your times."

There is nothing I can do here. I'm backed into a corner. I've been where they are, but because I'm not there now, I'm an outsider. What more can I do, anyway? I've given up some Saturday mornings to help them practice and haven't even stepped into the pool myself.

I've been an outsider in many things before, but not my friendship group with Sophie and Haley.

I guess things change. A lot of things recently.

Too much.

We've gone backward now too. I got six days of a normal sister relationship. Is that all Iris is allowing us?

God. She didn't mean any of it, did she? Not that I'm surprised.

"Don't worry, girls," Iris says. "Now that I'm on the team, you'll fly past one Mason sister."

My heart misses a full beat.

She's on the team.

"What?" I heard that right, I'm sure. Iris said she's on the team. My jaw drops.

Haley stares at me. "You didn't know?"

Does this look like the face of someone who knows?!

"You're on the swim team?" I ask Iris, ignoring my friends.

"I spoke to Coach. She watched me in the pool after Sophie and Haley gave me some pointers."

I bet they were pointers I gave them.

I breathe long and slow through my nose. "You're on the team?"

She nods. "As of yesterday."

"You didn't tell me then because . . . ?"

"I barely saw you. Besides, I thought it might be fun for us all to celebrate tonight with milkshakes."

Sophie drops her straw from her mouth. "This is a great thing, Ivy. Iris is a pretty good swimmer. It's obviously in your genes."

"Ah, but I'm not even as fast as you two, let alone my shark of a sister."

I wouldn't say I'm the shark.

My brain is having all kinds of trouble processing this. Iris has never once mentioned that she wants to swim competitively. Haley and Sophie never mentioned helping her so she could try out. When was this decided? When did Sophie and Haley get involved? And why didn't my two best friends tell me?

They all kept this a secret until now. Iris wanted to watch my reaction and she wanted my friends here when I found out they helped.

My skin prickles, and I want nothing more than to leave. I'm sitting here in the middle of one of Iris's games, playing right into it in fact, and I can't leave because I'll be the unreasonable one. Besides, I think she wants me to leave, to make a scene so my friends will tell me once again that I've changed and they're worried.

Not happening.

She can take my spot on the team from me, and I still won't react.

"Hey, Sophie, is it still okay to go to your house tonight?" Iris asks. "The boys are coming too, right?"

Not reacting.

But who are the boys? Sophie's boyfriend and Todd, maybe?

Sophie winces. "Yeah. Though I am a bit nervous to watch the Scream movies."

Iris laughs. "I think we must be the only ones who have never seen them!"

Seriously? "I hardly think you two are the only ones who have never seen them."

I'm willing to put a lot of money on the fact that the Scream trilogy has been watched millions of times, but there are billions of people in the world.

Iris rolls her eyes. "Don't be ridiculous, Ivy. There's no need to be jealous. She's still your friend too."

I clench my jaw, my cheeks filling with heat. "I'm not jealous. You've never been interested in scary movies and neither has Sophie."

Why on earth would they want to get together and spend, like, six hours watching movies they don't enjoy?

"It's something different," Iris replies.

Sophie nods. "It's good to try new things."

Like having your hair down?

Didn't last long, though.

"When Haley and I ask you to watch scary movies with us, you always turn us down."

Iris doesn't give Sophie a second to speak for herself. "Maybe she wants to watch it with someone who won't be cheering for the killer. You two enjoy it."

"So you want to watch them with someone who will equally hate them?" I ask Sophie, not expecting her to reply now she has someone to speak for her.

"Why are you having such a difficult time with this?" Sophie asks.

I hold my hands up in surrender. "I'm just having a difficult time with your choice of movies, that's all."

Haley shrugs. "I think it's good. Maybe you'll actually end up liking them and we can all watch horror together in the future."

She can't be serious. Haley has teased Sophie for years about her being scared of Scooby freakin' Doo. How is she not finding this super odd?

"Sure," I say, fighting so hard to force a smile that my jaw aches.

My phone dings with a message. I glance down and read.

OK, I'll meet you.

Biting my lip to stop the grin, I turn the phone over so no one will see.

When I look up, I see Iris staring at me over her milkshake. I match her gaze.

Whatever you're doing, I'm about to find out.

38

Iris and my best friend are watching a Scream marathon at Sophie's house. I wasn't invited, which is so unlike Sophie.

Whatever.

Kat has finally relented and agreed to meet me.

I have to get out of the house at eight, which is not such a challenge, but I need to sneak back after talking to Kat, so there's the challenge.

When I'm trying to be quiet, I literally make the most amount of noise possible for a human, tripping over and knocking things down. So I don't really know how that one is going to go, and I'm fully prepared to be grounded again when Dad catches me, but it will be worth it.

If he does find me sneaking in or if Iris realizes I'm gone and tells him—which is more likely—I'll make something up.

Dad probably won't believe me unless I tell him I met up with Ty, but I don't want to drag Ty into this.

I'm lucky that Dad is working late at the office and not home; he's already told us to not wait up.

I hate lying to Dad, but I don't have a choice.

Tucking my long hair behind my ears, I straighten Ty's dark gray hoodie and slide my phone and keys into the pocket of my black skinny jeans. I'm in dark colors, and I'm not entirely sure why, but it seemed fitting.

Looking in the mirror, I take a long breath to calm the nerves buzzing through my veins. I don't know what I'm expecting, but I have too many questions to ignore. As an outcast of Iris's group before Mom died, Kat might be the only person who can answer them.

Showtime.

I leave the house, lock the front door, and get in my car.

Taking a jagged breath, I close my eyes. Things have escalated beyond measure. I'm sneaking away to meet one of Iris's old friends. Because nothing I do is working. Kat might be able to help. If anything, she might be able to back me up.

I pull off the driveway, pushing the edge of the speed limit.

Ed Sheeran blasts from my stereo. The music does not fit my mood, which is why I like it. You can't be angry when you're listening to Ed, and I need to slightly tamp the anger burning in my stomach.

The roads are relatively quiet, so I arrive a little earlier than I thought. Which does nothing but leave me with an extra fifteen minutes to obsess.

Kat wouldn't have agreed to meet me if she didn't know something about Iris. She must have dirt on my sister. My thoughts range from Iris must be suffering from some sort of breakdown as a result of ignoring her grief all the way to she's a psychopath in training.

I pull the car into the parking lot at the park where I'm meeting Kat. Clouds darken the sky as the sun sets. The night air is chilly, and I shove my hands into the pocket of Ty's hoodie. There are a couple of benches and a small playground. The place is deserted. I stick by a line of trees that surround the park to stay out of view.

I check my phone. It's 10:30. *Come on, Kat.*

The cooler summer night's breeze blows my hair in my face. I sweep it aside as a squeak fills the silent air behind me. I spin around.

"Ivy?" Kat asks, holding on to the metal chain of a swing. She's dressed head to toe in black like she's on a secret mission. A bit like me.

"Yeah, hi. Thanks for meeting me."

I walk toward her and she holds her hand up, blue eyes rounding in . . . fear?

Planting my feet, I frown. "What?"

"You look so much like her," she whispers.

Well, yeah.

"You're identical?"

"We are."

"She didn't mention that. Some twins don't look alike at all."

"Fraternal might not look similar. We were one egg."

But we're not the same.

"Well." She straightens her back. "You can just stay over there while we talk."

Kat is afraid of Iris.

"What did she do?" I ask.

Clenching her jaw, Kat looks away and her long hair falls in her face.

"You're scared of her. Why?"

"She's not as innocent as she makes out, but, God, she is a master of manipulation. You know, half the school and everyone in town still believes her lies. Sweet Iris has now turned into poor, sweet Iris."

Kat is me. The only one who believes there is much more to Iris than she allows people to see.

"I believe you. Please tell me what she did to you."

"Has she cried for your mom yet?"

Her question catches me off guard. I hadn't expected to talk about Mom.

"Um." I shake my head. "Not since the funeral. Where are you going with this? You think she's not sad that our mom is gone?"

Kat shrugs, her haunted eyes meeting mine. "One day I was running to class. I was the only one in the hallway. I was in a rush." She pauses, staring off in the distance.

Where is this going?

"Tell me. Please," I plead. "Kat?"

She inhales long and slow. "She pushed me down the stairs."

"What?" I gasp. "Did my mom know?" There would be a police report. Iris is a minor, so our parents would have been informed.

"Slow down. There was no evidence."

"What do you mean?"

"There was no one in the hallway. Everyone thinks I fell, but I was pushed. I felt it."

"Wait, so you didn't see her?"

Kat shakes her head. "No, but who else would it have been? I didn't have a problem with anyone else. There was a sharp shove to my back and then I was falling. Teachers heard my scream on both floors. The ones who came from above said there was no one in the corridor, but I could smell her perfume lingering in the hallway."

"Could she have got away that fast?"

"There are empty classrooms up there. She could have easily hidden in one until people came out of their classrooms and then joined them."

"Oh my God," I whisper as my heart races.

This is crazy. Iris is jealous and possessive, but would she really push someone down the stairs? Would she physically hurt someone to be the center of attention?

Kat could have wound up dead. Like my mom.

Oh . . . No.

Blood drains from my face. I fling my hand out and grip hold of a monkey bar support pole. Black spots dance in front of my eyes.

No. No. No.

"Ivy?"

I suck air into my mouth as my hand tightens around the metal bar.

Mom slipped.

My blurry vision sharpens, and Kat comes back into focus.

"Mom," I whisper.

Kat's eyes are wide like she's seen a ghost. "I only agreed to meet you to warn you. I couldn't keep this to myself . . . that Iris could have done something to your mom. Her death was ruled an accident . . . but are they *sure?*"

They seemed positive of the outcome. But what if they're wrong? Their investigation lasted all of three seconds when they saw the slip marks in the wet mud. Marks that matched Mom's sneakers.

But Iris has the same pair, just with a pink tick on the side instead of white.

What if Iris pushed Mom and used her own trainers to make the marks in the ground?

No, that is crazy. It's too much. I take the deep breath my lungs are screaming for.

"But why would she do such a thing?" I ask, trying to make sense of it all. "Was there something Iris was jealous of?"

I can see from the frown on her face and panic in her eyes that she's trying to talk herself out of what she knows. If she can convince herself that Iris wouldn't do that, then it's not real. Only it is real, and she can't lie to herself.

Kat shrugs. "We weren't exactly talking much in the end, but

I know your mom had started dating some guy. I heard Iris complaining about it to her friends, but I don't think it was serious. We had been pretty close friends and Iris never mentioned anything about a guy. Do you think that could have pushed her over the edge?"

I thought back to the way she reacted to Dad having a girlfriend. "I mean, maybe?" I'm breathing hard. "But maybe she didn't mean to. I mean, maybe she just wanted to scare her?"

Kat looks up to the sky. "I knew meeting you was a bad idea." She lowers her head. "You need to be so careful with this. Believe me, you can't get ahead of her. She sick but she's also far more conniving than you could ever imagine."

"What am I supposed to do? I share a house and a dad with her. How can I forget what you've told me? What she might have done to my mom?"

"You can't prove it, and if you try, she'll bury you. Iris has left town, but I still have no friends. Everyone in school still believes I'm the creepy one."

"All right. Okay," I say. There is no point in arguing. Kat is free of her in the sense that Iris isn't going to be around her again. But I don't have that luxury. All that separates us is a bedroom wall.

Kat backs away, and I know our conversation is over. "Be careful," she whispers as she retreats. I watch her until she's lost to the darkness of the night.

I stand perfectly still, as if moving will somehow make this real. It's already very real. Iris couldn't have killed our mom, though.

Could she?

39

Kat left about five minutes ago, but I'm still rooted to the spot beside the monkey bars. The swing sways eerily in the breeze.

I need to go to Mom's house. It's not far from the park; I can make it back in time if I hurry. I think Iris's old school is close by as well.

Why didn't Mom tell me she was dating? Not that she would have unless she thought it was going somewhere. But now I have to go through her things to find evidence of this guy and evidence of Iris hating them both.

If that even exists.

I clench my hands in the pocket of Ty's hoodie and turn around. Slowly, I make my way back to my car in the lot beside the park.

The city is still like a maze to me, but I recognize enough

after the years to find Mom's building easily. I park outside and go in. I know the door codes and I have a key, so getting in isn't a problem.

Taking the elevator to the third floor, I stop outside apartment 313. Every other time I've put the key in this lock, Mom has been on the other side of the door.

Taking a breath, I raise my trembling hand and stick the key in the lock.

The apartment is cold, like it knows the owner is no longer here.

The furniture is all pale green and gray, with rose-gold accents and a few pieces of modern art on the walls. Closing the door softly behind me, I step farther into the room. The apartment has three bedrooms but it's not particularly big.

We need to pack everything up. Iris has been putting it off, and I've allowed her to because I didn't want to push, but I need to push now. It's not right that Mom's things are just sitting here collecting dust.

I walk into Mom's room with guilt burning in my stomach. Looking through her stuff doesn't feel good. It's not like I'm organizing things to keep or donate. I'm searching for evidence of this boyfriend.

So I need to search Iris's room, too, but I don't feel any guilt for that.

In fact, I'm excited to do it. I want to root around her room and see if there is anything I can use to get her to leave me alone. I want to dig up the dirt I'm positive she has hidden away somewhere. She thinks she's the smartest person alive. I'm going to prove that she's not.

When a person gets overconfident in whatever they're doing, they make mistakes. Iris might have her mistake tucked away in her room where she thinks no one will look. We inherited the apartment so it's not like it *has* to be cleared.

If I was going to hide something, it would be here.

But before I get to the good bit, I want to get the bad bit out of the way.

Mom's king-size bed is made. Shimmering silver scatter cushions complement the dusty purple cover and pillows. Every morning, Mom made her bed before leaving her bedroom and going for a run.

I spent many mornings sitting in bed with her and watching TV. She adjusted her routine when I was there, pushed everything back a little to spend time with me. Iris never joined us. She became too cool to hang out with parents long before I did.

In fact, it was only a few months ago that I sat in this very room, tucked up with Mom, watching Judge Judy tear into people.

I take a ragged breath and press my palm to the ache in my chest. I want her back.

She's everywhere in here still. The faint scent of spring flowers from her air fresheners lingers, but it's not as strong as usual. I miss almost being squirted if I walked past it at the wrong time. The canister must be running out. I want to replace it but that seems pointless. There's no one home to appreciate the scent.

Get it together. You don't have a lot of time.

Pushing down the raw heartache, I turn and face Mom's

closet. That's the obvious place to hide things. I can't imagine her being super sneaky and having anything under floorboards.

I grab both handles and open the double doors. Her light blinks on automatically.

Mom's clothes are organized by season and color. I used to tease her about that. My winter wardrobe just means I throw a hoodie and coat over my T-shirt.

I run my fingers across the clothes, feeling soft cotton, wool, and satin as I go. She took good care of her appearance. I like a little makeup and have a good skincare routine that she taught me, but I wish I could be more like her. Every time I try, I get bored after a week, as it takes too long.

I kneel down and look under the clothes. Mom has transparent boxes filled with sandals, sneakers, and heels, and a few cardboard boxes. I pick up the first one. A shoe box that probably doesn't hold shoes since she has those organized so neatly in a place she can see them without opening anything.

Biting my lip, I lift the lid. Old photos of her and Dad from when they were together. I flick through the large pile, smiling and crying at the same time. They stopped loving each other but it's so good to see that she kept the memories.

I pop them back in the box and leave it outside the door. I want to keep them, and I know she would be okay with that. Dad might like to see them, too, or at least know that she has them.

I open the second box and I'm instantly hit by the smell of old paper. There are letters and photographs. They're things from Mom's teen years. I pick up a photo of her and smile. She looks a lot like me and Iris, though her hair was lighter.

I put it back and close the lid. This is private. I wasn't a part of that life. I don't know anyone from that time. She didn't meet my dad until college.

The last box is larger.

I pull it toward me and open it. Sweaters. And underneath one of them . . . a book.

Frowning, I pull it out. It's a book about mental health issues in children, covering topics like personality disorders and psychosis. I freeze, my fingers tightly clutching the book. Why did she feel the need to hide it? Why did she buy it?

She suspected something about Iris. Mom was a researcher. She never did anything without extensive reading. I remember her spending hours reading reviews on TVs before we went and bought her new one.

What did she think Iris has?

If Mom was researching this and Iris found out . . .

Could that be why Iris pushed her?

I flick open the page. The top edge is slightly curled, and the spine is bent. Mom had read this. If Iris knew that, she might have panicked and gone running with her that day.

Oh God. I have to go back to the little bridge where she fell. When I was there last, I wasn't looking at it as a murder scene.

Bile hits the back of my throat. Dropping the book, I slap my hand over my mouth and close my eyes.

One . . . two . . . three . . .

I count slowly in my head as I breathe deeply through my nose.

Mom had to have fallen. There is no way she could have been killed by her own daughter.

You wish.

All the signs point toward Iris doing something evil, but I don't want to believe it. Mom would have been heartbroken if she knew someone she loved hated her that much.

This can't be right.

But it is. I feel it in my gut.

My eyes snap open as a tear rolls down my cheek. Chucking the book back in the box, I put the lid on and swipe the tear away. No more crying until this is over.

There is way more to Mom's death than a freak accident, and I'm not going to sit around mourning her until I find out the truth. She deserves that much.

I push everything back and go into Iris's room.

Not that I expect to find anything since she's a master at deception. Rule one in the psycho's handbook has to be "hide the evidence."

I take a quick sweep, making sure to do it thoroughly. Just as I suspected, I find nothing in her drawers, closet, table, under her bed, under the mattress, hiding in her pillows, or behind any pictures. The floorboards are all fixed down, and the vents are sealed shut.

Jumping off Iris's bed, I grab my bag and head for the door.

It's dark but the flashlight on my phone is pretty decent. There won't be anything left by now anyway, the slip prints in the mud will be long gone. We've had rain and storms recently.

Yet I'm still going. I need to. I have to be where Mom died; maybe I'll know then. Or maybe I'll be just as confused, but doing nothing isn't an option.

I take the flights of stairs like I'm in some crazy race because it's faster than waiting for the elevator. When I hit the bottom, I sprint outside and get in my car. Light drizzle hits my face as I run.

I know the way. Dad drove before, but that journey is burned into my memory. It doesn't take me long to arrive. The roads are much clearer at this hour.

My heart is racing in the worst possible way. I was desperate to get here, but now I just want to run away.

Iris is sneaky, manipulative, and an attention seeker. I'm not ready to think of her being a murderer. There is no way. She wouldn't do that. There's a reason she chose to live with Mom. She loves her and couldn't stay away from her.

But the very fact that I'm here means I'm willing to consider the possibility. Doesn't it?

No, I'm here to clear Iris's name. Even if it's only to myself. Kat hates my sister—rightly so—but to accuse her of murder is overkill. No pun intended.

Mom fell. It was an accident. The police know more than a bitter sixteen-year-old girl. Kat is only speculating.

She has to be wrong.

There is light from the industrial buildings at the farm near the bridge, but I still hold my phone up, letting it light my way. I step slowly toward the bridge. The outskirts of the city are so quiet. I can see why Mom drove fifteen minutes out of her way to run here. It's much better than a concrete track near her house.

It's unusually cold for May tonight, thanks to the rain. Dark gray clouds gather with the imminent threat of a downpour. I wrap my free arm around my stomach, holding Ty's hoodie closer to my body.

The road, which is mostly compacted mud, veers off to the right toward the farm. I don't know Mom's usual route, but I do know that she ran across that little bridge. I walk closer, my chest tightening with every step.

I can picture her, blond hair tied up, black leggings and a neon top. Mom was a colorful person, always full of life and searching for the next adventure. She ran to keep in shape, though I suspect it was her way of forgetting everything that played on her mind too. Much like swimming is for me.

She was probably happy here, running her route in the countryside, getting away from the business of the city. Mom felt safe here, but she wasn't. Even if it was an accident.

I stop at the spot where she slipped, my hoodie now damp. The skid marks in the mud have long been washed away, but I would never forget the place. I crane my neck and look over the side. The rocks at the bottom are a long way down. It's deceptively high up here.

Last time I was here, I didn't get too close to the edge. I wanted to see where she died, but not the very spot she hit the ground. It's slightly higher than I thought. Probably just under a standard flight of stairs high.

Why would this be her usual route? She was deathly afraid of heights, wouldn't even use a stepladder. Even if she didn't look down, she wouldn't come here if there was an alternative.

There is just no way. I spin, taking in the surrounding area.

There is a large field beside the bridge, and along the far side is a track. A public walkway. That's where she would have been. I get why she would want to run in the countryside, but she wouldn't be in this part of it by choice.

Why was she here?

Something made her take this route that day. Or someone.

Iris?

God, am I really allowing myself to believe Iris is a killer? She's capable of making my life hell but to push your own mother off a bridge? No.

An ice-cold shudder ripples down my spine but it's not because of the chill in the air.

I don't have a single clue what I'm supposed to do now. It's not the kind of allegation you can just walk into a police station and state. What evidence do I have? A feeling from two people that something is up with Iris. My mom didn't like heights, but do I know that she *definitely* wouldn't run over that bridge? Enough to be positive that her death wasn't accidental?

No, I don't.

People conquer their fears. Perhaps Mom wasn't afraid of that bridge because you have to be right up to the edge to see how high it is.

Perhaps I'm trying to talk myself out of what I feel really happened that day.

I don't want my mom to have been murdered. And I don't want my sister to be responsible.

Taking a shaky breath, I press my fist into the swirling nausea in my stomach.

Accusing Iris of murder could ruin my life. How would it be proven? How will I not look like a jealous, vindictive sister?

Ty hasn't said anything about being uncomfortable around Iris yet, though he clearly is. There's a possibility that talking to him about this now is premature, but what choice do I have? There is no one else, and Kat has made it crystal clear that she doesn't want anything else to do with Iris.

I could try one last time. Send her a message and see if she would consider helping me. Before I bring Ty into this because I really don't want to involve him.

I pull my phone out of my pocket with trembling hands. Kat is probably going to tell me to get lost, and I can't blame her if she does.

> I know you said you don't want to hear from me again, but I need your help. Please don't say no right away. Think about it? We can make people believe us if we work together.

As if I'm conspiring to bring my twin sister down with her ex-bestie.

I stuff my phone away and the enormity of the revelation makes my legs give way. Dropping to the ground, I put my head in my hands and sob.

Please let me be wrong about this.

40

I get into my car and sit in the driver's seat without a clue as to how I got here. My mind is buzzing, heart racing, and my hand shakes as I close the door.

Gripping the steering wheel, I stare ahead. A light rain spatters the windshield. It hasn't rained harder—at least, not yet. Maybe we'll get away without a storm tonight.

It's getting late, and if I'm not home, Dad will go mad. But like at the park, I can't move.

Nothing quite makes sense. Then, at the same time, everything does.

Iris is responsible for Mom's death. No, Iris *murdered* our mom. She did it because she was angry that Mom had someone else and suspected there was something mentally wrong with

Iris. As much as I love my mother, she was crap at hiding things. Iris helps herself to things in my closet, so she could have easily found that book in Mom's.

What was Iris scared of? Admitting there was a problem? Getting help? How her mental illness would look?

I don't have the answer to that. All I have now is a massive, heavy responsibility to handle this properly.

My credibility is at an all-time low. Not even Dad or my friends believe me over her. Everyone, even Ty, has asked if I'm okay because I'm not *myself*. Only Ty believes that Iris is the one with the problem.

Mom believed it too, and it got her killed.

Would my twin do something to me if I confronted her? If I told Dad?

He would speak to her and she would know it came from me. Groaning, I slam my head back against the headrest and turn the key in the ignition.

I have to be very careful. Iris is dangerous.

She's alone with Sophie at her house right now. The thought makes me feel ill. Maybe my friends will believe me. Or maybe I'll make things ten times worse and put myself in the line of fire.

Shaking off my many thoughts, I put the car in drive and pull away.

Driving takes more effort than usual. I have to think hard about every turn of the steering wheel and press of the accelerator, and I reread every sign I pass to make sure I saw it right. I'm hyperaware of pedestrians, though there are very few at this hour, even in the built-up areas that I pass through.

But soon the landscape changes from tall buildings to farms, and I know I'm closer to home. Fields stretch out beside me for miles. The odd farmhouse with glowing light spilling from the windows is the only sign that I'm not alone on the planet.

When I get back an hour and ten minutes later, the driveway is empty. Iris isn't back. I let myself in, not caring to be relieved that I haven't been caught. That pales in significance now.

I drop my keys onto the side table, slip off my shoes, and head straight for the stairs. The bitch is going down. Iris might have killed my mom, and I need to know.

Her door is closed, but she's out, so I turn the handle and shove.

With my pulse throbbing in my ears, I stomp to her desk and rip open the drawer. Grabbing the flip phone, I take it back to my room. In my desk is a brand-new charger for it.

I sit on my bed, plug it into the wall and the cell, then wait.

After the longest twenty seconds of my life, the phone illuminates. I sit up straighter.

The cell belongs in a museum. It's pre-smartphone and only has texts and calls. There are no messages. I open the sent texts and my breath gets stuck in my lungs.

Ty's number. I click the message and my heart pounds. It's the photo of Logan kissing me. It was Iris and now I have evidence that she is messing with me.

"Ivy, we're home," Dad calls out.

Leaping out of bed, I rip the phone from the charger as I go. Holding down the OFF button, I dash out of my bedroom and into hers. I look over my shoulder, my heartbeat making it impossible to really hear if anyone is coming up the stairs.

Placing the cell in her drawer, I carefully push it shut and back out. I slip into my room and silently close the door. Getting into bed, I shove the charger under my blanket and lie down.

That was close. If I get caught, I don't know how I will explain it.

Well, I could explain it with the truth. I can get the phone.

But it's not the right time. I need to prove that she killed Mom, and if I go in now with a dodgy text, Iris will hide things better and I might never prove anything. When I go to Dad and tell him he backed the wrong twin, I want it to be for murder, not outing a kiss.

Nothing would happen to Iris for that. Sending a picture of me and Logan to Ty is nowhere near the worst thing she's done to me.

Right now, she doesn't know that I've seen the cell. She doesn't suspect that I'm finally one step ahead of her, and I'm not going to ruin that by getting ahead of myself.

It's better that she thinks she's smarter. Besides, there are more texts in the sent folder that I didn't have time to read. I want her to use the phone again.

Closing my eyes, I take a jagged breath as a tidal wave of emotion washes over me. Iris killed Mom. My heart tightens, and I curl my fingers into the blanket.

Lying awake, I listen to the sounds of the house. I hear Iris's and Dad's muffled voices downstairs. Then two sets of footsteps creeping upstairs.

I hold my breath. It's unlikely that Dad will check on me. He'll assume I'm asleep since I didn't answer him. There has only been one time he's woken me up before, and that was when Grandad went to the hospital in the middle of the night. He wants me to sleep as much as I can.

Their voices grow louder, and then, with the closing of two doors, silence. I hear only the rain tapping on my window and occasionally a car passes the house. The night rolls on and on.

Biting my lip, I turn my head, hating knowing that Iris is so close.

She killed Mom!

Tugging on my hair, I roll onto my side and press my face into my pillow.

This is awful. There is a tugging feeling in my stomach, and time is barely passing at all.

Sighing sharply, I look up and grab my phone off the nightstand: 3:16 a.m.

Outside the rain beats harder on my window. I love it when it rains. Give me water in any form, and I'm happy. Tonight, it's not working the way it usually does. I don't feel calm. I'm on edge. My heart is constantly beating a fraction harder.

Maybe I can sleep at Haley's or Sophie's tomorrow.

That is, if they're not still mad at me over something that isn't even my fault.

A part of me wants to be angry at them, but Iris is good at what she's doing, so I can't blame them for being sucked in.

I don't know what my next move will be. Proving my innocence is harder than I ever imagined it would be. I've lost all credibility. Everyone believes Iris and not me. These people have known me for years and her a matter of weeks. No matter what I say, I'm the jealous one. I'm the one who is suffering a breakdown over Mom's death.

How has she managed to do all of that so fast? It doesn't make sense.

She's a master.

Neither of our parents is manipulative, so I have no clue where she learned it. Must be a natural gift. I look over at my door. My desk chair is propped up against the door handle, making it impossible to open from the outside.

I can't say for sure whether she would hurt me, but I'm not taking the chance.

Turning onto my other side, I yawn. I thought I was tired before Iris moved in. Since she started screwing with my life, my sleep has been cut in half. I'm lucky if I get three hours a night.

When Iris is in the pool, practicing when I should be, I will get to be here alone. That hour will be blissful. I don't have to worry that she will appear. I can sleep in peace.

I rub my tired, stinging eyes and curl my fist around the quilt.

She has my life, and she is loving every second of it.

* * *

The next morning, I stay in my room. Chewing my lip, I grip the strap of my bag. I can't come out until she leaves because I hate her, but I want to eat something before I have to get to class.

My spine stiffens. I hear her before I see her. The front door opens and then slams shut. Iris skips to her car that she finally got Dad to buy her. I watch as she drives off; then I run downstairs.

"Morning, Dad," I say tightly as I walk into the kitchen and grab a coffee mug.

He looks up from his paper. It's a little late for him to still be sitting there. He's waiting for me. "Ivy," Dad says, the exasperation in his voice cutting through me. "Look at me. Please."

I meet his eyes.

"I'm worried about you. Maybe you should take some time off school. I think we should speak with Meera about getting some more help."

He might as well just stick a knife in my heart. "Excuse me?"

"You're not sleeping. I don't know what to do to help you."

"All you have to do is believe me," I whisper.

I feel like screaming. The desperate need to fix this and have everything go back to normal itches at my skin. I'm being accused of horrible things, I'm losing friends, losing my dad, and none of it is my doing.

"I'm trying to understand."

No, he's putting me in the box that Iris has created. I have been so deeply affected by Mom's death, but it hasn't made me seek out attention. How can he not see that? I wasn't invisible before, but I sure wish I was now.

"I want you to think about taking some time off. Half a semester. We can work with school so you don't fall behind."

My toast pops up. I turn back. "Dad, can we talk about this later?" I ask, my voice rough with betrayal.

If only he knew what I found on Iris's old cell. I want to get it and shove it in his face. At least let him start doubting her. But I'm not going to underestimate her.

The girl with all the secrets will only get better at hiding them if challenged.

Sighing, I hear him shuffle his paper. "Fine. You need to think about taking time off so that we can focus on your healing. Then we can get back to normal."

He's painting a pretty picture now. Make it all sound like a beautiful fairy tale so I'll go along with it. I don't even recognize normal.

What choice do I have if that's what he wants me to do? I'm a minor. I'm not in charge of my life.

Well, I already knew that. Iris has got her grubby little hands firmly on my present. She won't have my future.

God, I just need to get through the day.

I pick up my plate and sit at the table. I would walk out, but I don't want him to think I'm sulking. Meera is my only hope right now. Until she talks with him, I have to let Iris's games go over my head. I won't get sucked in. Later, I'll call Meera and explain what's going on, get her to talk to him.

Dad's eyes are on me as I take small bites of toast between long sips of coffee. His gaze is full of sadness, and it breaks me.

Iris is making me out to be the evil twin, and Dad believes her.

41

Walking down the hallway at school, I keep my eyes forward and my head high. Classmates stop and stare, and whispers echo behind me as I plant my feet one in front of the other.

I can't believe I ever worried about people talking about me when Mom first died. This is much worse.

On top of stressing that Iris has killed my mom, I do not need all the gossip to be about how Ivy has "changed." I'm sorry that I'm sad and grieving.

My heart races with every step. When I reach my locker, I almost fall into it. My legs are like jelly. Bracing myself with my palm against the door, I take a breath to try and inflate my lungs.

I look up. What the . . . ? Four teachers and the principal

swarm the corridor, one with a clipboard, another opening lockers. The principal standing behind, his shoulders tense and hands on his hips.

Haley stops beside me, her eyes wide.

"What is going on?" I ask.

She glances at me out of the corner of her eye.

"They're searching lockers," she replies.

"I can see that, but why?"

"A test was taken from Mrs. Lewis's office apparently. I overheard her and Principal Grant talking about it."

My eyebrows shoot up. "Someone stole a test?"

"It was probably Leo," she says. "Only way he's going to pass and stay on the team."

I scoff. "Like he'll get kicked off even if he does cheat. The football team gets all kinds of preferential treatment."

"Really, Ivy?"

Wincing, I turn around. Ty is behind me with his arms folded over his chest.

Great.

I groan inwardly. "Ty, you know I wasn't talking about you."

"That's what you think of us, huh?"

"Come on, Ty," Haley says. "You know this happens."

"That's not what I think of *you*," I tell him, and pull open my locker with a little more force than necessary. A white booklet flies out and whacks onto the floor.

"What the . . ." I bend down and pick it up and my eyes widen as I realize what it is. The stolen test paper.

"Ivy, oh my God!" Haley screeches.

I glance up, my heart racing and face heating to a hundred degrees.

Principal Grant swings his head in my direction. His jaw hardens as he sees me frozen, holding the test.

"Ivy Mason, come with me," Principal Grant says.

"No." I look to Ty and Haley. Both are watching me with wide eyes and open mouths. "I didn't do it," I tell them. "I don't know how this got in my locker, but I did not put it there."

Principal Grant clears his throat and takes the test from my hand. "Ivy, come on."

My legs feel like jelly as I take small steps toward him. With burning lungs, I suck in air. "Sir, I didn't take that. I swear."

"My office, Ivy. I'll call your dad."

"What? No. I didn't do anything!"

Around me the hall erupts into a chorus of echoes as I become today's gossip.

My heart pounds so hard my head feels cloudy, like I'm floating. Or about to faint. This is serious. I could be suspended. This will be on my permanent record. I can kiss college goodbye.

"Wait! Stop!" Iris shouts. "Ivy, what's going on?"

"Did you do this?" I ask her.

She scrunches her nose. "Do what? Where are you going?"

"Ivy, keep walking," Principal Grant orders, his voice firm and unforgiving. He's not going to give me any time at all to speak to Iris.

"Tell the truth," I hiss, and dash to catch up with the principal. If she doesn't come forward, I'm screwed. How do I prove that I didn't take it?

His eyes look through me, and I can tell that he believes I'm guilty. "Take a seat, Ivy. We're trying to get hold of your dad."

"I didn't take that paper. Please believe me."

"I rarely see you, Ivy. You don't get into trouble and I will admit, this seems out of character, but I cannot ignore the fact that the paper was in your locker."

"Someone else put it in there. I changed my code to my damn birthday!" Oh my God, I'm so stupid.

The phone rings and Principal Grant takes the call. "He is? Good. Thanks for letting me know." Hanging up, his eyes rise to mine. "Your dad is on his way."

Great, another day he's had to drop everything to race to school.

Slumping against the back of my seat, I close my eyes. "I didn't do this," I whisper.

"The test was in your locker, Ivy."

"I know, but that doesn't mean I took it. Someone put it there. Please, you have to believe me."

"You won't be rejoining class before your dad arrives. I've canceled my meeting with Mrs. Lewis so we can talk. I would like for you to tell me exactly what happened."

I scrub my palm over my face. "When I got to school, I noticed you and other teachers in the hallway. Haley told me you were looking for a test paper that was stolen from Mrs. Lewis's office. I opened my locker and it fell out."

"And you have no idea how it got in there?"

"No! I swear."

"I think you can appreciate how serious this is, Ivy. You have had a test paper in your locker overnight."

"But I didn't know that!"

His lips press together in a grim line.

"Principal Grant, I didn't steal anything. I have no idea how the test got into my locker." I exhale. I have a very good idea who put it there. I don't want to tell him that before Dad gets here, though.

He holds his palms up. "Perhaps you have some homework to complete before your father arrives."

My shoulders slump and I pick up my backpack as my heart sinks.

He doesn't believe me.

Not that I'm surprised. Maybe I should try and get ahold of Iris's current cell. Her Internet history will probably show a search for how to set someone up.

My teeth cut into my bottom lip as I force myself to remain silent.

Bide. Your. Time.

The door opens, and I tense. I don't turn around, but I feel the anger radiating from Dad. He thuds over and sits down beside me. "Why, Ivy?"

"Dad, I didn't do this." My eyes widen, and I turn my body to face him. He's always been able to tell when I'm lying. He'll know that I'm telling the truth now.

"How did the paper get into your locker?"

"I have no clue, but that doesn't mean I'm guilty."

"Who have you shared your combination with, Ivy?" Principal Grant asks.

"Just Ty. But I've unlocked it in front of my friends and my sister loads of times."

The principal and teachers know us all. They don't know Iris well. Surely someone can see that things began to go wrong for me when she arrived? That's not a coincidence.

"Do you think Tyler or your friends could have done this?"

"Not Ty or my friends, no."

Dad stares into the side of my head. "What are you saying, Ivy?"

"Oh, come on! It was obviously Iris! How blind are you people?"

"Ivy," Dad snaps.

I take a breath. "I'm sorry. I didn't mean to be rude." My heart thumps painfully fast. "Things have been different, Dad, you know they have. But can you please think about the one thing that's different."

"Your mother died, Ivy, and we understand how traumatic that is—" Principal Grant says.

"No," I say, cutting him off. "That's not what's happening here. I'm not having some sort of breakdown because my mom died. I'm not acting out because I want attention. I'm not jealous because Iris is living with us now. My life has changed in a way I could never have imagined, but *I* haven't changed. Please believe me."

"Honey," Dad says in a soft voice like he's talking to a toddler.

"You've had a hard time, we all have, but I need you to think about what you're saying. And I need you to be honest with us."

"Dad, I *am* being honest with you. Iris is behind this."

Principal Grant looks at my dad. "There will be an investigation. Ivy will need to take the rest of the day off."

And that's where I stop listening because my ears ring. A roaring fills them and black dots dance in front of my eyes. I'm being kicked out of school.

Is this what she wanted? What would be the point? My friends have welcomed her, everyone has. Why do I need to be out of the way?

"Ivy, come on," Dad says, rising to his feet.

I have to go. We're going to leave this school, and I won't be allowed back until they figure out I didn't take that paper. *If* they figure it out.

By now everyone in school will be talking about me. They already think I've done some pretty shady things recently. Nothing as serious as this. Maybe they won't believe I've stolen test papers. Ty, Haley, and Sophie should know that I would never do that.

Mom and Dad taught me about hard work. I would rather fail than cheat.

Dad walks a step in front of me, hands fisted like he's about to snap. When we get home, he's probably going to shout a lot. He never shouts. But then, I—or Iris—have never given him reason to.

Everyone is in class, so thankfully I don't have to endure even more whispers.

My shoulders slump as I follow Dad out to the parking lot. I don't know what happens now because I spaced in there when Principal Grant told me I can't come back until they've investigated, but I know more people will have to be involved. I doubt this can be contained within the school.

The worst part is that I can't do anything to fix it yet. I don't have enough evidence, and no one believes me.

42

Sitting at the table, I watch Dad make two coffees. He walks to me slowly, like he needs the extra time to figure out how to deal with me. He's never had to play the disciplinarian much.

He places my coffee in front of me and sits down.

"I don't know where to start, Ivy."

"You could start by hearing me."

His intense gaze pins me to the spot. "Why do you not think I'm hearing you?"

"Because you're blaming me."

"The test was found in your locker."

"I'm not denying that. But it wasn't me who put it there. Why would I leave it in my locker? I had just gotten to school when they found it. How would I have had time to steal it, put it in my locker, get outside, and pretend to come in again? It makes no sense because I didn't do it."

He clears his throat. "The test was in Mrs. Lewis's office on Friday, and when she looked again this morning, she found it to be gone."

"Oh right, so I broke in over the weekend, stole it, and left it in my locker."

"This is not the time for sarcasm, Ivy."

"When you're sitting on this side of the table, innocent with no one believing you, it is."

"So you think Iris did it?"

"Yeah, that's exactly what I think."

"Why, Ivy?"

"I don't know exactly. She hasn't been right and you know it."

He curls his hands around his mug. "She hasn't spoken about your mom or grieved. I'll give you that."

I narrow my eyes. "But . . ."

"But it's you I have seen the most change in. Ivy, you aren't sleeping well, you're distracted at school, you've shouted out and been disruptive in class—none of this is like you."

"Because it's not me. Dad, hear me. *Please.*"

"You want me to believe that Iris is setting you up?"

"It's that or you think I really did steal a test."

This is looking more and more like one of those pick-a-side moments, which I think are in poor taste, but he has to believe one or the other. He either takes my word or believes Iris.

Sighing, he glances down at the steam rising from his coffee. "I don't want to think either of you is capable of any this."

He's going to have to, though.

"Dad, you know me."

"I do, Ivy, and that's why I'm so worried about you. On my way to the school, I called Dr. Rajan."

"You called Meera? What for?"

"For her professional advice."

"And what advice did she give you?"

"We've decided that you will be taking a break from therapy sessions with her while I look for someone more suitable."

My heart skips a beat. "What? What do you mean by that?"

School isn't that far away. How did they decide all that in ten minutes?

"Dad, I want to keep seeing her. She helps."

"I don't know if she does, Ivy."

It's decided, then. He's Team Iris.

I turn my head away as his betrayal punches a hole in my chest. He's my dad.

"Wow," I whisper.

"This isn't a personal attack on you, Ivy. I'm trying to do what's best and get you the help you need. Once you're settled here, I'm going back to school to speak with Principal Grant."

"Why are you going back?"

"Because I don't want you to be expelled from school."

"I should move to a different school anyway, one Iris is nowhere near. You'll see how things are *miraculously* better then."

"I don't want to have an argument about your sister right now. Let's focus on you."

"Bloody hell, she really has got you wrapped around her finger."

"Ivy!" he snaps. "That's enough. I don't have time for this. I need to do damage control with your school. Do not leave this house."

He stands, leaving behind his untouched coffee, and walks out of the room.

I sip my drink, fuming on the inside but knowing there is no point in showing it. Dad has made up his mind. Iris has probably been in his ear, whispering lies about me the whole time.

The school has CCTV on the outside. They'll soon see that I didn't come in over the weekend. Maybe they'll find that Iris did. Or maybe she stole the paper and planted it in my locker before she left on Friday. We both hung around a while, her at cheer practice, me to finish up some reading because I couldn't focus in class. I left first because of my session with Meera.

I finish my coffee and try not to stress. Iris can't keep this up forever.

She's already caused me to lose so much, and now I have to do this without Meera. What did she say to my dad that made him pull me out of therapy with her? Or maybe Dad removed me because he doesn't think she's helping.

Hopefully Dad will fill in the blanks for me later.

Someone pounds on the front door.

I let go of the mug that has turned cold in the thirty minutes I've been sitting here.

The knock comes again, this time louder. I get up and walk to the front door. Ty is the other side when I look through the hole.

Opening the door, I look at him and wait. Who does he believe here?

"What is going on? I couldn't stay at school any longer. You stole a test paper?"

"No! You know I didn't!"

I step aside. Or rather he barges in and I have to step aside.

"Come in," I mutter.

"I need you to start talking, Ivy. Why was a test paper found in your locker?"

I cross my arms. This question is going to get old real fast. "Iris put it there."

"How do you know that?"

I start walking up to my room. Ty follows. "Who else could it have been, Ty?"

"All right," he says.

I make a left into my room and crash down onto my bed. "I hate this. She's crazy, but she's making me look like the one who's lost it."

"They'll get to the bottom of it, okay?"

He's not really saying much, nor is he getting angry, which is how he usually reacts if he thinks someone has messed with me.

"You should get back to school, Ty."

"Do you want me to leave? Because I don't care about missing a few classes right now."

"I want you to believe me. If you do, stay."

I don't meet his eyes because I'm scared of watching him leave. But a few seconds pass and he doesn't move. I raise my eyes.

"You want to watch some TV?"

His lip quirks in a smile. "Where's the remote?"

"Top drawer. I tidied."

He walks to my bedside table and pulls the top drawer open.

"Ivy, what are these?" Ty asks.

I glance up as he pulls a small stack of Polaroids out.

"I don't know," I reply, sitting up on my bed.

"Why do you have these?"

I take the photos. I gasp, my hand jerking, and I drop them like they're on fire. Pictures of my mom with a man. In three of them, they're kissing. The other seven are just of him. Why would these be in my room?

Shaking my head, I mutter, "I don't know."

So that's the guy my mom was dating.

"Iris," I say, lifting my head. "She must have put these here."

"Don't you set traps in your room to see if anyone comes in?"

"Yeah, but she could have put these here before that. Clearly she did, because I have never seen these before!"

"Why would she do that? It doesn't make sense."

"I don't know. I haven't been able to figure out why she does anything. Ty, I didn't take these photos."

"You think she followed them? The pictures of him were taken at different times. He's not wearing the same clothes."

I look them over again, scattered on my bedspread. "Do you think she was obsessed with him?"

"Do you know him?" he asks.

"No, I didn't even know she was dating until after she died."

"Looks like they've been together awhile, from all these pictures. How would she have kept it a secret for so long?"

His voice is low, the way Meera's gets when she's trying to get me to realize something I should know. When she doesn't think I'm telling the whole truth.

"I didn't know about him, Ty."

He raises his palms. "All right. So Iris put these here."

My mind spins. What possible reason could Iris have to put these here?

"Do you think it could have been mixed in with some of the stuff you brought home from your mom's?" he asks.

"How did you know I went there?"

Ty frowns. "When you brought Iris here to live. What are you talking about?"

He doesn't know I went to Mom's recently. "Nothing," I say. "This doesn't make sense. Why would my mom take so many candid pictures of him? And someone else had to have taken the ones of them both."

Ty watches me out of the corner of his eye and my heart rate spikes. He's questioning me.

"Tyler, I didn't take these photos."

"Ivy, I believe you."

No, you don't.

Smiling, I say, "You should probably go. My dad will be home soon."

Ty doesn't put up a fight or offer to climb out of my window for a few extra minutes like usual. That's a terrible sign. I'm sitting on this information that would make people doubt Iris, even just a little bit, but I can't do anything because I'm petrified of screwing up for Mom. She would be so disappointed in me if I accused Iris when she's innocent.

I don't really care what people think of me. Or not more than I care about finding out the truth. Mom is getting justice if it kills me.

"I'll see you tomorrow," he says, giving me a chaste kiss.

I scoop the photos together and stuff them back in the drawer.

Why doesn't Ty believe me?

I leave my bedroom door open a few inches so I can leave a small object behind it. A lip gloss. If Iris sneaks into my room, it'll move. I slip inside like a ninja to see if the lip gloss has moved farther than I pushed it.

That is why he doesn't believe me. Iris was in my bedroom the very first day we arrived home after Mom's funeral. She could have stashed them way back then.

My twin was behind this, and I have absolutely no idea why. But it's one more thing that I have against her. She's getting sloppy, hiding things in my junk drawer, assuming that I won't look.

From now on I'm taking an inventory on the contents of my room. I'm keeping everything she adds. And I'm bringing her down.

43

Since there is no evidence that I took the exam paper, although it ended up in my locker, there is little the school can do. It's a win for me, and I bet it's eating Iris.

One thing they have managed to do is suspend me from the swim team. Principal Grant called to inform me that I could return to school but not the swim team just yet. That's a win for Iris and something I'm trying not to focus on. I don't know how long it will be before I'll be allowed to compete again. I'm trying really hard not to let Iris know it's bothering me because I don't want her to feel any kind of victory. She will probably know I'm desperate for the Stanford scout to want me. So I pretend that I'm okay and could do with a little time off from competition, while inside I feel like I'm breaking.

It's fine. It's all fine. I can train in any pool.

I think Dad played heavily on the grieving daughter thing to get me back to school. You know, *if* I did take it, then it's because I'm extra stressed over my mom dying and end-of-year tests were too much.

I don't even want to think about Mom being used like that.

My head is downcast as I walk the hall. I can't stand to see so many pairs of eyes burning into my face. Everyone has questions. Why am I lying? Why did I cheat? Why is Ty even still talking to me? Why does Iris keep forgiving me after everything I've done to her?

I hate my sister.

This has gone way past sibling rivalry.

Not even my dad trusts me anymore, and I can see Ty's doubts every time he looks at me.

My heart skips a beat.

What, I'm left with no one?

I don't know how to repair my life and my reputation.

The fake cheating thing got me kicked off the swim team.

I have nothing left.

Nothing but the suspicion that Iris pushed my mom and killed her.

And who would believe me now? I have to find proof or get Kat to talk. She's the only one who can back me up, tell the world what Iris is really like. Maybe then I can rebuild my life.

But I think I'll be finding new friends. Mine wouldn't believe me on top of everything else.

Someone grabs my upper arm. Gasping, I spin around. "Ty," I breathe, my shoulders slumping.

"Sorry. I tried calling out, but you were somewhere else."

"I wish I was somewhere else."

"People will come around, Ivy."

So far, I haven't asked Ty whether he believes me about all the crazy stuff that has been going on. I have one person left in my corner, and I'm not ready to lose him too.

I'll fight to keep Ty, and I'll fight dirty if I have to.

"I don't care about people anymore. Nothing I say makes it better. Trying to tell my side only seems to dig me in deeper."

"Everyone makes mistakes, babe."

My face falls. "Is that what you think?"

He shakes his head. "That's not . . ." Sighing, he says, "What I mean is these people forgive actual mistakes. Whatever they believe about you doesn't matter."

"What you believe about me matters, though."

He steps closer and presses his forehead to mine. "I think you're under a lot of stress. I think your sister is also under a lot of stress, and those two things combined have made this toxic mess of drama and jealousy. She's adjusting to a lot and she's not doing it well."

"Do you believe she put the test papers in my locker?" I ask.

"I believe someone did."

"Not Iris?"

"She was swimming all morning. When would she have had the opportunity?"

I lick my dry lips. "She had help."

"From who, babe?"

"You don't sound like you believe me right now."

He backs up a fraction and shakes his head. "Not saying that. I'm genuinely asking. Who do you think she got to do that for her?"

"Ellie," I reply.

"Do you think she would do that? Ellie loves a bit of drama, but she prefers more of a spectator's role."

"I don't know," I say, rubbing my face.

"Did you sleep much last night?" he asks.

"A little. I got a couple of hours. That's beside the point. I'm fine with the lack of sleep. I'm just sinking here, Ty. I hate that people think all this crap about me when I haven't done anything wrong."

"Come on, I'll walk you to your first class."

Looking up at him, I smile. "Even though you'll have to run?"

His eyes glow with amusement. I've missed that. "Yeah, even though I'll have to run."

He wraps his arm around my shoulder, tucking me into his chest.

"Do you need me to do anything?" he asks.

"Just don't lose faith in me," I whisper.

"Hey," he murmurs, kissing the side of my head as we walk. "That'll never happen."

I can read between the lines. He might be telling the truth when he says he believes Iris is causing issues for me, but he also thinks there is something more going on with me.

Ty holds me tight as we head to my first of six classes with Iris. Despite my request to change all of my classes, I still share my schedule with Iris. I don't know why one of us wasn't moved but here we are. I'm not even going to mention it to Principal Grant or Ms. Hart.

I need to keep my head down until I can convince Kat to speak up. If she doesn't reply to me when I message her again, I'm going back there.

And I'm going back to Mom's too. There might be more proof. Things I've missed, things I wasn't looking for last time because I didn't think Iris was a killer.

We stop as we reach my class. The teacher gives me a look and heads inside. She thinks I'm guilty of stealing the test paper.

Whatever.

"You going to be okay today?" Ty asks.

I only nod because a wave of emotion washes over me, making my stomach churn.

My whole life has been turned upside down, and I don't know where I go from here.

The first four classes pass without incident. Iris goes out of her way to ignore me. And I'm totally including everyone whispering about me in the non-incident thing. I can handle that. A bit of gossip seems so insignificant now that my sister is trying to ruin my life. It really puts the minor things into perspective.

That's one positive to come from this, I guess.

During lunch, I meet Ty and we eat on the grass at the edge of campus.

He pops a grape in his mouth and leans back against a tree.

"You can go play ball if you want," I tell him, noticing his eyes wandering to his teammates, who are messing around on the field.

"I'm good here."

"Have you gotten a lot of crap for sticking by me?"

His eyes slide to mine. "I'm not going there."

"Yes, then."

"Ivy, it doesn't matter what anyone else thinks. This will blow over eventually, so focus on school, okay?"

"All right."

I'm not sure just focusing on school is going to cut it. Iris is probably still plotting. She has my friends and my swim team. What more is there for her to take?

My life?

I still can't bring myself to believe that she would kill so coldly like that. If she pushed Mom, it was because she felt threatened. Not that it's any better because she felt like she had a reason to. God, I want to scream it from the rooftops, but I can't accuse her of murder until I have evidence or my word actually means something.

Ty might believe me, but he's quieter than usual around me. He hasn't left yet but that doesn't mean he won't if I suddenly drop the M bomb. Iris *murdered* my mom.

There's a certain point where Ty might walk away, and I'm scared of pushing him there. Even if it's not my doing, he might have enough of the whole situation and decide I'm too much drama or that he doesn't want to be treated differently because he won't walk away from his crazy girlfriend.

I'm walking a tightrope, and I'm petrified I'll fall off.

Or Iris will push me off.

There has to be a way to expose her. She's so transparent to me. I can see straight through her little act. It's just a shame I can't see into the future, so I'd know what she's planning next.

But maybe it's time for me to start planning too. Do things that make her look bad, start planting doubt in people's minds about her. I've been on the defense for too long; it's time I started on the offense.

Ty would be proud of me for using a football metaphor.

"Did you manage to get in touch with Meera?" he asks.

"She wouldn't take my call, so I've emailed her. I hope she responds."

"It would be good to know what she and your dad spoke about."

I unscrew the lid of a bottled water. "I would love to know what he said to her. I don't think she would have ditched me as a client, so he obviously pulled me from her sessions."

"And Iris isn't talking to you?"

"I get the odd smirk here and there. Besides that, nothing. She avoids me, especially when Dad is home."

She has to show him that she's scared of me. I don't really mind that; at least she's out of my way. I can't stand to be in the same room as her and still sleep with my chair blocking my door in case she decides to smother me in my sleep. Okay, I don't even know if I'm kidding there.

I do fear her. She's proved in six weeks that she can make my life crumble. She has everyone at school on her side, including the teachers, and even made Dad doubt me. And she is the one who isn't dealing with Mom's death while I attend weekly therapy sessions. She deserves a freakin' Oscar.

The bell rings, so Ty and I grab our trash and throw it out on the walk back to class. I have a double math period. Hell for some, but at least I don't have to think too much. You can't question math; the answer is the answer.

Logan is in my math class, and a couple girls from the swim team. No cheerleaders, but the swim girls will probably be Iris's spies. I'm going to keep my head down and focus on passing this class. Maintaining As is exactly what I need to do in order to show Principal Grant that I'm the same Ivy as before and I deserve to swim again.

Logan sits down next to me, and I cringe.

"What are you doing?" I whisper.

"Math. What are you doing?"

"You're not funny. You don't even sit here."

"I do today. How are you holding up?"

"Why do you care?"

He shrugs. "Can I borrow a pen?"

I dig in my bag and chuck a black pen at him.

"Thanks, Ivy."

The last thing I need is for someone in here to tell Iris that I was speaking to Logan for two hours. That'll get back to Ty and Ellie. I don't want any more drama. And I don't want to give Ty a reason to doubt me. He's still touchy on the whole Logan subject. I've barely seen them talk since, and that's only because they have to.

"Are you going to the swim meet this afternoon?" he asks.

"Why do you ask that?"

"Look, last year I was kicked off the team for fighting with this older kid. I know what it's like to be banned from something you need. Go to the meets, support the team, and show them that your mistake doesn't define you. Be part of the team even though you're not in the pool."

All right. A lot of that makes sense. Actually, it does.

"Thanks, Logan."

"Yeah." He turns his focus to his work.

Looks like I'm going to the swim meet after all.

44

The smell of chlorine repels some people, but not me. It's as comforting as my warm bed or a mug of hot chocolate. The pool is home, and I miss it so much. The principal hasn't said whether I'll be allowed back on the team next year, but I've overheard things my teammates have said.

Some feel that I should be back because I'm fast. Not because they like me and believe I'm innocent, but because they want the win. Some would rather lose than ever have me back.

To be honest, I don't particularly care what any of them think. I just want to swim.

I walk through the changing room and head for Haley and Sophie.

Heads turn as I walk; dozens of eyes peek up. I can guess what they're thinking, but whatever.

"Hey," I say, handing them a bottle of water each.

Haley smiles. "Thanks, Ivy. I get so thirsty when we're competing."

"I know," I reply. "Are you both ready?"

"I think so," Sophie mutters.

"No need to be nervous. You've got this."

With a shrug, she turns around. "Not nervous."

I watch her walk out of the changing room with my heart in my stomach. "She's still mad at me."

Haley pulls her hair up into a ponytail. "She's worried about you, Ivy. Things have changed a lot recently."

"My life is barely recognizable now, I'll admit that, but I haven't done anything—"

"Ivy," she snaps, cutting me off midsentence. "You're my best friend, and I love you, but you have got to take responsibility for what's going on. We all get that you're having a rough time and there would be a lot of understanding if you'd own up to your part in the downward spiral."

My word holds no weight now. How do you restore trust in people when they don't believe what you're saying?

Averting my eyes, I blink to ease the sting of tears.

Haley sighs. "Forget that now. Just keep going to see Meera."

Right, because she's the miracle cure. If she was, I would sign Iris up.

She smiles. "How are you feeling being here but not competing?"

I look back at her. "Er, not great. It's going to be so weird being a spectator."

"You didn't need to come. We would have understood."

"Yeah, but I want to support you and the team still." Even if half of them would rather drown me. "I want to be involved in some way."

"Have you spoken to Coach? About helping her out?"

"I don't think she will allow that."

"Maybe not. You'll just have to let things settle before you try to get back on the team." She holds up the bottle of water as people filter out of the room. "Thanks again for the water. I'll see you out there."

Haley heads out, and I watch her go. The door slams shut, echoing through the room. I've spent so much time in here over the last couple of years. Now I can only come in to hand my friends bottles of water.

And none of it is my fault. It's so unfair.

"Ivy?"

My body freezes at the sound of my twin's teasing tone.

With fire in my stomach, I clench my jaw and turn around.

She's standing by the entrance to the pool, in team swimwear that I should have on, with her hands on her hips. "Are you, like, okay in here?"

Oh, there's no need for her to pretend now. We're alone in here.

"Fine, Iris. I just came to see Haley and Sophie."

"Really? They're both out by the pool. Are you sure you're okay?"

Like you care.

"Absolutely fine. Break a leg out there." *Please.*

Laughing, she drops her arms. "I'll do you proud."

Iris spins like a freakin' ballet dancer and skips out the door. Do me proud. Yeah, whatever, sis. She's been swimming for all of five minutes, so there is no way she will come anywhere near my time.

But she doesn't need to beat my time; she only needs to get close to Leah's, and she's already getting close to Haley's. Iris may not have swum competitively before, but she has always been in the pool growing up and you can tell.

It sucks. I really wish she bombed at it.

I take a long breath and my chest expands. Okay, time to do this.

Reaching my hand up, I push the door and step through.

The pool glistens as the water softly ripples. I would dive straight in if I could.

Coach lifts her eyebrow at me from the other side of the room.

Right. I'm not supposed to use that door anymore. I need to use the one for the people who aren't on the team. Because I'm not anymore.

I turn my head away and walk around the pool to find a space to sit. The bleachers are almost filled. The school we're competing against is good, probably the best, but we've beaten them a couple of times before. We're pretty evenly matched. Iris better hope that she can get near my times today.

Sitting down, I drop my bag between my feet and smile at Haley. Sophie is talking to Iris and Coach. Leah rolls her shoulders and glances at the other team. She's nervous. Before each competition, we size up the other team together. She's doing that alone now. Leah and I aren't exactly close, but we get along. We push each other. I'd like to think that she is one of the girls who's behind me joining again.

But with me out of the way, she's anchor, so who knows.

"Hi, Ivy."

"What do you want?" I ask Logan.

"That's not a very nice way to speak to a friend," he says.

"I didn't know we were friends."

"Seems like you could use every one you can get right now."

Rolling my eyes, I turn away. "I don't need a pity friend, but thanks."

"Good, because I don't pity you."

"Great. I'm glad we have that cleared up."

Logan narrows his pale green eyes. "Why am I getting attitude here?"

Honestly, I don't know. If someone is actually being nice and not treating me like I'm contagious, I shouldn't be a bitch.

But this is Logan, and Ty still isn't happy with the whole drunken kiss thing. It makes Logan a bit of a risk. I don't want to upset things with Ty. I need him more.

"I'm sorry, Logan. I'm just in a bit of a funk."

"Funk," he repeats, smirking. "So, did you do any of it? I've heard a lot of things. Ellie says a lot of things."

I roll my eyes. "I'll bet."

"It doesn't make sense. You and I are a lot alike. We both put everything into our sport, we both overthink, and we both need to fix things."

How does he know this?

Chuckling, he says, "You're not that much of a mystery to me, Ivy. Looking at you is like looking in a mirror. Only I'm hotter."

"Oh, please," I mutter.

"That's how I know it's completely out of character for you to purposefully sabotage your life."

"You believe me," I whisper.

"I believe something is off. Unless you've totally lost it, I don't think you could steal test papers or do any of the other crazy stuff you've been accused of doing."

"I haven't done any of it," I tell him.

"Who did?"

I glance back at the pool. Iris is on the diving block. She's not one of our strongest swimmers, so she's going first.

Do I tell Logan? Does he not already know?

Oh, he knows but he wants me to say it. Everyone thinks I'm crazy and a terrible sister for accusing Iris. People who have known me for two years and her for less than two months have chosen to believe her.

I'm trying not to take that personally because Iris is obviously a master of manipulation, but it's hard not to when you've never done anything wrong before.

"Iris," I say, turning back to Logan.

He stares into my eyes like he's searching for signs of a lie. Is he watching for a flinch? I'm not flinching. I'm not lying.

"You think it's your twin sister?"

I nod.

"Why?"

"Well, that's the million-dollar question, Logan. I think there's something wrong with her." And I think a lot more than that, of things that she's potentially done, but I'm not going to disclose everything. Accusing Iris of setting me up has come back and bitten me on the ass before, so I can only imagine what will happen if I tell people I think she's killed our mom.

"You must have a theory."

I shrug. Is he genuinely interested because he believes me or is he here for Iris? She's all buddy-buddy with Ellie, so it's possible she could have gotten to Logan too.

God, I don't know what to believe. Everything is such a mess.

"Do you think she's jealous?" he asks.

On an extreme level.

"Honestly, Logan, I have no clue. I haven't done anything wrong." I look away and then back at him. "Is there anything you want to tell me, Logan?"

His eyes narrow. "I'm just a jock. I don't see anything." We both know that's not true.

He might know something. But he's scared to tell. Maybe Iris has something on him. Or perhaps, as usual, I'm overthinking.

"You saw me. If I'm not allowed to pretend, then neither are you."

The sound of a whistle blows through the air and the crowd begins yelling. It's much louder from here. When I'm swimming, even when I'm waiting, I can tune it out.

Wincing, I whip my head around to see Iris disappear under the water.

My throat burns as I watch her.

That should be me.

Call me bitter, I am, but I'm so glad Dad couldn't get out of work to see this.

My sister's name is being chanted; I can hear it doubly loud over the name of her opponent. With every chant, my heart beats harder and my fingers curl into the palms of my hands.

I hate her with every fiber of my being.

I hate that she can take what she wants.

I hate that she doesn't care about me.

And I hate that no one can see what she is.

When I leave high school, I'm moving thousands of miles away, avoiding every college my classmates get into. I want somewhere remote, somewhere I can pretend that I don't even have a sister.

I get my phone out of my pocket as the sight of my twin swimming churns my stomach. Kat is going to help me whether she likes it or not. I don't care if she's scared. We can't let this continue. Something is very wrong with Iris and it needs to be exposed.

I type Kat's name into Facebook and find her profile.

I know she wouldn't accept my friend request, but she doesn't have the best privacy settings. I can still see her profile.

I scroll down and my heart leaps into my mouth. Standing up so fast my head spins, I grip my phone in my hand and try to force my blurry vision to focus.

No.

I'm too hot. It's boiling in here. My scalp prickles.

"Ivy, what's wrong?" Logan asks, rising to his feet.

Half the crowd is standing, so we don't look out of place. But I feel it.

I shake my head. "Nothing. I need to go."

Snatching my bag off the floor, I dart toward the door. Iris is out of the pool now, Sophie taking her place in the water. I don't seek her out, but I know her eyes are on me.

I burst through the door and slam into the wall across the hall. Placing my hand on the cool brick, I count in my head. *Breathe. In for four. Out for four.*

Lifting my cell, I reread the posts that Kat has been tagged in.

Everyone is devastated.

By her death.

45

Kat is dead.

I feel light-headed, like I'm floating out of my body. I'm scrolling without reading, comment after comment about how sad it is that she's gone.

Everyone by the pool cheers. I can hear them from out here, spurring on the swimmers. All I can focus on are the pictures and posts about Kat.

She was ostracized like me, but everyone is acting like they're her best friend.

Why do people care more when you're dead?

The door swings open and Logan rushes toward me.

Oh my God, just go away.

Having him anywhere near me feels like a trap. He might seem genuine, but Iris can manipulate people in her sleep.

He might not even be aware that he's her spy.

"Ivy, are you okay?"

I back up. "I'm fine. I just need to go home."

"Okay, let me drive you."

"No! My car is in the lot."

"You're shaking. I can't let you drive like that."

Taking another step back, I put my phone in my pocket. I need to pull it together. "That's not your call, Logan. You should get inside before Ellie realizes you're here."

"I can handle Ellie. Let me at least call Ty."

Stilling, I frown. "Why aren't you with Ty?"

"I hurt my foot and need to rest it for a couple of weeks. Thanks for noticing."

"Why would I notice? We're not friends."

He grips his heart with a little dramatic flair. "Ouch, Ivy."

"I'm not trying to be mean. We've never been friends." Why am I even standing here having this conversation with him?

"Wow. You really are too wrapped up in your unraveling life. I came over when I spotted you because I thought you needed a friend. I guess I shouldn't have bothered."

Turning around, he heads back poolside, shaking his head as he goes.

Leaning my side against the wall, I close my eyes and wince. I was horrible to him, and for all I know, he could be genuine.

I take my phone back out of my pocket, closing Facebook before I see any more tributes to Kat, and text Logan.

Having a bad day and took it out on you. I'm sorry

Then I walk quickly down the hall and out to the football field. Ty will know what to do.

Kat is dead.

Iris could be involved.

She tried to hurt her first. Maybe Iris found out that I met up with Kat.

No, I can't go there. If I got someone killed . . .

I reach the field and take a seat in the bleachers. Ty is running. I spot him immediately, and smile. He's safe, and right now, the only safe person in my life. Ty believes me. Despite the overwhelming evidence—planted by my evil twin—he believes me when I tell him I didn't do all of the crazy things Iris has made me look guilty of.

Maybe Logan does, too, but I can't bet on that. Trust isn't something that I'm handing out freely at the moment.

During one of Ty and his team's many still moments during practice, he looks up and does a double take. His forehead creases as he spots me sitting and watching. He knew I was going to the swim meet, so of course he's confused.

Ty was going to meet me by the pool after, as he finishes first.

He says something to his coach, who then looks up at me and scowls. *What did I do, dude?* Coach turns back to Ty and holds two fingers up as he says something.

Ty immediately spins around and sprints up the steps.

I guess he has two minutes to talk to me.

Ty takes off his helmet and runs his hand through his hair. "You okay?"

I shrug. "Fine."

Raising both eyebrows, he puts one foot up on the bench so he can lean his elbow on his knee. "You're here and not at the pool."

"And you're observant as ever."

"Ivy . . ."

"I prefer to watch you. Go back and finish, then we can go eat."

He hesitates with his lips pressed together and disbelief in his eyes. Ty isn't stupid, and I really am a terrible liar. It's unfortunate that no one else remembers that about me.

Apparently, I had a personality transplant as my mother was laid to rest.

I clench my jaw as the pain of losing her and losing my life cuts through my chest. Iris makes me so angry, but the worst part is that she's using Mom's death as an explanation for why I'm supposedly doing all this crap.

Mom's memory is going to be tainted and it will be all Iris's fault. Meera thinks that Iris is acting out, and, I mean, that much is clear. I can forgive her for making me look guilty, but if she's hurt Mom or Kat, that's not something I can forgive, no matter what is really going on with her.

"We can go to my house. My parents are out."

With a tight smile, I nod. "Okay."

I would rather be at his house anyway. Kat is dead, and I have to find out how that happened. That's not really something I want to be doing in a restaurant. I'd look on my phone now—there is probably a news article about it, but I'm too scared to. I want to be alone with Ty.

After practice, Ty follows me to his house. I get it together long enough to drive.

He lets us in the house and I immediately collapse on the sofa before I fall to the floor.

"Kat's gone."

"What? Who has gone?"

"Kat. Iris's old friend. She ditched her and turned the whole school against her. Sound familiar?" I run my hands over my face. "Oh my God, she's killed two people."

"What?"

I drop my hands and look up at Ty. "Iris killed my mom and Kat."

He takes a step back as if my words have pushed him. "Iris?"

"Yes."

"You need to start at the beginning, Ivy. I'm lost. You think your sister is a killer?"

"I know she is," I whisper. "And if I'm not careful, I'll be next."

"Stop." He kneels down in front of me. "I need you to start making sense. How do you know Kat?"

"I tracked her down on Facebook. At first, she didn't want to talk but then she agreed to meet me. She told me how she was once best friends with Iris until Iris turned everyone against her. No one believed Kat when she told them what Iris was doing. One day, Kat was pushed down a flight of stairs at school. Everyone thought she fell because there was no one at the top. They didn't believe her when she told them it was my sister."

"Why does that make you think she's killed her now?"

"I went to the bridge where Mom died. One side of the bridge has a tiny dip, but the other side is a long drop with rocks at the bottom. It's on the side of a hill that leads to a farm. Mom wouldn't have taken that route, not when in the next field there is a public footpath. Someone—Iris—made her take that route so she could push her."

"Babe, why?" he breathes. His eyes are wide and jaw hanging slightly open.

"I found a book in Mom's closet. It was about child psychology and mental illness in children. I think Mom suspected something was wrong with Iris and Iris found out."

"Ivy, you're accusing your sister of murdering two people—and one of them is her own mother."

"Yes," I reply. "I just need to prove it."

"How?"

"I don't know. But I have to figure out exactly what happened to Kat first."

"How do you plan to do that?"

I shrug. "I'll work it out. She must have at least one person in her school who was friends with her still. I'll find them and go from there."

"How did she die?"

"The posts on her Facebook suggest that she fell while taking a selfie. Iris doesn't have much strength, but she can shove someone."

"Jesus, Ivy."

"It's a lot, I know."

"How are you so matter-of-fact about this?"

"I have to be, Ty." It's eating me up. I can't think about much else other than what my sister is doing and has done. "I can either sit back and wait to see if anyone else figures it out, or I can take control. I haven't had control of my own life since she moved here, and I'm done with that."

He shakes his head. "If you're right about this, she could turn on you."

"She already has. Look at everything that's happened. She's alienated me from my friends, taken over the swim team, got everyone on her side, convinced the teachers I'm a test thief, and tried to cause problems between us by sending that picture."

"That was Iris?"

"I know it was. I found a burner phone in her room. A really old one that had the battery drained and no charger."

"Where did she get the picture?"

"My guess is someone on the football team. If it was a cheerleader, it would have been leaked by now. All she had to do is go through someone's phone at a party and find it."

"The picture was old, right? Wouldn't it be buried? The number of selfies people take alone . . ."

"Folders, Ty. I have tons of named folders in my photos."

"That's crazy."

"That's Iris."

"What are you going to do now? You should go to your dad."

I laugh, but there is no humor in my voice. "He doesn't even believe I wouldn't steal. You really think he, or anyone, would think I'm telling the truth when I spill this secret?"

His shoulders drop because he knows I'm right.

It's okay. I have time to make things right. Now that Iris isn't in most of my classes, I'm concentrating better. The teachers will see that; Dad will notice the change. I'm working on gaining trust all while snooping for things to cause doubt in Iris. I'm going to start by talking about her old friends to Dad. You know, why don't we reach out to them and see if they want to visit.

First, though, I need to back off from her and let her think she's winning.

Iris has started this at a sprint but in a marathon, you have to pace yourself. She's going to burn out and I won't have even broken a sweat.

My time is coming, and my sister is going down.

46

Iris followed me to school in her car. We have an unspoken rule to not leave our house together. Neither of us wants to be in the other's company. She can't have waited longer than twenty seconds.

Is it just my rule, then? We've been avoiding each other all week.

I get out of my car and watch her drive past to a spot closer to the building. She parks near Ellie's car.

I cross the lot, turning my head from the blistering sun. It's much hotter today than yesterday. The air is dry, and I think a storm is coming, but right now we're in the hotter-than-hell stage.

Jogging up the steps outside school, I shove the door open and walk toward my locker. Ty will meet me there, but until I see him, my heart beats with nerves.

I bite my bottom lip and keep my eyes on my end goal. The assistant principal's voice comes over the speaker. "Would Ivy Mason please come to the principal's office?"

I let out a small gasp. I'm not supposed to see him until the end of the month when he checks in to discuss my behavior. It's absurd. I've never been in trouble before. Now, thanks to Iris, I'm a regular in the principal's office. Yet, he doesn't see the connection either.

Everything is being blamed on Mom's death, not Iris's presence.

I turn around slowly because my locker is in the opposite direction of where I've been summoned. I'm not aware of Iris doing anything else, but when do I ever get a memo?

"What's she done now?" a voice whispers behind me as I make the walk of shame.

I'm not going to look back and see who it was. It doesn't matter. Everyone is talking about me anyway. People who don't even know me are talking about me. It's a small school, but I keep to myself.

I walk into the assistant principal's office, trying to stay calm.

"Ivy Mason is here," the secretary calls out, looking up at me over a folder.

It's a manila folder but I would assume mine is sitting on the principal's desk with him poring over it.

"You can go in, Ivy."

"Ivy, take a seat," Principal Grant says, clearing his throat as I open the door.

"Okay," I whisper, my throat suddenly dryer than the air outside.

My jellied legs carry me to his desk. I sit down opposite him. "What is this about?"

I sit down and curl my fingertips into my palms.

"This morning, when the pool was checked, it was found that the chlorine level was thirty PPM. We have had to cancel the next swim meet, and if the water cannot be treated, we will have to drain the pool."

My eyes widen. "Oh my God." A safe level is between three and five for our pool.

His dark eyes pierce into mine like he's waiting for something. Oh.

My palm slams down on my chest. "You think *I* did it?"

"We're speaking to a few people. But, Ivy, you have recently been removed from the team and there have been other . . . issues."

"I would never do that! I'm doing everything I can to prove that I haven't done all the things I've been accused of so I can get back on the team. I would never do anything to the pool or to hurt the team. Please, you have to believe me."

"Can you tell me where you were last night?"

"At home," I reply. "I didn't do this. I'm training hard to impress a scout from Stanford!"

My skin prickles from the heat flooding my scalp and fingertips. The accusation makes me feel sick. And what's worse is that it's going to be so hard to get anyone to believe me. I'm the obvious choice.

My lungs feel like they're being squeezed in a vise. The team will blame me. Coach too. I'll never get a scholarship.

"Who was with you, Ivy?"

I shake my head, tears welling in my eyes and blurring my vision. "No one until my dad got back at ten."

"Where was your sister?"

At the pool, setting me up.

I didn't think she could sink much lower than she has. I thought she would get bored when she got what she wanted. She has my friends, my spot on the team, everyone eating out of her hands. Even Dad is looking at me differently.

My heart beats too fast as my Stanford dream sinks to the bottom of the thirty PPM pool.

"I don't know. She said she was going out after school but didn't tell me where or with who."

She doesn't tell me anything these days. Unless Dad is present, then she's all about helping Ivy through her *breakdown*.

"Ivy, this is very serious."

"I know," I croak. "Hopefully they'll find out who did it because it wasn't me. I want my name cleared, and I want my shot at a scholarship. I've worked too hard to sabotage myself! I wouldn't do that to the team either. I love those girls."

He holds his palms up. "No one is accusing you."

My eye twitches. "You've called me in here to question where I was last night."

"Like I said, you won't be the only one I speak with."

"But I'm the first, so that tells me a lot. I know that things have been falling apart recently," I say, careful not to sound too defensive but also not admitting any fault, "but I'm not stupid."

"No one could ever accuse you of being stupid, Ivy. You're a straight-A student."

"What else do you need from me?" I ask.

He threads his fingers together and lays his hand on the desk. "Only the truth."

"I went straight home from school. I was going to watch Ty's practice, but I decided not to, since people—and by people, I mean cheerleaders—aren't that friendly anymore. When I got home, I worked on an essay for English Lit, made some pasta for dinner, and watched Netflix. I didn't leave my house again until this morning."

"Okay," he says, nodding. "Did you speak to anyone?"

"Ty, when he got home from practice."

"What time was that?"

This is sounding more and more like an interrogation.

"Around five. I didn't do this."

He looks straight through me like he doesn't believe a word I'm saying.

"I would never do anything to the pool."

"All right, Ivy. You can go."

"I can?"

No calling my dad in? No suspension?

"I have a few more people to speak to."

Reading between the lines there: *Then I'll come back and find you.*

• • •

The rest of the day passes so painfully slowly that I want to whack my head against something. I walk down the hallway, and at the end is Iris, standing with a big group of people and laughing. Haley and Sophie stand with her on one side, Ellie and cheerleaders on the other. A few of the football team are scattered around too.

I take a deep breath as my heart drops to the floor.

The whispers around school are obviously that Ivy ruined the pool out of revenge.

Is this what Iris wanted? To be surrounded by people who are eating out of her hand while I'm standing alone? It doesn't make any sense.

To get out of school, I need to walk past them.

I keep my head up and straight as I walk.

Whispers bite at my skin as I pass them.

Iris laughs and says, "I have no idea."

I'm unsure of the question, but her snarky tone makes me think it was about me.

Neither Sophie nor Haley jumps to defend me. The sting of their betrayal cuts through my heart, and I wince.

Nope, I'm not giving any of them the satisfaction of seeing me upset. If they can ditch me so easily, then they never were very good friends. That doesn't stop it from hurting, though. I thought they were real.

I shove the door open and my footsteps falter. It's pouring. Pushing off my back leg, I jog down the stairs.

Rain pelts my skin like hundreds of tiny darts. Covering what I can of my forehead to protect my eyes, I head for my car.

A chill runs up my spine as someone falls into step with me.

I glance to the side and see a mirror image staring back.

"What do you want?" I snap at Iris.

"To make sure you're okay."

I stop, half because I want to be able to hear her properly and half because her words have shocked me to my core. Not that I believe them for one second, but the very fact that she can even say them with a straight face is testament to her deviousness.

My muscles lock as I think about everything she has taken from me.

What would be the point in holding back now? I have no credibility; the whole world thinks I'm lying.

Haley and Sophie are still mad at me . . . all because of Iris's interfering. Like everyone else, they believe the wrong twin. I've lost the relationship I once had with my dad, my friends, my chance at Stanford.

I have nothing left.

"Did you kill Kat?" I ask.

There's a bigger question, one that hovers over my head like the gray clouds above me. I want to know. I want the truth about my mom's death, but I'm so scared that she'll confirm what I already know.

What do I even do when she admits it all?

Will the police believe me if my own friends and family don't?

If I tell, I will lose Dad.

Our relationship is hanging by a thread. He thinks I hate Iris and want her gone. Every time I bring something up, he shuts me down and acts like I'm the one with the problem.

She's manipulative, and I don't know how to take her down because I'm not pure evil.

"Iris, what did you do to Kat?" I repeat.

There's a reason we're doing this out in the middle of the parking lot.

Who could record a confession over the noise of vehicles driving past, students chatting, laughing, and shouting?

A slow grin tugs across Iris's lips. "I followed her. She had to know it wasn't nice that she was talking behind my back. Kat always said too much. You shouldn't have gone there, Ivy. Her blood is on your hands."

"What?" I spit. "You're trying to blame me for this? You are the one who killed her. Tell me what you did!"

"You already know, Ivy. She was taking a selfie and fell in a river. All for a silly picture."

"She didn't fall."

Iris laughs. "Well . . . she had a little bit of help."

"Did you push her? Did she even know you were there?"

"We spoke. She accused me of the most heinous crime. Children murdering their own parents." She shakes her head, and I press my hand to my stomach, which is roiling with nausea. "See you at home." She turns and slowly walks across the lot to her car, not caring that water is cascading down her.

She'll see me at home. She's going to start talking when we get home.

I unlock my car and jump in.

47

Iris gets home first because I was parked farther from the exit. Not that it really matters. We're having this out right now.

I pull the parking brake, leap out of the car, and run inside. She's already in the house, and I don't want to give her the opportunity to lock herself in her room.

She doesn't, though. She leaves the front door wide open.

I kick it shut behind me, and she stares back with her hands on her hips.

This is it.

The enormity of what she's done to my beautiful mom hits me like a freaking tsunami and I hunch like she's punched me in the chest. "Why, Iris?" I demand as tears roll down my cheeks.

She shakes her head. "Poor perfect Ivy. You had everything and you didn't care!"

"What makes you think I didn't care about what I had?"

"You have the perfect group of friends who would do anything for you. Tyler would cut off his arm to make you happy. You're successful on the swim team. You get straight As."

"Iris!" I snap. "Friendships work both ways. I put in the effort with them too. I study for those As, and I was in the pool every opportunity I got. Nothing magically happened for me. I worked my ass off for it all. You can look in and assume that I got lucky but that's not what happened. This is never going to work for you if you take what you want without earning it."

She tilts her head. "Look around, Ivy. It's worked. I've already taken everything I want."

"But why? What do you think you're going to get out of this?"

"I wanted what you have," she says without hesitation, no sign of guilt or remorse in her steady voice.

"You could have it. Why can't you see that? You don't need to make me look bad to make yourself look good. One day it will all fall apart—everyone will know what you've done, and you'll be left with nothing. Do you think Dad will forgive that? He won't. No one is going to be behind you, and it will be all your fault."

"Wow, you really underestimate me. Don't assume that anyone will find out anything. I know what I'm doing. I've planted exam papers and wrecked a pool without leaving a trace of evidence."

I smirk. Not because I'm sure of myself, but because I want her to think that I am. Besides, I already know what she's done. But the reality is, I have no idea what's going to happen. I'm not underestimating her. I'm scared, but I will never allow her to know that.

"Iris, I saw through you. I knew there was something wrong with you, and a couple of people have been asking me rather interesting questions about you recently. Especially after your old bestie was found in a river. It's only a matter of time, and I can't wait."

Iris's eyes narrow into slits. "You have no idea who you're dealing with. Be grateful it's only your friends and swim team that you've lost."

Is this it? Is my sister about to admit to murder?

"Please, what else are you going to do? Cut my hair in my sleep? Tell everyone what a terrible person I am? Oh, wait, you've already done that and I'm still standing."

Her nostrils flare. "Don't push me, Ivy."

"Me push you? I'm pretty sure you're the one who's been doing all the pushing. You know, I have no idea how the police haven't connected the dots yet. Mom falls. Kat falls. Now, what or who is the link between those two? Oh, that's right . . ." I stare into her cold, heartless eyes. "It's you."

"If that could be proven, you would have gone to the police by now."

Her words punch the air right out of my lungs. She isn't denying it. Our mom and her old best friend. If she's willing to hurt—*kill*—them, she's willing to do anything.

What's her goal? "You want my life. Iris, you have it. So what's next?"

"What?" she asks, as if she's never thought about anything past stealing the world from me.

"You have my life. Now you have to maintain it. You get to spend the next two years swimming four times a week, meeting up with the girls at the diner, pretending to care about Leo's interests, and busting your butt to maintain my grades. For someone who doesn't want to put the effort in, it seems like an awful lot of work."

Her face pales but she holds eye contact.

Nope, she hasn't thought this through. It's one thing to take everything I have, but it's another to keep it.

"Enjoy your weekly milkshake and listening to Leo give you a play-by-play of every game. It's exactly what you deserve."

"My God, you're a bitch. I should have killed you when I had the chance."

My spine straightens. When did she have the chance? I mean, she can't exactly suffocate me in my sleep. That would be far too obvious.

She could be messing with me, of course.

"Like you did with Mom and Kat?" I ask. My voice is unbelievably calm considering my heart is racing so fast I feel dizzy.

"You have no idea what Mom was really like, Ivy."

"What's that supposed to mean?"

"The boyfriend, Carl, became much more important than me. She was so blinded." Iris rolls her eyes. "She couldn't see what was going on."

My blood runs cold. Carl. That's the man Mom was seeing. The man in the photos. "What *was* going on? Iris, did he hurt you?"

She recoils, her head whipping back like I'd hit her. "Of course not! Carl and I were going to be together, but she always got in the way of us."

I shake my head. "Be together?" That sure sounds like he was being inappropriate. Grooming her.

"I know he wanted me too. I could tell."

Wait, what?

"How do you know that? He was with Mom. What did he do to you?"

She rolls her eyes. "He did nothing to me, but he wanted to. I could tell every time he looked at me that he wanted to kiss me. Carl took me on dates."

"Dates?" I think I'm getting whiplash with all this conflicting information.

"If my car was in the garage, he would pick me up and take me for coffee, or order in when Mom was away, and we'd eat in front of a movie."

"Iris, that sounds like normal things you do for your girl-friend's kid."

"You don't know what you're talking about. You weren't there! He was only with her to spend time with me. There were looks. He tried to deny it, but you can't deny chemistry like that. We fell in love."

That doesn't sound like love to me. "So he never touched you or told you that he wanted you?"

"God, Ivy, did you hear what I just said? He didn't need to tell me. It was clear from everything he'd done for me that he wanted me. I wanted him too, but Mom was in the way."

So Iris was obsessed. He wasn't interested in a schoolgirl, but she wouldn't accept that. My god, she's delusional, mistaking kindness for love.

"Can you hear yourself? He never touched you or gave you any indication that he was interested, yet you still believed he wanted you? He wanted a sixteen-year-old psycho over our kind, driven, *sane* mother."

Her pale eyes seem to darken with evil. "She was sending him away!"

"What?"

"She was cheating on him and he was going to leave!" she screams.

"You're lying!"

She laughs. "Our mother was a slut."

I grind my teeth, my fists clenching.

"He was the best man I have ever met, and she was sending him away because she was sleeping with her personal trainer!"

"What?"

"He wanted to be with me, but we would never have a chance if she made him leave. Coming to the apartment to see her was his cover to see me."

Slowly, I shake my head. "Can you hear yourself right now? You sound so naïve."

"Shut up, you don't know anything," she spits. "She ruined everything for me. She deserved to die!"

Anger swallows me whole. Fire burns in my veins and I launch myself forward, slamming into Iris and curling my nails into her skin.

She screams, but her shock only lasts seconds before she grabs my hair and pulls.

Pain slices through my scalp, and I push myself forward with such force, Iris tumbles over.

I land on top of her and claw at the skin covering her shoulders.

"Ivy!" Dad bellows. I hear his voice, but Iris has her hand fisted in my hair, and I can't move. "Ivy, get off her."

Oh God. My heart sinks.

"Let go!" I scream, whipping my body from side to side to get her away.

I might be the one on top, but Iris is making sure I can't get off.

"Ivy, no!" Dad's arm wraps around my waist and at that very second, Iris's grip loosens. He lifts me off her like he's just rescued her.

Iris burst into tears, her chest caving as she sobs.

Oh, so we can control the water works, can we? Crazy witch.

Dad grips my upper arm, forcing me to look at him. "What the hell were you doing?"

"Defending myself! She ran at me after she admitted she pushed Mom off that bridge and Kat into a river!"

Iris's mouth drops wide open.

"Ivy!" Dad glares at me like I'm some stranger.

Granted, I should have had that conversation with him in a different manner, but he has to know what she's done.

"No, Dad. I'm so over being the bad one when I have done nothing wrong. All I have done since she first arrived is try to make things easier for her. Everything that has happened has been her! You know me and you know this isn't who I am."

He shakes his head. "Ivy, you have been caught doing some of those things."

"No, there has been convenient evidence. That's completely different. No one has seen me do anything because I haven't done anything."

Iris holds her cheek and pushes herself to her feet.

I roll my eyes. I guess I'm supposed to have injured her cheek. There is no mark but I'm going to take a shot in the dark here and say that doesn't matter.

It's like she has some sort of spell on everyone.

"Okay," Dad says slowly, letting go of my arm. "No one is to move until I say so. You both need to calm down, and I need to get to the bottom of this."

"Dad, she has accused me of *killing* my *mom*," Iris says, her voice rough like she's recovering from a throat infection. I stop myself rolling my eyes this time. "How can she say something like that?"

"I also accused you of killing your ex–best friend. You know, the one you cut out of your crew and tried to push down the stairs. There seems to be a bit of a theme, don't you think?"

"Ivy, enough," Dad snaps.

Really?

Crossing my arms over my chest, I take a breath. I'm not sure Meera's breathing techniques will work right now. They're good, but they're not showdown-with-your-murderous-twin good.

Dad's eyes glaze over as he stares at me.

My face falls and my scalp prickles. "Dad," I whisper.

He believes her and not me.

"Dad, come on."

"Ivy, I walked in here and saw you on top of your sister. What am I supposed to think?"

"Dad, you have to believe me," I say, adrenaline coursing through my veins. I don't look at Iris—all my energy is on Dad. "Iris killed Mom. Iris killed Kat." I take a deep, shuddering breath. "When I confronted her about everything, vandalizing the pool, Kat, *Mom,* she admitted to it all. All the crap that's gone wrong, the test papers, messing with my friends, planting pictures of Mom and her boyfriend in my room, making you think me and Ty were having sex, telling Ty that Logan tried to kiss me at a party. All of it was her." Everything is pouring out of me.

My dad is quiet for a moment. He isn't looking at my sister. "Ivy, why would she do that?"

Iris is suddenly very quiet. Now she gets to sit back and watch the show she's directing. Well, I'm taking over from here.

"Jealousy. She did the same to Kat, making people think she'd done all of this crap and then cutting her out."

He rubs his forehead roughly. "Why is she jealous, Ivy?"

"Because I had my spot on the team, excellent grades, awesome friends, and a great boyfriend. In her eyes I had it all and she had nothing. She was obsessed with the guy Mom was dating. He turned her down, so I think that's when she knew she had to get Mom out of the way." I address my sister. "Only it didn't go to plan, did it, Iris? He rejected you and moved away." Turning back to Dad, I add, "That's why Iris was out so much those first few days."

Dad looks at Iris.

Yes, come on, Dad. See through her lies.

"Iris?"

I put my hands on my hips. *Time to answer, bitch.*

Slowly, she shakes her head. "Carl? You think I wanted Mom's boyfriend? Ivy, he was, like, old and stuff. I mean, he was cool and all, but ew. Look, Ivy, I get why you're so upset, but I haven't done any of those things. You're not thinking straight. Ever since Mom died, you've been so different, and we know you barely sleep anymore. You need help, Ivy. More help than Meera can give you."

Of course. Here comes the denial.

"I would applaud if this wasn't so freakin' tragic, Iris. Can you even hear yourself? Take a step back and think about your life choices, because this is all going to bite you on the ass."

"Stop," Dad says, raising a palm at each of us. "Ivy, love, I do think we need to seek out some more . . . professional help for you. No one is here to blame you, but this has to stop. You're accusing your sister of murder. Do you understand that?"

Fire burns in my chest. "I understand that perfectly! I'm not the one who needs locking up. Iris is!"

"No one is talking about locking anyone up," he says, his voice soft yet firm. He's doing that thing where he treats me like a child again.

I meet his eyes, pleading with him to believe me. "Dad, I'm telling the truth. She admitted it."

His forehead creases, but he doesn't react beyond that. "Ivy, think about this. We've never heard of this Carl, and Iris has never mentioned him."

"I've done nothing but think about this!"

Oh my God, what is going to happen to me now? He's going to side with her. I gasp for breath, my lungs feeling like they've collapsed under the weight of Iris's lies. The room seems smaller, shrinking by the second as the air in one massive rush sends me plummeting to my knees.

"Ivy!" Dad shouts, crouching down. "Iris, call 911."

I shake my head, my eyes so wide they hurt. "Dad, I—"

They're talking about more help. What help? Will I be sent somewhere? They can't just get rid of me like I'm a nuisance pet. Dad wouldn't do that to me; he couldn't.

Iris might have everyone fooled, but she can't stop him from loving me.

"Ivy, breathe in and out," Dad orders, his face pale with worry.

He's scared. But his fear is nothing compared to the chilling terror I feel as I finally realize Iris has won.

I try to suck in a breath, but nothing is happening. My eyes widen and I slam my hand into my lungs. Oh God, work!

Dad's face blurs; then I'm falling into the abyss.

48

When I wake up, my head is throbbing. I press on my temple and groan. The last thing I remember is fighting with Iris. Then Dad split us up.

My mouth parts in a gasp. He sided with her. Even though I told him everything, all of the crap that she's done to me, the fact that she killed Mom and Kat . . . he didn't believe me.

I flick my eyes open. What the . . .

I'm not in my room. The walls here are a pale sage green. The sheets over me are white and stiff. Hospital.

"Dad?" I croak, sitting up. I hold my head as the world slides to the side. It hurts so bad. I run my fingers over my hair, feeling my head, looking for a cause of the pain.

"Hello?" I call, looking around.

I'm not hooked up to anything, so I can't be injured that badly.

"Ivy, hi," a lady in blue scrubs says as she walks into my room with a wide smile. She looks like she's glad to see me.

"Where am I?"

"You're at Rose Haven Institute. Don't worry, you're going to be okay. You collapsed at home and hit your head. How do you feel?"

Rose Haven Institute? That's not a regular hospital. "My head hurts. Why am I here?"

She smiles gently. "You're here for a forty-eight-hour observation."

"What? Why are you doing that? What are you observing?"

"Your dad tells us that you've had a difficult time recently."

Heat rushes to my face. I grip the sheets underneath me. No. "She's gone and done it."

"What's that, Ivy?"

"Iris . . . This is what she planned all along."

The nurse smiles again. "Let's get you out of the first aid suite and to your room. You'll be able to see your dad then. The doctor will be by in an hour to speak with you and explain in detail what's going to happen."

I barely hear her because of the shrill ringing in my ears. *This can't be happening.*

The nurse leads me to a room. My legs move on autopilot. I can't believe I'm staying here for two days. There is nothing wrong with me.

Dad is standing in the room with his hands behind his back.

When he hears us walk in, he turns. "Ivy, how are you—"

"Why did you bring me here?" I snap.

"I'm sorry. I don't want to do this, but I have to get you the help you need."

I shake my head, my eyes filling with tears. "Dad, this is a mistake. I shouldn't be here. You can't leave me here!"

My eyes fly around the room. The walls are plain, not white like I expected, but it's not many shades off. There is a single bed and a desk. A couple of books sit on the desk, but I have no desire to sit here and read.

I have no desire to be here at all.

"Right now, this is where you need to be, Ivy. I promise everything will be all right once you're better."

I stare at my dad, wondering how he could have let this happen. When did he stop being able to see the truth in my eyes? "I'm not sick, Dad."

"This is only a small chapter in your life. When you're out, the three of us can start afresh."

I'm in an institution.

They've locked me up because I didn't pass whatever observations they've been doing. No one believes me. They believe Iris.

For him to believe that a few days of therapy will make all this better is laughable. Why would I want to share a house with my twin after this?

This is what she wanted all along. I take a raspy breath and steady myself against the wall with my palm. She wasn't satisfied to take over my life, to steal my friends, to make me look bad; she wanted me out of the way.

Iris doesn't want a twin, and now she doesn't have one.

"Dad, please take me home," I plead. "You all have this so wrong. I haven't done anything."

"I can't, Ivy. As much as I want to, I can't."

"Sure, you can. Just go and discharge me."

"That's not how it works, sweetheart. This isn't forever. You have all the help and support you need in here. When you're ready, we'll be waiting."

We. Him and Iris.

She's not going to want me home. My sister is the reason I'm here. Everything she has done was designed to make me look crazy.

I can never go home.

I turn away from my dad. I don't recognize him at all anymore. The man who would fight for me, take my word above all else, is gone. If he can be manipulated by his other daughter into something this big, then I don't need him.

"Ivy, love, don't be angry. Your doctor thinks it would be a good idea if you allow Iris to visit. She's desperate to see you."

"She's desperate to gloat."

"Ivy, Iris does not—"

"Save it, Dad," I say, cutting him off. "One day you'll see that you locked the wrong daughter up, and it'll be too late for us." It's already too late. Iris has taken everything from me. but she won't have my sanity, and I won't give her the satisfaction of seeing me in here.

I'll play along. I'll get *better*. I'll get out. Then I'll get revenge.

49

Today's my sixth day here. I'm trapped in my room until we're allowed out for breakfast. They think I'm too dangerous to be on the outside, but no one seems to question whether we're all too dangerous to be around each other in here.

When I finish breakfast, I return to my room.

"Ivy," Dr. Finney says. She leans against the door frame and offers me a kind smile. Her graying hair is pulled into a bun. "You have a visitor this morning,"

I sit up straight as Meera walks into my room. "Hello, Ivy."

"Meera!" She's my last hope. Meera has been inside my head since Mom died. She will be able to see the truth here.

The doctors will listen to her; she's a professional, like them. Her opinion matters.

"How are you doing?" she asks.

Dr. Finney leaves us to it, and Meera takes the seat by my desk. She turns it around to face me.

"Not great. No matter what I say or how many times I tell them what Iris has done, no one believes me. They mostly keep telling me to take medication. That's not going to do anything because I'm not ill."

She tilts her head to the side. "No one thinks you're ill, Ivy."

"They think I've had a mental breakdown after Mom's death."

"That doesn't make a person insane. Please don't think of yourself as that."

I don't. I think Iris is that.

"I think you should have a supervised conversation with Iris. It will provide you with the clarity you need."

Clarity? What is she talking about? I'm totally clear.

My pulse quickens. "What are you saying?"

"Ivy, I'm trying to help you." She stands back and nods to someone in the hallway.

No.

Iris walks into my room with a victorious smile. She's wearing a dark skirt, pink tank top, and high heels, her lips a glossy nude. Her hair is pulled up into a bun.

"I have nothing to say to her," I tell the traitorous Meera.

"Ivy, facing up to reality is the first step to getting better. No one wants to see you in here indefinitely."

"Iris does."

My twin rolls her empty eyes. "You're ill, Ivy. Take the help. Me and Dad want you home."

"Shut up!" I snap. "Why did you bring her here, Meera? I don't want to see her ever again!"

"Iris and I have been meeting for a few weeks now. Having both sides has been very enlightening."

A few weeks? I shuffle back on the bed. She's been plotting much more heavily than I thought. Meera was my last hope, my chance to get out of here. Iris knew that; she knew where this was headed and planned accordingly, getting to Meera herself.

"You're finally seeing things clearly," I whisper. "All you're seeing is what she wants you to. How can *you* not get that?"

Meera is smart; she's supposed to read between the lines and see what's in the shadows.

Iris has charmed her, spun the whole thing to make me look like the one who has been setting her up.

"Get out," I tell them. "Don't ever visit me again."

Meera holds her hands up. "Ivy, I want to help you."

"Get out!" I scream.

"I'll get a doctor," she says softly.

Meera can get whoever she likes as long as she's gone.

Iris's smile grows as we hear Meera's footsteps echo down the hall and fade.

"You look awful, Ivy."

"Screw you!"

She laughs, and the sound makes my stomach roll with nausea.

"Seen Tyler lately?"

The pain in my chest spreads, radiating through my whole body. I haven't seen him at all.

"He doesn't want you anymore, not since you made all of this stuff up. He's angry that you sent him the picture of Logan kissing you."

My face falls. "What?"

"Duh, the burner phone in your desk."

"Your phone."

She shrugs. "No, I'm pretty sure it belongs to you. Why else would it be hidden in your desk with old pictures of Mom and a charger?"

"You need to be tested."

She rolls her vacant blue eyes. "You'd know all about that." Folding her arms, she scans my room with her nose slightly upturned.

I can't wait until everyone realizes the wrong twin is in here.

"Looking at your future, Iris? This room will be yours soon."

"Oh, please. You've proved you're unstable on more than one occasion. Thinking someone is after you in the locker room."

I tilt my head, a small smile pulling at my lips. "How would you know about that? I mean, you weren't there, right?"

"I wasn't . . . but Sophie was."

The smile drops in an instant. "You're lying."

Is she, though? The following day Sophie could barely look at me. After that she was more distant. But she wouldn't do that to me.

"Nope. It was my idea, of course. I take full credit. Sophie has been angry with you for a while. It was surprisingly easy to get her to freak you out and put you in your place. You think you're so much better than her." Iris laughs. "That's basically all I had to say to get her to agree. Ellie was obviously much easier to convince. Though getting her to pick up the mouse was a night-mare!"

"No." I shake my head as bile hits my throat.

God, she's not lying. Sophie really did that to me.

My eyes prickle with tears that I will not allow Iris to witness me shed. I take a deep breath. Sophie was manipulated; it's not her fault.

It still hurts so much, though.

"You're sick."

"Sure, sure. But you're the one in the hospital. Funny, right? Logan sends his love. Surprisingly, he's the only one who still asks after you." She laughs. "To think that he was on your side when you got booted from the team." Iris rolls her eyes. "He was so easy, it was almost embarrassing, telling him you said he's a crap kisser. All I had to do to turn him against you was bruise his ego. It was then that he admitted to knowing about the photo of you two all along."

What? Is that the truth? Because he seemed shocked when Ty received it.

But there isn't one person in my life who hasn't surprised me by turning their back on me.

My friends, Dad . . . Ty. None of them believe me even a little anymore.

Iris laughs. "Your face is priceless. Todd took the photo and Logan found out ages ago. I knew there was something between you two when you acted weird around him. So I helped him open up by giving him beer at a party, and he showed me the picture." She shrugs one shoulder. "It didn't take much to send it to myself after that. I must admit, he's a better actor than I thought, pretending he knew nothing about it."

I look away, each confession like a blow to the chest.

"Leave, Iris."

She grins. "Now, you're going to take your meds and play chess like a good girl. You ever think about trying to get anyone to believe your story and I'll end you. You're the crazy sister. And remember, hon, if you ever get 'better'"—she uses air quotes—"you'll be tried as a sane person in the death of Mom and Kat. I've heard awful things about juvie."

My chest burns. I curl my hands into fists. "Their deaths were ruled to be accidents."

"Only because they never found the shoes from the second set of prints. I made it look like the owner of those shoes ran a different path and not with Mom, but if they found them with the same dirt from the farm and from the riverbank in your bedroom . . ." She shrugs.

"What is wrong with you?" I breathe, my body frozen with shock.

"Looks a bit odd that crazy Ivy Mason would have dirt on her shoes from the scenes of two accidental deaths. Couple that with Kat's old sweater she lent me found in your room along with pictures of Mom and Carl . . . Who knows what the police will think of all that?"

Oh my God.

Iris shrugs and spins on her heel. Glancing over her shoulder, she chirps, "Stay crazy, sis."

ACKNOWLEDGMENTS

I first have to say a huge thank you to my husband and sons for supporting me through late writing nights, cranky coffee-filled mornings, and celebrating each step of this process. I love you guys.

To Kirsty, Vic, Zoë, and Kim. You ladies are the reason I'm still sane(ish). Thank you for always being there whenever I need advice, or to celebrate my achievements when I'm too British to do it properly!

My Venga Bus girls. You guys are ace, and I love you. Thank you for inspiring me and lifting me up. Never change . . . and never leave me!

Jon and Rosa, working with you both has been amazing. Thank you for always believing in me. This wouldn't be possible without you two.

Wendy, I can't thank you enough for taking a chance on me. I have loved working with you and can't wait for the next book!

Regina, you left me speechless when I saw the cover. It's GORGEOUS. Thank you for making *The Twin* look this good!

And to you, the reader. I cannot express how much I love you. Your enthusiasm for my books means everything to me. Thank you for every message, tag, tweet, and review. And THANK YOU for reading *The Twin*.

NATASHA PRESTON

THE #1 *NEW YORK TIMES* BESTSELLING AUTHOR OF
THE CELLAR AND *THE TWIN*

THE LAKE

DELACORTE
PRESS

Steve, Kyra, and Abbi. Thank you for visiting my books in Barnes & Noble while you were on holiday in NYC! You guys are the best. Steve, you'll be missed always and remembered forever.

1

We're returning to camp, to new friendships, to
songs and s'mores around the campfire . . . and to the scene of
our crime.

I lean between the front seats to get a better look out the
windshield. "There it is," I say as we drive under the large
CAMP PINE LAKE sign. It's exactly as I remember it, the name
carved into the wood.

Glancing down, I trace one finger across identical bold letter-
ing on the pamphlet I received earlier this year. Kayla and I both
got letters asking us to consider becoming counselors-in-training.

We're back.

My best friend of fifteen years glances at me as the cab crawls
to a stop. She pouts her glossy lips, which makes her eyebrows
pull together. "Does it seem, I don't know, *smaller* to you?"

"Everything seems bigger when you're a kid, Kayla," I remind
her. The last time we were here was nine years ago.

Compared to the other camps nearby, which really aren't that near, we're the smallest. But the best. Camp Pine Lake takes girls and boys ages seven to ten. Kayla and I spent two epic summers here when we were seven and eight.

We didn't come back when we were nine or ten.

We didn't dare.

But we're seventeen now. It's time.

Kayla squeals as she opens the cab door. "Yes! This summer is going to be amazing." She winks at me. "We can even stay up late this time."

"We stayed up late when we were campers."

The very second I open the other passenger door and we lose the AC, I feel like I'm going to melt. At least our uniforms are shorts and T-shirts. Texas summers can be brutal. I forgot how insane the heat is.

"Yeah, but this time we're actually *allowed* to."

Kind of. "We have to stay in the same cabin as the kids," I remind Kayla. It feels like more of a lateral move.

Kayla grins. "Esme, we'll be in our *own* teeny room, though. A bedroom in a bedroom. We'll have some privacy." Her eyes flit over the grounds. "I hope they have some cute counselors here."

There's my bestie. Kayla is boy crazy, loves pink and heels, and falls in love about every three minutes.

We thank the cabdriver, then pay and tip him as he removes our bags for us.

I lick my lips, swallowing as I take a look around. *I'm really back.* I feel a little ping in my stomach. I reach for Kayla's arm as she goes to pick up her pink camo suitcase. "Kay . . . are we doing the right thing coming back?"

She groans. "Don't overthink it. We're going to be fine. Everything is going to be *fine*."

Nodding, I pretend to agree. "We're not kids anymore."

"Exactly. No one here knew us back then, so no one knows what happened. Chillax."

"Do people still say 'chillax'?" I let go of her and smile as she glares. "All right. I'll *chillax*. We'll be fine. The last of my nerves have officially gone, *I promise*."

What a stupid promise.

"I did not miss the Texas heat," she says, her shoulders slumping.

I wave my hand in front of my face like a lunatic. "Can air be on fire? Because I think it is. Why has no one put more research into outdoor AC? . . . Look, there they all are. The counselors and the other CITs."

Kayla squeals and we drag our suitcases across the grass to the group gathered outside a cabin. How can they stand to be exposed in this heat?

"We need to find Andy," Kayla tells me.

Andy Marson is our boss. His name is on all the starter paperwork we were sent. He's the one in charge. Kayla and I have been paired together and assigned a counselor we'll do most of our activities with, along with our small group of campers.

"Which one do you think is Andy?" she asks.

I scan the group. "My money is on the redheaded guy with the clipboard."

He lifts his chin as we approach, and his pale eyes light up. "Ah, our final CITs are here. Kayla Price and Esme Randal?"

"Kayla," she says, lifting her hand.

"I'm Esme," I say.

Andy scribbles something on his clipboard. "Glad everyone is here. We're going to have a blast this summer, but first we need to get to know each other. Then I want to run through some rules and safety information."

He motions to two girls behind him. "This is Rebekah and Tia. And over there are Olly and Jake. They're all CITs too. You'll have your free evenings with them." Andy then rattles off some rules, but I know Kayla isn't listening. Her eyes are firmly on the two *very* cute guys standing behind Andy. Olly and Jake.

Camp just got a lot more interesting.

Rebekah and Tia step up to us with identical toothy smiles. That's the only thing similar about them. Rebekah is tall, with pale skin and shoulder-length ash-brown hair. She looks kind and a little bit lost, with her gentle, nervous blue eyes. Tia is petite, with black skin and large brown eyes. Her silky dark hair is so long it almost touches her butt.

"Hi," Rebekah says with a Southern twang.

"We're going to have the best summer," Tia says.

"Absolutely. Do you know which cabin is yours yet?" I ask.

"Rebekah and I are in Verbena. You're in Bluebonnet, the one right next to the food hall." Tia leans in, and I realize we're about the same height. "They're kind of small, but the beds look comfortable enough. Me and Rebekah are sharing a cabin with those two, and they're a little scary."

Tia points at two older girls who are full counselors. They both have dark heavy bangs and short bobs. One is pale like me, and the other has a gorgeous olive tan, the kind that Kayla pays for every six weeks.

"Mary and Catalina," Tia tells me. "Otherwise known as the Buttercups. Like the Powerpuff Girls."

I laugh. That's exactly who they look like. "Why are they scary?" I ask.

"Kind of intense when they're talking to you. You'll see what I mean."

"I wonder who we'll report to," I ask, looking around.

"Oh, I heard Andy talking. You guys report to Cora. She seems supernice. I think she just went into the food hall. It's kind of a mess in there, with a lot of equipment that needs sorting before the campers arrive. Final checks apparently."

"You get the impression that this is, like, the tenth final check?" I ask, watching Andy rushing from cabin to cabin with his clipboard.

Tia laughs. "Oh, for sure."

Rebekah and Kayla are chatting, having a similar conversation to ours, but Kayla is doing all the talking. My bestie can *talk*. Rebekah seems kind of overwhelmed, with her arms curled around her body and her eyes darting everywhere like she's trying to figure out all the escape routes.

Tia laughs and pulls me to the side. "Rebekah's from Kansas and applied to be a CIT because she wants to gain confidence before college. She's so sweet I feel like I'm getting a cavity just talking to her."

"Well, we can definitely help her out," I say. "We get our evenings off together. I wonder if we'll be allowed to leave camp."

Tia groans. "Apparently not. But I did a little research before I arrived, and there's a shortcut through the forest, right by the bramblebush at the side of the lake. It takes you to the edge of town, and there are no lights up that way."

I remember the shortcut. . . . But I don't want Tia to know I was a camper here. My eyes widen. "I have heart palpitations already."

"You don't want to come?" she asks.

"Oh no, I'll come."

She smirks. "Do you scare easily?"

"No, but it's not often that I walk through an unfamiliar forest at night. Kayla is going to freak out."

"We'll be fine. Why is Kayla going to freak out?"

"Shh," I hush Tia, and tug her closer. "I'll tell you another time."

Kayla is *so* scared of any kind of danger. It's a fear that not even extensive therapy has managed to calm. She doesn't need to be worrying about sneaking through a dark forest yet.

Rebekah glances at us both like she knows exactly what we're talking about. Tia has already had this conversation with her.

"CITs, if you can finish unpacking and then head back out to the fire for lunch, we'll eat and then go to the multiuse cabin so I can assign you a job!" Andy shouts, looking at something on his clipboard.

Tia cuts me a look. "He's going to be a nightmare."

Yeah.

Kayla and I head to our cabin to unpack. Kayla stands in front of the full-length mirror in our little room. The separate room gives us a little privacy while also making it easy to keep an eye on the campers.

We'll be sharing a bunk bed and a minuscule dresser since the cabin is so small. Cora, full-fledged camp counselor, has the other tiny room in the cabin.

Kayla and I will be rotating nights off with Cora so there is always a counselor in the cabin with the campers. I remember being so jealous of the counselors and CITs whenever it was their turn to sit by the campfire after hours. Now I get to do it.

I take the top bunk because Kayla doesn't like heights.

The cabin smells like wood and pine trees. Big surprise, right? The bunks look new, not like the old ones with names and private jokes scribbled in Sharpie on the sides.

"Which one do you like?" Kayla asks, and because I know her, I know she's referring to Jake and Olly.

"That didn't take you long."

She arches one perfectly shaped eyebrow in the mirror and fluffs her blond hair. Kayla is gorgeous, with fake tanned skin, huge blue eyes, thick lips and a killer figure with curves in all the best places. I'm pretty sure I'm going to look like a middle schooler—petite, skinny and pale—in the camp uniform, especially next to her. Texas might give me a nice tan, though.

"Which one, babe?" she asks.

"Hos before bros," I tell her, shoving my few belongings in the closet. I place my parents' picture on top.

"Fine. I like Jake."

Like I didn't know that. Tall, sandy blond hair, blue eyes and built like a football player, Jake is definitely Kayla's type.

394 • NATASHA PRESTON

"Shocker," I say sarcastically. "Go for it."

Kayla has unpacked all her clothes and hung them neatly.

"Summer's going to fly by, Esme. We have to move fast."

"So does that mean you'll sneak out with me into town one night?"

Her eyes narrow. "Seriously? Nothing good ever happens when you sneak into a forest at night."

I give her a nudge. "Things are going to be different this summer. Please, you baby, there's nothing scary in the woods."

2

Another minute slowly ticks by on my watch. Lunch is dragging.

I'm sitting under a pine tree with Kayla, Tia and Rebekah.

Olly and Jake are close by, a couple of trees over with the other male CITs, Marcus and Lorenzo. They seem more interested in spending time with each other than getting to know us. They might be a little older.

We've been here for about an hour and the counselor cliques are complete.

On my little paper plate there is a hot dog smothered in ketchup and charred corn. The second I take a bite out of the hot dog, I'm eight years old again. The taste brings me back to long summers swimming in the lake, and Kayla and me as skinny kids with dirty knees and wild hair. We'd eat hot dogs almost every day at camp, along with mac and cheese.

I loved it so much, and I can't wait to give the campers the same experience.

"He keeps looking at you," Tia sings.

"What?"

"Olly. He's talking to the guys, but about every three seconds his eyes wander your way."

I'm not even going to pretend I'm not interested in tall, dark and handsome. I would have to tilt my head up to talk to him, but I have to do that with almost everyone.

"What about you, Tia?"

She shrugs. "I'm not really into guys."

"There are girls here."

Her cheeks turn pink. "Well . . . Cora."

"How old is she?"

Tia sighs. "It's just a crush. I think maybe twenty? And *straight*."

I pat her arm. "Are you seventeen?"

"Yep. All of the CITs are sixteen and seventeen except Lorenzo, who's eighteen."

"You know everything. How long have you been here?"

"I arrived early this morning. I work fast." She taps her head. "Knowledge is power."

"You here as a CIT or as FBI?"

That gets a laugh. "You stick with me, girl."

"I'm going to talk to them," Kayla says, standing up and taking her plate to the boys.

Andy watches her from where he's sitting by the campfire. His expression is hard and his head tilted. Oh, come on, he can't possibly want to separate us. This whole camp is coed.

I'm not spending the entire summer pretending that boys don't exist.

"Shall we?" Tia asks.

Rebekah looks up and her eyes widen. "You wanna join them?"

"Yes, come on," I say, standing up. With one hand I hold my plate and with the other I offer to help Rebekah up.

"All right, I'll go with y'all." She places one hand in mine and I tug her to her feet. She towers over me. "Thanks, Esme."

Tia, Rebekah and I take a seat on a log bench. I strategically sit next to Olly. He *has* been looking at me, and he is totally cute. He looks athletic. I'm betting on football.

"Hey," I say.

He glances sideways and smiles. "Esme, right?"

"Should I be flattered that you remembered?"

Laughing, he says, "You should actually. I forgot my cousin's name once."

"How do you do that?"

"I have fourteen. Most of us live on the same street."

"Yeah, I only have five. Where are you from?"

"Missouri. You?"

"Pennsylvania. So, what made you want to be a CIT?"

He rips the end of a hot dog bun off. "I went to a camp when I was thirteen. It looked a lot more fun being a CIT. I guess I'll find out. How about you?"

I think of the pamphlet, now buried away in my tiny dresser. "Pretty much the same as you."

His insane green-blue eyes drift to the bramblebush that is probably going to shred my skin. I hope we don't have to go through it to take the shortcut.

"Tia told you, too?" I ask.

He grins. "I think before she even said hello."

"All right, guys, let's finish up and organize the multi and the food cabins," Andy says. "There's lots to do before the campers arrive the day after tomorrow."

Olly doesn't move. He does glare at Andy's back, though.

I sit straighter. "I guess we should . . ."

"Finish eating, Esme," Olly replies.

My glance drifts between him and Andy. "Did you know him before you came here?"

"Kind of. Only through one of my cousins. They went to college together and I met him at their graduation. He talked to me a little about camp. When I got a pamphlet about becoming a CIT earlier this year, I figured he was the one who sent it."

"He really likes this job, doesn't he?"

Olly laughs. "Yes. He spends about ten hours every day promoting it. You should see his social media, it's nothing but camp."

"I don't think I want to see his social media."

I finish eating. The Buttercups—Mary and Catalina, I need to use their actual names!—follow Andy, almost tripping over themselves to get in first.

Is there a prize for best counselor or biggest suck-up?

That's not a medal I'm likely to win.

Kayla and I dump our plates in the trash and head into the hall with our newly formed coed group.

Jake and Olly have broken away from the guys to stick with us four girls. We really don't mind.

Inside the multiuse cabin is a sea of equipment. Tents, canoes, kayaks, sports gear, ropes, camping stoves and pans are spread out. It smells like a gym.

"Er, we have to check *all* of this?" Kayla mutters to our group.

"What qualifies me to assure anyone that a kayak won't sink?" I mutter.

Olly chuckles, but I'm being serious.

Andy claps his hands. "Right, CITs can start by putting tents up and checking that they're intact. I want to know if anything is missing or if there are rips, et cetera, et cetera. Counselors are to check outdoor equipment, and I will check the cooking equipment."

We pair off and get to work. Kayla makes a beeline for Jake, so I end up with Olly. Not that I'm going to complain when his crazy shiny eyes keep making my tummy flip. I smile as I grab the first tent and try to hide my face with my long hair. My cheeks are probably tomato red.

The first tent goes up without a problem. It's a small, simple four-person one.

We walk around it checking for rips, and Olly ducks inside, checking there too.

"It's fine," I say.

"Yep," he agrees, poking his head out of the opening. "On to the next one, Esme."

I like the way his rough voice says my name.

Enough, you weirdo!

The day rolls on, and we keep making good time with organizing. It's nonstop work, but I'm enjoying it.

Nerves are swimming lengths in my stomach, though. What if I'm not good at this? What if my little team of campers doesn't like me? I have to guide them and make them feel safe as well as learn new skills and have fun.

This isn't just something that will look good on my résumé. I want to be good at it. I loved it here. I loved *almost* every part of Camp Pine Lake. There was just one thing. One night picked from a horror movie that still freezes my heart.

By nightfall we're officially ready for the campers. Or at least the camp and equipment are.

We pushed on and got everything done. I'm a hot, sweaty, gross mess of a human, but because we finished, it means tomorrow we can have some fun. Then, it will be all about the young people we're caring for.

After a refresh in the communal showers, we gather back outside. The air is a lot cooler, though I'm still in shorts and a T-shirt.

Tia grabs my elbow and I startle. "Let's take a walk."

I do a double take as she pulls me in another direction. "What?"

"Around the lake."

She doesn't wait for me to agree, but all right.

"What are we doing?" I ask when she lets me go.

"Walking."

"I got that. Why?"

Grinning over her shoulder, she replies, "We're checking out the shortcut. You just go straight along a man-made trail right through the trees. We should wait a week before we sneak out."

Her voice is animated, and she waves her arms as she speaks. Her hair is tied in a messy bun.

"Make Andy think we're good little CITs and following the rules," I say.

"Exactly."

"What happens if we get caught?"

"We'd be in a lot of trouble, I think. I doubt we'd get kicked out, though."

I take a breath. "I hope not."

My mom and dad would be *so* mad.

"Don't worry, Esme, we won't get caught."

I mean, the chances are high. If someone else is outside, too, they will see us disappear into a bush and not come out for a couple of hours. Maybe they all do it.

We walk along the edge of the oval lake with trees to our left and water to our right. It's beautiful, peaceful.

In a couple of days, we're going to be swimming out here. We even have an inflatable obstacle course for the water. We didn't have that when I was a camper, so I can't wait to try it. I can get a bit competitive, so I need to remember to play fair with the children.

"Are you going to college after summer?" I ask.

"Yep, in New York. Big change from Oregon. I can't wait. What about you?"

I nod. "Denver. I'm from Pennsylvania, so a big change for me, too. It's so pretty in Colorado. I can't wait to see mountains."

"We'll have to keep in touch."

"Definitely. Is this it?" I ask.

"Yep. Must be."

Thankfully, the track is just behind the bramble.

Tia and I continue to walk around the lake. It's dark over here without camp lighting, but the moon is bright, so there's enough light to see where we're walking. The scent of pine is stronger away from the cabins and campfire. I breathe it in.

It takes about ten minutes to walk all the way around the lake, probably quicker now that I'm not eight.

"Next week," I say with a bubble of excitement. This summer is going to rock.

≈≈≈

Back at camp, some of the CITs are down by the lake, while others are playing cards.

"I'm not jumping in the water tonight, I've already showered," Tia says.

"I'm with you," I say. We take a seat with Kayla, Rebekah, Jake and Olly. They are sitting to the side of the campfire in a little circle.

"Campfire games," Tia says. "We can play Which One Is the Lie. You have to tell two facts about yourself, but only one can be an actual fact. The rest of us have to guess which one is the lie."

Rebekah interjects. "I have a better one for y'all, a way for us to really get to know each other. But we have to all agree to be completely honest and no one can judge."

I'm not sure I like the sound of that.

"I'm game," Jake says, rubbing his hands together.

Good for him.

Kayla and I share a look. There are some things we won't *ever* be telling anyone.

"Come on, it'll be fun." Rebekah sits taller if that's even possible. "It's something I've played before with my best friends. It keeps us close."

"All right," I concede. I don't have to lie to anyone. Kayla and I just won't tell *everything*.

Kayla's eyes snap to mine and I see her body visibly stiffen. *We're obviously not going* there. I subtly shake my head, telling her it's okay.

"I'll go first," Rebekah says. "My greatest fear is that I will never be happy. Really, truly happy."

Her confession knocks the air out of my lungs. "You've *never* been happy?"

She shakes her head, eyes downcast. "I don't think I know how. Since I was young, I knew there was something wrong with me."

Well, this got dark fast. I want to ask what she thinks is wrong with her, but her eyes fill with tears and I don't want to make her cry.

Olly purses his lips like he's deeply uncomfortable and doesn't know what to say. Jake clears his throat and looks longingly at the lake as if he wishes he was in it.

He's not alone.

"You will be happy," Tia tells Rebekah, giving her shoulder

a squeeze, and then quickly moves on. "So, my big confession is that my parents still don't know I'm gay." She laughs. "In fact, no one does but you guys."

"What, no one at all?" I ask.

She shrugs. "I guess being here and being out will give me the kick in the ass I need to live this way back home, too. What's yours, Esme?"

I clear my throat.

My biggest fear is that someone will find out what I did ten years ago.

3

I wake in the morning in the top bunk with a crick in my neck. The beds aren't too bad, but the pillows are. Tilting my head from side to side, I kick off the thin blanket and climb down the ladder.

Kayla is still asleep. I don't want to wake her, so I take my clothes and toiletries and go to the bathroom to get ready.

When I get back to the cabin, I notice how eerily quiet it is this early in the morning. Every bunk bed in the main room is neatly made, blankets and sheets tucked in, ready for the campers tomorrow.

I dump my bag back in our room and shake my head at Kayla's soft snore. She could sleep in for hours. Getting her beauty rest, she calls it. She doesn't need it, though; she's naturally model material. Her Insta following grows with every selfie.

I take the few steps to our dresser and open my drawer. From it, I pull out the pamphlet Kayla and I received a few months earlier asking us to consider positions as CITs. They arrived at our houses on the same day. We assumed most ex-campers received them. I run my hand over the laminated cover. It's a picture of the lake at sunset, campers jumping off the dock. Inside is a bunch of information—about schedules, pay and benefits. I flip the brochure over and a chill runs down my spine, just like it did the first time I read it.

In big block letters are the words **COME TO CAMP PINE LAKE . . . YOU'LL REGRET IT IF YOU DON'T.**

The first time I pointed this out to Kayla, she told me it was nothing. Just cheesy copy. But something about it rubbed me the wrong way. By the time I realized why, Kayla was already in love with the idea of coming back. I agreed to come too, but for different reasons. I had the feeling this pamphlet was a threat. That if I didn't come back, something bad would happen. Like maybe someone would reveal my and Kayla's secret.

But who would do that? Only one other person knows what happened the last time Kayla and I were here. A girl from town named Lillian Campbell. I remember her being a little bit . . . off. Kayla would use the word *weird*. But Lillian would want to keep what happened a secret just as much as we do. Unless . . .

No. I shake my head, clearing away the thoughts. I am just being paranoid. Being back here must be having a stronger effect on me than I had anticipated.

I put the pamphlet back in the drawer and head out the door.

The landscape takes my breath away for a second. Blue sky at first light, with lush pine trees surrounding us and a peaceful lake in the middle.

I'm not the only one up early. Rebekah is with Andy and a

couple of other counselors who I haven't had a chance to speak to yet. They're standing by the lake, on the beach area. I quietly close the cabin door and take the steps down to the grass.

Last night I learned that Tia is scared her parents won't accept she's gay, Olly won't be as successful as his cousins, and Jake won't make it in football.

I told them I'm scared of disappointing my parents because of how seemingly perfect they are, always doing the right thing and advocating for 100 percent honesty. They totally lied about Santa, the Tooth Fairy and the Easter Bunny, but whatever.

My confession wasn't technically a lie. The thought of disappointing them does actually make me nauseous. They can never know what I did. No one can.

My personal favorite revelation was Kayla's. She told everyone that her greatest fear is she'll need Botox before the age of forty. Now, I have no doubt she *is* worried about that, but I'm pretty sure her *greatest* fear matches mine.

I slide my sunglasses down over my eyes and walk to the little group. "Morning," I say.

"Mornin', Esme. You're up early." Rebekah looks relieved to have someone else she knows up. She stands and takes my wrist. "Let's go get coffee. Do you drink coffee?"

Another one of my fears is people who don't drink caffeine. Like, how do you function?

I nod. "Absolutely. Too bad there's no Starbucks here."

"Did you sleep okay?" she asks as we walk.

"Okay. My neck is hurting, though." I tilt my head from side to side.

"Mine, too. I'm on the bottom bunk and had to listen to Tia toss and turn above me. We're on the lake today, right? I'm kind of nervous."

"It'll be fine. I think Andy will make us wear life jackets even though we could stand up in it."

"The middle is deep. Be careful." The middle of the lake is cordoned off. There were lots of wild rumors and ghost stories about it when Kayla and I were here. One was that some hybrid shark was down there. The other part of the hybrid was never mentioned.

"Have you been here before?" I ask.

Rebekah flattens her straight hair. "No. I did spend a lot of my childhood in summer camps, though."

Maybe it's because she seems so nervous that I decide to open up . . . a little. "I was a camper here with Kayla when we were younger. My parents couldn't afford to send me every year, unfortunately."

The truth is, I *couldn't* come back.

Rebekah scoffs. "My parents are more than willing to pay to get me out of their hair for a summer."

Wow, okay. Her parents don't sound like fuzzy, loving people.

"Why did you decide to train to be a counselor here?"

"I wanted something different. As soon as I looked the camp up, I fell in love with the lake. It's got such a traditional camp vibe, right? Like this place could be used as a set for a movie."

Yeah, a movie where you either swap with your twin you didn't know existed or you get murdered. Both are super farfetched, but, yeah, this place would totally make a great movie set.

"I heard you're from Kansas," I say.

"Yep. How about you?"

"Lewisburg, Pennsylvania. Kayla is too."

"Have you been friends for long?"

"Yeah, we met in preschool, actually."

Her smile doesn't touch her sad eyes. "I wish I had a good friend."

Didn't she say she played the game of fears with her friends? "There's no one back home?"

"Not really. I have a few friends, but we don't confide in each other."

Nope, I'm calling her out on this. "But I thought you said you did the secrets thing?"

We walk into the hall. A few people are milling around, eating cereal and fruit. Rebekah and I go straight for the coffee.

With a sigh, she admits the truth. "Okay, confession time. The game last night. It didn't exactly come from my friends, it's what my cousin does. Her and her friends are tight, and they tell each other their deepest, darkest fears. I tried it once with a group back home in the hopes that it would tie us together and we'd be close."

"What happened?"

"They were the wrong people to try it with; we weren't tight enough. We grew apart, but we all know each other's secrets so we're all fake nice to each other, talking about the weather and how lame school is. I don't even think school is lame."

I pour two mugs of coffee. "So why did you do it with us?"

She shrugs. "I just felt, like, I don't know, that we clicked. Our little group of six. I've never had that. The only thing I had in common with my high school 'friends' was that we were all running from the same bully."

"I'm sorry high school sucked." I was never bullied, but I know it's traumatic, never being able to get away from the people making your life a misery, not even at home thanks to social media. Feeling alone is awful; feeling alone *and* hated must be unbearable. "You have us now." I hand her a coffee. "And soon you'll be in college."

"Thanks. I sure hope college is different."

From what my mom has told me about her office environment, I don't think anything is too different from high school. But I don't tell her that.

Kayla and I weren't part of the popular group. Well, she could have been, but she stuck with me. We were somewhere in the middle. It was the best place to be. We didn't have to pretend the way the popular people did, and we didn't have to fear anyone like the unpopular people did.

Rebekah and I grab some breakfast and sit down. I sip my coffee and dig my spoon into my cereal.

Over Rebekah's shoulder I see Olly walk in. The khaki shorts and white T-shirt look great on him. He scans the room and his bluey-green eyes settle on us. I get a mild electric shock.

"Olly's here," I say as he makes his way toward us.

Rebekah takes a quick look and turns back. "He so likes ya," she sings quietly.

I wide-eye her, telling her to shush as he approaches.

"Morning." He sits down next to me. "You two okay?"

"Yep," we reply at the exact same time.

His smile widens. "How's the coffee?"

"It's fine," I reply.

Rebekah adds, "It's no Starbucks, right, Esme?"

I groan. "Don't remind me about Starbucks. I would kill for a vanilla latte."

"*Kill* is a little strong, isn't it?" Olly asks, lifting his eyebrow.

"No, I don't think so."

Rebekah eats her banana in silence, watching us like we're in a play.

"We have a whole day to hang out . . . and do final *final* checks, apparently. I'm going to grab some food, and then we'll head out there, yeah?" Olly says.

"Sure," I reply as he heads for the cereal.

Rebekah smirks.

"Don't say a word." I'm pretty sure I'm blushing a very unflattering shade of red.

She puts her banana peel in her bowl. "Okay, I'm going to see if Tia is up. Meet you at the dock?"

I know exactly what she's doing.

"Rebekah!"

Laughing, she adds, "Enjoy breakfast."

She leaves just as Olly puts down a bowl and coffee. He sits. "Hey, where's she going?"

"To find Tia."

To leave us alone. Why? What does she think is going to happen over breakfast? He kisses me? Announces love at first sight? No. Insta love is dumb.

"Do you know what jobs we have to do today?" I ask.

"I don't think we've been assigned anything yet. Andy did say we could get on the lake, explore the camp and the forest if we want, get to know the place before the campers arrive."

We have a grand total of seven cabins. I don't think anyone is getting lost.

I nod. "Good. I'm going to spend the whole day chilling around camp. There won't be much chance for that later."

"That's true. What have you and Rebekah been doing this morning?"

"Not much, I haven't been up long. She seems really nice."

Nice and . . . something. I haven't figured it out. It's probably her shy nature and desire to please. When someone is like that, it's hard to know the real them.

4

My eyes are saucers.

That is a lot of children.

Today the campers are arriving—all fifty-six of them. Although I knew how many were coming, actually seeing them all in one place makes it seem like a lot more.

I tie my hair on top of my head and smell the coconut-scented SPF 50 on my skin.

I'm both excited and nervous. Then I suddenly realize that I'm one of the people responsible for keeping all these kids alive for six whole weeks. My chest tightens.

What if I lose one on a hike? What if one drowns?

They're everywhere, hugging parents and chatting enthusiastically with their new camp friends. Andy and his clipboard are out in force. He's frantically ticking people off and telling them where to take their things. No one else has been trusted to do that. He's a bit of a control freak, I think.

The camp is buzzing with excitement and nerves.

"What were you expecting?" Kayla asks, taking in my panicked expression.

I shake my head. "I don't know."

She laughs, wrapping an arm around my shoulders. "We're going to be fine. We'll have a small group each and be with counselors the whole time."

"You look like you're going to pass out," Olly says, stopping beside Kayla and me. "Second thoughts, or Andy's cooking last night?"

"No, I'm good. Got a little worried there, but I'm over it now. I will not lose a child," I say.

He dips his chin. "Good. That's good."

While the campers get settled and say their final goodbyes, half of the counselors stay outside and half are in the cabins helping. We want it to look like there are plenty of CITs and counselors. The parents of these children are trusting us.

My eyes drift to the shortcut through the woods. Are we terribly irresponsible to sneak off? I mean, we're not on duty every night.

Stop overthinking!

A little girl, probably eight or nine, clings to her mom's waist. Her big green eyes shed tear after tear while her mom tries to reassure her that she'll have a good time.

A lot of the parents are leaving or have already left.

In the clear blue sky, the sun shines down, making this the most beautiful day for the campers to arrive. The whole camp looks bright and inviting.

"Hi," I say, walking over to the little girl and her mom. "I'm Esme."

The mom looks up. "Oh, Esme. Andy just told us that you're Isabel's CIT."

I smile, trying to look friendly and reassuring. "Hi, Isabel. This is my first time being a counselor here, so you're not alone, okay? It's new for me, too." Her eyes meet mine, but she still keeps a tight grip on her mom's T-shirt. "We're going to have the best summer ever. Remember you can write your mom anytime you like, so you're not saying goodbye right now, you're only saying see you later. Would you like to come with me?"

Isabel presses her lips together, completely unsure.

I add, "I think we're going to do some 'getting to know you' games before we cook a welcome lunch on the campfire. You could help me until you feel like joining in, if you like?"

"Go on, Isabel. You'll be fine, my darling," her mom prompts.

"The trees are scary," Isabel says.

I shake my head. "I promise you, there is nothing scary in the woods."

"Okay." Isabel lets go of her mom, giving her one last kiss on the cheek before she leaves.

"Let's go find the rest of our group. We're looking for Maisie, Addison and Audrey," I tell her.

"Do you know who they are?" Isabel asks.

"Not yet, but we can find them. They're also part of the E Team."

Isabel follows me as Andy shoots off more instructions, calling out names and telling children which staff member to go with.

I find the three other girls, then stand with Kayla and her group.

There are a lot of children. I hope I can remember them all. Or at the very least remember the ones I'll be spending the most time with.

I wipe my forehead as the heat scorches my skin. None of the campers care how hot it is.

I don't know why Andy insists on cooking on a fire in this heat.

Tia rocks on her heels, grinning at her little group like she wants to corrupt them all. I'm sure she won't. Well, I'm not *sure*. She's standing next to a petrified Rebekah, who periodically glances at one of her campers, a girl with makeup, glossy, straight hair and low heels. A queen bee type. She's going to have to change into tennis shoes soon.

I can't help feeling sorry for Rebekah as she glances worriedly at a girl nearly ten years younger than her. The kind of girl who probably made Rebekah's life miserable in school. That's unfair, though. The girl isn't necessarily a bully just because of her stereotypically popular-girl appearance. Kayla isn't.

We're split, Kayla and me with Cora's group. Three adults and twelve children. Olly and his group head toward the lake, but we're staying near to the tennis court to play our "getting to know you" games.

Cora takes over, but Kayla and I stand with them. Cora explains what we're going to do. We're playing All About Me tennis. Each time you hit the ball, you have to call out something about yourself, like your favorite vacation destination, animal, color, food, class at school, celebrity, etc.

I remember playing the exact same game when I was a camper.

The girls split easily into groups of two, each twosome taking a tennis racket. I stand on the sidelines with Kayla. The girls call out random facts with every hit of the ball. Laughter fills the stifling-hot air, and none of the campers seem to care about the heat.

"They're all so adorable," Kayla says.

"Remember when that was us? You spent the first few hours crying because you missed your mom and then forgot to write to her the rest of the summer."

"Oh, but she wrote to me. *All* the time!"

"She's your mom."

"And you," Kayla says, "were so cute, the smallest one here with the biggest green eyes that matched the leaves on the trees. You looked around as if you'd never seen a lake or forest before."

"Okay, so I didn't get out much. I was way less tragic the second year we came."

But we don't need to talk about that second time.

Kayla laughs. "All right, I'll give you that. I'm so excited these girls get to experience this. They're already making friends."

"So are you," I say, arching an eyebrow.

"You're talking about Jake."

My smile widens. "Ding, ding, ding."

"He's hot." She side-eyes me. "Almost as hot as Olly."

"Don't start."

Andy calls an end to the games after an hour. Most of the kids have swapped partners and met new people. The rest of the afternoon is spent splashing in the lake, and the evening toasting s'mores on the campfire and telling crazy stories about killers in the woods.

There aren't killers in the woods, but I did lie to Isabel.

Bad things do happen there.

5

Yesterday was tiring, yet here I am, wide awake at five a.m. Below me, Kayla's deep breathing vibrates through the room. If I didn't love her, I'd throw something at her.

No one is getting up anytime soon, and I'm bored. There is no rule about me leaving the cabin in the morning. I won't go far, just outside to see if anyone else is up. Besides, Kayla and Cora are still here.

Twisting my body, I carefully climb down the ladder, holding my breath as if breathing is the part of my escape that could wake Kayla. I don't think a marching band could wake her this early.

My feet touch the cool wood floor. I quietly change into my camp T-shirt and shorts and creep out of the room. The door creaks when it opens and I wince. I'm sure it doesn't do that during the day. After a quick head count—every camper is still in their bed—I leave the cabin.

Even though the sun won't rise for at least another hour, it's not too dark.

I pull my jacket on and walk down the few steps to the grass.

Rebekah is up early again. She's sitting on the beach, by the firepit. She has a blanket around her shoulders and her eyes are fixed on the center of the lake.

"Hey, are you okay?" I ask, walking toward her.

She jolts and looks over her shoulder. "Hi. Esme. Yeah, I've just never been able to sleep late when I'm away from home."

I sit on the sand and curl my arms around my legs. Me neither, apparently. "Nothing beats your own bed."

"How come you're up so early?"

I shrug. "I can't sleep. Excited, maybe?"

"I wish the hall was open so we could at least make coffee."

"Andy probably sleeps with the key on a chain around his neck."

That gets a laugh out of her. "He loves it here. He's not so bad, though."

Rebekah seems like the type of person who would bite her tongue so that she doesn't end up in the middle of any kind of conflict. Hopefully, that's something she will leave here. It doesn't seem like she stood up to her bullies.

"The lake is eerie first thing in the mornin'. Dark and quiet, like it holds a lot of secrets," she says.

Okay . . .

"Have you been all the way around it?" I ask.

"No, not yet. The other side is owned by the camp, right?"

"Yeah, about a full five-minute walk past the lake. After that, it's a public forest and the locals use it to hike and camp. I remember when I was here last, an old couple wandered onto camp land. I think they put up even more signs around the perimeter after that."

The land is far too big to put a fence around, so signs are necessary.

Rebekah nods. "Didn't something happen over there, past our site? I overheard one of the counselors mention there was a fire or something."

I shrug and swallow acid at the same time. "No idea."

"So, Esme"—she sits straighter—"tell me more about you. What's the plan after college?"

"I'd love to be a journalist. I love the hustle and going out on the hunt for stories."

Her light eyes watch me carefully. "But you seem too honest to do that."

I laugh and hope it sounds normal. "I want to write facts. There are still some news outlets that do that." And probably four times as many that don't.

"You might be the first."

I raise my eyebrows. "You don't like journalists?"

Rebekah turns away, her eyes settling back on the middle of the lake. "I don't like lies."

"What's your plan, then?"

She blows out a breath. "I wanted to swim in college."

"Not anymore?"

Shaking her head, she replies, "No. Now I don't know what I'll do."

"What made you change your mind?"

She hesitates. "I didn't get a scholarship. I like where I'll be going, but there's no chance for swimming. I'm going to take all the classes I can and see what I like."

"That's cool. You can go wherever your heart takes you."

"Do you have siblings?" she asks. "I only have a brother."

"I'm an only child, but Kayla feels more like a sister than a friend."

"Well, you're not missing much."

"Don't you get along with your brother?"

"We'd do anything for each other, but he's twenty-eight, so we don't have a lot in common."

"I always wanted a protective older brother."

Rebekah scoffs. "Trust me, you don't. Hey, do you think Tia is going to make us sneak out tomorrow?"

"She can't *make* you do anything, but I think we're going next week. We need a couple of nights to figure out what happens after lights-out, make sure no one sees us breaking out."

"By that you mean when Andy goes to bed."

Nodding, I say, "Precisely."

"Do you even know where we're going?"

"Apparently there's an arcade and bowling alley on the edge of town. Tia looked it up. So we're basically sneaking out to be thirteen again."

With a soft giggle, Rebekah stands. "Andy is up."

I follow her gaze over my shoulder. Andy walks from the staff cabin where he has a room next to the food hall.

His step falters as he spots us. "Rebekah, Esme, what are you doing out here?"

I stand and head toward him. Rebekah follows, staying a step behind me. "Neither of us could sleep. Do you need us to do anything?"

He nods. "I could use some help setting up for breakfast," he says as he lets us into the hall.

That's in two hours. This summer could pass very slowly if I keep getting up before the sun. Though I like the peace first thing. The lake is quiet, like it's sleeping.

The key is returned to his pocket. Not around his neck, then.

I wonder where he keeps it at night. In his shorts?

I'd love to be able to get in a late-night snack, but the thought of going through his shorts is nasty. They're a little shorter and tighter than they need to be. Ew.

Rebekah and I begin to bring tubs of cereal into the dining hall. There will be pastries too, but we don't need to get those out until closer to eight.

Andy hums as he works and pushes one hand through his red hair.

"I was impressed with how you both performed yesterday. You made your groups feel welcome. Were there any issues last night? Homesickness?"

"Nothing," Rebekah replies.

"I've never seen anyone fall asleep so fast," I say.

He laughs. "The first night is always like that. I assure you it won't be the same tonight."

"When Kayla and I were campers, we never fell asleep before lights-out. We'd whisper for hours," I say. It seemed like midnight back then, but in reality we were probably all asleep before ten p.m.

Rebekah adds, "The same with my camp."

Andy shakes his head. "It's been a long time since I was a camper."

"You came here?" I ask, surprised.

"Yes, probably before you two were even born."

"How old are you?" I ask.

Rebekah's eyes go round as if I've just asked Andy to strip.

"What?" I mouth at her.

"Almost thirty," he replies, not taking his eyes off the notice board where he's pinning up camp expectations.

See, he didn't care. He knows how old we are anyway.

"The boys snore."

Rebekah, Andy and I all startle at Olly's voice.

He walks into the hall, rubbing his eyes. "Is there coffee?"

Andy laughs. "Not yet. I've opened the hall so you can make some. I moved the coffee maker into the kitchen now that the campers are here."

Olly frowns like that was a dumb idea.

"We don't want a bunch of seven- to ten-year-olds caffeinated to their eyeballs," I tell him. And I don't want to share with even more people.

Andy nods. "The coffee is for the staff."

I'll never get used to that being me.

"Please hurry," I tell Olly. "I'm dying for coffee."

"Well, if your life depends on it . . . ," he says, smirking at me as he walks past. His eyes are playful, and I turn away before I blush brighter than the bottles of ketchup on each table.

Rebekah's gaze moves between me and Olly. When I look up, she turns around as if embarrassed to be caught looking.

6

You know what sucks?

Volleyball in thirty-thousand-degree heat.

All right, I don't know the *exact* temperature, but thirty thousand feels pretty damn accurate.

The campers still don't seem to care. They all have water and hats and are young enough for extreme heat to take a backseat to fun. I can't remember being like that, but I must have because I definitely didn't complain about the weather when I was here as a kid.

Maybe I really *am* an almost-adult. Is that what seals your grown-up fate? Being too hot or too cold?

"Well done, girls," I say to my group as they play against Cora's.

Kayla and her group are off with Tia and Mary's. They're swimming in the lake, where normal people are in high temperatures. There's an instructor teaching the campers the butterfly stroke.

We're in the lake after lunch, and I cannot wait.

Cora calls another point for my team and the girls play on.

Cora blows out a breath and wipes her forehead with the back of her hand. "I'm dying."

"I know the feeling," I say, sucking on the straw of my water bottle. "I should have picked a cooler state to be a CIT."

Laughing, she replies, "Yeah, it's *hot*. Stick to the shaded areas and drink plenty of water. As far as I know, we've never had anyone suffer sunstroke."

"The first will probably be me."

"Take a drink." She turns to the girls. "All right, great game. Let's wrap it up and go inside for lunch."

There's a collective cheer as we head to the hall for food.

Cora and I follow the girls inside.

We're a little late. Everyone else is already sitting down. The air-conditioning welcomes me, making the skin on my forearms pebble.

It's loud, with dozens of conversations merging together to make one big chorus of noise.

The girls get food and head to a table together. Cora and I wait until they've gone to get ours. I add some salad to my plate of mac and cheese and sit at the table with Kayla, Tia, Rebekah, Olly and Jake.

"Tomorrow night, we're going around the lake and into the forest on the other side," Rebekah tells me, her eyes wide like she's not at all comfortable with this.

I don't like it around there, but I say, "Sounds good."

I look over at Kayla. She has a brilliant poker face, but her anxiety shows physically. She will trip on air or fall up steps. Basically, she turns clumsy when she's anxious.

Kayla stabs her fork into her pasta, but the fork slides and she flings a noodle into the center of the table.

And there it is.

She looks up and her worried eyes meet mine.

A couple of the others chuckle. No one but me picks up on her nervous energy.

"Slippery?" I ask.

She clears her throat. "Mascarpone sauce."

She worries about me overthinking and blurting the wrong thing out. I worry about her clumsiness giving us away.

I want to ask her again if we're sure being here is a good idea.

We're guilty of a crime that no one even suspects us of.

My parents are superbig on honesty. "The truth always comes out, Esme."

Cold cases get solved. Not many—2 percent according to TV documentaries I've watched—but better technology means criminals are being caught years later.

Could our DNA *still* be at the scene ten years later?

Unlikely.

7

The next morning is filled with excitement. It's like the kids think we're going to Disney World, not hiking.

Kayla and I will be with Cora. I don't think we're trusted to take a group off into the woods alone yet.

Despite being a competent map reader, I'm really okay with this. I don't remember the trails from before. Back then I was messing around with Kayla and the other girls from our cabin.

The campers chow down on breakfast like they're fed only once a day. I'm sure they eat about as much as the staff.

I'm sitting at a table with Olly and Tia. The rest have finished and gone back to the cabins.

"We have the night off," I say with a grin.

Tia's dark eyes light up. Her hair is tied back in another sleek bun today. "Oh yes. Remember, we're going around the back of the lake tonight."

"Sure."

I look out the large window in the hall, my eyes following

the dock, then out across the lake to the line of trees that hide a secret.

I gulp down the last of my water and pick up my plate, the half-eaten croissant now unappealing.

"You're already done, Esme? You've barely eaten anything," Olly says.

"Too hot," I reply, as if it's perfectly reasonable to go hiking on a few bites of pastry. "I'll see you guys outside."

I dump my food and put the plate on the trolley.

Andy raises one hand as I walk past him. He half covers his mouth, chewing at the same time as he says, "Esme."

I stop beside him. "What's up?"

He stands. "Are you feeling okay? I noticed you throwing away your breakfast."

I blink. Is there anything he doesn't notice? When we leave camp, I hope he's not as sharp-eyed.

"Um, I'm fine, just not very hungry."

"Perhaps you should take something? We're going to be hiking all morning."

I nod. "I'll grab an apple."

I know he said to keep an eye on the campers and make sure they're all eating enough and especially drinking enough water, but I didn't think he would be policing me, too.

Weird.

Andy smiles and moves out of my way. I duck past and leave the hall with a Granny Smith apple in my hand.

Kayla is ready when I get back to our room. She's sitting on her bunk chatting to Cora.

"Esme, good. We were just going over a few things," Cora says, leaning against the wall.

"What's that?"

"You and I will walk at the front of the group; we'll try to keep them in twos, but it doesn't always work. Kayla will be at the back."

"Okay."

"We need to check their backpacks and make sure they have the appropriate gear: a compass, map, sun hat, sunscreen and water. If we each check bags, that would be great."

"I think they're ready," Kayla says, laughing and nodding toward the sudden noise in the room adjoining.

"Let's do it." I grab my bag and we all head into the main bedroom.

The girls are stuffing things into their bags. I go straight to the two bunks right at the end that sleeps the four girls in my group.

I take Isabel's bag first and look inside. "Okay, everyone make sure you have the map and compass on your bed and put it in." I run through the final few things and double-check that we're all set.

Once we're done, we meet up outside with the other groups, and Andy assigns trails to us. There are four trails in total.

I pull my cap on my head. Cora and I lead the group along the red trail. Inside the forest there is welcome shade.

The girls behind us are superexcited for a little trek in the woods. Getting away from the camp for a while was one of my favorite things as a camper; it kept it exciting rather than seeing the same campsite and activities for weeks.

"How long have you been a counselor here?" I ask Cora.

She smiles. "Three years full, one CIT. Do you think you'll be back next year?"

"I'm not sure yet. I am enjoying this, but the responsibilities counselors have scare me a little."

"By the time the campers are picked up again, it won't seem scary at all. It's like that for everyone. You'll realize soon that the kids actively prevent themselves from starving, and drowning too."

Laughing, I reply, "Well, that's good to hear."

I don't know why I worry so much. At eight I was relatively independent and fairly good at knowing I shouldn't run toward danger.

But then I got tangled up in something bad . . .

"You should definitely consider coming back next year," Cora says. "You're great with the girls and they love you. It's always easy to figure out who will make it. I can tell ten minutes after they've met the campers."

"Are you ever wrong?"

She straightens her back with pride. "Nope."

"So, you've worked with Andy a lot." I want to ask about the Buttercups, but I don't want to seem nosy, and I don't want her to know that we've nicknamed them.

"Yeah, Andy, Mary and Catalina have been here for years."

So they have all been here before.

"Cool."

She side-eyes me and lifts one dark eyebrow. "What do you want to ask? I can tell there's something."

"No . . . Yes. Well, it's just that I can't figure him out," I say, stumbling over my words.

"Andy's cool. A little old school sometimes, and he loves rules. I don't think he has broken one. *Ever.*"

I nod and step over a fallen log. Ahead I see a red rag tied around a tree branch.

When we get past the trail, the girls will have a go at orienteering, leading us away from the mapped-out path to get back to camp. At least, that's the hope.

"Are the other groups near us?" a girl asks.

"Not really, we're all spread out," Cora replies.

"I saw someone."

Cora stops and everyone else does too. I turn around with Cora and see Ava's big eyes looking up at us.

"What's going on?" Kayla calls from the back.

"What did you see, Ava?" I ask.

I don't like this.

With a frown, Ava steps up to me.

"Someone in the woods. They were really far away, so I can't be sure, but I think it was a boy."

"It was a child?"

She shakes her head. "Um, no, a grown-up. They were tall."

My heart sinks.

Cora tells the girls to sit down and take a water break.

Kayla joins us, her face full of worry.

"Ava, are you *sure?*" Cora asks.

"Yeah. I was going to point the person out, but when I looked back, he was *gone.*"

The girls are all chatting about who it could have been. The word *killer* almost makes my eyes roll. They'll be telling campfire stories about this all summer, imaginations going wild.

Cora and I look at each other. Some trees have fallen; others have been cut down. Ava could have seen one and thought it was a person. When she looked again, she saw nothing because there are only trees.

The land we're on is private. It belongs to the camp.

"Ava, what did the person do?" Cora asks, wrapping one arm around her.

Her head tilts all the way up. "He was just standing there. I'm not making this up."

"No one thinks you are," I tell her, glancing back in the direction she said "he" was. I point. "Do you think it could have been a tree? You see there, the tree stump with no branches nestled between the normal ones?"

Ava frowns as she looks. "You think it was that?"

"It could have been," Cora says. "I've done the same thing. Some of the trees are cut down for firewood, which makes a few of them human size. You did the right thing telling us, though."

"So there's no crazy guy out there?" Isabel asks.

"Definitely not!" Cora says. "All right, girls, everything is fine. The forest sometimes plays tricks on you, so remember you can come to us if you're ever unsure of *anything*. Let's get going again or we'll be the last team back. I might have heard Andy saying there's a surprise for the first team home."

The girls leap to their feet, the madman in the forest forgotten as they try to guess what the treat will be.

We've just stopped for five minutes to play Find the Human-Looking Tree. We might not win.

Cora and I lead the girls, with Kayla taking her place at the back.

I look at the trees, toward where Ava thought she saw something.

It would be very easy to hide.

8

Cora doesn't seem to give the idea of a person running between trees watching us a second thought.

I've given it a third, fourth and fifth thought.

I know what Ava saw wasn't really a person the way I know that I won't be instantly killed the second I turn off my light. But does that stop my imagination from trying to convince me otherwise? Nope.

My eyes dart back to the woods, getting lost in the density of the trees.

Why would anyone be watching us? It could have been someone passing by; we're close to the camp's perimeter. Perhaps they veered off course, saw us and realized where they were, then dashed back onto public land.

Cora has switched from small talk with me to singing with the girls. I wish she would stop that and ask me random questions again. I don't much feel like joining in with their poor rendition of "Alice the Camel."

They finish the tenth song and Cora takes a breath. "Okay, I don't think I can do another one," she says.

She doesn't need to. The girls start to sing their own, "Baby Bumblebee," which has to be one of the oddest and grossest camp songs. Why would anyone lick a smashed bee? You deserve to throw up, in all honesty.

"We're almost to the orienteering point," I say, glancing at my map. The red trail curls back around, but we're not going there. We're going to go off course and find our own way home. Hopefully, we should arrive back at camp in time for lunch. That's if the girls don't get us lost.

Five more minutes of walking through shaded heat and we reach a clearing. It's a man-made area with a firepit. It belongs to the camp and we'll use it for building dens and cooking later in the summer.

The girls cheer from behind me.

"Thank goodness for that!" Cora says. "Okay, everyone have a drink and then we'll let small groups of you lead at a time. Make sure you have your map orientated. If you start off wrong, you will never find where you want to be."

Isabel stops in front of me, her big eyes as worried as the day she had to say goodbye to her mom.

"Esme, was that really a tree Ava saw?"

My heart pounds. "Of course. It's easy to assume something perfectly innocent is something really scary in situations like this. Don't worry."

I smile to load up the reassurance. All the while my mind is going, *Killer in the woods.*

Isabel smiles, her posture relaxing as she takes a breath. "Okay. Good. Can you help me with my map? I don't know which way it's supposed to be."

"Sure," I reply, really hoping it will be obvious. With few landmarks, it's not likely to be straightforward.

Isabel holds out her map. My three other girls shuffle over to us, and I take a look at the map.

"Ah," I say, pointing to the trail. "This is where we've come from, look. We took the red trail to this clearing. Straight ahead is where it continues, but we're not going to go that way. We want to head directly back, so where would you go to do that?"

I peer up from the map and all four girls are staring at it with matching frowns.

Maisie points. "Well, this would be a straight line back to camp." She looks up. "I'd go between those two big trees with curly branches."

"Good, Maisie."

Cora, hearing us, calls, "Girls, Maisie has figured it out first, so we're going to let Esme's team lead for the first part. Make sure you follow on your maps as you'll all get a chance to take over. Now, the little crosses along the map represent landmarks. Where those crosses are on the map is where red ties will be on trees."

"Score for the E Team," Isabel says.

"Let's rock this," I cheer.

The other groups walk behind us. We have an hour before lunch. If we don't go wrong, we should make it back on time.

Kayla and Cora switch places. I think that shows Cora trusts us if she's willing to fall back and let us little CITs lead. Not that we're leading, four seven- and eight-year-olds are.

"How's it going, May-May?" Kayla asks, using my very old nickname.

I think she stopped using it after the last time we were here.

"Feeling pretty good, actually. I can't wait for tonight." I'm absolutely not thinking about someone else in the woods.

My group leads us through the forest, and we find each flag shown on the map. They have confidently chosen the correct path. I give each girl a high five as we hand the map reading to Cora's group.

"You guys did so good," I tell my group. Four toothy smiles beam at the praise.

I fall in line with Cora, who's leading now.

"How many of these hikes have you done?" I ask.

"I'm pretty sure I could do this without a map. Well, not this route; I'm usually on the north side. The flags aren't spaced too far apart, though."

"Yeah, I noticed that."

"The next hike we do, we remove every other flag to make the girls rely more on the map rather than just walking and looking for a colored rag."

"That's the all-day hike?"

Cora nods. "They'll all make their own shelters. Sometimes the shelters even last the whole night."

Great, I'm going to sleep under the stars and get eaten alive by bugs.

Cora laughs at my expression. I'm sure I look like I want to run home. "You'll be fine. Don't worry."

"I'm not sleeping in a tent without my hair straighteners," Sophia says. She is in Cora's group and although she is sweet, she's high maintenance and kind of a princess. It came as no surprise to learn that she's an only child and here purely because her parents wanted her to experience something different.

I'm glad the girls in my group don't mind getting their hands dirty and their hair messy.

"You'll survive too, Sophia," Cora replies, laughing.

"Are we doing anything fun this afternoon?" she asks, running her fingers over her long black plait.

"We're on the lake."

"Do we have to do anything on the lake?"

Cora's smile tightens and I can tell she wants to roll her eyes. "No one is going to make you do anything."

"You might enjoy it if you try," I tell her. "You can always get out if you don't."

Sophia shrugs. "Maybe."

She has probably lost where we are on the map now.

Cora takes a deep breath. She's makeup-free and wears shorts and T-shirts exclusively, so I can't imagine she has a lot in common with Sophia.

The girls ahead stop and look around.

"Where are we, girls?" I ask.

My group turns to me, their foreheads furrowed. "Er . . . I have no clue," Audrey says. "There should be a flag here.

Look"—she points to the *X* on the map—"the flag should be right in front of us."

I walk up to her and look at the cross. She's right, we should be standing beside a flag on a tree that Kayla is currently scowling at.

"Are we lost?" Isabel asks.

Cora looks up, alarmed. "No, we've just gone wrong a step, but don't worry, we have the map and there are plenty of flags. If we pick up another color flag, that's fine. We'll just take that route."

Cora sounds so sure. She is right to be—I'm sure too. But the girls do not look convinced.

"Hey, it's fine," I tell them. "Cora is right. There are plenty of paths out here and they all lead back to camp."

They nod, satisfied with my answer. For now.

"Okay, we're going to go east and pick up the other trail," Kayla says, scanning her map. "It looks like the flag is gone . . . or we've detoured."

Cora gives her a thumbs-up. "See, girls. We'll be back on track in a few minutes."

Cora and I resume leading and take us east.

I lick my lips and take a sip of water.

"You know this new trail?" I ask Cora as we get a few steps ahead of the girls.

"Kind of."

I frown. Her "kind of" is not at all selling it to me. "Why would the flag not be here?"

All we can see around us are tall trees. The flags are the landmarks.

Cora shrugs. "It probably is. I think it's most likely that we've veered off course. We might see it in a minute and pick up the track again. If not we'll move to green flags—those are on the trail nearest to us. It doesn't matter how we get back."

It only matters that we get back. We've been walking deeper into the forest for about an hour now, without knowing where we are on the map. How do we find our way back if we don't see another flag? We could go in circles until we pass out from the heat.

I swallow the hysteria conjured by my own damn imagination, and push forward.

Our bodies would decompose quickly in this heat.

Shut up!

Kayla is always telling me to calm down. I'm terrible. Whenever someone is late, I assume something bad has happened.

Because sometimes bad things *do* happen.

Cora's lips press into a thin line. Her eyebrows knit together. She's getting worried.

She is not alone. No one is saying anything negative, but we're all wondering why we haven't seen a red or green flag yet.

Kayla, Cora and I don't want the girls to be alarmed. They're young and they're likely to be scared if they knew the truth right now. We don't know where we are.

Cora has very cleverly started a conversation about Roblox. Most of the girls play it or want to; they chat incessantly about the game, telling each other what they've done on it and what they want to do. They swap tips and tricks and it leads them away from our reality.

We are lost in the forest.

9

Cora chews her lip, visibly uneasy now.

Her head swings around every few minutes, making her hair sway. She's scanning the trees for evidence of ripped flags.

"How much longer?" Ava asks.

I make myself smile. "Shouldn't be too long now. Are you getting hungry?"

"I'm starving!" Sophia answers for us all.

Lunch was supposed to be fifteen minutes ago.

When will Andy begin to worry? We have a phone for emergencies. Cora has placed her hand over her pocket a few times. She's probably considering when the right time to call would be.

I know what she's doing. She wants to show the girls how to orient yourself when you're lost.

But there's a reason we haven't found a single flag landmark yet.

Someone has removed them.

It's so obvious. Why else would they be missing? Colored rags do not untie themselves from tree branches. I'm no wildlife expert, but I do know that squirrels can't work knots.

"Esme," Cora calls, and she comes to a stop. Her voice is sharp, and a cold shiver ripples down my spine.

Her eyes, round and brimmed with defeat, stare back at me. With a quick nod, she gives me the answer we've all been longing for. Yes, we can call for help now.

"Hey, look!" I say, my eyes catching something red. Cora is a step behind me as I jog to the scrap of material on the ground by a tree.

"Is that the flag?" Maisie asks.

I swipe the flag off the ground and hand it to Cora.

"Someone ripped this off the tree and left a piece behind. Who would do that?" Cora says.

I shrug one shoulder. "We're on track, though. Just a shame we don't know which cross this relates to on the map."

"Yeah. I think we should still call Andy."

Kayla catches up to us.

The girls are whispering about what's happened. Hushed voices are spurting all sorts of crazy stories.

"It was definitely ripped off," I tell Cora and Kayla, keeping my voice low. The girls are already suspicious and pretty much think there is a madman after us, especially since Ava thought she saw someone watching us.

Did she?

"Do you think that Ava could have seen a person?" I whisper. "The same person who's taken the flags off, so we got lost?"

Cora shakes her head, frowning like I've just asked if she believes all of those Area 51 conspiracy theories.

I do not. If I'm an alien visiting Earth, I'm going to the Bahamas, not Nevada.

"Drink some water, Esme," Kayla tells me.

Now she thinks I'm delirious.

I take my water bottle out of my bag and pretend I can't see Kayla's tight lips and tense eyes. It's her way of telling me to get ahold of myself.

That would be wonderful, but I can't until we're safely back at camp.

"All right, girls. It looks like we've veered off course, so we're going to make a call to Andy for some assistance," Cora tells them. "For now, take a break and hydrate. You should all have a protein bar, so have at it."

"Wait, what is that?" Isabel asks.

Ava stands on tiptoes. "Yeah, why is the flag on the ground?"

Cora tucks the marker into her pocket. "It's made of thin cotton, so it isn't a flag. Must have been left by someone."

She's quick with the lie there. She didn't even blink.

I should take lessons from her. When I lie, I'm sure my face is as red as a London bus. Kayla says it isn't, though. She has told me I'm quite a good liar. I've never quite known how to take that.

"Really?" Isabel asks.

I step up to her. "Really. I checked it myself. Take a seat with everyone else and rest. Once we have our bearings, we'll set off and go get some lunch."

She does as I say and takes a seat with the others. All of them look suspicious as hell.

"How do we know you three haven't taken us out here to do something?" Sophia asks.

Cora tilts her head. "Seriously, Sophia? I know you might be worried right now, but we're here to take care of you. Everything is fine and soon we'll be back at camp."

She huffs and sits down next to Ava.

I sip my water as I walk back to Cora and Kayla.

"Doesn't that thing have Google Maps?" I ask Kayla.

She smirks. "I asked the same thing. We won't get service, but Cora's going to ask Andy to message our location and the direction we're supposed to head."

"How's he going to do that?"

Kayla shrugs. "Do I look like a tech geek?"

With her glossy hair, manicured nails and hot pink sunglasses, no, she does not.

Cora is still talking on the phone. Her voice is as calm as always, as if she's letting Andy know we're almost there, not that we got lost in the forest with twelve young girls.

This isn't going to look good on my CIT record.

"Yes, that's correct . . . Looks like it was," Cora says into the cell.

I'm guessing Andy is asking about the ripped flags.

"All right, Andy has tracked the phone number and is sending us the directions back to camp."

"He tracked us?" I ask.

"Camp cell phone," she replies, holding it up.

Okay, that's less creepy.

"Good," I say, sliding my water bottle back into my bag.

"Looks like we need to go southeast and we'll be back shortly," Cora says after the phone beeps. "We're minutes away!"

She puts the phone away, opens her compass and starts to walk slowly.

"All right, we know where we are, and we're off. Up we get, girls," Cora says, waving her arms as she passes them.

"Are we close?" Ava asks.

"Ridiculously close," I reply. "Despite the lack of flags, we almost got back."

Sophia's shoulders drop. "But we didn't."

"But we will. Come on, do you want a big bowl of mac and cheese or not?"

Her eyes widen. "I do."

"Then let's go!"

Four minutes. That's how far away we were. If everyone was out on the lake or outside, we probably would have heard them.

"Mac and cheese," Ava cheers, followed by whoops and squeals from the other girls.

It's funny the psychology of being lost to post-lost.

The girls had been hunched, looking around, whispering, worrying. I was convinced we were goners and now I can see us splashing around in the lake this afternoon without a care in the world.

Now it's no big deal. The knowledge that we're almost back and there's mac and cheese waiting has them forgetting one very important thing.

The fact that someone wanted us to lose our way hasn't changed.

Whatever they think they believe because Cora told her white lie with conviction, they'd realize the truth if they thought about it for a second.

Red material dropped by someone else at the same time our red flags go missing? Unlikely.

Kayla falls in line with me. This time Cora trusts both of us to be at the back and make sure none of the girls decide to run away. As if at this point they would be so stupid.

What with a flag-stealing stalker maniac out there and all.

"Something is off, right?" I whisper.

Kayla shrugs. "Think about it logically."

"I have."

"Who could it be?" she asks.

"I don't know who!" Not *exactly.* "People do all kinds of crazy stuff for all sorts of reasons. Some just because they're bored. Maybe someone from town is trying to make it an eventful summer."

"Then don't worry about it, Esme. They've had their fun."

"Yeah, but what if they're just getting started?"

"Babe, stop. You're going to fry that big brain of yours if you don't stop thinking."

I'm not usually this bad. It's being back *here.*

"Okay, I'm done," I tell Kayla, mostly to stop her from thinking too much about who could be out here. And I'll do my best to ignore what my mind is trying to convince me of. It's like my mind and I are separate entities sometimes. The battle of staying sane versus letting hysteria take over.

I don't want to think the worst. This summer is supposed to be fun and I'm letting what is probably some innocent prank get to me.

Kayla and I pulled pranks when we were here. Everyone does. It usually starts with the counselors once the campers have settled in. Then it goes back and forth.

The most likely culprits are teens from town who have wandered onto camp property and stolen some flags from the trees.

A cheer from the girls jolts me from my incessant thoughts.

My muscles unlock.

We're back.

The trees give way to open land and a glorious body of water. I am so freaking happy to see the lake!

The girls run for the food hall chanting about mac and cheese. Andy laughs and steps out of their way before they trample him.

He waits for us to catch up.

"Thank God we're back," Cora says. "Thanks, Andy."

"What happened?"

She takes the scrap of red material out of her pocket. "Looks like someone has been having fun on camp grounds."

Andy takes it from her hand. "Someone has taken the flags off?"

"Yeah."

Muttering something under his breath, he straightens his shoulders. "I'll deal with this. We'll have Garret and Ward come in and set the flags up again. Go eat. And well done on staying calm and getting help when you needed it."

I smile at Andy, feeling like a bit of a fraud for accepting his praise along with Cora and Kayla. I didn't show the girls that I was worried, I suppose. That's what counts.

"You good?" Kayla asks me.

"Yep. You?"

"I'm fine," she replies, and trips over the threshold of the food hall.

Yeah, me neither.

10

It's nine at night. I'm outside with Kayla, Tia, Rebekah, Olly and Jake. We're going for a walk.

The campers are tucked in bed and it'll be lights-out soon. Not that they'll stop whispering and go to sleep. It's such a relief to be able to relax after all of the lost-in-the-woods excitement. Except I didn't find it very exciting.

Kayla has stopped being clumsy, so I'm pretty sure she's moved on. She's very good at pushing something out of her mind if she doesn't like it. I wish I could do the same.

It was probably someone from town messing around. At least, that seems to have won the whodunit votes. It's not the first time that teens have wandered onto camp property and messed around, according to Andy; occasionally they've been caught and cautioned by the cops.

Now that we're out of the woods and I've eaten, I can see how over the top I was being. Kids have been hauled away by cops and taken back to town. The path through the forest leads our way, so it's easy for townies to reach the camp.

The fear of being lost and thinking that Ava saw someone got to me in a big way.

Just because the camp looks like a horror movie set does not mean it is one.

I don't know exactly when we're going to sneak into town. There was talk of next week, but after we got lost today, I think the others are hesitant.

It better be worth it. I'll probably stress the whole damn time that we'll be caught.

"Almost to the other side," Rebekah says as we walk around the lake.

I hate being this far away from camp.

Every day after the accident I would almost hyperventilate being so close to where it happened. I still remember taking this very route, then Kayla and I veered left into the woods and things got . . . bad.

But that was years ago. I'm not the same person I was back then.

It was easier to be on this side of the lake earlier, when we finally arrived back from the hike. Everyone was so relieved to have found camp again, I didn't think about how close we were to the accident site.

After getting lost in the forest, I don't much feel like being very close to that place again. But that doesn't mean I need to fear it.

The others turn, and I follow them between the trees, my stomach tightening.

"Will you stop stressing," Kayla hisses in my ear. "I can see those dark eyes filling with anxiety."

"Kayla, I don't like this—"

"Stop. You always look on the negative side whenever something is even slightly suspicious. Or not suspicious at all!"

"This isn't about the forest thing. I get what that was now, okay?" I shake my head. "It's passing that place. . . ."

"Don't. We're not talking about that ever again, remember? We made a pact. A *blood* pact."

It can hardly be called a blood pact. We both cut ourselves while we were running through the edge of the forest to get back before the counselors woke up. We promised not to tell and shook on it. There was blood on our hands.

"Fine. Okay, you're right," I tell her. "I thought it would be easier to be back here after so many years."

"It freaked me out too at first, but you have to get over it. What happened wasn't our fault. We were kids, Esme."

Smiling, I nod. "I'm forgetting it. Let's join everyone else; they're ahead."

Olly looks over his shoulder as Kayla and I speed up.

His frown is wiped away by a smile. "Come on, Esme, we're almost there."

"Almost where?"

"To the fire damage."

Kayla's steps falter at his words and she trips. I grab her elbow, holding her upright. "Tree roots," I say aloud to cover up the real reason Kayla almost wiped out.

That's where we're going?

No way.

"You okay?" Jake asks, jogging back.

Kayla blushes. "I'm so clumsy!" Jake holds his hand out and she takes it.

Can't she pretend to faint and get us out of this?

Jake and Kayla walk ahead of Olly and me.

"Why are we going there?" I ask, trying to keep my voice even and not Minnie Mouse high. Olly doesn't so much as blink, so I know I sound normal.

"Andy won't say much about the fire. I think he's embarrassed on behalf of the camp that it happened. Kids alone in the woods, starting a fire, almost burning the place down . . . It doesn't look good."

"Huh? How do you know?"

"People talk, Esme," he says.

Do they? No one was caught. There were rumors circulating, but no one talked. Kayla and I have never talked.

"What happened?" I ask, trying to figure out how much Olly knows. He thinks the fire was started by someone at camp?

"Word is a group of kids from town snuck into the woods and their campfire got out of hand."

Yeah, that's what everyone thinks. The fire department and police. I remember the cops the morning after the fire talking to the counselors.

Kayla and I were petrified that they'd come for us, but the damage wasn't to camp property.

"There's another theory, however," Olly continues.

I hold my hands behind my back. "About campers?"

He nods. "Some people think a group of campers snuck out of the cabin and lit a fire in the woods in the middle of the night. It got out of hand, but by the time counselors were alerted, the campers were already back in their beds."

I lick my lips. *Diffuse, diffuse, diffuse.* "How could they sneak in and out during a fire and not be noticed?"

Olly shrugs. "Kids are sneaky."

Play. It. Cool.

I gulp down what I think will come out as manic laughter. "True. So, we're going to look at burned wood. We've really peaked on the boredom scale, huh?"

Olly laughs. "All right, there's not a lot to do, I'll give you that. We're out of here soon and heading into town."

"What happens if we get caught?"

"Andy will likely tell us how disappointed he is. Then we'll never be allowed out of our cabins in the evening. We'll have to be asleep by nine like the campers."

"We're not getting caught, then."

He laughs again. "No getting caught."

I'm good at that. So is Kayla.

I take a deep breath. Everyone still thinks the fire was caused by kids from town, which means Lillian never spilled either. I just need to get through these six weeks and never return.

"Here it is," Tia says, bouncing up and down. She shines her flashlight around. There is a large clearing. A five-minute walk from camp.

I stand at the edge of the forest and do a three-sixty, looking around in every direction. This is crazy.

My heart thumps against my rib cage. My chest tightens. A lot of work has gone into these woods to make sure forest fires don't get out of hand—strips of land between the trees, large circles of rocks around campfires, and fire prevention signage.

Those rocks saved the woods that night. We accidentally set fire to only three trees. It was contained.

But that wasn't the worst thing that happened here.

11

Today we're going to the lake for swimming lessons. Thankfully not taught by me. I'm confident I could swim to save my life, but I'm nowhere near good enough to be able to teach. Besides, I'm not qualified.

We also have water volleyball. The lake is very deep, and dark, in the middle, but about three-quarters of the way in, there's a ring of rope that we're not supposed to go beyond.

"I remember being excited for a day on the lake," I say to Kayla, and take a big gulp of my second coffee.

"Yeah, it was so much fun. The kids are going to love it."

This is our first full day in the water and around it. We're having a picnic lunch on the beach and dinner around the campfire. Andy had a *lot* of burgers and hot dogs delivered early this morning to feed hungry children.

I can almost taste the lightly charred hot dogs just from thinking about them.

"I can't wait to get in the water. Texas is so hot," I say.

Kayla smirks. "You're getting in?"

"Totally. I can referee volleyball or something." I haven't been able to focus on anything since last night. Not even sleep. I see angry orange flames consuming three trees so clearly that it's as if it's happening right now. The screams are imbedded in my memory, refusing to leave no matter how hard I try.

"Ready to go get changed?" Cora asks, stopping by our table.

I nod and grab my empty bowl and mug.

"See you out there," I tell Kayla.

Cora and I head out. As we walk, she asks, "Where did you go last night? I saw you guys walking around the lake and into the woods."

I lick my lips. "Tia wanted to see the old fire damage."

"Gosh, that was so bad. It was lucky the fire didn't take hold."

"Seemed to be held up by the rocks," I say as if I have no idea.

"Yeah. The trees in the middle of the clearing were the only ones that burned, thankfully."

Cora knows a lot about this.

My heart skips a beat. "Were you here then?"

I don't remember her.

"No. I had a good look around when I first came as a CIT, though. It's such a nice man-made campsite, shame the dead trees ruin it."

That's all that's left. The forest has recovered; new growth has long hidden the mess left behind on the ground. But the burned trees are still there, one of them just a stump. I'm hit with a pang of guilt whenever I think about it. Which has been often lately.

If the site hadn't been man-made and the ground cleared to

protect the forest when campfires were used, the whole woods could have gone up.

Kayla and I almost destroyed acres of forest and the campsite.

Cora heads down to the lake while I return to the cabin to change into my bathing suit. I tie my long hair up on my head, pinch my pale cheeks to give them some color and stare into my green eyes. They really are the color of leaves on a tree. As if I need more reminders of what I've done.

Grabbing my towel, I head to the lake. Some of the campers are in the water already, with the swim instructors taking groups of eight each. The other campers are by the two volleyball nets and split into teams. The Buttercups, who aren't actually twins or even related, are in the water near the volleyball nets, as are Olly and Jake. I bet Kayla regrets her decision to be on swim watch now.

Out of nowhere, a young girl from Cora's group runs in front of me and trips on a large rock. She lands on the ground with a thud. For some reason, when she falls, I startle more than I should.

"Alana, are you okay?" I ask.

She's a shy girl. She looks up from the ground and I can tell she's holding back tears.

I sit down next to her. "Let me see."

With trembling hands, I inspect her knee. There's only a slight scrape and it's not bleeding. Still, I can hear my heart beating in my ears.

"I'm okay," Alana says.

"Do you want me to get you an ice pack?"

She hesitates, then shakes her head. "I want to get in the lake."

"Great. Our groups are doing volleyball first. Shall we go?"

She stands and her eyes dart to the swimmers. "I can't swim. I've never had lessons."

"You'll be able to by the end of the summer. There are lessons three times a week."

We walk around the lake to the others.

"Most of my friends can already swim," she says.

"You'll be able to tell them you can too when you go back to school."

Alana beams, her big eyes alight with the excitement of such a simple skill. She doesn't want to be the best swimmer in the world or go for the Olympics, she just wants to be able to do it like her friends.

She seems to have already forgotten about her fall. But I haven't.

"Stay waist-high, Alana," I tell her as she splashes into the lake.

She shouts a very quick okay over her shoulder and joins her team.

"All okay?" Cora asks.

"Um, yeah. Just a small scrape," I say.

Cora nods. "Thanks for taking care of her. I'll follow up later and see how she's doing."

"For sure."

I barely hear Cora tell me she is going to check out the water. My mind is still elsewhere. Back at the night of the fire. Only now, new memories are surfacing. They came to me the minute Alana hit the ground and have only grown clearer since. Kayla and I had snuck out. When we reached the clearing, we built a small fire, but we used too many logs. Only after the fire was burning did a young girl come out of the woods. She told us her name was Lillian and that she had run away from home. She wanted to show us something. Something . . . horrible. Kayla called her a freak and pushed her. Lillian fell, knocking the wood from the firepit. The flames started to spread, hot and vicious, and we all ran.

Or at least I thought we all ran.

But now something nags at my mind. The image of Lillian sprawled on the ground.

Did she run?

And if she didn't, what happened to her?

Where is Lillian now?

12

Kayla and I are sitting on the bottom bunk in our room. The campers are having s'mores after dinner and we've come inside while Andy tells some of his "infamous" ghost stories. I haven't heard any of them yet, but Cora says they're pretty lame, though highly entertaining.

"So, you don't think Lillian ran?" Kayla asks. Her fingers knit together and then she unfolds them like she's performing jazz hands.

Her back is straight as a board and I don't think she's blinked in the past few minutes.

"I can't be sure. But I don't remember seeing her get up," I say.

"That doesn't mean she didn't."

"I know that."

Kayla shakes her head.

"She could have." I take a breath that feels like I'm swallowing razors. "But she was already hurt."

"Maybe she was still there when the cops arrived and they picked her up?"

I kick my feet up on the mattress. "Maybe. But last night Olly said that no one knows who started the fire. If the cops picked Lillian up, then surely they would've pinned it on her."

"What if the cops couldn't say anything publicly because she was a minor?" Kayla says.

"Okay, I'm not really interested in what the cops think."

"You should be, Esme!"

"We know she didn't light the damn fire—we did! What I'm worried about is what happened to her after we ran. Were we the last ones to see her? Did she get into some sort of trouble?"

Kayla and I panicked and ran, flattening ourselves against trees and watching to see whether any lights came on in the cabins. We never bothered to look back.

"Why didn't you tell me any of this before?" she says.

I shake my head. "I guess because I wasn't sure. But every time I think about it, I hear the roar of the fire and those screams."

"Okay. Okay." Kayla sits even taller. "Right. Okay. Right."

Ugh, I want to throw something at her. "Kayla, use other words!"

"I'm thinking! You know, it wasn't our fault. We weren't the ones who started the trouble that night."

That sounds like something you say to justify your actions. Are you guilty because you didn't stop something from happening? Yes. We had the power that night to help and we didn't do *anything*.

"We need to find out where Lillian is," I tell Kayla.

I can't stop thinking that maybe she was injured more than we thought.

"I'm going to Google her. There could be an article about it, right?" I say, pulling my phone out of my bag on the floor.

Kayla leans forward to look over my shoulder as I type *fire, Texas* and *Lillian Campbell* into the search bar.

I shake my head, scrolling as I pass names and faces that don't match.

Come on.

I bite my lip in frustration. No one looks familiar.

Please.

"None of these kids look like Lillian," I say.

"Well, that's good. We don't want to find her in the news."

"True," I mutter. I sigh and drop my phone in my lap when the internet comes up empty. "Okay, I've got nothing."

"Good." Kayla brushes her hair over her shoulders. "That means we didn't do anything."

I side-eye her. "It only means it's not online. What we did was very real."

"Esme." Kayla says my name like all of this is exclusively my fault.

We were so dumb that night, thinking we were cool for sneaking out like the older kids. Kayla was so excited as we left the cabin, thinking about how she was going to tell them the next day.

But when we got into bed that night, we vowed to never tell anyone.

That night she also lost her desire to be popular. Mostly.

Kayla wants this to all go away, for it to be a buried memory that she never digs up.

Something is wrong here. I feel it in the skittering of my heart whenever I think about that night. Lillian was a little girl alone in the woods. We had no idea who she was; we only spoke to her for about five minutes before the fire got out of hand.

"Come on, let's go join the others before they get suspicious," I say, sliding my useless phone back in my bag. This is getting us nowhere.

Kayla hops up and knocks her water bottle off the dresser at the end of our bunk. It rolls under her bed.

"Damn it," she hisses, kneeling on the floor to reach under the bed and pick the bottle up.

At this point, we don't even need me to state the obvious. Kayla is worried too.

She ducks her head, refusing to meet my eye. I wasn't going to say anything to her anyway.

"Let's get a s'more," I say as we walk outside.

That's code for "let's act normal."

"All right, campers," Andy says. "We need you to get a good night's sleep tonight because tomorrow there is a summer school exam you're required to take."

A rumble of unhappy conversation tears through the groups of kids.

Kayla and I look at each other.

"What's this about?" I ask Cora as we sit next to her.

She shrugs, her mouth failing to hide a smile.

Oh, I get it. Andy's pranking them.

"Settle down, settle down," he says, waving his arms up and down. "This will be the only test you have to take and it's for us to see what math group to put you in."

"Math!"

I don't know who said it; I only know that the sound pierced my freaking eardrums. Wincing, I plug my knuckles into my ears and rattle them until the ringing stops.

Andy laughs and addresses the loud child. "All right, Cady." He turns to the group. "I was, of course, joking. There are no tests at camp."

The children grumble at his lame attempt to prank them but cheer for the lack of tests.

"We're going to get you back, Andy!" Zak from Olly's group shouts.

Andy smirks. "I invite you to try."

The mood lifts. A tinge of excitement makes my heart leap. I loved getting involved in silly pranks. Some of my favorites were putting food coloring in the milk dispensers, icing cleaning sponges to look like cake and stuffing counselors' shoes with tissue.

Now it's on.

Kayla rubs her hands together. "We need to think of something to do to them."

"There is plenty," Cora replies.

We sit and plot pranks by the fire, eating s'mores and chatting about how much fun the next few weeks are going to be.

I only forget Lillian for a second.

We don't know that she was *really* hurt that night. She probably ran away too. There is nothing to suggest that she didn't get home safely.

I am letting this thought reassure me when I look up and find Rebekah staring me down from across the campfire.

13

Three guesses for who didn't sleep well last night.

I hug my mug of coffee in my hands and wish I could have it in an IV.

The girls are learning how to make safe campfires on the edge of the forest. The counselors have got this one since they're trained. That means the CITs are free for the morning and we're in the hall having a late breakfast.

I'm sitting at a table with Kayla, Tia, Olly, Jake and Rebekah. After I caught her staring at me across the fire last night, Rebekah quickly looked away and it hasn't come up since. I was probably overreacting anyway, considering the state I was in last night. A leaf falling on my shoulder would've made me jump ten feet.

"I've missed sleeping in," I say, yawning behind my mug.

Olly laughs. "It feels like it's been weeks. Hey, do you want to take a walk before we have to build dens with the campers?"

I nod as the back of my neck heats. A walk in the woods is

about as close as you can get to a date here. Not that he's asking me out.

Is he?

Don't act weird.

"Sounds good," I say.

The very last thing I'm about to do is make eye contact with Kayla. She will absolutely be giving me *the look*. That goofy expression your friends give you when your crush talks to you. It's a dead giveaway.

"You ready now?" Olly asks.

He keeps eye contact so casually, like this is no big deal.

Because it isn't a big deal. Chill out!

"Uh-huh," I mutter as words fail me.

I sip the last of my coffee and Olly takes my bowl, stacking it on top of his.

My stomach flutters.

"Have fun," Kayla sings. Tia and Rebekah giggle behind their spoons, dropping cereal onto the table.

I ignore them and get up. Olly dumps the bowls and we leave the food hall. The heat hits my face. I'm glad I tied my hair up this morning and applied the standard thick layer of sunscreen.

"They've gone east, so let's go west," he says.

I turn and smile. "Okay."

"You cool, Esme? You haven't been yourself the last couple of days," Olly says after a minute. We walk into the forest, where the air is slightly cooler, more bearable.

Not been myself? He's only known me for a week. "I'm good. A little tired."

"Did sleeping late this morning help?"

Nodding, I say, "Yeah, it was awesome." It wasn't. I stayed in bed but didn't sleep in. "Hey, what's your favorite movie?"

"Are you going Ghostface on me, Esme?"

A twig snaps under my sneaker. "I didn't ask your favorite *scary* movie."

"Horror isn't my thing. My favorite is *The Godfather Part II*. What's yours?"

"You're going to think I'm superlame."

He chuckles. "It's a chick flick, isn't it?"

"I'm a total sucker for them. *Pretty Woman* is genius. And *27 Dresses*."

"You're a romantic."

We head deeper into the forest, keeping camp just in view. "Guilty. My parents have always been supersweet to each other."

"You're lucky. Mine divorced when I was a kid."

"I'm sorry," I tell him.

Olly shrugs like it's no big deal. "What pranks do you think the campers are going to pull?" he asks, changing the subject.

"I don't know, but always check the toilet thoroughly before you pee."

"Saran Wrap?"

I nod. "Would make a hell of a nasty mess."

"I'll be checking."

I grab his wrist when something crunches deeper in the forest. My gaze flies in the direction the sound came from. "What was that?"

"What?" Olly looks around. "Esme, what did you hear?"

"Twigs breaking."

Olly's shoulders relax. "It's probably an animal."

I slide my eyes to him. "Animals usually don't come too close with all the noise at camp."

It's bright this morning, but the trees block the sun. The forest is swallowed by darkness.

"Whatever it is, it's probably gone. Why are you freaking out? Seriously, I didn't hear anything, Esme," he says.

You won't if you keep talking!

I drop his wrist. "You're right. It was probably an animal. Sorry, it just spooked me."

"I've never minded hot girls grabbing hold of me."

His words light up in my mind like the Las Vegas Strip.

He called you hot. Don't cackle like some nervous witch. Play. It. Cool.

"How often does that happen? Or is that your tactic?"

Laughing, he starts walking again. "You mean do I take girls into the woods so they'll get scared and jump me?"

"Seems to be working for you."

"I live in a city, but I'm considering moving."

I shake my head. "Cities are way worse, just take them to a bad part at night."

"You can't get lost in a city," he says. "I mean, you can lose someone, but you'll always be seen. Deep in the forest, you could live the rest of your life with only the birds and squirrels."

"Can someone survive on their own like that? I'd starve in a week."

Olly laughs again. "I'm sure you'd make it. Just don't eat any berries you're not sure of."

"It's kind of scary to think that there could be a whole bunch of people living out here."

"You think people aren't? There are whole tribes who live in the Amazon."

"Yeah, but that's not on my doorstep."

"You want to go and see if we can find them? I'll get a map."

"Nope," I say, playfully slapping his arm. "When are we going to town? It's been a week."

Olly arches an eyebrow. "You itching to play arcade games?"

"I have a lot of pennies I want to exchange for a crappy plastic Slinky."

"Tomorrow?"

Okay, that's soon. But it gives me a thought. When we go into town, maybe I can find Lillian. She's the one who can put my mind to rest. If she's okay, then I can forget all about the fire.

Olly and I get back to camp just as we have to join the campers in the food hall. They're baking cookies.

Each group is at a table, with all the necessary ingredients and equipment in the middle of it. The room is a cloud of flour.

"Esme, Kayla is in the kitchen getting extra bags of chocolate chips. Can you join her and get another bag of flour? Catalina's group is missing one," Andy says.

"Yeah, sure."

I skip into the kitchen, still high from my walk with Olly. Pushing the door open, I stop dead in my tracks as Kayla almost slams into me. The door clicks shut. "Whoa, Esme!"

"We need more flour," I tell her.

"How was your date?"

"It wasn't a date, but it was nice."

Kayla hands me the chocolate chips and pulls at her sweater. "I'm too hot in this now."

"Why are you wearing a hoodie?"

"I was helping Andy print the recipes for the cookies in the staff cabin and he has the AC on ice-cold." She whips the hoodie over her head and a piece of paper falls to the floor.

I bend down and pick it up. Thick black writing catches my eye.

"Kayla," I breathe.

YOU'VE BEEN VERY BAD GIRLS

"What the hell!" Her eyes widen and she snatches the paper from me.

"Who put that there?" I ask.

"I don't know." She throws the hoodie on the floor. "Someone put that in my pocket!"

"While you were wearing it?"

"I've only had it on for, like, ten minutes. I was alone with Andy in the staff cabin, but he didn't come that close to me."

I close my eyes and take a breath. *Stay. Calm.* "Someone put it there when the hoodie was hanging up in our room."

"Ew. No way. That's *not* possible."

"Should we be freaking out?" I ask. "Because I'm thinking this is all about Lillian."

And I am so freaking out.

Kayla's wild eyes meet mine. "No . . . it can't be. This is just someone pranking me," she says.

"Then why does it say *girls*? Plural, Kayla. If it was just for you the note would say 'You've been a very bad girl.' Read it again. Read it!"

She shoves the piece of paper in her shorts pocket. "I don't need to read it again and we don't need to obsess over some stupid prank."

"Prank? You think this is one of the kids' pranks? Kayla, this is—"

"Over," she snaps, cutting me off midsentence. "Grab what you need and forget this. Please." She snatches the chocolate chips from my hands.

I watch her with my mouth wide open as she storms out of the kitchen. What did I do?

I gasp for a deep-enough breath and brace my hands on the wall.

Someone out there knows what we've done.

14

Kayla isn't my biggest fan right now.

Yesterday she thought I was being crazy and obsessive. It's clear from the silent treatment I got this morning before she left for breakfast that she still does. She stomped around our tiny room getting ready, making as much noise as possible, letting me know that she's not happy with my Lillian theories.

Kayla doesn't want there to be anything wrong, so she pretends everything is fine.

I don't want there to be anything wrong either, but we can't ignore a creepy note.

"Esme!" Cora whispers as I leave the cabin. She runs toward me from the staff cabin. Her eyebrows are pulled together like she's stressed.

"What's wrong?"

"Come here!" She beckons me, waving one hand in circles like she's about to take off.

I jog toward her. She instantly spins and runs toward . . . whatever she wants to show me.

"Cora, what are we—" The words die on my tongue. Painted on the back of the staff cabin is THE LAKE NEVER FORGETS.

My mouth parts and my fingers curl into my palms.

An ice-cold chill ripples down my spine. First the note, now this.

I shake my head, willing the message to change, but I haven't read it wrong. "Who could have done this?" I ask.

"I know we're all pranking each other, but if one of the campers managed to get out of their cabin and do this, we have a big problem," Cora says.

"Yeah," I agree.

This wasn't one of the kids.

"Should I get Andy?" I ask.

Cora's shoulders sink. "We have to tell him. He's going to be angry and he's going to want to keep this under wraps."

I clear my throat. "Right. The campers don't come around the back of the staff cabin, it's too out the way, so if we don't make it public knowledge, we either catch the culprit when he or she mentions it, or the rest of the campers go home unaware of what happened."

Cora smiles. "You're good at this, Esme."

"Thanks."

"You go get Andy, I'll get some cleaning supplies and paint so we can try to remove this crap. Whoever it is, they get points for creepiness."

The lake never forgets.

How much trouble could Kayla and I even get into over something that happened ten years ago? I don't want anything to go wrong for us . . . but maybe it should. Karma could finally be coming for us.

"Esme?"

I jolt. "Sorry. I'll go get Andy."

What if Lillian *was* hurt worse than we thought?

What if she didn't get up in time and was burned?

Or worse.

Shut up, Esme!

I run around the cabin and jog into the food hall. Rebekah almost bumps into me. "Sorry," she says, laughing and stepping back.

"Me too." I scan the hall. "Have you seen Andy?"

"He left a minute ago. Is everythin' okay? You look . . . pale."

I'm so not okay.

I pull on her hand. "Come with me, we need to find Andy."

"Huh?" Rebekah dashes after me. "This sounds a little ominous."

"It's more than a little."

"Officially intrigued."

"Andy!" I call. He's standing by one of the boys' cabins, digging his foot into a floorboard. A creaky one, maybe. He's very big on keeping the camp in top condition despite its age.

He looks up. "Everything okay?"

"Could you come with us for a minute, please?"

"Of course."

"Where are we goin'?" Rebekah asks.

They follow me around the food hall to the back of the staff cabin. "Cora found something."

Andy's eyes tighten in alarm.

"What the . . . ?" he says, and his jaw hits the ground.

"I saw this about five minutes ago," Cora says. She already has a bucket of soapy water and three sponges. Will that even work? There's a tin of brown wood paint and a brush, so I guess we'll be painting over the graffiti if it doesn't wash off.

"Who would do this?"

"One of the kids thinks they're funny," Rebekah says, shaking her head.

Yeah, only problem with that theory is the writing is at my height. A kid could have reached up to do it, but the natural way to graffiti is at your own height.

Could this have been done by one of the counselors or CITs? But who, and why?

The person in the forest watching us hike and removing flags?

Or maybe . . . *Nope, not going there.*

Andy takes his phone out. "I'll get a photo and then we'll clean it off."

He snaps a picture and slides his phone back into his pocket.

"The campers will be outside soon; I need to get the canoes ready. Esme and Rebekah, do you think you could take care of this? Cora and I will need to be on the lake with the campers."

I nod and Rebekah says, "Sure."

As soon as Andy and Cora leave, muttering about what's happened and who could have done it, I dunk a sponge into the water.

"This is insane," I say, dragging the soggy sponge across the first letter. The metallic taste in my mouth makes me gag. I drop my head so Rebekah can't see my reaction. I'll look like a crazy person if I panic over a little graffiti. Or a guilty one.

"Yeah. I know we're all in for the pranks now, but I don't know, maybe this is too far. Do ya think?" she says.

"I *really* do. Why do you think that it would be written *here*?" I ask. "It's not like it's out in the open for all to see." I want someone else's thoughts on this, someone who will give me all the reasonable explanations for why a camper had done this.

Rebekah shrugs, scrubbing with all her force at the letter *R* at the other end. It doesn't come off. "Maybe they don't need it on display. They're pranking us and we're pranking them. No reason for them to need all the other campers to see."

"Yeah, that makes sense." It actually does. Campers are pranking us, not each other. "Why say 'the lake never forgets'? What does that even mean?"

Her pale eyes cut sideways at me. "Why do you think it means somethin', Esme?"

Um . . .

I scrub harder, the sponge almost shredding against some of the rougher parts of wood. "I don't know, it just seems like an odd thing to say."

"We're at a lake."

"Right," I reply. I haven't forgotten about the massive oval of water I walk around every day.

Rebekah glances at me and then back at the writing. Then back at me again.

"What?" I ask, my stomach lurching.

"Huh?"

"I can tell you want to say something."

She sighs. "Are you okay? Your reaction . . . Esme, are you worried about this? Do ya think it's more than a prank?"

"I don't know," I whisper.

There are a lot of dots here and I'm not sure whether I'm trying to force them to connect.

I dunk the useless sponge. "What do you think about this?"

"I think one of the campers likes horror."

"What about the fact that this is written at adult height?" I ask.

Rebekah stills. "What?"

"The writing is at our height. The campers are shorter, so wouldn't this be a little lower down if it was one of them?"

"Hey, maybe that's how we find out who did it. Maybe it's one of the taller ones?"

I shrug one shoulder. "Could be."

"What's your theory?"

"I don't have one," I lie.

"I know we're not really close yet, but I would like to change that. You can talk to me, Esme."

Rebekah said that she doesn't have friends. No one to talk to and here I am closing up on her. That can't feel good after years of being bullied.

"Totally. I'd like that. Hey, I think it was someone else who wrote this," I tell her.

"Someone else?"

"Yeah, like someone from town. It just doesn't add up. Why

would someone working for the camp want to remove flags and get us lost? Ava thought she saw someone in the woods when we were hiking."

"Really?"

"There was no one there when Cora and I looked. Cora said it was just the trees."

"But you don't think it was a tree?"

I dunk the sponge again, getting frustrated. "I mean, it could have been, but then the trail was tampered with, and now this."

"Who else have you told?" Rebekah asks.

"No one," I say, not wanting to drag Kayla into it. "They will probably think I'm crazy. I have the tendency to overthink. My mom is the same; anytime I'm late she calls, worried something has happened to me."

"At least she cares."

"I'm lucky. So . . . do you think I'm crazy?" I bite my lip in anticipation of her reply. Sometimes *I* think I'm crazy.

"I don't think you're crazy at all. I can see how you got there."

"Do you think I could be right?"

"It's not impossible."

"But?" I prompt, wanting the rest.

"But *why* would someone do all of that?"

I shrug. "Good question."

That I can answer.

"I don't think this is going to come off," I say, exasperated. We decide to cover it with three thick coats of paint and that does the trick. It's not perfect, but at least the words aren't visible. I wish they would just disappear.

As we walk away, Rebekah turns to me. "Hey, maybe Andy has annoyed someone. He comes to camp early from what I overheard. He spends a lot of time in town."

"Really?"

Her eyes glow. "Uh-huh. Maybe he slept with someone's wife."

"Nasty."

She guesses again. "Maybe he offended the whole town, called them hicks or somethin'."

Or maybe this has nothing to do with Andy and everything to do with Kayla and me.

15

"I can't believe anyone would do that," Mary says. Her dark eyes narrow under her fringe.

I look away from her, but I feel her gaze long after she's turned away.

Jake shrugs. "It's extreme but a good prank, to be fair."

I've heard enough.

It took a lot of scrubbing to make the words fade even a little. Then we had to paint over them.

I get up, walk away from the table and dump my plate and cup on the trolley. The counselor tables have one topic tonight: our not-so-friendly graffiti artist. Some think it's a bad joke; others are horrified. One thing we all agree on is that they went too far.

With a prank you should be able to laugh. No one is laughing at a creepy message smeared on a wall in blood-red paint.

"Esme, wait up," Kayla says. She runs after me as I head to our cabin. I wanted a few minutes to myself before the guitar lessons by the campfire tonight.

"Yeah?" I say, folding my arms.

Sighing, she tilts her head. "Are you okay?"

Oh, now she's concerned for me.

"Yep. You?"

"I know what you're thinking. That the message was for us."

I look over her shoulder to check that no one else is coming outside and duck into our cabin. Kayla is hot on my heels.

"How can you not?" I ask.

"It's a weird message to leave."

"That's not what I asked, Kayla."

"Okay." She throws her hands up. "Okay, I'll admit it. Maybe you were right and it was for us. Bad girls and the lake never forgets." She shudders. "Who could it be? Lillian? No one else knows."

I arch one eyebrow. "We can't be sure. Lillian could have told someone what happened that night. Or maybe someone saw."

"What about the man Ava thought she saw in the forest? Maybe it was him."

I bite my lip and sit on the bottom bunk. "The man in the forest could have easily been a woman. Ava only assumed it was a man. Lillian could be out there watching the same way she was ten years ago." A shiver rips through my body. "She likes to keep to the shadows, remember?"

"I can't forget," Kayla replies. "But why would she say the lake never forgets instead of '*I* will never forget'?"

"I don't understand her shady mind! She's obviously trying to freak us out without advertising what happened."

"Why?"

I shake my head, then stop dead as a realization slams into my mind.

Oh no.

My hands shake. "Because she isn't finished. This is just the start. Think about it, if she wants revenge it would be dissatisfying to come out and tell everyone what happened straightaway. Proper revenge is messing with someone's head, ruining their life *before* the big reveal."

"I think you need to get some sleep."

I grit my teeth. "Kayla, don't play dumb. You want to pretend, but we both know you can't, so let's move past that. Okay? This is happening and we need to figure out what Lillian wants."

Kayla sighs and slumps onto the bed. Her glossy blond hair falls in her face. "Esme, I don't want this to take over our experience here if it doesn't have to. You can't be *sure*, and you're going to let it become an obsession."

My obsessions used to be fun. There were my One Direction, piano, *Riverdale* and, most recently, adult coloring book phases. I should have brought some coloring books with me. I'm not even sure my mom's Valium would help at this point.

"If someone is out there and they're trying to mess with us, we need to deal with that. Lillian has every right to be angry with us," I say.

"Unless she *did* run and you're freaking out over nothing!"

I want to curl up inside myself. "After . . . what happened, I tried to look back once the fire spread, but I couldn't see through the flames. I wanted to be sure, but we ran back to camp. I don't know what happened to Lillian next."

"Do you even understand what you're implying?"

"Yes. Maybe . . . she was *really* hurt."

Kayla's eyes are big and full of concern. "I think you should have an early night, Esme. You're pale and you have dark circles under your eyes. I'll tell everyone that you have a headache."

I tap my fingers under my eyes. "No, I'm fine."

"You're not! I can see this on your mind all of the time! Sleep!"

"I get eight hours a night, Kayla. I don't need more rest."

Okay, it's more like six hours, but that's still enough. It's more than I used to get around exam time when I'd cram in last-minute studying until midnight.

"Maybe we can arrange for you to see one of the counselors?"

My jaw drops. "Are you serious? You don't believe me?"

"I'm not saying that. I think you're right and someone *is* pranking us, but I don't think there's anything more to it than that."

"But what if there *is* more to it?"

Kayla tilts her head the way you do when you think someone is ridiculous. "Like what?"

"Like it's Lillian and she wants us to pay!"

"For what? We didn't do anything to her. If anything, it was *her* fault."

Her words chip away at my sanity. Kayla is mostly right, I suppose.

"Hey, it's okay. I understand why you think all this stuff, Esme. You just want to protect us."

"I want to come into town with you guys tonight."

Kayla stands up and sighs. "If you promise to rest now, I'll wake you before we go."

"Thanks."

She leaves the room, and I climb up to my bunk and settle in.

I close my eyes, listening to the faint sound of terrible guitar playing and laughter.

They all sound so happy out there, without a care in the world.

Sighing, I turn onto my side and take my cell from under my pillow. Maybe I can find Lillian on social media. All I know is her name and that she lives around here. That might not be enough, especially if she doesn't state exactly where she lives, but it's worth a try. If I can get in contact with her, then maybe I can fix whatever she's angry about.

If there even is anything.

This still could all be random, just bored kids from town looking to get their kicks by spooking the campers.

I commit each face of a girl named Lillian who lives in this area to memory. None of them look like the girl who Kayla and I saw ten years ago, but yeah, ten years is a long time. She could have changed a lot, dyed her hair, gained or lost weight.

Kayla will worry if she knows I'm still obsessing, but I hate that we've potentially hurt someone. Whatever really happened that night, I want to make it right.

An hour later, the cabin fills with girls. I listen as they chat excitedly about the guitar lesson. I didn't hear anyone playing well, but that's the point of learning, right? You're terrible until you're not.

Kayla creeps into our room and whispers, "You awake, Esme?"

I sit up. "Yep."

"You feeling better?"

She asks that as if I've been ill. There is nothing wrong with me. "Much better," I say to appease her. "Is Andy in his cabin?"

"Yeah, and the counselors with the night off are all in the staff cabin playing cards. They invited us, but Tia said we wanted to take a walk and then use the multiuse cabin for dodgeball. I was sure they were going to bust us then. Who *wants* to play dodgeball?"

"It's good for aggression," I say, and climb down the ladder.

"Are you feeling aggressive?"

"What? No. I was just saying. I don't want to play dodgeball. I want to kick your ass at air hockey."

"As if."

I grab my jacket and pop my cell in my pocket. "Let's go."

I'd be lying if I said I wasn't slightly nervous that we're finally doing this, but a rush of adrenaline keeps telling me it's a good idea.

Even if I don't find Lillian maybe I'll experience this little thing called fun. I'm in dire need of getting away from camp for a while. The isolation could be the reason for my latest stretch of paranoia.

Everything is worse when you're trapped.

16

Olly, Jake, Tia and Rebekah are waiting by the multiuse cabin, which is the closest to the man-made path between town and camp. It isn't really a path, but instead a thin strip of mud that's been trampled down.

We're all assuming it was made by CITs wanting to get out for the night. No one but me—*hello*—seems to think it could also be used by people from town coming in.

"Your headache gone?" Olly asks. He steps close to me.

"Yep, I feel great."

"Let's go then!" Tia cheers quietly.

"We're doing a lap of the lake first, right?" I ask. "The counselors think we're going for a walk."

Rebekah nods. "Good idea, Esme. Let's make it look like we're good little CITs."

She looks happier now than I've seen her since we arrived.

I link arms with her as we walk, despite wanting to be near Olly.

"How are you doing?" I ask.

She smiles tightly. "Me? Oh, I'm fine. This is cool and scary. Should I be scared? Are you?"

Laughing, I nudge her with my shoulder. "Breathe. No one has ever come checking on us before. There's no reason why they would now."

"That's true. I still feel like a criminal, though."

"Actually, it's not a crime what we're doing," I inform her.

We do one lap and stop by the shrubs that are doing a poor job of hiding the sneaky little trail. Kayla and Tia are animated, talking loud and fast.

I look over my shoulder. The camp looks deserted, like one of those creepy abandoned theme parks, but without the roller coasters. Above the lake a large bird glides in a circle and crows.

"Let's get out of here," Jake says. "Coast is clear."

He ducks between the bushes and Kayla follows straightaway. Rebekah takes a breath, but she doesn't have time to chicken out: Tia grabs her hand and pulls her along.

"Shall we?" Olly asks, nodding to the trail.

Biting my lip, I grab his hand and we disappear into the bushes.

He doesn't let go of me, and I'm not about to complain. His hand is warm; his grip firm yet gentle. He feels safe, which is nice since I haven't felt that today.

We walk quickly through the forest. Jake has a flashlight, but he's keeping it low to the ground in case anyone sees us. It's not that dark, but as we go deeper, we lose a lot of light.

The temperature has dropped to a comfortable heat, and I find myself smiling in the darkness.

This is what I'd hoped camp would be: hanging out with new friends and doing something fun. Olly squeezes my hand as we come out the other side of the forest. Across the quiet road is the teeny town. It's quaint and cute. From here, the streetlights make it look prettier, like the town is dotted with fairy lights.

"Okay, there's a little arcade on the outskirts. They have Rollerblading too, if anyone wants to break an ankle," Tia says.

"I'll pass," I reply as we cross the deserted road.

Kayla's eyes dart from my and Olly's joined hands to my eyes. *Don't say anything!*

She presses her lips together, stifling a smile. Tia nudges Rebekah.

Great, everyone has seen.

Olly either doesn't notice or doesn't care that we're being watched.

"Lead us to the arcade then, Tia," Jake says. "I'm dying for a drink."

I want to ask how he's going to get a drink, but my filter kicks in before I open my mouth. Yay for that. There might not even be a bar or restaurant nearby.

Fake IDs are a thing and Jake, being one of the popular kids at his school, is likely to have one. Kayla and I thought about it once, but we were both too scared to buy one from Mason, the dude at school with a supersketchy private life.

"Easy, Esme," Olly says, shaking our joined hands.

I release my death grip a smidge. "Sorry, didn't realize I was squeezing."

I'm not sure what I expected, but a run-down arcade on the very edge of town was not it. The place is huge, but the games are old, and the patterned red carpet is so worn in areas there are bald patches.

"Right," Tia says. "It's . . . nice."

Jake laughs. "It's not Vegas, but it'll do."

"Come on, Esme, I'm challenging you to a game of table hockey," Olly says.

"Does anyone even have cash?" Rebekah asks, looking around as if we could be busted at any moment.

She and Tia follow closely behind us. Jake and Kayla stop by a claw machine to try to win a stuffed animal.

"I do, but I need change," Olly replies.

Tia grabs Rebekah's hand. "I already have change. Come on, Rebekah, I see Pac-Man and I'm awesome!"

Rebekah follows without a word.

"This has always been my favorite game," Olly tells me as he picks up a puck.

"Mine is the claw."

He looks up from across the table. "You know they're rigged, right?"

"Yes, but it's so satisfying when you finally win."

"After twenty dollars."

I roll my eyes. "Okay, so once my dad did spend twenty-three dollars before we got a prize, but I still have that little stuffed pony."

"Your dad rich or just enjoy burning money?"

Laughing, I grab the other puck and send it flying to his side.

"He's never been very good at saying no to me, and I wanted that pony more than anything," I say.

I glance up quickly as Olly positions himself to hit the puck back to me.

The chances of Lillian being in here are small. What is she doing, messing with camp by day and hitting the dance mat by night? There is a chance, though. In this small town, there isn't a lot to do.

Olly and I play two games, each winning one, and then we move on.

"Olly," Jake calls, "basketball!"

He's standing with Tia and Kayla.

"I'm going to see if Rebekah is okay," I tell Olly. "I'll meet you over there."

He walks off to the basketball hoops and I split, heading to Rebekah. She's in a corner with her back to the room and her hands up to her face.

"No, they don't know . . . ," she mutters.

Is she talking to herself?

"Rebekah?" I ask.

Startled, she jolts and spins in my direction. One hand clutches tightly around her cell phone.

"Sorry, I didn't know you were on a call," I say.

"Esme." She smiles and her finger hits a button on the screen. "It's okay, I was just speakin' to my mom. She worries if she doesn't hear from me."

What did she say? *They don't know.* Who doesn't know what?

"Shouldn't you call her back? My mom would go crazy if I hung up on her."

Shrugging, Rebekah tilts the screen so I can't see. "I'll send her a message. We were almost done anyway."

I watch her tap away and then she slides the phone in her pocket. "Okay. Hey, you want to play Whac-A-Mole?" she asks.

"Sure."

"So, are you havin' fun?" she asks, glancing behind us.

I follow her line of sight and there is no one there. "Yeah. You?"

"Yep. Tia and I played a couple games and then she wanted to find Jake and Kayla. I don't think she enjoys my company that much."

I start the game and pick up the giant spongy hammer. "Of course she does. She probably saw some girl she likes and went to talk to her."

"Thanks, Esme, but I saw her with Jake and Kayla two seconds later. I'm not the most fun person, I know that."

We whack moles, Rebekah as if she's actually trying to kill them, teeth bared and eyes narrowed. I wouldn't like to be on the end of her anger.

Her phone buzzes in her pocket, but she continues hitting moles.

"Don't say that," I tell her. "I thought we were all having fun together. It wouldn't be the same without you."

"Thank you," she says quietly. With a frown, she adds, "You're so *nice*."

We spend an hour at the arcade, and I have the face of every person in here memorized. I age them, or rather de-age them ten years and none look like Lillian.

She isn't here unless she's had facial reconstruction.

"We should get back," Jake says. "It's been almost two hours."

When we get closer to the entrance, my heart stutters. On the sidewalk, right outside the open door, is a blond girl, around twenty. Suddenly, she whips around and runs.

I do a double take, my pulse racing.

Lillian?

"Let's go now," I say, jogging outside.

"Esme!" Kayla calls after me.

I hear their footsteps close behind.

The slightly cooler dry air hits my face. I whip my head in both directions.

Rebekah steps in front of me. "Esme, are you okay?"

"I'm fine. I needed air."

"All good?" Olly asks.

I take one more look around, but there's nothing in the empty parking lot. "Yep, let's get back to camp."

Was that her waiting outside the arcade. Watching us?

17

Rebekah dashes across the road, calling, "Let's go before Andy realizes we're gone!"

"Where's the fire, Rebekah?" Tia says, running after her.

We cross the road and race into the forest.

They're running so Andy won't realize we're gone. I'm running from Lillian.

Dry grass and sticks crunch beneath our feet.

"How much further?" Rebekah asks.

"We've only been in the forest for five minutes," Tia replies.

It took us about twenty minutes to reach the road from camp. It's darker now because we're not using the flashlight, and we're slower. The last thing we need is someone noticing us.

"I hate this part. What if we make too much noise gettin' back into the cabins?" Rebekah says.

"Don't," Olly replies.

I nudge his side. "Unhelpful. Just say you were going to the bathroom and heard a noise outside."

Olly grins. "Ooh, I like it, Esme. You're good at being sneaky."

"Is that a compliment?"

I can just about make out Kayla looking over her shoulder at me.

"It is," he replies.

To the left of us something flashes, lighting up the forest like freaking fireworks. I blink and a dot of white dances in front of my eyes.

"What the hell was that?" Jake says, whipping the flashlight from his pocket and turning it on. He shines it in the direction of the flash.

I gasp, my free hand flying to my throat. "Was that a *camera?*"

Another flash.

"Shit, it is!" Olly hisses.

"Who's there?" Jake calls.

I push against Olly, my hands shaking. "We need to go *now!*"

"Shh, Esme."

"Someone is taking our picture!"

Another blinding flash.

"Go!" Jake snaps, turning around and running in the direction of camp. He's holding Kayla's hand and practically dragging her. We all take off after him.

We sprint single file, and I wince every time another flash of light hits the forest and casts long shadows between the trees.

My stomach churns.

I push my legs to go faster and faster to keep up with the others.

The forest lights up again. My pulse is thudding loudly in my ears.

Someone is taking photos of us.

Another light makes me gasp again and turns my blood to ice. What if the next flash reveals the person behind it? If they're standing between the trees we'd only see them when the flash went off.

I want to know who it is, but I'm also scared to know.

"Almost there!" Jake snaps in something between a shout and a whisper.

If I fall over now, I'm going to kick myself.

I dart between two trees behind Rebekah. Olly's footsteps are thundering right behind me. My thighs scream in protest of the pace I'm keeping.

I ignore the pain and press on, gulping air and trying to remember if you should breathe in through your nose and out through your mouth when you're running or the other way around.

"Go, go!" Olly says, putting one hand on my lower back.

I push harder, gritting my teeth. My legs feel like they're going to snap off. We burst from between the shrubs and run along the forest, toward the cabins.

The flashes stop abruptly.

Jake slows and turns. I almost run into Tia as everyone else slows down too.

"What?" I ask, bending over to catch my breath.

Olly and Jake exchange a look, one that turns their faces red with anger and makes me flinch.

"Oh no. You cannot go back," I tell them. Are they crazy?

Their male pride has been hurt. We were chased out of the

woods by someone with a camera. But it's not like we can afford to be caught. Andy wouldn't be too happy that we went to town in the middle of the night.

He's big on responsibilities, and he has one to keep us safe, too.

Olly's jaw clenches in the dim light of the wood lamppost. "We can't let whoever that was get away with it."

"Why would they want photos of us anyway?" Rebekah asks. "What were they trying to do?"

"I intend to find out," Jake replies.

Kayla puts her palms on Jake's chest. "Wait up a second. We don't know who it is or what they're capable of. They might be dangerous."

"Me and Olly can take him."

I throw my hands up, annoyed with all the testosterone flying around. "And if he has a gun? You stronger than a bullet, Jake? Let's go inside and pretend this never happened."

She could have just been trying to scare us.

It was a success.

"It's probably just someone trying to freak us out," I say.

"Esme is right," says Tia, backing me up. She points toward the forest. "We don't know what that person is capable of. It's most likely that he was there to freak us out, but I don't want to take that chance. Do you?"

Jake growls a no that sounds like it wounds his ego, while Olly grits his teeth.

Tia shakes her head. "What if they send the pictures to Andy?"

"Even if they do, all they got is us running through the forest and we told everyone we were going for a walk."

"That's true," Kayla says.

"Let's just go to bed, I'm over it," Jake mutters.

I take Olly's hand and he grips mine tight. I'm just happy to help calm him down. "Hey," I say, leaning against him. "It was just some crazy guy in the woods. We don't need to get mixed up in whatever he was doing."

Olly's green-and-blue eyes slide very slowly to mine as if he needs a second before dealing with me. My mom did the same thing when I was nine and I accidentally smashed her very expensive eye shadow palette.

"If he comes back . . ."

I nod. "Then you can kick his ass."

Rebekah peers over her shoulder and into the forest. "Can we please get to bed before someone hears us out here?"

We split up and head to our cabins. The boys' cabin is closest, but Olly and Jake stand on the porch, watching us get inside safely before they go inside. *That is so cute!*

Rebekah and Tia tiptoe into their cabin and close the door.

I can hear my ragged breathing as we walk up to our door. Kayla and I walk up the two steps at the same time, carefully placing our feet in case the wood creaks. I look back at Olly and Jake as Kayla slowly turns the door handle.

With a quick wave to the boys, I turn and slide through the small opening. Kayla didn't open the door wide; I'm guessing so the light from outside wouldn't creep in.

The room is filled with heavy breathing and soft snoring. I glance at each of the bunk beds in the large room. The girls are all very still. It's sometime after one in the morning.

Kayla and I pad into our room. We undress in silence; I clumsily pull my pajamas on and climb up to my bunk quickly and quietly. Neither of us speak. We usually say good night, but tonight we're too scared.

Lying on my back, I replay the events of the forest in my head. I can't remember exactly how many flashes—photos—there were, but it was a lot.

Somebody wants evidence that we snuck out.

Evidence that Kayla and I snuck out.

Like we did ten years ago.

18

Edge, meet Esme. Yep, I'm on it, the edge, in a major way.

It's morning and no one but me is acting strange. Andy is his usual self, which tells us he has no idea what we were up to last night. But still, I can't calm down.

Every time a noise comes from the woods, I jump. Which is freaking often since the kids are collecting sticks and branches to make dens.

Olly and Jake are with some of the other guys, lugging larger branches for the structural parts of the dens. Once each group has four large branches and a bunch of medium and small ones, they have to make their own den and it needs to stay upright.

It's a little challenge that Andy told the campers about over breakfast, and it's caused a lot of excitement.

I haven't spoken to anyone about last night yet, not even Kayla. We haven't had any time alone, and to be honest, I don't think anyone wants to relive it.

In the cold light of day, we seem a bit dramatic, not even asking whoever it was to show themselves. We all ran as if we were being chased by zombies. Not that I was ever going to ask the cameraman if he wanted to chat over an iced tea.

My little group of four are piling up medium sticks on the beach.

Andy stops beside me with his clipboard. "Good haul," he says. "Looks almost there."

"Yeah, I sent them on one last trip."

"Excellent. How are you today?" he asks.

My heart misses a beat. I blink heavily. What does he know? "I'm fine, thanks," I croak. "How are you?"

He smiles. "I'm well. Are you ready for a day of camp building and fire lighting?"

"I am."

Dipping his chin in a curt nod, he says, "Well, shout if you need anything."

I watch him walk off and my tense shoulders relax a fraction. If Andy knew we had snuck out he would definitely say something. I don't know why I'm so jumpy around him. He's the kind of guy who sorts things out right away, not someone who waits and sees how it goes. We would have all been in the staff cabin first thing. Hell, he would have had us in there the second we got back in the very early hours.

Inhale, exhale, act normal.

Guilt doesn't feel good on me. It's a shame I can't remember a time before it.

I watch my girls carry back armfuls of sticks that are about as long as their legs. "Well done, girls. I think we're ready."

They wait with me. I'm not allowed to leave the beach because I'm in charge of making sure all the groups have enough sticks and that the campers who dump them here don't wander off.

A little bit ironic that I'm in charge of keeping them out of trouble when I can't even manage to do that myself. Still, what Andy doesn't know . . .

When everyone else gets back from gathering wood, Andy instructs the groups about what they will need and sends each merged group of eight to different parts of the forest.

Cora and I follow eight massively hyper girls who are bouncing, dropping sticks and talking a million miles an hour. I bend down and pick up another dropped stick.

"What did you do with your night off?" Cora asks, brushing one hand over her smooth ponytail.

It's an innocent enough question, but my mouth goes dry in a nanosecond.

"We just went for a walk."

"Yeah, there isn't much to do. When I was a CIT, I think I played Go Fish about a thousand times. I was so jealous of counselors who could get dressed up and go out for the evening."

My hand tightens around the stick. "Maybe next year I'll get to go out."

"Oh, you think you'll come back next year, then? To here or somewhere else?"

"I like it here," I tell Cora, even though I'm almost positive I will never return. I love camps, but this one has way too much baggage.

"That's great, Esme. I love it when I hear that people want to return. You're so good with the girls and they all love you."

We're halfway to our designated den area, the furthest from camp.

"Okay, girls," Cora says, and launches into instructions.

We can use whichever trees we want in our area and the den has to be big enough for all the girls to sit under.

Cora and I help them with the large logs since it took four girls on each end to carry them up here. Why we weren't just sent to our zone to collect sticks there, I do not know. Andy might have some control issues, wanting to see each freaking stick before we took them away to use. Or maybe he was promoting teamwork, getting everyone together to gather the most suitable materials for everyone to use.

"Ew, look," Alana says, pointing to a collection of cigarette butts on the ground.

I bend down and count five of them. "No one here smokes, right?"

Cora folds her arms. "They're not supposed to."

Alarm bells chime a very loud song in my head: It's the creepy cameraperson!

This was the direction that we came last night. Did they stick around and watch us? But who hangs around long enough to smoke five cigarettes when everyone has already gone inside?

Unless this isn't the first time they've watched.

"That's not safe," Isabel says.

"You're right," I tell her, collecting the butts and trying not to gag. Someone's mouth has touched them. "I'm going to throw them in the trash and disinfect my hands."

"Will you let Andy know too, please?" Cora asks.

"Sure thing."

The second I turn around, the girls have forgotten. Cora gets them on task and they fuss over which sticks to use first.

At least our phantom smoker had the good sense to properly extinguish the cigarettes. They're almost flat they've been stomped into the ground so hard.

I walk back toward the cabins in the thick heat.

"Found these by our den," I tell Andy, opening my hand so he can see what I'm holding. Then I dump them in a trash can near the multiuse cabin where he's scribbling something on his clipboard.

His frown makes his whole forehead crumble. "Who's been smoking?"

I shrug. "I'm not sure. Us CITs walked around last night, but no one smoked, and we didn't see any counselors doing it either."

Sighing, Andy nods. "Okay, I'll have to make sure I speak with each staff member today and remind them that it's forbidden to smoke on campgrounds. And in the forest too," he grumbles, tutting. "Thanks for cleaning them up, Esme."

"No problem."

"There's someone there! There's someone there!" Isabel screams.

My head whips in her direction. She's pointing into the forest.

Cora steps in front of the girls, her head bent forward as she tries to get a better look.

Jake and Olly are running toward them. Andy and I take off too, with him shouting at everyone else to stay where they are.

"Mary, watch the campers," he says as we pass her.

"Where?" I ask when we reach Cora. I've got a stitch in my side and ice in my heart.

There has to be someone out there watching us. Ava's sighting in the woods, the creepy message, the pictures that were taken.

Kayla can't explain it away with coincidences. Lillian is trying to mess with us.

Olly and Jake are in the forest, and spread a little too far apart for my liking. Does safety in numbers mean nothing to them?

Andy follows them as Mary looks at us from the other side of the lake.

I put my arm around Isabel. Her slender frame is shaking. "Hey, it's okay," I tell her. "Remember, we don't own all of this forest."

She looks up at me with fear in her eyes. "He was walking."

"Toward us?"

"Um, kind of, I think. I saw the side of his face."

Cora turns. "It was definitely a man?"

Isabel nods. "I think so. I couldn't see his face very well."

Translation: It could have been a woman or a man.

"Okay." I look at the twelve girls huddled together. "Look, there is no reason to be alarmed. I'm sure people go on hikes all the time out here and not everyone pays as much attention as they should. Sometimes they miss the sign saying this is private property. I'm sure Jake and Olly will find him and remind him that he shouldn't be here."

Biting my lip, I watch the spot in the forest where the boys disappeared.

Five tense minutes later and my arm is still around Isabel. No one is building anything, and I can't take my eyes off the last place I saw Olly.

"All right," Cora says. "I think we should all get back to camp and wait."

She takes out her walkie-talkie and speaks to the other counselors, who are dotted around the forest.

"We all agree," she says, finally putting the device away. "We're going to go into the food hall and grab a snack until the guys get back."

"Good idea," I say. "Come on, girls, who needs some sugar?"

They cheer, but their hearts aren't quite in it.

Cora and I walk behind them, slowly joining the other groups as we all trudge back.

My heart flutters wildly and my stomach sinks. Am I going to have to tell everyone what happened? Maybe Kayla and I should leave.

I should have thrown that damn pamphlet in the trash.

"It's okay, Esme," Cora says. "This happens sometimes. I swear some people think they're above the rules. If a sign says private property, keep off, you damn well keep off!" She shakes her head.

"Now our activity has been interrupted, and I don't think the girls are going to want to go back out there today."

I can't blame them. I don't want to go back out there either.

We enter the food hall and gossip flies as quickly as the candy wrappers. At least the campers are all happy with a midmorning treat.

I wash my hands and then sit at a table with Kayla, Rebekah and Tia.

"This is crazy!" Tia says. "So much drama over a dude getting lost on a trail."

Rebekah's mouth pops open. "After last night you're seriously trying to make this sound random?"

"Oh, come on, you're not telling me you think that guy was here to pick us off one by one?"

"Okay, I wasn't thinking we're in danger like *that*," Rebekah says.

"What are you thinking?" I ask, desperate for other options that don't involve Kayla and me.

"He's a weird dude who gets his kicks from people watching," she says.

"He's watching a camp full of *children*!" Kayla squeals.

"No, he was watching *us*. Same as last night, and he wrote on the *staff* cabin. The dude is here to freak *us* out, not them. What's scarier than having to deal with something like that all while making sure the children don't worry?" I say.

"Esme's right," Rebekah says. "This is about the counselors. Do you think he could have been one?"

"A disgruntled counselor from the past. Maybe he did something and was made to leave," I say. "He might think that he was treated unfairly."

Rebekah nods. "Kayla and Esme, you've been here before. Anyone you can think of?"

I can't be sure, but I think I sense an edge to her voice.

"No," we reply in unison.

I swallow and add, "We wouldn't have known about any issues with the counselors. You know how well we hide that from the campers. This guy saw us out there doing a job he thinks he should still be allowed to do."

"You two are getting ahead of yourself," Tia says. "It might not be that."

"Maybe, but it's possible," I reply. "Cora?"

She looks over from where she's sitting with a few other counselors and immediately gets up.

"What's up?" she asks.

I tell her our theory and she sits down at our table. "Okay. That's a possibility. I don't like that we've had two sightings of someone in the woods, trails tampered with, and cigarette butts left. Andy radioed a moment ago; he and the guys haven't found anything, so they're coming back. Andy is going to head into town and talk to the cops to see where we stand."

"Whoa, you think we need to involve the cops?" Rebekah asks.

"We're responsible for the safety of children, so we have to. Even if Andy just files a report. Sometimes the police will ask him to put a post on the camp's Facebook page about the land being private and they share it. I'll speak with him when he gets back and see if he can think of any counselors or CITs who left on bad terms. I know I don't need to say this . . . but not a word of this in front of the kids, okay?"

She gets up and goes back to her table, leaning in and whispering to the rest of the counselors, telling them our theory.

So, we're running with this one. Going for the angry ex-staff member. I like it, and I want it to be true.

It certainly fits better than the Lillian thing. I mean, she isn't a dude and the motive is weak.

This isn't Lillian and it's not about what Kayla and I did ten years ago.

It can't be.

19

Olly and Jake walk into the food hall as Cora walks out to meet Andy.

I sit taller when they reach us. "What happened?"

Jake turns to address the room.

"Everything is okay. We caught up with the guy; he'd taken a wrong turn on a trail from the other side of town. He was apologetic, and we helped him get back to where he needs to be."

"He's gone?" one of the boys asks from across the room.

"Yeah, he didn't mean to be here in the first place."

The room erupts with chatter again, this time voices are higher and filled with laughter and about Olly and Jake chasing away the "stalker man."

Olly sits close to me, his arm pressing against mine.

"That's great," I say.

Olly subtly shakes his head.

"It's not?" Rebekah asks.

I sink into my seat, understanding. "You were just saying that so they wouldn't worry."

Jake rubs his jaw. "It was Andy's idea. I'm going to go and tell the other counselors."

He walks away, heading to Mary's packed table first.

I place my clammy palms on my knees. "What happened?"

Olly clears his throat. "We couldn't find anyone. But we did find a box of matches that he must have dropped."

"Esme has a theory that it's someone who worked here and was fired or whatever, since this guy seems to only be messing with the counselors," Rebekah says.

Olly glances at me, smiling. "Good one, Esme."

"Cora is telling Andy."

"This jackass is going to get hurt if he comes back here again. Did Isabel mention anything about a weapon?" Olly asks.

"What?" Kayla hisses.

"Last night you didn't want me and Jake to go after him because we couldn't be sure he wasn't armed," Olly says.

"She didn't say anything about a gun, but that doesn't mean he didn't have one. It could be concealed," I tell them.

Olly leans back, effectively ending our little arm cuddle. I do my best not to pout.

"This is insane. I came here to help kids have an awesome summer," he says, shaking his head. "I didn't sign up for some freak in the woods."

"I'm sure the cops will do something now," Kayla says.

Tia huffs. "What can they do? We don't know who it is or why he's doing this."

"Andy will have records of who's worked here and how they left. They'll start there," I say, backing Kayla up, although I'm not at all convinced there is anything the cops can do.

We have two sightings of a man, one of which was uncertain and possibly a tree. We can hardly say we were chased through the forest at one a.m. by someone taking our picture.

Still, the police might take it seriously because there are children here.

"What's the relationship like between camp and town?" I ask.

Tia shrugs. "I don't know, why?"

"Well, my cousin was a counselor at a camp in Michigan and said that the camp and local community hated each other," I say. "The town was mad because of the noise or something stupid like that. There were arguments and a lot of bad blood between staff and residents."

"Where are you going with this?" Olly asks.

I shrug. "I just wondered if it could be someone from town. Andy visits, so they know him and maybe someone there is tired of staff getting wild in their town. Did you hear that Cora and the others go drinking there?"

Tia ties her hair into a bun on top of her head. "Ugh, I wish we could go drinking."

I ignore her. "Maybe someone has a grudge against Andy?"

Olly leans forward. "Maybe."

He doesn't sound like he believes me. But it's a totally plausible explanation for the strange things happening around here.

So is Lillian.

"What do you think?" I ask him.

"I have no idea, Esme." Olly looks away, toward the table of food. "I need something to eat."

I watch him with narrowed eyes as he gets up and walks away.

Rebekah's eyes slide from Olly's vacant chair to me. "That was odd."

I turn to her. "What do you think?"

"Well, I think the same as you. Maybe someone in town is annoyed with the camp. We're close to town. They can probably hear us sometimes, smell smoke from our campfires if the wind is in the right direction."

"We should find out if there is a grudge. Maybe Andy has been invited to town meetings or something," I say.

"How would we find that out?" she asks.

Tia rolls her eyes. "We ask him."

Such a simple response.

"I vote Esme has that discussion with him," Kayla says.

"Why me?"

She arches a plucked brow. "You're the one who's going full Sherlock."

"I'm not," I defend weakly. "Don't you want to know who's behind the graffiti?"

"I can sleep without knowing who's been turning innocent pranks creepy. Now, if I wake up to find a bloody deer head on my pillow, I want to know."

How can Kayla say that?

Has she forgotten all about the note we found in her jacket pocket?

Despite my best attempts at distracting myself with theories, the more I think about it, the more I think Lillian *is* behind this.

Why else would this all be happening now?

20

Andy wanted a full staff meeting. It turns out that's no simple task.

So here we are, hours later, *finally* sitting outside the cabins at ten-thirty at night. The children are tucked up in bed and snoring.

We're in a circle. I'd like to think that's because we all want to be involved, but really, it has more to do with the fact that we have eyes in every direction around camp this way.

Let's say hello to pessimistic Esme.

As the meeting starts, I plan how to catch Andy after and ask about the camp's relationship with town.

Andy speaks in a low voice so we can hear but not be overheard.

"What are the cops doing?" Cora asks as he finishes explaining that they didn't find anyone in the woods.

"They're going to look into some names I've given them."

"Who are they?"

He dips his head. "I can't say. Both worked as counselors be-fore any of you started. Both left on unhappy terms."

"Can you tell us what those terms were?" Jake asks. He and Kayla are sitting side by side, holding hands. She hasn't told me that anything happened between them, but it sure looks *on* now.

Andy presses his mouth into a thin line before he looks at Jake. "I'm sorry, I can't. But rest assured that the police will speak with both of them in person. For now, we're going to make sure that groups are doubled up. CITs *must* be with their coun-selor when doing any activity with the campers. We're cancel-ling our hike this week, unless the police have good news, so we'll have kayak races, extra swimming time and cooking lessons instead."

"Should we inform parents?" Mary asks.

"The police didn't seem to think the campers are in danger and neither do I, but we have to take it seriously. We will inform parents if there is another sighting or any evidence that he's been back. Security will be upped, no campers will be allowed to go into the cabins alone, and we'll remain vigilant at all times. For now, we just need to carry on as we are and make their summer the best it can be."

My stomach twists with unease.

"I'm glad the cops don't think the campers are in danger," Rebekah says.

"But are *we*?" Tia asks.

I hold my breath.

"I really don't think so. There's a big leap between wanting to frighten people and wanting to harm them. The two suspects never showed any signs of violence and were let go for a number of minor grievances," Andy replies.

But let's face it, it's not the two former staff members who are doing this.

Rebekah curls her arms around her body and nods.

"Everyone stays in their cabins tonight. Does anyone have any other questions?" Andy asks. No one says a word. "Right, let's all get some sleep."

I stand and turn to Olly. "Are you okay?" he asks, brushing his knuckles along my jaw. His fingers leave a warm trail behind them.

Don't faint!

"I'm all right. This is all a bit scary, though."

"You'll be fine, Esme. I'll watch you go into your cabin."

"Thanks. Night."

He smiles. "Night."

I link Rebekah's arm with mine as we walk toward the girls' cabins. "You okay?"

She looks straight ahead, nibbling her lip. "Yeah, I guess. I'll see ya in the mornin'."

"Yeah."

"You doing this?" Kayla whispers to me as we walk on to our cabin.

I look back and locate Andy. What choice do I have? Everyone has volunteered me. "Yeah, I'll be there in a minute."

"Esme?" Cora asks when I stop following her.

"Oh, I just need to speak to Andy real quick, then I'll be right in."

She nods and follows Kayla into our cabin.

"Esme, is there a problem?" Andy asks.

"I just wondered about the graffiti and the guy in the woods. Could it be someone from town? I know a lot of camps don't have the warmest and fuzziest relationship with nearby towns."

He frowns. "We've had a few small issues, but nothing too bad. I can't see why a local would want to do this."

"How small were the issues? Maybe a local thinks they're major?"

"Yes, perhaps they might. I'll mention it to the police," Andy says.

Wow, he really isn't going to tell me what these "issues" are.

"Are you going into town now?" I ask.

It's a small town; there is no way the police station will still be open.

"No, I have a contact I can call," Andy says.

"Good."

He smiles and his thin lips disappear. "Great thinking, Esme. You're smart."

"Er, thanks," I reply.

"Get some sleep. And don't worry—I'll sort this out."

He turns and walks away. *Don't worry?* Sounds like Andy *really* doesn't know me at all. My nan, my mom and I are Olympic-level worriers.

I sneak into the cabin, tiptoe through the main room and climb up to my bunk. My body is heavy and aches. I sink into the mattress and sigh. Every part of me is tired.

"You all right?" Kayla whispers in the darkness.

I left our door wide open so we can see and hear the campers.

"I am, but I don't think Rebekah is," I say, keeping my voice quiet. "We should check on her first thing."

"What's wrong with her?" Kayla asks.

"I don't know, but she seems really scared. During the meeting she looked like she wanted to hide, and she was chewing on her lip and staring when we walked back to the cabins. I know that she was bullied in school, and I've noticed that when someone disagrees with her, even nicely, she tends to go inside herself."

"You notice everything, Esme."

I turn onto my side and am confronted with something that steals my breath.

I stare, unblinking, until my eyes sting and water leaks from the corners.

No.

I suck in air as fear clutches my stomach in a vise-like grip.

Carved into the wall by my pillow are the letters *LC*.

They were not there before.

I freeze, staring at the letters while anxiety curls in my stomach.

Lillian Campbell.

I lick my dry lips and force my breath to slow down. In for five, out for five.

God no.

She has been in our room, in my *bed*. I want to jump out of the bunk, run away and never look back.

She was right here.

Nausea rolls my stomach.

Kayla is in bed. Do not freak out.

I reach out, my hand trembling as it gets closer to the wall. My index finger pokes into the rough scratches and loose shavings drop to the floor.

No.

Retracting my hand, I ball it into a fist.

My shoulders hunch.

What do I do now? Someone here besides me and Kayla knows what happened ten years ago. Maybe it's Lillian, or maybe it's someone else—someone she told or a witness we didn't know existed.

Ten years. That's a long time to carry anger.

"Esme?"

I clear my throat, but I'm unable to look away from Lillian's initials. It takes everything I have to keep my cool. "Yes, I notice things. And you only notice when cute guys are around."

"It's a talent, I have a cute-guy radar. Night, babe," Kayla says.

Her voice is barely audible over the shrill ringing in my ears.

"Night," I whisper as my shaking finger curls around the *C.*

Why am I not telling Kayla about this?

21

In the morning, we're in the lake. The sun shines brightly through a thin smattering of fluffy clouds. Andy thinks it's a good idea to keep the campers' minds off the person in the woods by switching our hike today with the water sports that were scheduled for later in the week.

My fingertips graze the lake's surface of the water. I know the water is smooth, but all I feel is the rough texture of the carved initials. Lillian has been in our room.

I'm in up to my knees watching my and Cora's group swim the length of the lake.

On the other side of the lake, four merged groups of boys are having a kayak-racing mini tournament. Andy said the winners will get extra s'mores, but we all know he'll let everyone have extra.

The inflatable water course is coming out soon. Some of the guys are setting it up.

The atmosphere is somewhat tense. The staff have information that the campers don't and it's making us slightly paranoid. Well, it's certainly making *me* paranoid.

If I had a dollar for everyone I witnessed looking at the forest, I could buy a beach house in Malibu.

"Keep going, girls, you're doing great," I call as they swim back to me. The trained instructors and lifeguards watch closely and occasionally tell one of the girls how to improve their stroke. Bless, some of them still look like they're drowning.

"Did you manage to speak to Rebekah?" Cora asks, staring ahead at the girls. Or maybe she's staring beyond them, into the trees. "Kayla mentioned at breakfast that you were worried about her last night."

"Not yet. She got up late. She seems okay now, though, cheering her girls on in the race," I say, blinking my heavy eyelids. I'm tired after last night and can barely focus on anything.

I remember how weird Rebekah was at the arcade. And the possible sighting of Lillian outside.

"Good," Cora says.

"Is it always like this? Not the 'someone's watching' thing, but are there always issues coming from all directions?"

She laughs. "Pretty much. How are you handling it?"

"It's slightly exhausting, but I'm much better at helping other people with their problems than I am with my own."

"You can talk about yours with me, if you want."

"Thanks, I'll keep that in mind."

Yeah, no. I don't think I'll be doing that. Talking to Kayla right now feels weird and we share everything. How would she react to the initials on the wall?

Not great.

I shiver at the thought of Lillian creeping up onto my bed and carving those letters. Was she snarling as she dug into the wood? Did she pretend she was cutting into me?

"It's good to talk, Esme," Cora tells me.

I clench my jaw. "I agree. I'm fine for now."

"You're a fixer."

"Sorry?"

Laughing, she turns to me. "You fix things for other people, you're good at it. Unfortunately, that usually ends with neglecting yourself."

Ugh, really? We're going there. I can't have her worrying about me or telling anyone that she has Esme concerns.

"I overthink," I tell her. "So right now I'm convinced that something bad is going on. Like, more than pranks."

"Ah. My sister is just the same. If I don't check in, she thinks I've drowned in the lake or something."

"That sounds like me."

"You care, that's not a bad thing. And bad stuff does happen at camps."

"What?"

"Accidents, I mean. We're doing games and sports in the water and in the woods, and that brings more dangers."

I gulp. "Has anything really bad happened here?"

"We've had a few near misses. Last year a kid got into trouble in the water and almost drowned. That's why we test their swimming ability before they get in and have the waist-high rule for non-swimmers. Another camper tripped over a branch when she wasn't looking and broke her ankle."

I'm looking for something more sinister. Besides, I don't think a camper is behind what's going on.

Lillian. Obviously. Hello, you have her initials carved into your wall!

"There's a shoe! Gross!" Ava shouts.

Cora and I look up.

Ava drops the shoe that she's holding back into the water. She and Addison back up.

"What?" I ask, wading over to her. The water hits my shorts. "A shoe?"

"Ugh," she mutters, and bends down, keeping her head above water as she reaches into the water. "Here."

I take the tennis shoe that was probably white once but is now green.

"Wonderful."

"You think someone threw that in?" Ava asks.

I nod. "Yep."

Addison's eyes widen. "I would be so mad if someone threw mine in the lake."

"Me too," I tell her. "Looks like it's been here a while, though, so it was probably from years ago." The shoe is slimy. "I'll chuck this. You two go catch up with the others. You're both doing so well."

"Thanks, Esme," they chime in unison.

They dive back into the water belly-first.

I manage to turn before I get a face full of water.

Holding the shoe by the heel with two fingers, I take it out of the lake and dump it in the trash.

Andy shakes his head. "I once found a T-shirt and a hairbrush in the lake."

"I guess it's not one big happy family all the time," I say.

"We have our fair share of arguments among the campers," he confirms. "It usually happens week three, when they really feel like they're family."

"A week of peace left."

"Enjoy it while it lasts," Andy replies.

"Have the cops got in contact yet?"

"Not yet. I called last night, and they said they'll keep me informed. I'll let you all know when I hear from them. No one has noticed anything so far today."

"The forest seems quiet," I say. Since I've been out here this morning not once has the hair on the back of my neck stood up.

"Let's hope it stays that way. The last thing the camp needs is a reputation for having a stalker lurking around. We're the best youth camp in the area and I intend to keep it that way."

"Are you worried?"

His red eyebrows meet in the middle. "No. Are you, Esme?"

Yes, I'm worried. I'm scared for the campers, I'm scared for Kayla and I'm scared for myself. Mostly, though, I feel guilty. If I weren't here, would any of this be happening?

"A little." He can tell that I am, so lying isn't going to help me. "I don't want the campers to be frightened."

"It's okay to worry. In fact, it's normal. This isn't the first time I've had to deal with the public wandering onto camp land. It just takes a conversation. Plus, we have cleaning staff, cooks and de-livery people coming and going, the campers rarely notice who's supposed to be here or not."

Isn't that *more* dangerous? If the campers assume everyone here is part of the camp, they could trust someone they shouldn't.

"Don't look so concerned," Andy says. "It really is fine. You'll come to realize that in time, especially if you come back next year. There are things that are part of being a counselor that the campers have no clue about." He smiles. "I bet there were people closer to camp than you think when you were last here."

I know there were.

22

Jake and Olly help the guys set up the inflatable obstacle course on the lake.

All of the campers are standing on the edge of the water, bouncing.

After anchoring the course, the guys test it, climbing up, running through and around obstacles and sliding down the slide into the water at the end.

Andy laughs. "Okay, looks like it's ready to go. Four at a time."

Two counselors stand by the start and two by the finish.

Kayla and I wade into the lake and stop about halfway along the giant orange inflatable. The water is almost up to my shoulders, but I love being in the lake, so I don't care.

I watch as camper after camper runs along the obstacle course, some making it and others falling in.

When they get off, I'm getting on it.

Kayla moves along the inflatable, a little further from me, getting a better look as the campers go by.

My eyes drift to the forest, to the entrance of the trail that leads to the green flag route. It also leads to the site of the fire.

I blink, my eyes flitting past and then shooting back. Was that a flash?

I turn to face the forest, and through the pine trees, I see it again. A glint, like light bouncing off glass.

Lillian is watching.

I'm about to call to Kayla when the inflatable suddenly dips toward me. I gasp and hold my hands out as if I can single-handedly stop it from tipping over. The four campers on it scream as they're thrown into the lake. It's too deep here for some of them.

I grab Ava as she kicks to the surface. The other counselors rush over, and Andy shouts orders to the rest of the children to get out of the lake. Kayla has two of the campers who fell in, and Isabel is tall enough that she can walk on tiptoes back to land.

"Are you okay?" I ask Ava.

"That was so cool!"

That's great, they loved it.

The inflatable shrinks as it loses air.

All of the campers are standing on the beach, laughing and chatting about the "inflata-fail." At least they're not scared.

Cora takes over from me and Kayla. She sits the girls who fell into the water down with a towel and asks them what happened.

"What the hell was that?" Olly asks me.

I shrug. "I have no idea. One minute I'm watching them and the next minute the thing is falling toward me."

"There must be a hole in it," Kayla says.

Andy shuffles over, face ashen. "Are you two okay?" he asks me and Kayla.

Kayla nods, linking arms with Jake.

"Do you know what was wrong with it?" Jake asks.

"I had a look and found a small hole." Jake shakes his head. "I must have missed it when doing my checks."

Or Lillian did it after his checks. Then she watched from the forest as the thing went down.

I shiver and wrap a towel around myself, though I'm not actually cold.

"It might have torn on the way out there. These things happen, Andy," Mary says, joining our group.

They don't, actually.

Are none of them concerned that this could be more than an accident?

How did it stay up for so long, though?

The guys tug the inflatable to the beach and pull it up onto the grass.

"All right, campers," Cora says. "Let's get changed and head back out for lunch. Hot dogs and s'mores!"

There's a collective cheer before the campers bundle into their cabins.

I walk away from the group, my hands in fists, and head over to the inflatable.

Marcus and Lorenzo are frowning at something.

"What is it?" I ask, crouching down next to them.

The inflatable material is slit.

I take a deep breath through my nose. "What could have done this?" I ask.

Lorenzo shakes his head. "I dunno. It looks like a neat cut but could have been a rock."

There are a few rocks on the beach, but none of them look particularly sharp. Something near the slit catches my eye.

"Let's leave this here until it's dry, then see if Andy wants to get a new one or have this one repaired," Marcus says.

He and Lorenzo walk away.

I run my finger over a sticky residue around the slit. It looks like the material was cut and then shoddily fixed. Someone taped it so it would stay inflated temporarily, until the water ruined the tape. It was probably masking tape, which wouldn't hold for too long in water.

"Esme, come on, we need to get changed," Kayla calls.

I stand and nod. "Okay."

What should I say to them all?

I'll tell Kayla while we're getting ready and see what she thinks.

I jog to our cabin and Kayla closes the bedroom door behind us.

"That was insane," she says, stripping off her soggy swimsuit.

"Uh-huh," I say, pulling clean underwear, a pair of shorts and a T-shirt from the tiny dresser. "It's actually more insane than you think. . . ."

"Oh no," she says, rolling her eyes. "I don't want to hear any more conspiracy theories, Esme."

"It's not a conspiracy theory. The cut looks like it was done with a blade and there was this residue on it, the kind you get when you try to wash off a sticker. It was taped, badly."

Kayla shakes her head. "You need to stop with this."

"Can you please listen to what I'm telling you? Right before it went down, I saw a flash in the woods."

"It's daylight, a flash wouldn't be visible."

"No, not like the camera the other night. This was like the sun bouncing off a lens. I'm telling you Lillian did this. She watched and took photos too."

"Okay, stop!" Kayla pulls on a T-shirt and scowls at me. "If *we* stop talking about this, then it didn't happen. You're playing with fire, Esme, and it has to freaking *stop*! Forget this and forget Lillian. The whole thing was her fault anyway. I'm not risking my time here or my relationship with Jake over that crazy freak."

I stand there, speechless, as she whips the door open and slams it behind her.

Kayla has checked out. The games are getting more sinister.

And I'm alone.

23

I spend the rest of the day avoiding Kayla, and she does the same.

Andy sees no reason why we can't have the night off as planned. The inflatable was an accident and the campers are all fine. He said the cops are looking into the ex-counselors.

But I know they won't find anything.

I'm by the campfire with Tia, Rebekah, Olly and Jake.

Kayla is getting changed into sweats and meeting us out here.

The flames crackle gently as the last of the fire struggles to stay alight.

I watch the embers float before disappearing into the air.

Olly nudges my side with his. "What's going on?"

"Huh? Nothing."

"We can tell it's not nothing, you know," Tia says, scooping her long hair over one shoulder.

I raise my eyes to hers. "I've been distracted, but I'm fine."

I'm on my own and have no one to talk to. Kayla has made it clear that she's done with the whole thing, and I can't bring anyone else in on this.

Mostly I feel horrible for keeping the inflatable tampering a secret.

Rebekah twists her hands together like she's trying really damn hard not to voice her opinion.

I'm not sure I want to hear it right now.

There are more important things I need to worry about. Like Kayla.

"What's happening?" Olly asks. "Please tell us."

"We . . . I thought we were closer than this, Esme," Rebekah says. "Whatever is goin' on, we can help. Are you homesick?"

That sounds much better than the truth. "I'm close to my parents," I say. "I've missed my nan's birthday. It was last week."

Actually, it was two months ago and I was there, at her place. We ordered Mexican food. She drank a lot of tequila and sang sixties songs on her karaoke machine until three a.m.

"I'm sure she won't be angry with you," Tia says. "You can always celebrate when you get home."

"Yeah, I will. Thanks. What do you guys want to do tonight? No walks in the forest!"

Please go with the subject change.

Jake laughs. "The next time we go into the forest, I'll find that creep."

"We don't need to go search for anyone," Tia says. "Town is a bad idea after last time."

"Does that mean we're not goin' back?" Rebekah asks.

Tia's smile widens. "Not at all."

I'm not going back.

"Are you sure that's it?" Olly asks me while the other three argue about whether we would be crazy to go back to town.

"Uh-huh," I reply, looking at the dimple in his cheek because I can't meet his eyes.

He nods. "There's something you're not telling me."

There's a lot I'm not telling you, to be honest.

"No, it's just . . . Some things are complicated."

"I understand that we haven't known each other for long, but you can talk to me."

It's kind of weird, being secluded with these people twenty-four seven. It feels like I've known them for years. It's the oddest feeling ever.

"I can talk to you, and I'm grateful for that," I say.

"You want to start doing that now?" Olly asks.

I really don't.

Olly thinks I'm a good person, and I'd like to keep it that way. He would hate me if he found out what I had been involved in. Maybe he could look past the accident, but his opinion would change if he knew I lied about it for *ten years.*

"I'm freaking out that we were chased and watched. Okay, there you have it. I'm a massive baby."

Chuckling, he lowers his voice. "We're all a little freaked out. Even Jake, but he will never admit it."

"What the hell is this?" Cora's voice isn't particularly loud, but it's heard clearly by us and by a group of counselors on the dock.

She comes running down the porch of the staff cabin holding a piece of paper in one hand and a kitchen knife in the other.

I push myself to my feet, feeling gritty sand embedded under my nails.

"What's wrong?" I ask.

"This was *stabbed* into the door!"

The counselors run toward us and we all meet a pale Cora. She turns the paper around with shaking hands. It reads:

> We're going to have some fun
> Alert the cops and you'll be done

My heart thuds.

I try to take a breath, but it's like breathing through a blanket.

"That's creepy as hell," Jake says, snatching the paper from Cora. "Who do you think wrote it?"

"What do you think it means?"

"Could it be one of the kids?"

"Why would kids write that?"

"Is it the stalker in the woods?"

"What do they want?"

"You guys need to calm down."

I stand back and listen to the comments flying all around me.

My head is spinning so fast, I'm dizzy.

Lillian wants us alone out here.

24

We're outside in the middle of the night with the campers fast asleep in their cabins because Andy has called *another* emergency meeting. I think he actually likes calling them.

He's holding the note in one tightly clenched fist like it's a prize he never wants to let go of.

I'm still sitting on the tampered-with-inflatable information.

I've left it too long and now I don't know how to speak up or what I would say.

What a nightmare.

"All right," Andy says, clearing his throat noisily. "We received this note this evening, and I find it completely unacceptable. Pranks are fine. I started them and encourage everyone to have silly fun." He holds the note up. "This is going too far, though. We need to find out who's responsible for it."

Why does he think it's a camper or a counselor?

"What will happen to the person responsible?" Jake asks. "Do they get booted?"

Andy shakes his head. "No, we will speak to them. *I* will speak to them. We're not about punishment, but the young person responsible has to understand that a prank like this won't be tolerated."

The prank angle seems to be the only one he's willing to accept.

Kayla hasn't said a word since she walked out of the cabin and into the middle of this mess.

I can see in the tightness of her eyes and her hard jaw that she's thinking. Maybe she's finally accepting that this is about Lillian. That this, quite possibly, *is* Lillian.

So many scenarios run through my mind about what happened after we left, what Lillian wants to happen now and what could happen if I react in different ways. Does she want to talk?

"Esme?" Olly says.

"Huh?" I look around. Everyone is gone. Well, they're standing up and chatting in smaller groups.

Tia, Rebekah, Jake, Olly and Kayla are still sitting with me.

"You haven't blinked in five minutes," Rebekah says.

"Sorry, this is all a bit crazy."

Kayla shakes her head. "This isn't happening."

"What isn't happening?" Jake asks.

I widen my eyes at Kayla, telling her to shut up.

Of the two of us, the most likely to crack is me. *What is she doing?*

"Can't you see? All of this is connected. Someone is trying to hurt us," Kayla says.

Tia laughs. "Don't you think that's a bit dramatic?"

"How? The missing tags, the photographer in the woods and now this note."

And the inflatable. And the initials on our cabin wall. And the note in Kayla's pocket. I swallow all the secrets I'm keeping.

Rolling her eyes, Tia tilts her head like she thinks Kayla has lost it. "I'm not denying that someone is messing with us, but that doesn't mean they're an ax-wielding murderer."

I hold my hands up. "Calm down. No one said anything about a murderer or axes!"

"All right, let's stop with the wild theories," Olly says. "No one is talking about anything as crazy as that. Let's think rationally."

"I am!" Kayla snaps.

Her hands curl into fists and she takes deep breaths, like she's trying to calm herself down. She is getting more and more agitated.

"What do you think Andy is going to do?" I ask. "Do we believe the threat?"

Jake snorts. "Why would we believe this? It's clearly someone screwing around, just like the graffiti."

"Well, I think the fact that Andy called *another* meeting shows that he believes there is some threat," I tell the group. "I don't know that this creep will do anything to us, games or whatever, but I do think they want something."

"We should find out what and give it to them," Rebekah says, looking between Tia and me. "Right?"

I shrug and look away.

"What do we do?" Jake asks. "Leave a reply stabbed to a tree?"

"You're not helping," I tell him.

"No one is helping because there is nothing to help. We ignore the note and burn it, like we hid the writing on the staff cabin."

Rebekah shakes her head. "You want to pretend nothing is wrong?"

"I don't want some idiot who thinks they're freaking Jason Voorhees getting in the way of our summer."

"Jason Voorhees, really?" Tia scoffs.

Jake's eyes turn black and he grits his teeth.

"All right, everyone get some rest!" Andy shouts. "We'll do the same as when we saw someone in the forest. Always double up with teams, CITs with counselors."

"We're not going to the police?" Mary asks, her piercing eyes wide below her bangs.

Catalina puts an arm around her and stares at Andy.

"Not tonight. I'll go tomorrow if anything else happens," Andy replies.

He walks off and half the counselors follow.

Mary doesn't move.

"Are you okay?" I ask.

"We should go to the police now! They can protect us better than Andy. Why would he want us to keep this quiet?" she says.

"He's scared for the camp and its reputation. *His* reputation," I say.

She grinds her teeth so hard I hear them creak together. My stomach lurches.

"Mary," I say, shuddering. "Stop. You can talk to me, but I really need you to stop doing that."

Snapping her lips together, she looks away, her cheeks turning pink. "Sorry. I do it when I'm stressed."

"What are you going to do?" I ask.

"I think we should all agree to go to the cops," she says.

"That might not be a good idea."

"Or it might be the only thing we can do to stop this weirdo from hurting us."

Rebekah and Jake stop dead in front of us. Jake tilts his head. "Are you seriously thinking this crap is real? This dude wants us to panic. He wants to watch us run around, paranoid and worried about what he'll do next. Mary, he's just going to play games. We can beat him at that."

In my mind, I substitute *he* for *she*.

"Beat him at his games?" Mary says. "What does that even mean? Do we play along? Pretend that we don't see whatever he does? That doesn't work for me. I won't stay here in fear and allow someone to *threaten* us."

"You're right," I tell her. "We shouldn't allow anyone to make us live in fear. But we have to be sure of what's going on. If we go to the cops, tell them there's a new crazy development, cause panic and this turns out to be a hoax, someone with a sick idea of fun, then who will trust us with their kids again? This is bigger than us, Mary."

I'm so scared that Lillian will follow through with her threat. Before we do anything, I have to know how far she will go for revenge. I'm also totally not on board with the cops finding Lillian. Once they do, she'll talk, and then it's all over for me and Kayla.

We could end up with a criminal record.

My parents preach honesty and truth about every five minutes. If I lie, like *ever*, they are right there to set things straight. Which usually means I'm guilted into telling the truth and then chastised for not doing it earlier. They make their disappointment clear.

It's no fun.

I can only imagine what they'd do if they found out I've been lying for *ten years*.

"Not yet. Andy wants to wait," Mary sneers. "All the while this freak is watching us." She looks at the forest again. "He's probably watching right now."

"Okay, let's not get too ahead of ourselves," I say. Her words send a shiver right down the center of my spine.

"Someone has left a goddamn threat at a kid's camp!" Kayla snaps. She throws her hands into the air. "We are in danger and we're sitting here having a chat about it?"

"Okay, Kayla," I say, grabbing her hand. I tug her closer and she doesn't resist. Suddenly, I feel like our roles have switched. "I'll take her to bed," I tell the others. "She's tired."

Cora nods. "That's a good idea. Get some rest."

Kayla doesn't need a good night's sleep, she needs to see clearly. We can't go telling people about any of this stuff.

No one can ever know what we did.

25

"Kayla?" I say once we close the door of our small room.

She completely ignores me and changes into her pajamas, punching her legs through the leg holes as if she's angry with them. She rams both arms through the sleeves and tugs the top over her head.

"This is too much, Esme!"

"I know, but we *have* to keep it together."

She swings around to face me. "What's going to happen?"

"We'll be okay if we stick together and *stay calm*."

"They're going to find out what happened that night."

My heart misses a beat. "No, they won't."

I don't believe my own words, but I want to calm her down.

"Of course they will! How can they not?"

"If Lillian wanted everyone to know, she would have said something by now. She isn't trying to out us; she's trying to scare us. She wants payback. If they find out and Andy kicks us out, her game is over."

"You think so?"

Maybe.

"I do."

"She was the crazy one that night, Esme."

I take a deep breath as I change into my pajamas. "I remember. That doesn't mean we're innocent. We did something wrong as well."

"We didn't mean to . . . ," she whispers as she slips under the covers.

"I know that, too," I reply. "We need to get some sleep. We're not going to figure anything out tonight."

Kayla rolls over and faces the wall, away from me. "Night, Esme."

"Night," I reply, climbing up the ladder.

The last thing I see before I close my eyes is Lillian's carved initials.

~~~~~

I jump, awake and gasping and clutching my blanket as a loud thud seems to echo outside.

"What the hell was that?" Kayla asks.

I chuck the blanket off and scramble down the ladder.

She's already out of her bunk, waiting for me, and we run into the main room.

"What's happening?" Alana asks.

All of the girls are awake and sitting up in bed.

Cora comes out of her room sliding shoes onto her feet.

"Stay in bed," I tell the campers. "We'll go and see."

Kayla, Cora and I go outside. It's beginning to get light out. The sun is peeking through the trees.

What was it? I look around, scanning the area. The lake is fine, the beach, the outdoor equipment. What . . .

"Oh my God," I breathe, finally locating the cause of the noise.

Wedged into the door of the shed by the road is an ax.

Cora turns around and says into the cabin, "It's all right, girls. It was just some equipment that has fallen over." She glances back at Kayla and me with a look that means "sort this out *now.*"

By the time we reach the bottom step, counselors from every cabin are outside. So is Andy.

The air is warming.

"What on earth . . . ?" Andy says.

The staff cabin is next to the shed, so he gets there first.

Written on the door just above the ax in red paint:

I SAID NO COPS

"I don't like this at all," Mary says, pressing one hand to her mouth. She turns in a circle, looking into the forest. "Last night I said I wanted to go to the cops. He was out there. He's out there now. Watching."

Paranoia will drown you, and Mary is starting to sink.

"Hey," I say, laying my hand on her tense back.

She flinches away from me, spinning around as if she's afraid I'm the one stalking the camp.

Jake steps forward, places one foot on the door and pulls the ax from the wood.

Andy nods at him. "Marcus, Lorenzo, can you deal with the door quickly? The campers will be up soon."

Olly isn't here. I guess he's the one staying with the boys in the cabin.

Mary shakes her head, cowering.

"It's going to be fine," Catalina says, but her quavering voice suggests otherwise. "I'm going to check on Tia and the girls."

"Are you okay, Mary?" I ask.

"An *ax*."

The other counselors disperse, either going to tell the campers nothing has happened or to conceal the evidence.

Andy takes the ax from Jake and heads into the staff cabin.

Jake shakes his head and touches my shoulder as he walks past.

It's just me and Mary now. Kayla walks off with Jake.

Mary hugs her arms around her stomach. "This isn't right. What if the man in the woods comes with a gun next time?"

"Mary, he won't. Okay? We'll figure this out, find whoever it is and stop them without putting the kids in danger. We have to stay strong for them."

Lorenzo and Marcus come running back with a bucket of soapy water and two sponges. They dunk the sponges and start scrubbing immediately.

Mary takes two deep breaths and closes her eyes. "Okay," she says, opening them again. "I'm giving this a couple of days and then I'm taking things into my own hands."

"Let's talk about it again later. Right now we need to make sure the campers are getting dressed and then feed them. It'll be breakfast time soon."

Mary's worried eyes look straight through me. She glances toward the forest once again and then walks away.

If she's not careful, she's going to push Lillian even further.

26

Tonight is . . . what's the best way to describe something that's on a downward spiral? We're in a tornado about to touch down.

The day was fine, after the door was scrubbed. We hiked close to the forest's edge, made campfires, built dens and ate bowls of chili with nachos.

The campers are happy.

The counselors, behind fake smiles, are not.

We seem to be divided, too, figuratively and literally. On one side of the campfire are the counselors and CITs who are pro-cops, and the other side—hello, my side—are those of us who think cops are a bad idea. You could also divide the no-cop camp into two groups. There are the no-cops basing their opinion on this being some dumb, harmless joke, and the no-cops who think it's more than that.

How can anyone think this is nothing more than a silly prank? I don't know how to handle this. Maybe if Kayla and I tell everyone what happened with Lillian this will be over. Or maybe it will anger her and she'll hurt someone.

It's a huge gamble.

Lillian is messing with us, and I don't know how far she will take it. I still haven't told Kayla, or anyone, about the LC carved in the wall. She was *in* our room. Kayla wouldn't be able to relax if she knew that; she would be petrified that Lillian would smother her in her sleep.

It would set off the anxiety in Kayla that she's fought so hard to get under control. She was in a bad car accident as a kid, one that killed her nana. It took years of therapy for her to get to where she is now. That could all be undone if I'm not careful.

Never again do I want to see her sobbing hysterically on the floor because she can't deal with the possibility that something bad might happen.

Kayla and I should leave. What would Lillian do if we tried? I think back to the CIT pamphlet both Kayla and I got. It said we'd regret it if we didn't come back. What if that *was* Lillian making a threat? Would she make our lives even worse if we left?

Besides, how would we explain coming home *weeks* early to our parents?

They would call camp and boom, suddenly we're having a lot of talks. Or rather an interrogation. Mom and Dad would not let it go lightly and they would absolutely not believe I was just homesick.

My dad is quite literally a human lie detector. He's a polygraph examiner and conducts the test for hopefuls applying for a job with the FBI. That makes him sound a lot cooler than he is, like he's *in* the FBI and could be an extra on *Criminal Minds*. It's not like that at all.

He conducts the test and sends the results off.

"What are we going to do about this?" Jake asks.

"We?" Tia curls her top lip.

He scowls. "I'm not sitting here waiting for some creep in the forest to take another picture or stroke my hair while I sleep!"

"Let's not go there," I say.

"Whoever it is, they can't get into the cabins," Rebekah adds.

Untrue. Lillian carved her damn initials into the wall by my freaking pillow.

I bite my tongue. Rebekah doesn't need to be worrying about the very real fact that our resident stalker can get inside the buildings we sleep in.

"You sure about that?" Olly says. "I don't think it would take much."

My jaw drops as I twist my head toward him. "Can we not? How would someone sneak into a cabin of twenty people? Also, the doors are locked at night."

"If it was an ex-counselor, they might have a key," he replies.

Groaning, I close my eyes. But then I'm hit with a thought . . . how did *Lillian* get a key?

Was she a CIT?

She must have been about a year or two older than us. She might have worked here last year in order to get a key, to learn the layout and routines of the camp.

My rapidly thudding heart is making my head spin.

Andy has staff files in his office. Which is a locked filing cabinet inside the staff cabin.

I have to get into the files and find out if Lillian was here in the past couple of years.

"Andy!" Tia calls, standing up.

Silence falls. A sea of heads whip her way, mine included.

Andy, frowning, says, "Yes?"

"Your theory about it being someone who worked here is right. Only, they might not have been a 'bad' one. Which means they could have a key to the cabins."

"CITs aren't given keys, Tia," Andy says.

"That doesn't mean he couldn't have gotten one when he was working here!"

Andy chews his lip.

I glance at every member of cops and no-cops. They're all thinking the same thing, that this person might be able to get to us. Even the doubters have frown lines.

"I think we should go to the police *now!*" Mary says. She stands and folds her arms, her pursed lips and darkening eyes a warning to Andy: *You go, or I will.*

"Shh! We don't actually know anything for sure," I say. "All we have is a lot of speculation."

"And we should let the cops find out if there's anything behind this threat!" Mary throws her hands up in the air, exasperated with all of us. "What's wrong with you people?"

"Mary," Andy says softly, "let's calm down so we don't wake the campers. I understand you're worried, but there is nothing to suggest that we're in danger."

"This guy tried to get a group lost, graffitied a cabin, watched us from the forest and left threatening notes stabbed and axed into doors. What more do you need, Andy?"

Well, when you put it that way . . .

No one actually moves, but a few on the no-cops side nod. The balance is shifting. We were about even, but Mary's little speech has them spooked.

"There has been nothing that's an actual threat to our safety," Andy says.

"All right," Jake says. "What if a few of us go into the forest and check it out, see if there's anything suspicious? Would that make you feel better, Mary?"

"Are you crazy?" Kayla snaps. "You can't go out there in the dark."

"I'll take a flashlight," he says. "A group of us guys will have a look."

"I'll go," Olly says. Marcus and Lorenzo offer too.

"In a world of evolving equality, I'll be going with you," I tell them.

Olly shakes his head, but I raise my hand.

"I'm not a damsel in distress. I'm going. We have kids here and I won't figure anything out just sitting around." And if Lillian is out there, I need to get to her before they do.

Andy nods. "All right. I want you to have radios . . . and pepper spray. Actually, I'm going to come; I should be with you. Cora, I need you in charge here. Have your radio on and we'll keep in constant contact."

"What about weapons?" Mary asks.

I side-eye her. "We're not taking weapons!"

"We don't need any," Jake says.

"Pepper spray is all we'll take," Andy says sternly. "All right, everyone who is coming wait by the staff cabin. I'll get the supplies."

Cora walks with Andy and they chat in hushed tones.

I start to follow Olly, Jake, Marcus and Lorenzo, when Kayla catches my wrist.

Her eyes are wild, freaked. "You can't go out there, Esme."

"Yes, I can. I'll be fine."

"What if she's out there?" Kayla whispers, her eyes wide.

"Maybe that's a good thing. If I can talk to her, find out what she wants and apologize for not making sure she was okay that night, maybe this will all be over," I reply in a hushed voice.

"I don't like it."

"Not exactly wanting to sing from the rooftops either, Kayla, but I have to try *something*."

"You're absolutely, one hundred percent sure it's her?"

"Yes. *Absolutely*," I say. "I'll be with the others. It's fine."

She drops her arm. "Please, *please* stay safe."

Kayla would never come. She won't do anything remotely dangerous.

"You sure you're coming?" Olly asks.

I turn to him and smile. I probably look like that cringing emoji. "I'm sure."

"All right, let's head out," Andy says. "We stick close together.

Cora, stay with Tia and Rebekah, watch the cabins, make sure no one gets near the campers. Mary and Catalina, watch the forest but don't go into it."

Olly holds my hand tight and we follow Andy.

I take a breath as we step into the dark woods.

The temperature drops.

Goose bumps raise along my arms.

27

A thick white blanket coats the ground ahead of us.

"Mist," I say, swallowing a lump of fear. Well, that's not at all ominous.

I wrap my free arm around my tummy and squeeze Olly's hand.

"Do you want to go back, Esme?" Andy asks.

"No, I want to keep going."

Want isn't quite the right word.

You are fine.

"Where are we going?" I ask.

"We'll check this area and see if there's anything suspicious. I don't think we'll find anything, but it will make everyone back at camp sleep much easier."

Does he think that the stalker dropped their driver's license in the forest?

Our feet disappear as we walk into the mist.

"If I was terrorizing a camp, I'd be very careful about leaving Scooby-Doo clues everywhere," Olly says.

I smile at his Scooby reference.

"If this asshole has left anything, we're going to find it and catch him," Jake says.

"I'd like to get my hands on him," Olly agrees.

Andy looks over his shoulder. "I'd like that too, but we have to be careful with this."

I can't imagine Andy in a fight. Not winning one, anyway.

Snap.

We all turn to the left at the sound. My long hair whips against my face.

"What was that?" Olly mutters.

I blink as a sudden flash of light blinds me.

Pictures.

This time the flash is brighter, like our stalker is much closer.

Flash.

Not again.

I spin around. This one came from the opposite direction.

Flash, flash, flash.

I slap my hand over my eyes. The onslaught of light from both directions makes it almost impossible to see. The fraction of a second between each one isn't enough for my eyes to adjust.

There are orbs of red behind my eyelids.

"Back to camp!" Andy shouts.

I let go of Olly's hand and we all turn around.

I blink again, wincing at the light. How is it possible that it's this bright? The flashes are constant.

Without thinking, I take off. My feet thud against the ground as I sprint, the wind whipping at my face.

I can't see, and I don't know where the others are.

My stomach coils around and around.

What is she doing?

Does she want to get to me?

The air is cold, and I can barely see between each painfully bright flash of light.

Flash, flash.

Flash, flash, flash.

They're nonstop now, one after the other, like a rave without music or fun.

"Olly!"

Where is everyone?

"Olly! Andy!"

I cover my eyes with one hand, leaving a small gap at the bottom so I can see the ground a little. My other hand is stretched out in case I hit a tree.

"Where are you?" I call.

Whimpering, I push forward and shout, "Answer me! Olly! Jake!"

Flash, flash, flash, flash, flash.

My head hurts from the bright light, and I cry out.

Biting my lip, I stumble forward.

I can't hear anything but my own heavy breathing and my own heavy footsteps.

"Andy?"

Where are they?

The light stops.

I gasp and squeeze my eyes shut. When I open them again, all I can make out is the outline of trees and dancing circles of light.

Turning around, I look for the others.

But no one is here.

A chill travels down my back.

Where am I?

I turn my head and crouch on the ground. Fear claws my throat.

Where is everyone?

Where is camp?

I'm lost.

Digging my fingernails into a tree, I say a silent prayer. I've never thought much about whether I believe in God, but I will start if I can just get out of here.

In the distance, a sharp *crack* sends goose bumps up my arms. I turn my head and strain to see into the forest.

My heart stutters.

I don't know which direction the noise came from.

Whoever is out there, they could be anywhere.

I want to go home.

I flatten myself against the tree when another crack comes closer. Pressing my palm against my mouth to stifle a scream, I slowly lean my head to one side to look around the tree. I stay close to it, my forehead touching the rough bark.

In front of me is someone dressed head to toe in black, with a hood pulled over their head.

I press my lips together as my stomach bottoms out.

Please don't see me. Please, please, please.

"Esme!" Olly calls in the distance.

"Where are you?" Jake shouts.

Their voices echo through the forest.

My heart leaps. They're not too far away.

The figure—I'm fairly certain it's Lillian, even though I can't make out her face—turns in the direction of their voices.

"Call out, Esme!" Andy orders.

I can't!

I don't know how far away they are. I can't hear their footsteps and their voices aren't close yet. Lillian is maybe twenty feet away. I can't move an inch in case I make a noise.

Lillian looks around, the hood still obscuring her face. She doesn't appear to have a weapon, but there is no way I'm taking that chance. Just like there is no way I'm making a run for it. Stupid people run through a forest when their assailant is just feet away. Then they fall and we all know how that ends.

I don't need to outrun her, I need to outsmart her. And I will do that by pretending I'm not here.

"Esme?" Olly shouts again.

My eyes widen. His voice is much fainter than before.

No, this way! Come back. I wince, willing myself to breathe quietly. *Please come back.*

Lillian moves very slowly in my direction.

Ice-cold fear slithers down my spine.

I steady myself against the tree.

Branches and sticks snap beneath Lillian's feet.

We must be in the publicly owned section of the forest. The

camp's section is kept somewhat maintained. Now I'm out of bounds, away from any kind of safety.

I press my side against the tree and place one foot a step to the left. Lillian is going to pass me, and I have to make sure she doesn't see me.

It's too dark to make out her face. She's tall and slim. I can still only just make her out. She's like an evil paranormal presence in a horror flick. If she began to float and disappeared in a puff of black smoke it wouldn't surprise me. In fact, I would love that.

I want her gone.

Her footsteps are light, but I feel each one vibrate through me. *Crunch. Crunch. Crunch.*

I curl smaller inside myself and say another silent prayer.

My grandparents would love to know that I'm praying.

Will I get a chance to tell them?

Flattening myself against the tree, I wait.

Please leave.

Her footsteps slowly get fainter and fainter.

I let out a quiet breath and swipe a single tear from my cheek.

Crouching in the mist, I count in my head.

She must be gone now.

I'm alone again.

My heart thumps.

It's scarier to be alone than it should be. I'd rather be on my own than have Lillian near.

How did she get away just now?

When I reach one hundred, I rise to my feet. The lingering

orbs are gone. I can see normally now, despite the fact that it's dark.

I look around and decide to walk forward. I'm sure that's the way back to camp.

You can do this, Esme. Keep moving.

I clench my hands and run to the beat of my thudding pulse.

28

My feet hurt from running on uneven ground. Sharp pains shoot along my shins. I round a thick bush and whimper, but I can't stop. If I stop now Lillian might catch me.

I run as if she's barely a foot behind me, as if she can reach an arm out and touch me.

Oh God.

"Olly!" I shout, spotting him up ahead.

He spins around and his eyes widen. A fraction of a second later, he's sprinting toward me.

"Esme!"

I'm vaguely aware of the others calling my name and saying how relieved they are, but all I can focus on is Olly.

His arms shoot out to catch me as I run straight into him. My legs give out and he's all that's stopping me from hitting the ground. I lean into him, feeling his warmth seep into my clammy skin. I sob, the relief of being safe drenching me.

The static from Andy's radio crackles as he makes a call to Cora to tell her we're almost back.

"What happened? Are you okay?" Olly asks.

You can't be a big baby now after insisting on coming.

I stand. "I don't know. One minute you guys were there, and the next I—I couldn't find you."

Should I tell them what happened?

No. No, I can't.

"We're so sorry, Esme, we thought you were with us," Andy says, stopping beside me.

I wipe my hands on my shorts and take a ragged breath. "It wasn't anyone's fault, and I'm fine."

"You sure about that?" Jake asks.

"Yeah."

"Did you see anything?"

My body turns cold. "Just a whole lot of trees after the lights."

And the dark figure of Lillian.

"Us too." Andy takes a big breath. "Looks like this person isn't done with their pranks, though."

I nod. "What do we do now?"

"We remain vigilant, stick together and make sure the children are safe," he says.

If I can't get my heart rate under control, I won't be doing anything at all.

"I agree," I whisper. But do I?

Jake scowls. "We ride this out, let this freak have his fun and keep the campers safe. The day they leave, we find out who's taking pictures and leaving notes."

Andy says, "That's settled, then. Let's get back to camp and have a hot drink and let everyone know there's nothing out here."

I look behind me. Somewhere in the distance, Lillian is probably livid because I made it back to the others. She was right near me. I shudder at the thought of her being so close. What would she have done if she'd found me?

I keep a small smile on my face and walk beside Olly, his hand in mine, trying not to crush his bones as I hold on.

"That was eventful," Jake says, his voice brimming with sarcasm.

I wish my evening had been as uneventful as his.

God, I wish I could speak with Kayla right now. She's the only person I can talk to about what just happened. Only I can't really, can I? I was supposed to talk to Lillian and clear this up. I was going to tell her how sorry we were that she got hurt and ask her to forgive us. But when it came down to it, when I was separated from the others, I was scared and hid rather than confronting her. I. Was. Scared.

There, I've admitted it to myself. Esme is a big chicken.

I pretended to be tough and unafraid, but I'm a phony.

Kayla can't find out what happened. She was counting on me to make this stop. I don't know how much more she can take if she knows that Lillian stalked me through the forest like she was stalking her prey.

No, this I have to keep to myself.

We walk into the clearing and the first thing I see is the

bright-white reflection of the moon on the lake. Small ripples in the water make it look jagged, like it could cut into you.

The second thing I see is the remaining group of counselors running toward the staff cabin.

"Shit!" Andy mutters.

What's going on?

We sprint around the lake.

"What is it?" Andy calls when we get close enough that he won't wake the campers up.

"The radio!" Cora says from the porch. "Someone just came on the radio telling us to get in the staff cabin or they'd start a fire. We heard rustling in the forest."

My eyes widen.

How did Lillian get back here so fast?

"What? Okay, I'm calling the police," Andy says.

His response is met with a wild and collective no.

"Get inside," Cora says. "I'll tell you everything."

We stampede into the multiuse cabin.

"What happened while we were away?" Andy demands, pulling the door shut. "We can't all be inside here. No one is watching the campers' cabins!"

Cora shakes her head. "It's not *them* this person wants. They're safer if we're not with them."

"What's going on, Cora?" I ask. "Where are Kayla and Rebekah?"

"They were very anxious out here, so I told them to go in and get some rest a while ago."

Bed? Kayla went to *bed*?

"About ten minutes ago, the first message came through the radio. This voice, it sounded like someone using one of those voice-altering things. They said if we contact anyone, wake the campers or alert the cops or anyone else, we're dead. *Dead.* We didn't know what to do, so we tried to look around, to see who was out there."

"How did this happen?" Andy asks.

"They must have our frequency."

"Why didn't you call me?" he demands.

"I knew you would be back." Cora drops her eyes as she speaks. I don't think she was certain that we would be back.

"When did this person threaten fire?"

Lillian, I correct him in my head.

"Before you came back, literally seconds before. He said, 'Everyone into the cabin or I'll send the food hall up in flames and call the parents.' Half went in the campers' cabins and the rest went in the multiuse to see if we could spot anyone lurking."

"Parents?" Andy's eyes bulge.

"This person has the parents' contact details?" I ask.

Cora shrugs. "I don't want to find out."

"It has to be a former employee," Andy says. "I just can't figure out why he would go to these lengths."

"Do we believe he would actually set the food hall on fire?" Jake asks.

Cora raises her eyebrows. "We *have* to."

"Whoever this is, they want us to be alone," Mary says from the back. "They want us trapped here, slowly going insane from paranoia, constantly worrying what we're going to have to do next."

"Wait, if they want that, then surely they won't set a fire?" Tia says.

"She's right," I say. "How would he do that and get away with it? There would be smoke, and the flames would be seen from town; the fire department would come. It would all be over for him. That one is for sure an empty threat."

Andy is a bobblehead as he agrees with me. "I think you're right. But we shouldn't ignore it. Four years—*four years*—I've been here, and it's always been a safe place. I can't believe this is happening."

"For what it's worth," Jake says, "I don't think this creep is going to hurt anyone. This bullshit is all about fear and every time we have conversations like this and run off into the woods, we're feeding his sick little fantasy. I'll have no problem kicking his ass."

"That may be true," Andy says. "Still, I don't think it would be right to ignore this."

"We can't ignore it," Marcus replies. "He's everywhere."

Lorenzo shakes his head. "Enough of this for tonight. Let's not give him any more attention."

Mary folds her arms and glares at Lorenzo. Catalina puts an arm around her shoulders. "Come on, he's right," she says to Mary. "We should get some sleep. Let's make it look like we're doing what he wants and keeping quiet."

"We *are* doing that," Olly says.

We have no choice.

29

I dig my fists into my stinging eyes and rub.

Man, seven- to ten-year-olds have a crapload of energy.

I'm drained. The incident with Lillian in the woods has me on edge. I woke about every hour, panicked that she was searching for me again. Everyone looks on edge.

But the kids are as excited and loud and bouncy as ever. I feel like I'm hungover, although the only thing I've had to drink since I arrived is water and coffee.

I don't know how the campers haven't realized that every one of our smiles is forced. I'm positive I look like I'm grimacing.

I care about them all, but I'm finding it really hard to bounce off the walls over a new fastest win of tennis.

Lillian is out there, somewhere close I'm sure, watching the morning after her night of insanity.

She's loving it, I'm sure. I bet she's drinking in every second that we look around for her.

It could come back to bite me and Kayla in the ass eventually, if Lillian decides that she wants to make herself known. Which, let's face it, she will. I just hope the others aren't around to hear it when she confronts us.

We're standing by the tennis court in the shade of the trees. Kayla's arms are wrapped around herself like she has to physically hold all of our secrets in.

"How are you doing?" I ask, still looking at the girls and smiling. My jaw aches. I don't know how models do it.

"All right," she mutters. She was awake in bed when I got back, chewing her nails to the quick. Mine are about the same.

"You can tell me the truth, Kayla."

"Can I?"

I fight the urge to push her. "Really, dude? We've known each other since we were obsessed with *High School Musical*. Hell, we have a blood oath!"

"Oh, now it's a blood oath."

Before we decided to become CITs, we hadn't talked about the accident for years. I hate that we spent so long ignoring what we'd done. I *hate* that we ran.

Dipping my head, I wince against the sting of regret.

"Kayla," I prompt.

"What do you want me to say, Esme?" She looks across the court as her girls cheer for another point and purses her lips. "I'm scared. We both know Lillian is going to do something bad. We burned her!" Her voice is low, a whisper, but I feel it in my bones.

"We don't *know* that." I don't say it with much conviction. I'm shocked to hear those words come out of Kayla's mouth. She's always been a total pro at denial.

"Yes we do! If we hadn't been out there that night, then none of this would be happening now. She wants revenge. I still don't think we're to blame, but *we* didn't get hurt."

"We never meant for anything bad to happen."

"Esme, can we not talk about this anymore, please? I'm totally over it."

We never talk about what we did anymore and it's slowly driving me crazy. You're supposed to talk, everyone says so.

Kayla storms off, leaving me with a burn in my chest that makes me resent my best friend just a little. I need her support right now.

I've spent so much time and effort making sure things aren't too much for her. I never get that in return.

Fine. Whatever.

After games outside, we go in for dinner and then to the beach for a campfire.

We finish up the day with s'mores. It's a pretty standard end; there haven't been many evenings that don't include marshmallows.

"Esme," Mary says behind her massive bangs, "can you pop into my cabin and see if Phoebe is there? She went to get her hoodie and hasn't come back out and I need to help Ava."

"Sure," I reply.

Kayla walks past me to join our girls by the campfire. They're mostly split up tonight, though, mixed heavily with the boys.

Jogging up the cabin steps, I twist the doorknob and let myself in. "Phoebe?"

My eyes bulge. Through a crack in the door to Tia and

Rebekah's tiny room, I catch a glimpse of Rebekah pulling her T-shirt down over her head. Her side and most of her stomach is burned.

"Esme?"

My pulse skitters as Phoebe walks up to me. She smiles.

I jump away from Rebekah and Tia's room. "Are you okay?" I ask her.

"I was getting a sweater."

Burns!

"You ready to join us?" I ask.

Rebekah has burns!

She nods. "Yeah."

What does this mean? I dash out of the cabin with Phoebe right behind me. I don't think that Rebekah saw me. She didn't turn around.

I walk with Phoebe until she sits down with her group. As soon as the other girls embrace her, I dart around the campfire and scan the crowd for Kayla. We need to have a conversation right this second. Whether she wants to or not.

"Kayla, can we walk?" I say when I find her.

Olly and Jake, who are sitting next to her, look up too.

Her shoulders slump like I'm the last person she wants to see. I'll try not to take that personally. "Er, sure, Esme. . . ."

She stands up and puts on a fake toothy smile that almost makes me roll my eyes. Doing the bitchy smile to me, really? Is she doing the popular thing now?

I grin back and grab Kayla's arm. "This will only take a minute."

The guys watch us suspiciously. Come on, we could be talking about anything. I'll tell the boys it's something menstruation related, that'll shut it down real fast.

Someone who knows the routine of camp and has access to cabins is doing this. . . .

"Jesus, Esme, what's going on?" Kayla asks, stumbling behind me as I tug her by the hand. She pulls out of my grip and glares.

"I know who Lillian is," I say.

"You what?"

"Rebekah."

30

"It's *Rebekah*!" I say her name again because Kayla is looking at me the way you look at people arguing in Walmart.

She blinks and shakes her head. "What are you talking about?"

"It's *her*! Lillian. Rebekah *is* Lillian. They're the same damn person. Catch up!"

Throwing her head back, Kayla laughs. "Oh, come on, Esme. Rebekah was with us when we were chased through the woods."

This is it, time's up. I can't keep hiding things. "But she wasn't there when I was stalked in the forest last night."

"What?" Kayla steps closer, tilting her head.

"When I got separated from the others, someone was stalking me. I saw her. Well, it was dark and misty, but I saw someone dressed in black. Tall and slim. She was so close."

"Esme, Rebekah was with us last night." Kayla says it like I'm slow.

"No, she went to bed early, remember? And she has *burns on her side and stomach. . . .*"

"Lots of people have burns. How do you explain the night of the photos? Rebekah was there that night."

"Right." I hold one finger up, cracking it. "There's two of them; that's how they're able to do so much. She—Lillian—would need help. There is no way she could do this alone. I don't know if Rebekah is Lillian or one of her cronies. Yet."

Kayla frowns, her once sparkly blue eyes now full of doubt. But I see it in there too, a little flicker. She's starting to believe me. Kayla is considering the possibility that we've been living with one of our stalkers for weeks.

"What did you see *exactly*?" she asks.

I don't like her emphasis on *exactly,* and her tone is the one she uses when she thinks someone is an idiot.

"Mary asked me to go to her cabin and check on Phoebe. Rebekah and Tia's door was open a little and I saw Rebekah putting on a T-shirt. There's a burn all down her side and her stomach. Like all down it, not just, 'Oh no, I spilled coffee on myself.' It was *bad.*"

Kayla blows out a breath, her eyes darting to Rebekah's cabin. "Does she look like Lillian?"

I shrug when she looks back at me. "Maybe. Her hair is darker, but so is mine now. . . ."

"What color eyes did Lillian have?"

"I . . . Light-colored, maybe? Blue or green. It was dark that night."

I remember the orange reflection in her eyes from the flames and the look of terror in them.

"That's not good enough," Kayla says. "You have to be *sure* about it! We can't just accuse her of something like this. I mean, how many burn victims do you think there are? How could Rebekah do all this stalking anyway? The girl is petrified of confrontation."

"Yeah, well, even introverts can be crazy . . . and what better way for an introvert to attack than to watch from afar and send creepy anonymous messages. Besides, she's not working alone!"

Kayla shakes her head. "She would need pretty regular contact with whoever her partner is. I don't think I've seen her use her cell once."

"You and I used to text each other through entire classes and the teachers never knew a thing."

"This is—"

"Yeah, yeah, yeah, get past that. We need to figure out a way to prove that Rebekah is Lillian before anything else happens. From this minute on, we don't give her a second to breathe. We stay with her and watch her."

"Esme, if what you're saying is true, we need evidence."

"I totally agree. That's why I'm going to steal her phone."

"What? You can't. The burns might be a complete coincidence."

"And all the weird 'what's your biggest secret' crap that she was going on about when we first arrived? What was that about? She was trying to see if we'd lie."

"Which we did," Kayla replies. "We've lied a lot."

"Sometimes the truth can do more damage."

"Even if the truth is about an *accident*?"

I blink hard to stop myself from rolling my eyes. "Kayla, the fire and Lillian getting hurt was an accident, sure. Keeping quiet about it for ten years *wasn't*."

"I don't need the abridged version, I was there," she snips.

"Whatever. I need you to distract Rebekah."

"I really don't think that's a good idea. Why can't we just ask her about the burns?"

"How likely do you think she is to say, 'Yes, Esme, I am the one creeping off into the woods.' Come on," I say, throwing my hands up. "Rebekah isn't going to admit anything. We have to find out. Keep her busy."

I start to turn away, but Kayla grabs my wrist.

"Wait. How?"

"I don't know! Ask her to talk, tell her you're homesick. She likes to share feelings . . . even if they're made up."

"All right. Be careful."

I'll be the one in the cabin; she's the one who's going to be with Rebekah. It's not me who needs to be careful.

We part ways: she heads to the dock where Rebekah is dangling her feet into the lake, and I go inside Rebekah's cabin.

The campers are in the multiuse cabin having a dodgeball tournament.

A dodgeball game doesn't require every counselor and CIT, so we've split up. Half of us are supervising the campers and the rest are taking a break. That's code for watching the forest. Kayla and I have been tagged in for first watch.

Andy is flitting between checking the campers and making sure there's no further danger. He's clutching his phone and the damn clipboard like he has a clue how to handle this situation.

He hasn't mentioned the cops again, so I guess he's not telling them anything else besides what he's already told them about the guy on camp property. Which is hardly likely to be up there on the cops' list of urgent incidents.

"Esme," Andy says, walking toward me as he makes another round, "where are you going?"

"Oh, Andy," I say, pressing one hand to my throat and acting startled. "You scared me."

He didn't. After two weeks at camp, I no longer jump when he pops up like a ghost.

Think! Why are you going into a cabin that isn't yours?

"I'm sorry for frightening you," he says.

"That's okay, I was just going to go check inside, you know?" I scratch my jaw. "That makes me paranoid, I get that, but we have kids here."

"I think it's prudent to exercise caution, well done. I can take on cabin checks."

Seriously?

I run my hand through my hair. "Even the girls' cabins? The girls might be more comfortable if it was a female going into their room."

His pale eyes widen a fraction. I guess the thought of someone witnessing him looking through the girls' cabin does not appeal to him.

"Ah, right. I didn't think about that. Very well, I'll take the boys' cabins. Let me know if anything is amiss."

I smile. "Will do."

That was too easy.

Andy walks off, heading toward the boys' cabins.

After taking one quick glance over my shoulder and seeing that Rebekah is occupied, I open her cabin door and slip inside. I've been in Rebekah and Tia's room once, shortly after we arrived.

I press my lips together hard against the rolling in my stomach. Some people love snooping, but I hate it. It feels so wrong, and I always worry that I'll find something nasty.

If I find something in here that I don't want to see, how will I look Rebekah in the eye again?

I'd rather find evidence that she's the creep in the woods. At least then this would be over.

I walk through the main room and go into Rebekah and Tia's bedroom.

Their beds are made and there is nothing on the floor. Kayla and I are messy. I think I have at least three T-shirts on the chair.

Rebekah's is the bottom bunk; I remember her mentioning Tia was above her.

I pick up her cream-colored pillow and stuff my hand inside the case. If I were hiding things, they would be in here or under the mattress. Not original, I've made my peace with that, but our options here are limited. The floorboards are fixed tight, probably thanks to Andy.

The pillowcase is empty, aside from the pillow, so I drop it back on the bed and move on. I grip the thin mattress and tilt it, leaning it against the wall.

Wooden slats are all that's beneath.

Okay, Rebekah, where are your skeletons?

I drop the mattress and remake the bed. She has two draw-ers, but she shares the small dresser with Tia, so it's unlikely she would keep anything in it.

Or it's the perfect cover. Isn't there something about hiding in plain sight?

What would she hide in there, though?

A voodoo doll of me and Kayla would be a dead giveaway.

I open the first drawer. There's a photo of Rebekah with who must be her mom and dad. It's framed in pink glass, so I don't know why she wouldn't display it.

Why hide your parents?

I put the photo back down and root through the rest of her stuff. Deodorant, headbands, toiletries, a charger—Kayla and I keep ours in the wall socket—a notebook, wire-bound with doodles on the front.

Her diary?

I open the notebook, ignoring the pang of guilt in my gut. The first page has her name drawn graffiti-style.

I turn to the second page. There's a doodle of herself, I as-sume, and another little girl. Rebekah's good at drawing, her sketches are so lifelike, every pencil stroke is precise. I wish I could draw like her.

Turning the page again, I almost drop the book. Fire. She has drawn *fire*. No forest, no campers running away, just fire. Jagged flames take up the whole page. I run my finger over the raised, angry ink.

This is something.

Why would she have drawn this?

I know she's been burned. I have zero idea of burn victim statistics, but I'm willing to put everything I own on it being higher than one. Rebekah was burned; Lillian was burned. That doesn't make them the same person. But it does mean they have something in common.

I think about the flames that night—how vicious they were. If Lillian was burned—and I am pretty sure at this point that she was—and Rebekah is Lillian, wouldn't her burns be worse?

My stomach clenches as the memory flashes through my head over and over, like a horror flick on repeat.

As I start to turn the page, the cabin door creaks. Someone has opened it.

My heart leaps. I drop the notebook back into the drawer and push it shut.

"Rebekah?" Kayla calls from outside.

No!

Rebekah cannot find me in here.

I have no reason to be in here.

Rebekah calls back to Kayla from the doorway of the cabin.

Kayla replies with a question about going for a walk. I don't hear Rebekah's reply because the sound of her opening the door has my pulse racing.

I look around. The window in the bedroom is big enough for me to climb out of—it's a fire escape route—but it's too far away for me to make it there in time, and I certainly wouldn't be able to do it quietly anyway.

Her footsteps thud closer.

I freeze.

31

I'm about to be busted.

I scramble, shoving her sketchbook away.

Hide!

Dropping to my stomach, I wriggle sideways under the bunk bed.

Kayla says something, but her hurried voice sounds quiet from where I am. She's trying to stall Rebekah. I press my lips together as the door to the bedroom opens.

Rebekah steps over the threshold. Her gray and pink tennis shoes tread lightly, but they make a ridiculously loud noise in my ears.

What the hell do I say if she finds me under her bed?

Her feet pass me, and I bite my bottom lip.

What is she doing? *Please leave.*

Where the hell is Kayla?

Rebekah sits on the bottom bunk and the mattress depresses, almost touching my head.

I lie flat, with my head turned sideways.

Why didn't Kayla keep her outside? They had looked deep in conversation when I snuck into the cabin.

Does Rebekah suspect us?

No. If she did, she would be looking for me.

I can hear her fingers tapping something. Her phone?

She's hiding something.

"Hi, Mom."

She's calling home.

Listening to Rebekah talk to her mom feels like a step too far.

"Yeah, I'm okay," she says, though her voice is low and she sounds anything but okay. "Honestly, I am. Things are just kind of full-on, that's all. . . . No, I don't want to come home. . . . Some great friends, yeah . . ."

Will she say something about me and Kayla? If she is Lillian, will she say something that gives her away?

"How's Dad? . . . Good. Yeah, I'm using the cream. I never forget."

Cream for her burns? Does she use it daily?

I close my eyes. We did that to her.

Well, *if* she's Lillian.

"I'm remembering to take my meds, yeah. . . . Yes, Mom," she says in exasperation.

Rebekah hasn't mentioned anything about medication, but then, no one has. It's not something she needs to share. Still, I am curious.

Could it be a condition related to the accident?

"I have to go—we're about to head into the conference room. Okay, speak soon. . . . Love y'all too."

Conference room?

I hear her tap the screen and then she stands up. I can't see her, but I think she puts the phone in her pocket, because I don't hear her put it down.

I watch her tennis shoes walk past me and leave the room. The door bangs shut.

I wait until I hear the cabin door close before I slide from under the bed and stand.

In hindsight, I should have brought my phone with me. That way, I could text Kayla and ask if the coast is clear.

"Esme?"

I startle and grip the doorframe, my fingers digging into the wood.

Kayla opens the door and walks into the room.

"What are you doing?" I hiss.

"Don't worry. The others are walking around the lake."

"Why did you let Rebekah come in? I had to hide under the bed!"

Her eyes widen. "Let her? *Let?*"

"All right, all right, you didn't *let* her. What happened?"

"We were talking, and I mentioned that I miss my parents, like you said to, and then she suddenly got up. She told me she was late calling her mom. I tried to stop her, but she was adamant that she needed to speak to her mom that second."

I nod. "Let's get out of here."

"You *are* going to tell me what happened, right?"

"Yes."

We leave the cabin and I close the door, glancing around. Rebekah and Tia are with Jake, Olly, and the others, walking clockwise around the lake.

Kayla and I head in the opposite direction.

"Well?" Kayla asks.

"She sat on the bed. I was under it and she almost hit my head. Then she called her mom. I found out she uses a cream for her burns."

"Breaking news," Kayla mutters sarcastically.

"Did you expect a full confession? She assured her mom she's still using the cream and taking her medication."

"What medication?"

"She didn't say the name. Her mom would already know what it is."

Kayla sighs. "All right."

"Then she told her mom she had to go because she was needed in the conference room. That's weird, right?"

"Maybe she meant the staff cabin and just misspoke."

I shake my head. "I don't know, there are so many theories in my mind. Anyway, she keeps her phone on her, even though the rest of us leave ours in our room, and she's drawing pictures of herself and a little girl . . . and one of a fire."

"A fire?" Kayla rasps.

"Yep. I couldn't tell if it was in the forest, though, so I can't be sure she's Lillian."

"Who was in the drawing of the fire?"

"Rebekah and a girl around ten years old."

"Was Rebekah ten in the drawing too? Did she look like Lillian?"

"No, Rebekah was the age she is now." Maybe she's not Lillian but her helper?

"Maybe she knows Lillian? Maybe they're sisters?"

I shrug. "I have no damn clue. She said she only has an older brother, but she could be lying. Maybe she has a sister and that's Lillian. But what are the odds of sisters being burned in different accidents? Probably not that high."

"This is so messed up, Esme," Kayla says as we walk in the stifling heat.

"We just need to figure out Rebekah's deal."

"How do we do that?"

"Don't know." Why am I always the one who has to come up with the plans?

"Awesome."

"But now we know she keeps her phone on her. Constant contact. But with who?"

Kayla scrunches her nose. "Esme, what if we're wrong about her and she's just regular Rebekah with a burn?"

"Then we'll find no evidence and we'll say a very silent sorry to her."

I don't say it, but I *know* there is something wrong here.

We reach the halfway point around the lake; the others are heading toward us. The trees smell like freedom, and for once, the hot air doesn't prickle my skin. It's not as hot today, even though the sun is shining away.

Rebekah smiles freely, walking arm in arm with Tia.

"She looks very pleased with herself," Kayla says.

"Nothing like threatening your newest friends to relieve pent-up stress," I mutter.

"It sounds like you're already sure it's her."

"I'm not *sure* of anything, Kayla, and I hate that."

"Not having a party over here either."

I plaster a smile on my face as we reach the others. Since the note incident, Olly and I haven't spoken much. Things were looking good at first; he's sweet and supercute. Now . . . I'm unsure whether he wants to spend time with me or to run away. Maybe he's just spooked too.

"Hey, Esme," Rebekah says. Her smile is normal, but I look deeper. Is it genuine or does she know that I was just hiding under her bed?

"Hey," I reply. "Seen anything weird?"

"Not a thing."

"You want to walk back the other way together, Esme?" Olly asks.

Well, that sounds like he wants to spend time with me.

"Yeah," I reply. "Let's do it."

Kayla chuckles under her breath as she walks off with the others.

I wrap my arms around my stomach as we walk.

"You freaking out?" Olly asks.

Only a lot.

"There's a weird vibe here, you know?" I say. "All the campers are carrying on like normal, getting excited for *everything,* and we're pretending this is the best place on earth. It's a lot. I'm not sure if we can keep it up for weeks, let alone days."

"We might not need to. The cops might find out who it is," Olly says.

"They have one report of a trespasser who they think was an ex-counselor. Once they clear the two names Andy gave them, they'll write it off as someone getting lost on the trail. How much manpower do you think they're going to put into this?"

"I'll give you that. Are you saying we're out here alone?"

Sweat breaks out on my forehead. "Sorry to be the bearer of bad news."

"This feels so wrong, not going to the cops with all the information."

"Have you changed your mind?" I ask.

Olly shakes his head, taking a step closer to me as we walk. "No, I just don't think this is a good option either. You still think staying quiet is the best thing to do?"

"Yes," I reply.

I have to protect the secret I've been carrying around for ten years.

"We need a real break," he says. "Do you think anyone would be up for taking the trail into town?"

Laughter bursts from my diaphragm. "Is that a trick question?"

"You're not up for it, then?"

"After last time? And with someone in the woods?"

Why would he even suggest that?

"Well, I figure it's the best time to go. No one would think we'd be that dumb."

Because we're not going to be that dumb!

"Olly, really?" Why is he even going there?

Chuckling, he shakes his head. "Not one of my better ideas, I get it. Can we forget I said it?"

Not really.

"Totally, it's forgotten."

He really wants us to go back into the forest? That would be crazy.

"What's your favorite book?" he asks.

"What?"

"I realized we haven't had much time to talk about random normal stuff."

"*The Great Gatsby;* born June fifth, Gemini; tacos," I say, and his smile widens. "I don't know if I believe in God, but I do hope there's something after. Light blue; I hate sliders because they look like toddler shoes; Britney is still relevant; and Harry Styles should be my husband."

Laughing out loud, he replies, "All right."

"You go."

"*It;* May seventh; I have no idea about my star sign; with you on tacos; my family is religious but I'm unsure; dark green; sliders are the devil; Britney was hot; don't want to marry Styles."

I laugh, linking my arm through his. It feels like a bold move. Up until now, it's been him who initiates any physical contact.

"Where do you want to live after college?" I ask.

"Anywhere but here. If you could go on vacation anywhere in the world, where would it be?"

"I've always wanted to go to Iceland. . . ." I trail off before I can tell him it's because of the northern lights.

My stomach twists. Wait . . .

Anywhere but *here*?

32

Anywhere but *here*. That's what he said. His *exact* words.

Olly told me he lives in Missouri. Why would he say that if he lives in Texas?

Olly hasn't noticed the slipup. Maybe he just said it because we're here now and he wouldn't want to *live* in this heat?

"Iceland because of the northern lights?" He takes a guess at why I want to go.

"Yes," I reply. *Does he live around here?*

Why the hell would he lie about where he lives? He has a slight Southern accent but not what you would expect from someone from Texas.

Heat creeps up my neck.

What is going on?

Olly could be the one doing all of this. Maybe *he* is the accomplice.

I bite my lip as my mind storms with stupid theories.

Rein it in, Esme.

My paranoia is so strong that I'm suspecting everyone for little to no reason. Accents! That's what I'm basing my suspicions on.

I slip my arm out of his and shudder. "Jake just jumped in the lake."

"He's always in the water."

Olly was with us the night of the photos, though, and the time I saw Lillian in the woods. How could he and Rebekah be working together?

Unless only one of them is in on it and the other is innocent.

I need to find out where Olly is from.

And what handy ID lists your home address and state?

I have to sneak into Olly's room and find his driver's license.

But am I really ready to go there? I've already been through Rebekah's things. When I came back to Camp Pine Lake, I'd hoped to find a better version of myself.

"So you've only known everyone since we got here?" I ask. "You and Jake seem tight."

Olly side-eyes me, and I don't know whether I've said too much.

"I didn't know anyone before the beginning of summer. Jake and I are similar. I knew we'd be cool when he told me that Xbox has nothing on PS."

Of course.

"You're a gamer?"

"Yeah, but not massively. My brother is eleven and would play all day and night if our parents allowed it."

"What's his name?"

He replies a heartbeat later. "Daniel. Danny."

"Just you and Danny?"

"Yeah. Just me and him."

His posture is relaxed, voice light.

He doesn't have a tell. Why doesn't he squint, croak or look to the left—aren't people supposed to avoid eye contact when they lie?

Only that's not foolproof. My dad says since everyone knows that now, they make sure they don't do it.

I wish I'd been more interested in Dad's work. If he were here, he'd know in a millisecond if Olly was telling the truth.

"Who do you think is doing this?" I ask.

"I don't know, but I think we're on the right track, that it's someone who worked here. How else could they get into the locked cabins and know our routines, right?"

Or they might work here now and be feeding their partner in crime information.

Olly or Rebekah?

Or both.

Or neither.

Not him.

I blink hard. This is going well.

At this point I wouldn't be surprised if my brain imploded. Just a big *boom* and that's the end of Esme.

"What's your most-watched show?" Olly asks.

"*Friends.* Hands down. My mom watched it when she was

younger and starts from the beginning at least once a year. She got me into it."

He chuckles. "Here I was thinking you'd say *Riverdale*."

"Probably a close second. What's yours?"

"The Walking Dead."

"I think I stopped around season three thousand."

Laughing, he tilts his head back. "It's not that bad."

"I know, but you kill Glenn, you're dead to me."

"Never get attached to a character in *The Walking Dead* or *Game of Thrones*, Esme."

"Tyrion lived. I'm fine with *Thrones*. You know you can tour the city where King's Landing was filmed?"

"Croatia, right? We should go."

"Bit presumptuous to think I'll want to vacation with you, isn't it?"

He laughs again. "Who wouldn't want a trip to Croatia?"

I'm not going anywhere with Olly until I know he's not torturing me.

"Do you think Rebekah is okay?" I ask.

"No idea. Why?"

"I don't know, she seems weird," I say, and watch his reaction.

He shrugs one shoulder casually. "She's scared. No offense to her, but she seems like the type of person who freaks at everything."

"Don't you think there's a very good reason for us to be scared?"

If he isn't scared, why not?

"I do. Why do *you* think something is wrong with her?"

"I don't know. She seems . . . distant. I guess I don't know how she handles stressful situations. I forget we've only known each other a matter of weeks."

"Camps have that effect on you."

Is he speaking from experience as a camper or as a CIT? He couldn't have been here before, though. Andy, Cora and Mary are the returnees.

There is no way Olly could have been here before now; he's the same age as me. Unless he's lying and has a fake ID that says he's a year younger.

No, not Olly.

We reach the others. I have to get Kayla to sneak into the guys' cabin.

"Esme, want to go watch something? I brought my iPad and we have a couple hours until we have to be in the food hall for dinner," Olly says.

Result. I can be in his room without sneaking in.

Ignoring Kayla, Rebekah and Tia, who are waggling their eyebrows, I reply, "Sounds good. If we start a new series, we both have to swear not to watch an episode alone. *No* skipping ahead."

He holds his hands up. "I swear."

I nod. Today I snoop through his things. Tomorrow I go back to Rebekah's room and find her phone.

I follow Olly into his cabin. It smells like feet covered up with pine air freshener. The bedding is pale blue; the girls' is cream.

He stands outside the door to his room and lets me enter first.

I clench my fists as my palms sweat. Nothing is going to happen in here, so I don't know why my nerves are racing.

What if Lillian is someone he cares about and this thing between us is him trying to get me to trust him? He could shut that bedroom door and strangle me. Okay, obviously not. I need to start getting some decent sleep at night.

That does seem a little excessive over some burns. I really don't think Lillian died, and although my mistake was a big one, I was scared, and just a kid.

I want to believe that no one would kill over that.

Olly might be innocent.

"Okay, pull up Netflix," he says. "Mine is the bottom bunk. Jake shotgunned the top."

I turn to him and grin. "I did too."

He chuckles. "I believe it."

I grab the iPad sitting on his bed and open Netflix. "What do you want to watch?" I ask. "Ooh, what about *The Circle*?"

He shrugs. "Sure. Whatever."

"You have no opinion on this?"

"It doesn't matter what we watch, Esme."

I'd swoon if I weren't worried that he's been leaving creepy notes and chasing me through the woods.

But Olly couldn't have been the chaser either time. He was with me. There can't be three people involved, surely? Or more?

I shake my head and swallow bile at the thought of a whole group. I press Play, trying to ignore where my mind is taking me. The suspicious side of me really sucks right now. It's like it overrides logic and all I'm left with is a big pool of suspects who don't quite fit into the mold.

Olly sits beside me. We lean against the wall and I rest the iPad on my legs.

"Wait," I say, pressing Pause. "Do you think you could grab us some water before we start? I dehydrate in seconds here."

I don't think I've heard Olly mention the heat once.

Could my newest Netflix buddy be used to this climate?

He smirks. "Fine, but no snooping through my stuff. A guy's underwear drawer is private."

Damn it.

"I wasn't going to. . . ."

"I'm kidding, Esme!"

My throat goes dry.

His eyes linger for a second too long on mine, then he gets up.

33

Olly specifically told me not to snoop when he left.

Am I listening?

Nope.

The second I see him pass the window and head toward the food hall, I drop the iPad and slide off the bed. Olly isn't a mattress or pillowcase kind of guy, so I go straight for the dresser drawers.

Biting my lip, I pull open the third drawer down. The top two are likely to be Jake's since he took the top bunk.

Or that's what Kayla and I have done anyway. Rebekah and Tia too.

The wood makes a scraping sound as I gently tug the drawer toward me. Wincing, I slow down. Why is it so loud? But I'm alone; no one will hear it. I dig one hand in and root around.

I'm a terrible person!

An iPad case, pack of gum, penknife, deodorant.

Come on, Olly, you must have something personal.

I root deeper and come in contact with a small leather square. Bingo.

The black wallet is worn and curled at the edges like he's had it a long time.

Okay, his license must be in here.

And that's the exact moment the door creaks.

Olly's rough voice asks, "What are you doing?"

I drop the wallet and close my eyes.

Shit.

Face up to it.

Standing, I turn to him. "O-Olly," I say, my heart in my throat. "I was just . . ."

"Snooping," he says. "Why?"

He leans against the doorframe, his expression blank. I don't think he's mad.

"I like you." I sigh.

Not at all a lie. I do like him, and I want my doubts to just be in my head.

"I'm sorry, okay? I saw an opportunity to see your stuff. That was crappy of me. I don't know why I did it."

He steps into the room, his eyes sharp. "I don't have anything to hide. No secret girlfriend's pic in there."

"That's not why I was looking." My cheeks flame. "Wouldn't you be curious if we were in my room?"

"Is this what girls do to guys they like?"

"It's what *everyone* does. When you like someone, you want to know everything. Sometimes you can tell more about a person by what they own than what they say." I'm lying. I don't enjoy snooping at all.

"I'll tell you anything you want to know, Esme. You don't need to sneak around."

I try to ignore the cold, sinking feeling in my stomach.

Well done, you've screwed this one up royally.

He takes another step and reaches out. I watch his hand curl around my wrist and unfold my arms.

"I just want to know you. The last guy I liked . . . it didn't end well."

"I'm not him."

"No, you're not. Can I have a do-over?"

He lets go of my wrist and pulls the drawer open all the way. "Go for it. Tell me what you learn."

"I don't want to," I tell him, and I mean it.

"Sure you do. I have nothing to hide. Snoop all you want. I'll even leave the room if you'd rather do it alone."

"No." I shake my head. "I'm sorry. I don't want to be that girl. I trust you."

I'm an idiot for thinking he's involved because of a slip of the tongue. He's been open with me and he's not even angry at me for going through his stuff. He wouldn't tell me to look if he had something to hide.

"Were you looking for something in particular?" he asks.

When is the ground going to swallow me? "No. You must think I'm crazy."

And I might be, you know. Since all of this started, the threats and stalking, I haven't felt very sane. I'm paranoid and jumping from one dumb theory to the next. It doesn't take much to make me suspicious, despite there being a serious lack of evidence with Rebekah and Olly.

"I don't think you're crazy. A little sneaky maybe," he says.

"I didn't mean to be."

That sounds so lame. I didn't mean to be sneaky? I freaking planned it!

"Ask me anything," he says. "Whatever you want to know."

"What song can you listen to over and over?"

His lips curl with a smile. " 'Bohemian Rhapsody.' It's timeless and brilliant."

I touch my heart. "Hail Freddie. What's your sick food?"

"My what?"

"The only thing you can stomach when you're ill."

"Oh. Dry toast, I guess."

"Mine is plain pasta. What's your favorite thing about your hometown?"

"That it's called Springfield. I like *The Simpsons.*"

There's a Springfield in Missouri. I know because my dad likes *The Simpsons,* too.

I nod. "My hometown has this little bistro called Dante's, and they serve the best Philly cheesesteaks in the world."

"How many calories are in those things?"

"About a whole week's allowance, but it's so worth it. Do you count calories?"

"Not religiously. Our old coach was big on living a healthy lifestyle. He liked to win."

"Football, right?" I ask.

"I was the running back."

"Did you want to be quarterback?"

"Never appealed. Besides, I was the fastest on the field. I could get that ball far."

"Do you love it?"

"I do. Football is big at home."

"Maybe I'll watch you in the Super Bowl one day."

"I'm not sure I'm *that* good."

"I wish I was sporty. I used to run track for school, but now I just do it for fun."

"I thought you had runner's legs." His eyes dip to my legs, then snap back up.

Smiling, I look away.

I don't mention him checking me out as I pass him. "If you could have dinner with any actor, who would it be?"

"The questions keep coming, huh?" Olly teases. "Dead or alive?"

I shrug. "Either?"

"Robin Williams. He was brilliant."

"Who is the person you can be one hundred percent yourself around? No hiding, no judgments? Mine is my nana."

"My dad. We're alike," Olly replies.

"What was your favorite thing to do when you were younger?"

"Six Flags Fiesta. Yours?' "

"The zoo with my nana. We went a lot, even sponsored some of the animals. Do you think we're in danger here?"

His attention drifts to his iPad. "I don't know."

I think we are, but I don't say anything to him because he's already clicking on Netflix.

So instead of pushing it, I watch *The Circle* with Olly until we have to go back to the food hall.

And I try to forget that I ever suspected him.

34

A slow two days later, I'm chewing my lip to the point of pain. No need for red lipstick when blood will do the trick.

The campers are asleep, and the day was pretty standard. Nothing out of the ordinary, unless you count one of the boys getting a Cheerio stuck up his nose.

Nothing out of the ordinary. That's what's making me sweat now. I'd prefer things to just happen. The wait for Lillian's next move makes my stomach churn constantly.

Kayla, Rebekah, Tia, Olly and Jake are sitting on the dock, dangling their feet into the water.

I'm supposed to join them.

Instead I'm sitting on the porch of the food hall, just out of sight of my friends.

"Esme?" Mary says as she walks past.

"Hi." I sit straighter.

She tilts her head. "Are you all right?"

"Fine. Just having a drink," I say, holding my mug of hot chocolate up.

She nods.

I'm sure she's about to leave—she should be in her bedroom with Catalina—but she sits next to me instead. "I thought you would be with your friends?"

Okay, she's staying?

"Yeah, I'll join them in a minute."

"You haven't had a falling-out, have you? Totally normal if you have, it happens from time to time when we're all in such close quarters."

"Nothing like that. I just needed a minute."

She huffs like an exasperated teacher. "Anything the matter?"

I shake my head, my long hair blowing around my face in the breeze.

"I know we haven't spent a lot of time together, Esme, but you can talk to any counselor here. Confidentially, if that's what you want."

Why does she assume I need a confidential chat? Because I'm sitting alone?

"I appreciate that."

Mary's big dark eyes watch me and wait, like she's thinking I'm about to spill my life story. I look away when her gaze starts to feel like it's boring into me.

Finally, she smiles. "Okay. I can tell something is wrong. Will you speak to someone if you need to?"

I don't want her to start telling the other counselors that I'm not okay.

"We haven't heard anything from this person in a couple of days," I say. "In theory that's a good sign. But it doesn't feel good, you know?"

"We were told to keep quiet and then nothing else would happen," Mary says.

"No, he said that if we don't alert the cops or anyone else, then the campers would be fine. What's the point of making us keep quiet and doing *nothing*? What does he get out of that? It doesn't make sense."

Not knowing what Lillian has planned is driving me *insane*. She could tell everyone what Kayla and I did at any moment. Would Andy kick us out? Right now, our friends think we're good people.

I drop my head. Am I not a good person?

Can one stupid decision really define you? Kayla and I never intended any harm.

Mary purses her lips, clearly turning my words over in her mind. I can see her making sense of them. "I don't think you're wrong, but none of this makes sense. Unless this person has a personal grudge against someone here, why would they continue to harass us?"

"You think they're just messing around?"

"No, I definitely think someone is out there and they want us to be scared. I'm unsure if I believe they want to hurt us."

I want to believe that Lillian just wants to scare us.

"Are you still Team Cops?"

Her lips slide into a smile. "Yes, I'm still Team Cops."

"They're not always that helpful. Sometimes the law doesn't allow them to be."

"Oh, I know. I had a friend once, this girl whose ex wouldn't leave her alone. There was nothing the cops could legally do unless he threatened her, or worse."

"What happened?"

"The ex strangled her to death, exactly one month *after* the restraining order expired."

I swallow. "Oh."

"It's not a nice story."

"So you're saying that the cops can't do anything unless this freak hurts one of us?"

It all sounds rather contradictory. If Mary knows that nothing can be done, why does she want to go to the police?

"There has been a direct threat, and children are here. I think more can be done in this case," she says.

"Even though we don't have a clue who it is? Or how many of them they might be?" I ask.

"How many?" With a shudder, she adds, "There's a chilling thought."

"I think it's more than one. Do you?"

"I doubt anyone could do this alone."

Good, she's got there, too.

"Do you think two people could do all of this?"

Her lips part in a small gasp. "I can just about deal with two, not a whole group."

Lillian lived around here. Who's to say she hasn't brought her friends in for a little revenge?

"You think they'll show themselves?" I ask.

"You said yourself that it doesn't make sense to threaten us, then walk away."

"Perhaps," I say, frowning. "You mentioned them having an issue with one of us. How would they know we'd be here?"

"It's likely teens from town getting their sick kicks from scaring us, Esme. But I don't think it's smart to ignore the possibility that one of us in particular is being targeted."

I need to change the subject.

"It's so pretty here," I say.

"Do you want to come back next summer?" Mary asks.

Absolutely not.

"I think so. How long have you been coming here?"

"Three years." She laughs. "I think Andy was born here."

"Yeah, he loves it."

"He's good at his job. There's a lot more to it than just making sure the campers have fun and learn new skills. He's managing staff too . . . and *this* situation. The past few days, he's looked tired."

"No one is getting much sleep. Besides the campers, that is."

"Ugh, my cabin is terrible for whispering until eleven at night."

"Mine too, but they usually quiet down before ten. I think all the physical activity wears them out."

"Whatever happens, we have to keep them safe," Mary says, wrapping her arms around herself.

"Of course."

The campers, the *kids,* are awesome. Some are cocky and full of attitude, but under the pretense, they're children. I won't let Lillian harm a single one of them.

I'd gladly expose my own secret before that happened.

And that could well be what she wants. The whole point of this is to make Kayla and me so paranoid we reach a breaking point, to watch us suffer before she forces us to speak up.

We can't even leave now.

We're completely at her mercy.

Mary walks along the beach. I watch her make eye contact with Catalina as she comes out of the cabin. Without a word, Catalina follows her. They said everything with a glance like some freaky Powerpuff juju.

They go into the multiuse cabin and close the door.

Okay.

"Esme!" Rebekah shouts, waving from the dock.

I plaster on a smile like the one Kayla used at school when talking to the popular kids. She was very good at their game. Sometimes a little too good.

Kayla stands and walks to meet me. "What were you doing?"

"Just talking to Mary."

"What about?"

"Three guesses, Kayla!"

"You look obsessed and soon people are going to be asking why."

"Don't worry about me, I have it under control."

"Do you?" she asks, her eyebrows lifting.

"I'm fine, Kayla."

"Maybe you should have an early night."

"Excuse me?"

"It's not good for you to be out here. You look pale and you're biting your nails again."

I hide my hands behind my back. "I told you I'm okay."

"And I'm telling you that you're not. I'm your best friend, Esme, and I can see what's going on. You're losing it." She steps even closer even though we're far enough from everyone else that they can't hear us.

I take a step back.

"People are going to get suspicious," she says. "You're constantly getting in the middle of every creepy situation and it's all you talk about to anyone."

"It's not *all* I talk about."

"It might as well be. Rebekah asked if you're okay. She said she's worried that you're not coping."

I bet she did.

"When did Rebekah say this?"

"Just now, while you were sulking over there."

My eyes slide over Kayla's shoulder. Rebekah and Olly are sitting together chatting. He throws a stick into the lake.

"Esme, I'll tell them you got too much sun and need to rest."

Kayla's hands are on her hips when I look back at her.

Am I unwelcome now? She's not really leaving me much choice. Not that I want to hang out with them right now. Not when Rebekah is analyzing me.

"Fine," I say through my teeth. "I'll go."

She sighs. "Don't be like that. I'm protecting us both."

"Night, Kayla," I say, and turn away from her.

No one calls my name as I head for my cabin.

$$\approx\approx$$

Dinner has been served after a day of baking, den building, dodgeball and tennis. The campers chat happily as they feast on Mexican food.

Taco Tuesday is the best day in camp.

But not for me.

Olly is finishing his fourth taco. The cooks here have to respect his and Jake's appetites.

Everyone's spirits are raised ever so slightly when we have a good meal. I pretend like mine are, too. This evening's conversation is about what we would do in the event of a zombie apocalypse. Half my table would go to the city and the other half would set up camp in a remote forest.

I'm Team Forest. Fewer humans to turn zombie and eat me. But I definitely wouldn't camp. I'd strap myself high up in a tree to sleep, like Katniss in *The Hunger Games*.

After dinner and music around the campfire, the kids go to bed.

It's my night off tonight, but Kayla and I have been asked to help tidy the outside area before we turn in. Cora is inside with the girls until we switch. I don't want to be outside; I'd rather be tucked up in bed.

It's not particularly messy out here, but I think Andy wants the creeper to see numbers. The more adults that Lillian and her cronies see, the less likely she is to follow through on any threats.

That's what I think, anyway.

I pick up a couple of tennis balls that have been hit over the fence.

As I turn to take them to the multiuse cabin, I see Olly walking toward me.

"Hey, Esme, you need a hand?" he asks.

I smile as he approaches. If I didn't need my friends right now, I would be pissed at them for how they treated me last night. "Yeah, can you grab those rackets, please?"

He picks them up and we walk back to the cabin.

"You shouldn't be out that far alone, especially not at night," he says.

"It's not too dark yet and I didn't go into the woods. There might be some balls in there, but hell no am I checking tonight."

"I'll take a look in the morning," he says.

We pass Mary, Catalina and a few others in canoes, letting off some steam.

They look so carefree.

I wonder what message that's sending to Lillian? We're still having fun. You don't scare us. Do your worst.

But how bad is her worst?

Olly holds the cabin door for me and I flick the light on. "Thanks."

He's acting normal. I'm not sure if they really were talking about me last night or if Kayla was just trying to make me feel bad.

We take the rackets and balls into the storage closet. It's full of sports equipment and smells like rubber and sweat. I turn to leave, but Olly steps in front of the door, blocking my exit.

"What are you doing?" I ask, my smile dropping.

"I've wanted to do something for a while."

Strangle me?

My eyes widen as he steps closer.

I brace myself for a fight.

Why aren't you running?

He looms over me. My mouth goes dry.

He *is* the one in on it with Lillian.

Fab time to find out that when it comes to fight or flight, I'm not a flight.

I've always had a lot of respect for the fighters. Turns out we're just stupid.

My heart races, and I clench my hands into fists.

I've taken self-defense classes, and I'm going to kick his ass.

His hands never reach my neck, though. They slide around my back.

What is happening?

It takes me a second later to really get it—I *am* that stupid—Olly doesn't want to hurt me. His lips touch mine.

Oh.

Code red! Code red! You're fraternizing with the enemy!

I relax into the kiss a second later and feel his smile against my mouth. He tastes like Dr Pepper and smells like a campfire.

Olly pulls back for a second. "I didn't expect complete shock, Esme. I thought I made it kinda obvious that I like you."

Do not tell him the shock is because he isn't choking the life out of you.

"I'm sorry," I say, shaking my head to try to get a little clarity.

"I'll stop if you want me to?" He looks at me, his eyes soft.

I don't swoon easily, but I am right now.

"You may continue."

He laughs and brings his lips down on mine again.

I step closer, closing any distance between us. I snuggle into him as he kisses us both breathless.

"We should get back," he says, minutes, hours later, I don't know.

He's taken my mind off last night and that's all that matters right now.

"Right. We have a job to do here and all that."

His mouth curls. "We should go and do that."

Neither of us moves. "Olly," I say. "I need to tell you something."

"Go on."

"The other day when we were talking about where we'd like to live after college . . ."

If we're going to start something, and it feels like we are, I want to be as honest as I can.

"Yeah?" he prompts.

"Well, you said you want to live anywhere but here, and for a second I thought you meant you lived here. In Texas. In this town."

"I'm not sure I'm following."

"We said that the person who could be watching . . . um . . ."

Lowering his arms, he breaks all contact and steps back.

"Me?" He turns and runs his hands through his hair. "Wow. You thought *I* was messing with camp?"

"No. Well, I'm sorry, but just think about how it sounded."

"I don't care how it sounded! Why didn't you just ask? I would have told you I just don't want to end up in a dead-end town like this. Jesus, Esme."

"I'm sorry."

Disappointment fills his eyes. "You actually thought I could threaten you all? That I would put *children* in danger?"

"No!" I say, but it doesn't mean anything because that is *totally* what I thought.

We haven't known each other long, but I really don't think Olly would be part of something as terrifying as this. Lillian wants to turn us against each other.

And I did exactly that.

"Please, can we just talk about this?" I plead. "I've been paranoid and scared. I like you and it was dumb. Like really dumb, but I haven't exactly been thinking straight."

He takes a step toward the door.

"Olly, don't leave, please?"

"I wouldn't hurt *anyone.*"

"I believe you."

He clicks his tongue against his teeth. "The first girl I've liked since my ex thinks I'm a deranged stalker."

I dip my head, wincing. I've made a huge mess of this.

"Olly," I whisper.

"Why didn't you just ask?" He sounds defeated, like this is all over and he's telling me it's my fault. I could have avoided this by talking to him. He huffs, his eyes flashing to mine. "That's why you were going through my stuff."

Crap.

"I was looking for your driver's license," I say. "I wanted so badly to prove my dumb theory wrong. The last couple of weeks with you have been awesome, and I was terrified that you might be the one doing this and that you hated me."

He tilts his head. "Why would that make me hate *you?*"

Oh God.

"No, I mean all of us. Whoever is out there clearly doesn't have warm and fuzzy feelings for any of us."

His sneakers thud on the floor as he walks closer to me.

"Why are you lying to me?" he growls.

I gulp. "I'm not lying."

"Then tell me what you meant by that. Why would this person hate you?"

I press my lips together.

"You acted weird when we were in the forest," he presses. "Sometimes you're off in your own world, and I can see the panic you're holding in. Last night you bailed on us and today you've been jumpy as hell."

"You're wrong," I tell him. But my words hold no weight because my voice cracks and betrays me.

"I'm not wrong. What's going on? You know more than you're telling me. Is someone threatening *you?*"

"Olly, no."

He shakes his head. "We're not leaving this damn closet until you tell me the truth."

I squeeze my eyes shut. I can't tell. I've never told anyone, ever.

"I can't," I whisper.

I keep my eyes closed, but I feel him getting closer. His breath cascades over my head and then I'm in his strong, warm arms.

"You're scaring me," he says into my hair. "If someone is harassing you, I can help. I won't let anyone hurt you, Esme. I promise."

After a mere two weeks, if something happened to me, he would get over it fast. We're not even together. I barely know the guy.

"Hey," Olly presses. "Please tell me."

His body is rigid.

I sink into him and feel my tears seeping into his T-shirt.

"You'll hate me," I mutter against his collarbone.

"Tell me." He pulls back. "It's bad?"

I nod. "I didn't mean it, though."

"What didn't you mean?"

"I lied about when I was last here as a camper," I whisper. "It was the year of the fire . . . and I was there that night."

36

The weight of the secret is heavy, but rather than feeling lighter now that I've told Olly, I want to crawl under a rock.

Realization hits and his jaw drops. "*You* were responsible for the fire?"

"It wasn't entirely my fault. I mean, it was, but it was an accident."

"What happened?"

"I—I was eight. The older kids had been sneaking out and bragging about it. I thought it would be cool if I did the same. It was so stupid."

Olly takes my hands in his and a glimmer of hope settles in my chest. Maybe he won't hate me. "What happened?" he asks.

"They used to sneak out the back window in the cabins and go down that trail. I didn't know it led into town back then. I went one night, past the camp's border and onto public land. I was a little scared but kept thinking about how the older kids would react the next day when I told them."

Meeting Olly's eyes, I wince. "I came to the clearing where people camp and no one was there. I lit a fire and it got out of hand."

Tell him what you and Kayla did to Lillian, you chicken!

"Whoa," he breathes. "Okay. Well, that was bad, but it was an accident."

"I never meant for it to happen. I added too many sticks to the fire. It collapsed as the sticks under the new ones gave way and the whole thing toppled sideways and hit that small group of trees." I gulp. "It was almost like adding gasoline, the trees caught fire that fast. It had barely rained all summer."

Olly squeezes my hands, telling me it's okay.

Nothing about that night was okay, though. He doesn't understand that because I can't find the words or the strength to tell him the rest.

We're new friends. What if he doesn't keep my secret?

"I hated myself for a long time after that," I say.

"What did you do once the fire spread?" he asks.

"I ran. Like a little coward, I ran back to camp and slipped through the window. By the time I heard sirens, I was back in bed. The whole forest didn't catch fire purely because of the number of rocks around the trees and the lack of debris. Any longer, though, and one of the trees could have fallen over and reached the others."

"Who called nine-one-one?"

"I don't know. There was a lot of smoke, so it could have been anyone. I heard a rumor that it was some people outside a bar who noticed the fire."

"You never told anyone?"

"No, never. In the morning there were a couple of cops at camp. I thought they'd come for me, but it turned out they were just asking the counselors if they'd noticed anything. Over breakfast we were all told there had been a fire off-site."

"And you decided not to tell."

Olly isn't asking me a question.

"I was so scared of what would happen. It was an accident, so there was no point in getting myself into trouble, getting kicked out of camp *and* giving the camp a bad name. How would it look when the counselors didn't know the campers were sneaking out at night?"

He frowns. "Do you think they're doing that now?"

"There never used to be locks on the windows. Now the only window you can get out of in their room is a fire escape with an alarm on it."

"Jesus," Olly mutters, dropping my hands.

"I regret it. Every day I've regretted what I did that night. I wish I could go back and stop it from happening. I was *so* stupid."

"You were eight."

"I still knew right from wrong."

"Damn, Esme." He rubs his jaw. "All this time . . ."

"I think whoever is doing this might know it was me that night," I whisper.

Olly's eyes snap to me and widen like an inflating balloon. "Why would you think that?"

"'The lake never forgets'? What other crap has happened

here besides the forest almost being burned to the ground?" *And someone getting hurt.*

"Probably lots of things."

I arch an eyebrow. "Such as?"

"I don't know, but I doubt you're the only one who has ever gotten themselves into trouble here." Olly blows out a long breath, as if there's something else he wants to say but won't.

I tilt my head, my eyes piercing into his as if I'll actually be able to read his mind. He looks away.

When he remains silent, I sigh. "Maybe we should go to bed."

"Are you for real? You think I'm hiding something again. You search my room because you think I'm a stalker, then you off-load your secret onto me, and still you think I'm hiding something."

"I can see that you are!"

"How?"

"Because you can barely look me in the eye!"

"I don't know what you're talking about."

I reach for him, but he backs up, shaking his head. "Please tell me if there's something, Olly," I say. "All of this is driving me insane and if we know for sure, once and for all, what this craziness is about, then we might be able to stop it."

"Esme . . ."

"Please?"

"There's nothing to tell," he says, scowling.

My jaw drops as he turns and walks out of the cupboard. He shuts the door a little harder than necessary.

And I know one thing for sure. Olly's keeping secrets too.

37

What is he hiding? Olly is lying to me, and I'm still half-lying to him.

When confessing my horrible secret, I left out the most important part of that night, and right now, I'm glad I did. Why would I tell him every gory detail when he's not telling me *anything*?

I open the cupboard door, flick off the light, and make my way outside.

Everyone is still in the same place as before. Olly is nowhere to be seen, so he must already be in his cabin.

I don't know what's happening with us now. I went in wary of him, then we were kissing, now he's mad at me. There's less back-and-forth in a game of Ping-Pong.

"Esme, you okay?" Kayla says as I walk into our little room, ready for bed.

The girls are still whispering to each other. Lights-out isn't for another thirty minutes.

"Ugh, not really." I drop onto Kayla's bed and put my head in my hands.

"What's going on?"

Tilting my head to the side, I peek up at her through my fingers. "I told Olly."

Her light blue eyes bulge. "You did *what*?"

I drop my hands. "Not about Lillian and I didn't mention you. I told him that I was in the forest and accidentally set it on fire."

"What the hell! Why?"

"I don't know. He could see that something was up, and he'd just kissed me."

"Wait, what? He kissed you? How was it?"

Really? I shake my head and ignore the question. "Anyway, he was understanding about the fire. He knew it wasn't intentional."

"Then what? You *definitely* didn't mention Lillian? We were supposed to take that to our grave."

"I'm sorry. It all got a bit much. I swear I only told him that I did it, no mention of you."

"Why do you look so down if Olly doesn't blame you for the fire *and* he kissed you?"

"Um . . . so I told him the truth about why I was snooping in his room, that I was suspicious. That annoyed him, but he got over it. After the kiss, when I dropped the bomb and said maybe what's happening now is due to that, he said something odd."

"Well?"

"He said that I'm probably not the only one to get into trouble at camp."

Sitting taller, Kayla tilts her head closer to me. "Like something else has gone down?"

"Thank you! That's exactly what I thought, too, but he got all shady and left in a huff, slamming the door."

"He's overreacting, right? That means the dude's hiding something."

"Do you think he was a camper here?"

"We'd remember those eyes."

"Yeah, I would, but maybe he was here after we were?"

"Isn't that a little too much of a coincidence? Bad stuff happened to three campers who all find themselves shiny-new CITs at the same time in the same place?"

"I guess."

"Ugh, I hate that I'm being sucked back into this . . . but what's the theory here, Esme? Olly's involved like Lillian, or he's like us?"

I'm not going to apologize for "sucking her back into this." She never should have left.

"I have no clue." I throw my hands up. "It's *so* frustrating because I know he's keeping a secret even after I told him mine. It wasn't easy to spill. Now he has a confession . . . maybe. Does it even matter?"

Kayla seems to consider this. "You have to talk to him. We need to know what he's hiding."

"How, though?"

"I vote for the direct route. Rip the Band-Aid off, Esme. Walk up to him and demand answers."

"Thank you," I say sarcastically. "That was superhelpful."

"Well, I don't think he's going to have it all written down for you to snoop again and steal!"

"That reminds me, I should try to get another look at Rebekah's diary."

"I love that almost getting caught isn't a deterrent for you."

"Getting caught just makes me sneakier. Besides, next time you're going to do a better job of keeping her busy."

"What do you want me to do, lie on the ground and hold her ankles?"

"No, start crying and she'll comfort you."

Kayla opens, then closes her mouth. Then she says, "That's actually a good idea."

"I know!"

I strip my clothes off and get into my pajamas.

"Fine, I'll do that," she says. "What do you want to do first tomorrow, interrogate Olly or ransack Rebekah's room?"

She makes us sound so delightful. At least she's with me again. I'm not sure how long it will last, though. She'll probably spook again with Lillian's next move.

"I'll start with Olly," I reply. "There's a hike tomorrow afternoon, and I'm going to have a very bad headache."

"I don't know if I should be proud of you or fear you."

I smile. "Think you can talk to Jake and find out if Olly has mentioned anything to him?"

"Sure."

"Just don't be obvious about it. Oh, and if you tell Jake about the fire, that's okay."

"Do you think Olly will tell him?"

"I hope not."

"I hope Jake doesn't know anything," Kayla says, sighing dreamily.

"That's going well, then?"

Her expression turns mushy. "I picked a good one that day. He's sweet and also has that alpha male thing working for him."

"Because he wants to go into the forest and pummel the person doing this?"

"He wants to protect us."

"Stop swooning long enough to keep a straight head, yeah?"

"What does that mean?" Kayla demands.

"Olly's not being honest about a lot. I think he might know Jake better than he says he does. They're very . . . in tune. They're a little too close for having only met a couple of weeks ago, don't you think?"

"Jake wouldn't lie."

"You've known him for, like, three minutes, Kayla."

"He *wouldn't* lie."

"You can't be certain of that."

"You need to stop pissing off all your friends, Esme."

Oh, come on!

Is she really arguing with me over a boy she barely knows? This is the last thing we need with all that's going on.

"Not trying to. I want to get to the bottom of this, same as you do," I tell her.

"Then can we agree to not accuse my boyfriend of being a liar?"

Boyfriend? Since when? Something tells me not to focus on that part or she might get cranky with me again.

"Yep," I say, smiling with gritted teeth. "We can agree to that."

I climb up onto my bed and scoot under the blanket.

"So, our suspect list is currently sitting at two? Rebekah and Olly?" Kayla asks.

"Yes," I reply, silently adding a third as I curl up.

Jake.

38

I jump awake, clutching the thin blanket to my chest.

What was that?

There was a crash. I'm sure I wasn't dreaming.

I throw the blanket off and climb down the ladder. Kayla is still asleep—she wouldn't wake if there were an atomic bomb. Surely I can't be the only one who heard the crash.

The girls are also asleep. But the noise was too real to just be my imagination.

Frowning, I pad toward the cabin door and slide the dead bolt open. The metal scrapes and I clench my teeth. *Shh.*

When I get the lock off, I pull the door open.

Be brave.

Stepping onto the porch, I glance around. It's early; the sun is still a while off from rising.

I look to my left. Olly is outside his cabin. Are we the only light sleepers?

"You heard that too?" he asks.

"Yeah, it woke me up. What was it?"

"I don't know. I think it came from your direction."

I glance the other way. Nothing looks off.

"Do you think something fell?" I ask.

Olly walks toward me. "Maybe. The thud sounded like something against wood, right?"

"Look," I say, as my eyes land on the food hall. Its door is wide open. "The door wasn't open when we went to bed."

Olly's eyes narrow. "Great."

What has Lillian done this time?

Olly stops when he reaches the steps of my cabin. "Okay. You wait here, and I'll go check it out."

"Wait, what?" I jog down the steps and grab his wrist. "You can't go in there alone. We don't know what's happening!"

"Esme, you can't go in there at all. Just wait until I've seen if it's safe."

My back stiffens. "Yes, I can go in there."

"I love that you have this super-chick thing going on and you don't need saving, but right now can you *please* stay here?"

I cross my arms. He's right about one thing. I don't need saving.

I watch him walk toward the food hall. Then I follow because there's no way I'm going to stay put. This is my mess.

Creeping closer, I try to look around the door as Olly opens it.

He looks over his shoulder and lifts his eyebrows like he knew I wouldn't do as I was told. "I mean it, Esme, wait until I've gone in."

"What if that's what they want to happen, huh?" I whisper, wrapping my arms around my stomach as I look back toward the lake.

"Don't be an ass," he hisses.

A smile touches my lips as I follow closely behind him.

Groaning my name this time, like he's beyond frustrated, he tilts his head back. "Can you not just do as you're told?"

"No. It's a curse."

He turns around and I follow close behind him.

Lifting his hand, he flicks on the light and we both gasp.

39

Is that what I think it is?

I blink hard, but when I open my eyes the image is the same.

This is very, very real.

The carcass of a deer lies in the middle of the floor between two tables. Blood pools in a circle around it like a grim rug.

I grab Olly's hand as my pulse thumps in my ears.

"What the hell is that?" he says.

I stare unblinking until my eyes sting. "It's a deer."

Doing a double take, he stares at me like I'm insane. "I know it's a deer, but *why* is it in the middle of the cabin, dead?"

Because Lillian is sick.

I should've known she would do something like this. The night of the fire, she terrified me and Kayla by showing us a poor animal that she'd killed and mutilated. It was the reason Kayla lashed out at her in the first place.

I should call an Uber right now.

"We eat in here. *Children* eat in here," I mutter. "I can't believe anyone would do this."

Olly covers his mouth. "I think I'm going to hurl."

Okay, get it together. You're not supposed to know who is behind this.

"L-let's look around. There might be a note like the one we got on the door."

He exhales. "Our resident psycho is getting bolder."

I walk around the tables, making sure to put as much distance between me and freaking Bambi as possible.

The deer isn't huge, but it's probably heavy. It's also covered in blood, so getting it here couldn't have been easy. It had to be a two-person job, surely.

"Esme, here," Olly says.

I turn to see him pick up a piece of paper from a table. He scrunches his nose. "Damn, that's gross. It's written in *blood.*"

"What does it say?" I ask, jogging over.

"It says, 'Someone here wants to talk.'" He looks up. "Who wants to talk?"

Someone. "Maybe it's about Mary? She's been very vocal about going to the cops."

"She's been vocal when we're around the campfire. How close is this person?" Olly asks, holding the note up.

I wave my hand at the dead deer. "Pretty damn close, Olly!"

In my room too.

"We need to get Andy," he says.

"I—I'll go."

Olly looks down at the deer with wide eyes.

Whatever his secret is, I don't think he was involved in putting the deer in the food hall.

I turn on my heel and race outside, down the steps and to the staff cabin, where Andy is sleeping peacefully. I almost feel bad for waking him up with this news.

Almost. I need someone else to deal with this, because I'll clean up the blood, but I'm *not* touching that deer.

I rap lightly on his bedroom window.

A minute later, the curtain is pulled to the side. Andy's eyes land on me, and he startles.

"Esme?" he says, opening the window and rubbing his pale forehead. "What are you doing?"

"I need you to come to the food hall," I say breathlessly.

His face falls. Shutting the window, he drops the curtain and I hear him bumping about, getting his clothes and shoes on.

I walk around to the front of the cabin and wait.

"What happened?" he asks, dashing through the door and down the steps.

"A deer," I say. "Dead."

"A dead deer?"

"Dead. Murdered. I don't know. It's *in* the food hall!"

"In it?"

"Yes, come on."

He runs past me and I follow, sprinting up the food hall steps.

I hear Andy say Olly's name and then he cusses the air blue.

"How did you find this?" he asks, sinking to his knees near the animal.

The blood is close to him. I squirm. *Move back a little.*

Olly crouches down. "I heard a crash. It sounded like chairs falling over or being thrown. Esme heard it too. The door was open, so we came in here and found this."

"Whoever it was, they couldn't have gotten far," I say, pressing one hand against my rolling stomach.

They both turn to me.

"God," Andy breathes. "All right. I'm going to get my phone and take some pictures, then we're going to clean this up. No panicking, we're not giving this person what they want."

"Okay." Nothing is okay, and that sounds like an awful plan, but I don't have a better one.

"You two stay here," Andy tells us.

I walk around the deer when Andy leaves, and Olly rises to his feet.

"Are you all right?" he asks.

"Are *we* all right?" I counter.

He was mad at me five hours ago.

Olly grabs my hand and pulls me in for a hug. I sink against him and my muscles relax. "We're cool, Esme. Does the deer mean anything?"

"What?" I mutter against his shoulder.

"You think the person doing all this knows about the fire? Is a deer relevant to anything that happened that night?"

Wow. What a question to ask. He's perceptive.

"What is it, Esme?"

"There was a dead deer near the fire site. But it wasn't significant."

Another lie.

The deer *was* significant.

My head spins. Of course it was significant. I should have known back then how troubled Lillian was. I was scared of her then. I'm petrified of her now.

"What do you think it means?" Olly presses.

I shrug. "I don't know!"

It's a warning just like that night: Fear me.

"Everything okay?" Andy asks, walking back into the cabin.

Olly looks up and rubs my back. "She's just a little freaked."

"It'll be fine, Esme. This person is just trying to scare us."

I turn around and Olly drops one of his arms from around me. "It's working," I say. "I'm scared for the campers. What if they'd found this?"

Andy shakes his head. "They're *never* in here first. Whoever did this knew that it would be staff who found it. This was all for us."

That makes sense. We always set up before the campers come in to eat. Lillian's knowledge of the camp is too great for her to not have been here. Or not to have an accomplice who's here.

There was no one else with Lillian that night in the woods. If Lillian isn't Rebekah, she must have told her everything.

I take a breath.

Andy shakes a blanket out. "Are you ready to get this deer into the woods, Olly?"

Wrinkling his nose, he replies, "Sure."

That is such a crap job. "How far will you take it?"

"Not too far. There's an area between two trails that's filled with bush. It'll be hidden in there."

"Great. I'll go and get buckets and cleaning supplies," I say. "The quicker we clean the blood up, the less likely it'll be to stain."

There are a lot of stains on the floor anyway. Hopefully the blood will blend in with them.

Or I could bleach the bloodstain and it would be lighter. That's preferable to a faded patch of blood.

I'm almost to the kitchen when I hear the front door creak open.

40

I spin around. Andy and Olly are already facing the door.

Oh crap, she's out there!

"Was that someone?" I ask.

Olly takes off running.

"Olly, no!"

Andy catches me as I make a run for it too.

"Stop, stop, stop. Esme, you can't go out there," he says, wrapping both arms around me.

I wriggle in his firm hold. He does not look this strong. "Let go! Olly could get hurt!"

This is all my fault. It should be me chasing her.

"Stay here. I'll go." Andy twists us around and pushes me deeper into the room. "I'll go, Esme."

Pressing one hand to my chest, I pant and my eyes sting with the threat of tears.

Do not cry.

Andy dashes from the cabin.

Walking backward, I let my legs hit a bench and then I sit.

I take a long breath and release it slowly as my head swims. This is all getting to be too much.

If Olly gets hurt because I wouldn't let go of my secret, I'll never forgive myself. Kayla and I need to have a chat, because we can't keep this up. We can't let someone else get hurt because of what we did.

I watch the door, willing Olly and Andy to come back. Maybe I should follow them? My getting lost in the woods isn't going to help anything, though. I've done that already.

What if Lillian's leading them away so she can get to me?

Calm down. Breathe.

With my heart racing a million miles an hour, I get up and walk into the kitchen. The cupboard with cleaning supplies is padlocked for safety. I twist the numbers to 9-4-5 and the lock springs open.

I grab two buckets, new sponges, rubber gloves and strong chemical cleaners. I've noticed the products used on the tables are *much* more eco-friendly. They won't cut it for this job, though.

I fill one of the buckets with hot soapy water and chuck the sponges into the empty one. Then I carry them both into the room, ready to clean when Olly and Andy get back.

I can't believe I'm having to do this.

Now there is nothing I can do until they return.

Unless . . .

No, there is no way I can roll that deer onto the blanket and wrap it up myself.

No. Way.

My eyes slide to the deer. It stinks like death, all musty and gross.

I can't sit and do nothing. I think about the last time I was this close to a dead deer and steel myself.

Taking shallow breaths, I pull on the black latex gloves, pick up the blanket and press my lips together. I wish I didn't need to breathe during this. The closer I step, the stronger the smell.

Laying the blanket out, I shake my head.

What the hell am I doing?

I walk around to the deer and reach down. My hands circle a front and a back leg.

The stench hits the back of my throat, and I swallow a gag.

Why would Lillian do this?

Leaning back, I pull the deer and it rolls effortlessly onto its other side.

Stepping to the side, I turn my head away and try to breathe some fresh air.

"Right, I need to wrap you now," I mutter, walking around to the deer's back. I can't get too close—I don't want to step in the pool of blood. But I manage to lean over and grip the edge of the blanket and then tug it up.

Gritting my teeth, I lift with every ounce of strength I have and push. The deer rolls again, and I cover it with the blanket. Now it can't be seen.

"I'm sorry," I whisper as if it can hear.

I pull the bucket of water close and get on my knees. Gripping the big yellow sponge tight, I wipe the blood with it. The sponge glides gracefully, picking up a line of gloopy blood as it goes.

So, so nasty.

The water turns pink as I dip the sponge into the bucket and squeeze it out.

Oh God.

"Esme?"

I drop the sponge and stand up as Olly and Andy come back into the room.

"You're okay," I say.

She didn't get them.

"We couldn't find whoever it was. No one else is awake," Andy says.

"You wrapped it?" Olly asks, smiling with pride.

"Yes. It was awful. You might want to roll it a couple more times before you take it out."

Andy clears his throat. "Thank you, Esme. Good job." He turns to Olly, who nods at his unspoken question. Yes, he is ready for them to dump the deer in the woods. I want to ask them to bury it, but that seems ridiculous and time consuming.

I get back to the cleaning and sneak a glance at Olly as he and Andy make light work of rolling the deer further into the blanket.

By the time they have the thing all rolled up and ready to go, I've got most of the blood up.

"I'd like to come," I say, taking the gloves off and putting them in the other bucket full of blood-soaked sponges.

Olly looks up through dark lashes.

"I'll bleach the floor after," I say.

"Of course, Esme," Andy says. "We'll all help with the floor once we get this little girl to the woods."

My heart pinches. I wish he wouldn't refer to the deer as "little girl." It's sad enough that Lillian did this to her. We don't need to make her sound like a pet.

Andy and Olly lift the deer and walk slowly outside.

I follow close behind. It's so dark out; the only light is the reflection of the moon on the lake. I squint to see. As it creeps closer to five a.m., we'll have some light.

Andy and Olly walk down the steps and we go around the food hall and into the forest.

"How far are we going?" I whisper, treading carefully.

"Only a couple of minutes," Andy replies, his voice strained due to the deer's weight.

We dodge smaller trees and bushes as we walk through the forest rather than on a trail.

"All right, about here, between those heavy bushes," Andy tells Olly.

They lay the deer down and gently pull the blanket, rolling her onto the ground. Andy gathers the blanket in a ball and sighs. "How has it come to this?"

I dip my head, guilt stabbing me in the chest, feeling Olly's intense gaze on me. Does he want me to fess up right now? Spill everything about that night to Andy? He must suspect there's more to it.

"Let's get back," Olly says. "We can discuss who, what and why later."

He says it to both of us, but I know it's for me.

We head back to camp in the dark. I breathe easier the more distance we put between us and the deer.

"Are you two okay?" Andy asks. "You should never have had to do that."

I nod and Olly tells him he's fine.

"If you need to talk, my door is always open. As CITs none of what happened tonight is your responsibility. I appreciate you helping me take care of it."

"No problem," I tell him.

"I don't really feel like a CIT anymore," Olly says.

"Yeah, me neither."

"I've got to say, you don't seem like it either. There has been so much more you've had to deal with than any other CIT any other year. All of you have taken on every challenge with grace and maturity. You're a credit to this camp," Andy says.

I'm a curse to this camp.

Olly and I glance at each other, then I look away. We're both thinking the same thing. It's my fault this is happening in the first place.

We get back to the food hall and put on rubber gloves. We need this place clean and sterile so that everyone can eat in here in four hours and thirty minutes.

I get onto my knees with tears in my eyes, while Olly gets a new bucket of water and Andy chucks the blanket in the trash. There's still a wet sponge on the floor near the trash bucket. I pick it up and freeze.

Written in blood are the initials LC.

41

Lillian snuck in here to write this when we left. If I hadn't gone with Andy and Olly . . .

Don't think about that.

"Esme?" Olly says, his tone asking what's wrong with me. He kneels down. "Oh my God. This wasn't here before, was it?"

"No. I *definitely* would have noticed."

"Andy, do you know anyone with the initials LC?" Olly asks as Andy walks toward us, snapping on a pair of rubber gloves.

"I'm not sure, why?"

"Look." Olly points to the letters on the floor.

"My goodness." Andy shudders. "Well, this could at least help narrow the search further. I'll have a look through the staff files and see who fits."

"Can I clean it up now?" I ask.

"Just let me get a picture." Andy takes his phone out and as soon as I hear a click, I dunk the sponge in water and scrub it over her initials.

"Didn't you want to bleach?" Olly asks.

"After this is clean," I reply, gritting my teeth.

Just. Go.

Whose blood did she write it with? I cleaned the deer's up. All that's left is a stain. Her blood? Am I washing away forensic evidence?

I use both hands and scrub as hard as I can. Andy and Olly help. Only one of them is aware that I'm unraveling.

If Lillian never worked here, Andy won't find her in the files. She'll want to remain hidden. I don't think she has been to the camp other than to snoop. I think that her accomplice is the one who worked here. Maybe *still* works here.

"All right," Andy says as we finish cleaning up and then wash our hands. "We should all get back to bed."

You would never know anything happened here. The floor is lighter and patchy where the blood was, but unless you were looking for it, you probably wouldn't notice. And if anyone does notice, we'll say food was spilled. The campers sure can make a mess.

Andy clears his throat. "I'll take the trash out. You two get some rest. Thank you for everything you've done tonight. It won't be forgotten."

That's what I'm afraid of.

Olly and I leave first. We walk in silence out of the food hall and down the steps.

I swallow a sob. *Don't break down!* "That was intense."

"Who is LC?"

"Olly, please," I whisper.

"Not happening." Grabbing my hand, he pulls me in the opposite direction to my cabin.

"What are you doing?" I tug my arm, but he doesn't loosen his grip, just keeps dragging me along with him. "Olly, let me go!"

"*Shh*. In here."

The multiuse cabin. We were in here last night.

"This is becoming our thing," I grumble as Olly shuts the door behind us and finally releases me.

He flicks on just the far lights, the ones that won't be visible from outside. The thick blinds are down too.

I fold my arms and glare at him. "What do you want?"

"The truth."

That's rich.

"Ditto!"

His eyes darken. He's mad . . . again. Well, so am I! "Esme, who is LC?"

I remain silent. Olly stalks closer. I narrow my eyes and hold my ground.

Stopping right before the toes of his shoes touch mine, he says, "LC just left a dead deer for us."

"I remember!"

Sighing sharply, he looks up at the ceiling.

"I didn't sneak out with anyone called LC," I tell him. "Now it really is your turn."

"Then who is it?"

"Olly! Where are you from?"

"Missouri."

Not buying it.

He said he wants to be away from "here" and he's super evasive. He probably chose Springfield because it's the same name of the town in *The Simpsons,* his favorite show.

He must be from Texas.

Oh God. That's it! How did I not connect the dots earlier?

"You said your favorite thing to do as a kid was visit Six Flags Fiesta. *Fiesta.* That one is in Texas," I say.

He winces, grinding his teeth.

"Tell me the truth. *Now.*"

"Esme, you're—"

"No! I don't want any dumb excuse or bullshit story. Tell me the truth, Olly."

"All right! Fine." He takes a long breath. "I moved from Texas to Missouri when I was fifteen."

I take a step back. I knew it. "Why would you lie about that?"

"I haven't been back here in a long time."

"Three years isn't a long time, Olly."

"It feels like it."

"You lived here? In this town?"

"No, the next one over. The towns share this forest. I wanted to come here without baggage."

Oh God.

"You said you didn't know your way around town."

"That wasn't a lie. I've only been there a few times in passing."

"Where is Jake from?"

"Texas."

Of course he is. Both of them are popular and athletic, and they're too close to be two-week-old friends.

"Right. So you *did* know each other before coming here."

"I've known him since we were about five. We kept in touch after I moved."

Great, twelve *years,* not two weeks.

"This makes no sense. Why would you lie about either of those things?"

"I used to go into the woods with my friends and older brother at night," Olly says. "Since I was about eight, we'd sneak off and hike or make a campfire. There was a large group of us."

My stomach clenches.

Where is he going with this?

"Olly . . . were you there that night?"

I turn around, unable to look at him. Shame washes over me, and I feel sick.

His footsteps creak on the wooden floor as he gets closer.

"Yes," he whispers, his breath blowing across the back of my neck.

I close my eyes.

"What did you see?"

"I got lost in the woods that night for the first time ever. We were walking, and I heard something. The others told me I was crazy and kept going, but I ditched them and came back. I saw the most beautiful girl—she looked like an angel—about my age, hanging out with her friend. You were both wearing pajamas, so I figured you had to be campers."

I look over my shoulder and he wraps his arms around me, hugging my back to his chest.

"It's okay, Esme."

"You saw the fire?"

"Yes. I saw you stack too much wood on the fire. I saw that girl come and talk to you and Kayla. I saw the fire get out of hand, and . . . I saw the fight."

I lick my lips, my heart thudding against his arm. "What else?"

"The branches fell, and the fire took the trees." He lowers his head, resting his forehead on my shoulder. "I watched you go to help the girl, but Kayla pulled you back and you both ran. Did you know that you are the only one who looked back? Kayla didn't."

Tears prickle behind my eyelids.

"What happened to the girl?"

"She was burned, but she eventually got up. But that's when I heard Jake shout my name and I left. I wish I had gone over to her. I'll always regret not helping her. What?" Olly asks as my body turns to stone.

"Lillian *was* hurt."

I have the same regret as Olly. The guilt of not helping her is something I live with every day.

"Lillian? LC? What was her surname?"

"Campbell. I tried to look her up on social media, but she's not there. Why didn't you tell me this when I confessed about the fire?"

"That was only yesterday, Esme, and we got into an argument. Remember, you thought I was the one messing with the camp." I start to pull away, but he stops me. "No, we're not fighting again," he says.

"I'm tired," I tell him. Suddenly I feel like I could curl up on the floor and sleep for a month. My head is going to explode.

"Me too, but we still have a lot to discuss. Lillian. That's who you think did this?"

"You knew this *whole* time."

"Yes. I was waiting for you to tell me the *whole* truth."

"I was waiting for you to tell me *any* truth."

Olly lowers his head closer to mine. "Lillian was burned. That's motive enough."

"I hate this."

His expression softens. "I know you do. What happened was an accident. You're not a bad person. In fact, you're one of the best."

"What do we do now, Olly?"

"I'm going to kiss you and then we're going to figure this thing out together."

I can't think of a better plan right now.

He closes the small distance between us and I sink into him.

Suddenly the light turns off with a snap, like the power has been cut.

I gasp, and Olly stands taller.

Lillian is still here.

42

"I swear if you suggest we go outside, I will throw you in the lake," I whisper while my heart tries to break out of my rib cage.

I can't see well in the dark, but Olly's arms are still very secure around me.

"I wasn't going to suggest *we* go out there."

"No way."

"She's just a girl, Esme."

I elbow him hard in the chest and he hisses through his teeth. "See, women can hurt too," I say.

"Unnecessary," he growls. "We can't stay in here, but who knows what she's got planned out there?"

"She's dangerous; we both know that. Let's call Andy for help," I say, checking my watch. We don't have long before sunrise.

"There are four cabins full of sleeping children between this cabin and Andy's."

He unwraps his arms from around me and I faintly make out him rubbing his chest. That will teach him for insinuating that women are weak.

I don't want to praise Lillian and Rebekah for what they've done here, but all hail girl power. I wish they would just use it for something good.

Rebekah might not be involved! I remind myself.

"What if we go out there and she has a gun?" I ask.

"How would that be revenge?"

"Isn't that, like, the *definition* of revenge?"

"No, and you don't believe it is either. You're letting fear talk now. She doesn't want to kill anyone; she wants to screw us up and turn us against each other. We're already divided: half want to go to the cops and the other half are scared to."

But Lillian must have an end game. In four weeks, we leave.

"What are we supposed to do with that, Olly? We need to do *something*. She could be out there now sacrificing more animals or writing threats all over the cabins!"

"I'm going outside."

"Bad. Idea."

He takes my hand. "Come on, let's look through the window and see if we can spot her."

The cabin is drenched in darkness. I can barely see an inch in front of me.

Olly and I shuffle forward. I reach my free hand out to feel. When it touches the wall, we move sideways. The window is only just visible, a thin strip of dull light around the dark fabric blind.

I hook the blind with one finger, wincing as I shift it out of the way. Olly's temple touches mine as we lean closer and look out.

My heart seizes and I jump back, letting the blind fall shut as a scream rips from my throat.

Olly makes a sharp *bah* sound and grabs hold of me, pulling me closer.

Lillian and whoever her accomplice is are outside, dressed head to toe in black, hoods up, facing us.

"Oh my God, they're out there!" I mutter.

"Okay. It's okay. Hey, look at me, Esme."

I can just about make out his face and meet his eyes.

"Don't panic."

"They're out there and they know we're in here! I *am* panicking! What are they doing? Waiting for us? To do what?"

I don't ever want to see Lillian again.

"Hey, shh. Nothing bad is going to happen to us. They're two girls our age. It's going to be fine."

"Y-you think we should go out there and talk to them."

"Yes."

Taking a breath, I place my clammy palms on his chest and focus on not freaking collapsing.

"All right," I say, and then regret it instantly. "Finding out what she wants is the only way to stop this."

"We go out together, but stay behind me. Please."

Holding my hand, he leads me to the door.

My pulse skitters as he pulls the door open.

Should we grab a weapon? There are plenty of bats in here. Though I'm hoping there won't be any need for that.

We step out onto the porch.

"They're gone," I breathe, doing a three-sixty to try to see *where* they went.

Olly creeps forward on the porch to peer around the side of the cabin. I do the same on the other end.

My footsteps are too loud, though I'm practically on my tiptoes and walking like a sneaky cartoon character. I place one hand on the corner of the cabin, my fingers digging into the rough wood. I peer around the corner and see nothing but darkness.

I turn to Olly.

Only, he's not there.

"Olly!" I whisper. Where the hell did he go?

I pad lightly along the porch, my side practically scraping along the cabin wall. "Olly?"

What is going on?

I strain my ears, trying to hear his footsteps, but I can only hear my ragged breathing. No matter how much I try to control it, I can't.

My stomach clenches.

I'm leaving tomorrow.

"Olly, where are you?" I whisper.

Please say she hasn't hurt him.

It's still dark out. I don't even know where the circuit box is to turn the electricity back on. That's what they've done, tripped the circuit . . . I think. It must be in the staff cabin. If I can find it, I can turn on the outside lights and find Olly.

"Esme?"

I startle, my body almost leaving the damn porch floor.

Pressing one hand over my pounding heart, I snap, "Jesus, Olly!"

"Sorry, I didn't mean to scare you."

"Where did you go?"

"Around the back of the cabin. They disappeared so quickly, I thought they went that way instead of around the lake. I couldn't see anyone, though."

I shudder. "It's so creepy knowing they're out here."

Not that I'll be doing much sleeping from this point on.

"The cabins are locked," Olly says.

"They have a key," I remind him.

"Which they wouldn't use with the campers inside. They seem to have a conscience when it comes to that, at least."

"What do we do now?"

"Andy."

We traipse back to the staff cabin again. I don't know what time it is, but I don't think we'll be seeing the sun anytime soon. It's not quite light enough.

Something catches my eye as we walk past the lake. "Olly, there's something in the lake."

I can just make out lumps of . . . something floating in the moon's reflection.

"Andy will have a flashlight," Olly says. "Stay where I can see you."

I wait while Olly runs to get Andy. When I say *wait*, I mean that my legs won't move anyway. My eyes strain as I try to see what's floating out there. It looks like a few small objects.

Andy comes rushing up with Olly a heartbeat later.

They take the steps quickly. Andy trains his flashlight on the lake.

"They were outside?" he asks.

A shiver rips through my body. "Yes."

"What were you doing in the multiuse cabin?"

"I needed to talk to Esme," Olly replied.

"I was freaking out a little," I add to give our story more weight.

The flashlight catches something that makes me lose my footing. "What the hell is that?"

Andy gasps.

"Oh my God, it's a doll," Olly says.

A *doll*.

No. It's not just one doll. There are five.

"Why?" Andy whispers.

"This is hideous." Five naked plastic dolls float on the lake. "There's something on two of them. Can you see?" I ask.

"Yeah," Andy replies. "I can't make out what."

"We need to go and get them," Olly says.

I knew that was coming. Of course we need them to be gone by the time the campers wake up. Can't say I'm particularly looking forward to fishing these out of the water.

"Esme, you hold the flashlight," Andy says. "Olly and I will retrieve them."

They wade into the lake and I shine the flashlight on the five dolls.

As I raise the light, it bounces off them and I can see clearly what's on the ones that are marked. Eight big black crosses over their eyes.

43

Creepy. Disturbing. Sick.

Five naked baby dolls, four with their eyes crossed out.

Who do they represent?

Me? Kayla?

Lillian?

Jake and Olly too?

Lillian was the one who was harmed that night.

"Are they American Girl dolls?" I ask.

Olly and Andy look up at me with identical frowns. Yeah, they wouldn't know.

"It's a brand. I had a couple of them when I was little. There are much cheaper dolls they could have used. Either they belonged to one of them or they spent a fortune to chuck these in the lake."

"What are we going to do with them?" Olly asks.

Andy huffs. "I'll bag them up and put them in my office. Once summer is over, we can go to the cops."

"Shh," I scold. "If they're watching, and I have a feeling they are, they'll hear you. No cops, remember?"

"God," Andy breathes. "This is out of hand."

"The next time we see them, we go for it," Olly says.

"Go for what?"

"Grab them, tie them up, hold them somewhere."

That sounds fun.

Olly's eyes meet mine. "We can take them."

"I think a woman is doing this. Or at least one of them is," Andy says.

Wow, he is several chapters behind.

"Why do you think that?" I ask, playing along with his great discovery.

"The dolls. Would a man think to use dolls?"

I shrug. "Maybe. Dolls aren't just for girls."

"Perhaps not. But it's most likely a female."

"Yes," I say. He's *not* wrong.

"Let's get the dolls inside." Andy looks Olly and me over and seems to make a decision. "You are both going to help me go through the staff files. We're looking for someone with the initials LC. Even better if we find a woman with those initials."

"Are CITs allowed to look at staff files?" Olly asks.

I want to punch him in the throat. I'm sure we're about to break all sorts of confidentiality laws, but *who cares?*

"Not technically, but I need help here," Andy says. "The faster we find out who LC is, the better."

"Can we please get some coffee before we start?" I ask as we walk to the staff cabin, each of us holding plastic dolls.

Andy nods. "That might be a good idea. It *is* five-thirty in the morning."

Fab, I've had about an hour of sleep. Will this night never end? Lillian's ramping up, her taunts coming thick and fast now.

Grumpy Esme will be coming out to play tomorrow. Or rather later today. Not that I'm planning on staying at camp.

We drop the dolls in the staff cabin.

"Would you two go make the coffee? I'll get the files out and we can get started," Andy says.

The last time Olly and I were alone in a cabin . . .

Olly senses my unease. "I'll go. It's probably best if Esme stays with you."

Andy's eyes drift to me and then Olly. "I agree. Take this radio and let us know if you have any trouble."

I have *no* objections. I don't want to go back out there. I want to sit in here, snoop through staff files and wait for my coffee. Maybe we won't find an LC in these files, but I might get some information on who Lillian's accomplice is. I'm pretty sure it's Rebekah, but I need evidence.

Olly takes the radio and clips it to his jeans. "I'll be right back."

"The files are in here," Andy says, leading me into his office. "Let's take them into the staff room and put them on the table. We'll need the space."

"Do I have a file?"

He smiles and unlocks the metal cabinet. "Yes. It's not very thick."

"Is that good?"

"This is your first year with us and you haven't done anything wrong, so I'd say yes, it's good."

"Does anyone have a thick file?"

Smirking, Andy says, "Take these to the staff room."

He stacks a bunch of files into my waiting hands and I carry them to the table. In the staff room there are two comfortable couches, a vending machine, a battered foosball table and a CD player. Yep, CDs. I don't think I've ever owned one. This room is stuck in the nineties.

"Do you think Olly is okay?" I ask.

"He would radio if he wasn't."

Olly has only been gone a couple of minutes. The coffee probably hasn't finished brewing yet.

I flip the first file open and stifle a yawn.

Misty Allen.

She's too old.

"Not this one," I say, putting the file on the floor. That can be the No pile.

"Nor this one. I remember her, lovely girl," Andy says.

I look at Andy over the top of the next file. "Please tell me you're not basing this on who you remember liking?"

"Her name is Sandie. No LC."

"Okay."

Andy leaps up to unlock the door as Olly returns. It's locked again straightaway. Olly comes into the room holding three cups of coffee. They're stacked on top of each other and his chin is resting on the top one.

Andy jumps up and helps him.

The second I thank Olly, I take a sip. Wonderful caffeine-laced liquid burns my tongue. Fatigue has begun to set in, and I need a pick-me-up badly.

Olly sits next to me.

"You okay?" I ask.

"Tired but ready to find our hugely unwelcome friends."

Me too. "I suggest we look for someone who's been here in the last few years," I say. "Things change at camp, and this person knows our current routine. And remember, this LC isn't alone, so we can't limit our search to just those initials."

"Why do you think only those initials were left?" Andy asks.

Olly clears his throat. "Maybe they didn't have time to write the other ones? I don't know. We shouldn't rule anything out, though, right?"

"Agreed."

I put my coffee down and open the next file.

Rebekah's file.

My face falls.

I pull the folder closer to my chest and scan it. I quickly find what I'm looking for—her home address. It isn't in Kansas. It's in Texas. *In this town.*

I close the file with a racing heart and put it in the No pile, but not before I memorize her address.

"Not this one," I say out loud.

Slowly, we make our way through the files. Even though I've found what I was looking for, I continue, which is tedious, but I need to keep up the pretense. I don't want Andy to know yet.

I'll tell Olly when I get him alone.

I roll my neck and yawn.

"It's six," Andy says. "We should try to get an hour of sleep."

"I *really* like the sound of that," I reply, covering my yawn with the back of my hand.

Olly stands and stretches. "All right, let's put these away first." He looks at me out of the corner of his eye. I pick up my stack of files and stand. Does he know that I'm hiding something? Hopefully he will understand that it's because of Andy.

By now he must know I'll tell him. I hope.

Andy locks the cabinet and we part ways. He goes into his room; Olly and I head out.

We walk to my cabin and I stop on the porch. "Go to yours and we'll head inside at the same time."

His lips quirk, amused. "You worried about me?"

"Yes. I'm worried about all of us."

I have so much to tell him, but right now all I can think about is sleep. Olly seems to sense this.

His fingertips trace my jaw. "Get some rest, Esme."

"I'll try."

I'm sure he's going to kiss me, but he doesn't. Instead he bites his lip, drops his hand and turns. I watch him walk along the trodden path to his cabin. He looks over his shoulder when he opens the door.

I do the same and we both slip inside.

44

An hour later, I wake with a foggy head but a clearer mind.

I found out that Rebekah is from this town. That at least gives me somewhere to start. This is something. I finally don't feel so far behind Lillian. We're closing in.

"Morning," Kayla says cheerfully.

I roll over and see her head peeking over the top of my bunk.

Whatever. It's been morning for what feels like five days already. I think I managed to get about forty-five-minutes' sleep. It's almost seven.

Groaning, I rub my tired eyes. "Morning. I need coffee."

She laughs. "Let's go get some then. Whoa, babe, you look awful."

"I didn't sleep well."

"No shit. Your eye bags are suitcases and you're washed out."

"Thank you."

I sit up and slide my legs over the ladder. Twisting, I climb down and stretch my arms over my head.

Do I tell her?

She'll find out. I don't think Andy and Olly will keep last night's insanity a secret.

We both get dressed and then head to the food hall for breakfast. Some of the girls are dawdling, getting ready slowly and messing around with their hair. That's pointless, we're swimming today.

In the lake of dolls.

Which I'm glad to see is American Girl–free.

The lake looks peaceful, as if it's frozen in time.

"Let's eat lunch outside today," I tell Kayla.

"Huh? It's hotter than lava."

"Trust me, Kayla."

She does a double take. "Why are you so tired? Oh my God, is it Olly-related?"

"*Nothing* like that."

"Then, what?"

"Not here. Too many people around."

Her eyebrows knit together.

"I'll fill you in on everything then, I promise."

"Okay," she says slowly. "Let's get you fed."

Olly is sitting at our usual table with a big plate of bacon and eggs. He's gulping down a mug of coffee like it's air.

I load up a plate with croissants and fruit. Then I get my beloved coffee and take a seat. Kayla has opted for a big cup of tea.

She didn't spend most of the night running around dodging Lillian's every move.

"Morning," I say to Olly.

He looks sideways with guilty eyes. "How are you doing?"

"I'm exhausted. You?"

"Same."

I sip my coffee.

"We need to talk today," he says, keeping his voice low so that the others won't hear. They're engrossed in their own theories about the person in the woods anyway.

"I agree." I turn to him. "Kayla too . . . and Jake?"

Olly subtly shakes his head. Does Jake not know about this? He was there the night of the fire, but Olly said Jake didn't see anything, that he called Olly from somewhere deeper in the woods. Maybe Olly never told him. But then why did Jake agree to lie about how long he's known Olly?

"All right," I whisper, nipping off a chunk of croissant.

"Morning, campers," Andy says as he enters the food hall with way too much energy for someone rolling on one hour's sleep.

I'm a zombie.

Olly and I exchange a tired glance.

"Who's ready for music and swimming?"

Not me.

The campers cheer, and I wince.

No one is particularly hyped about walking the trails anymore, so we've been keeping close to camp. This week, we're supposed to camp out in shelters we make ourselves. No freaking way.

It's on Andy's color-coordinated schedule that he printed for counselors and CITs. I want to scribble crosses all over it like the creepy dolls' eyes.

I don't know if he's thrown the dolls away yet or if he plans to store them. I couldn't care less about that, what I want to know is why Lillian put them in the lake. What kind of mind thinks that up? It's sick.

I pick at my food.

"You tired, Esme?" Rebekah asks.

Are you?

Tia must sleep like the dead if she's not waking up every time Rebekah sneaks out of their room and back in.

I have the upper hand here. Rebekah doesn't know that I've found out she's Lillian's accomplice.

"I'm fine," I reply with a smile. I probably look like I've been drugged.

She knows I'm not fine because she knows that I was outside removing the dolls from the lake. But neither of us can admit it.

We have to keep on playing the game.

"I'm going to go find the particular guitar that Ellen likes." Rebekah rolls her eyes. "She doesn't do well if she doesn't get that one."

"I'll come with," Tia says. "I need the bathroom before the campers make my ears bleed."

My eyes slide to Jake. He's still lying too.

Why, though? I guess he doesn't know that Olly told me the truth.

But why would he need to lie about where he's from in the first place?

It doesn't make sense.

There is something I'm missing, or rather something Olly hasn't revealed yet.

I watch Rebekah and Tia leave, and then I turn to Olly. It's on the tip of my tongue. I'd love to grill them both on why they lied.

"Let's go, man," Jake says to Olly. "I need to piss."

Lovely.

Olly doesn't look at me when he leaves with Jake, but he does chuck a "see you later" over his shoulder.

Is he mad at me again?

We were fine when we left for bed . . . I think. It was early and I was tired. Am I forgetting another argument we had?

"Something wrong?" Kayla asks.

"I don't know."

She glares. "Yes you do. Fill me in."

"I'm not sure that now is a good time. We're in a room full of people."

"No one else is at our table and no one is paying us any attention."

"I bet the diva inside of you is so mad about that fact."

Narrowing her eyes, Kayla replies, "Shut it."

Shuffling closer, I lower my voice. "Okay, so last night was . . . eventful. I woke up in the early morning because of a loud noise. Olly did too. We found a dead deer in the food hall."

"What? In *here*?"

"Yep."

"Like, it had died in here?"

"No, like Lillian had killed it and dumped it here. We're sitting quite close to where it was, actually."

Her pink-painted lips part.

"It was bleeding. Olly, Andy and I cleaned it up and put the deer in some bushes in the forest. When we came back, there were initials written in blood on the floor. You can probably guess which ones."

"LC," Kayla breathes. "Oh my God! Well, she *does* have a thing about deer."

I shudder, not wanting to think about that. "When we were all going back to bed, we saw five dolls floating in the lake."

Her eyes widen, but I don't slow down, because I'm on a roll.

"We got them out, and four had crosses drawn over their eyes, Andy hid them, and we went through the staff files. Kayla, I found out that Rebekah lives in town. Which means she lied about where she's from. She's definitely helping Lillian.

"Oh, and Olly admitted that he and Jake are from one town over. They were in the woods the night of the fire and Olly saw everything, including Lillian get burned by the fire."

"What?" Kayla hisses. "Are you . . . What? Last night? This all happened *last night*?"

"I finally got to bed at, like, six in the morning and had just under an hour of broken sleep. Tonight you and I have to sneak out and go into town."

"What? *No way*."

"Yes way, and we have to do it without anyone else. Just me and you."

She pales. "In the forest at night?"

"You up for it?"

"Not a chance, Esme," she replies, her voice thick with fear.

I raise my eyebrows. "We *have* to, Kayla. We need to end this."

We have to find Rebekah's house. I have the feeling that if we do, we're going to find Lillian.

45

Kayla is so not down with the idea of us sneaking through the woods alone at night while two people try to ruin our lives.

Can't think why.

I'm not entirely sure why I want to go. All I can think is that I'm so exhausted, I'm delirious. That's the only excuse for what I'm about to do.

I'm not ready to face the very real possibility that I'll be doing this alone tonight. I could take Olly. He would come, I know that for sure, but there is something about his secret childhood home that bothers me. And the fact that he and Jake are still pretending they don't know each other is shady and crazy suspicious.

I paddle in the edge of the cool lake, trying to keep myself awake by picturing all the ways Lillian could screw with me in the forest tonight. The sun shines brightly over camp as if it has no clue of the darkness lurking here.

Kayla is near but she hasn't said much to me since I told her I want us to go into town.

Nothing like fear to keep you alert.

My group is in the water and being taught by the swim instructors.

If they find a sunken doll, I'm going to throw up.

"How are you?" Andy asks, stopping dead in front of me. One more step and he'd be in the water. He's possibly paler than me this morning. But I think I win with the dark circles under my eyes.

I saw him walking around the lake with his clipboard earlier. He looked like he was checking things off, making sure equipment was safe and everything was in order. But I think he was actually looking for Lillian.

She won't be here now. Not after last night. She knows we're even more on edge, that we'll be watching like hawks.

"Exhausted but okay. You?"

He nods. "About the same. Who does something like this to a camp of kids?"

"There are a lot of crazy people out there, Andy."

"Yeah, no kidding. I just want to go to the police, but I'm too scared that this LC will realize what we're doing and react." He sighs and moves on, stopping by the kayaks and pretending to check them over.

Kayla grabs my hand. "Okay, my head is going to explode, and I'm still worried that you want to go back into town. Jake is being his usual sweet self to me, and I don't know how to be around him now that I know he's lying."

"Slow down, you really *are* going to explode."

"I can't believe he and Olly were there that night."

I nod. "Me neither. You know, there is one thing that is still bothering me."

"One thing?"

Rolling my eyes, I clarify, "Okay, one *new* thing."

"What's that?"

"Why are we all here? Lillian didn't just luck out that the three of us who were there that night are here now. I think she set this up."

Kayla frowns. "You're *beyond* obsessed with this, Esme."

Oh, I'm so far past obsessed it's not even funny. "How are you not? She's been stalking us and threatening the whole camp. Now we have an address. We know who her BFF is."

"We *think* we know."

I raise one eyebrow. "I have Rebekah's address! She's *from town.*"

Kayla's doing that thing again where she tries to deny the truth, and it's infuriating.

My chest burns. "Rebekah is the definition of BS. Look it up. Are you coming with me tonight or not?"

Kayla twirls her long ponytail around one finger. "Well, I can't let you go alone, can I?"

"You could. Maybe that would be better, actually. Yeah, I could swipe two radios from Andy's office, and you could keep watch. It's a bad idea for both of us to go."

"You're not going alone."

"I need you here. If Lillian thinks we're here she won't go looking for me. It's our night to be outside, unless Andy orders another freaking lockdown."

She opens her mouth to challenge me.

"Kayla, you know I'm right."

"Will you at least take Olly?"

"Hell no."

"It's him or me."

I roll my eyes. "We'll discuss this later, but I don't think Jake and Olly need to know any more than they do already."

"So it's all on me and you."

Now we're a team, huh?

"That's the way it's been from the start, Kayla. This is our responsibility."

"It was an *accident*."

"That doesn't mean we're not to blame. We didn't help Lillian."

"Because she was crazy and we were *scared*."

That's not a very good excuse.

We'll end up going around in circles if we keep talking. "Whatever. You should get back to the beach, your group is playing."

With a huff, she wanders off, whipping her hair the way mean girls in movies do. She's really playing the part now that she's dating the quarterback.

I've annoyed her. She wants a say in what happens next, but she doesn't want to step up and try to figure this out.

If she's not with me, then she can't make any demands. I'm

going into town tonight and she can stay here. And I'm not going to think about it so that I can't talk myself out of it. All I know is that I can't keep doing this.

"Esme, can I have a word?" Olly asks.

Cora looks up from where she's standing waist-deep near the girls. "Take ten, Esme, I've got this."

Well, I can't say no now.

I give her a tight smile. "Thanks."

Slipping my flip-flops on as I step out of the lake, I ask, "You want to walk?"

"Let's go to the food hall instead. I told Andy I would get the snacks ready for after the activity."

"Okay."

We walk up the steps and into the kitchen.

"What are we having?"

"Orange wedges, watermelon, crackers and yogurt are on Andy's list." Olly holds up a piece of paper with today's snack highlighted in case Olly didn't see the date beside it.

I bet Andy's never been late or unorganized in his life. Lillian is really messing with his order.

"I'll grab the fruit. Can you get the rest?" I ask.

"Uh-huh."

We work in silence at first. Olly glances at me occasionally as I slice oranges into wedges.

"What did you find?" he asks.

"Sorry?"

"Last night, in the files. What did you find?"

I put the knife down. "What do you mean? We didn't find anything."

His eyes narrow. *"Esme."*

"Can we please not have the same argument over and over? I didn't find anything. But while we're talking, do you want to go into more detail about why you and Jake lied about knowing each other? It can't just be because you were there the night of the fire. Why have you never said anything about knowing me? Didn't you think it was weird that we all just happened to be back at camp at the same time?"

He chucks the box of crackers down on the countertop and turns away from me.

"You'll think whatever the hell you want anyway, so forget it, Esme."

I watch with my mouth catching flies as he shoves the door open and storms out of the kitchen.

46

I used to love the mystery of night.

Things can exist in the dark that can't in the light. Elves and unicorns could be running around for all we know.

No, I haven't lost it. I know logically that's not true, but if you can't see something, then how can you be *sure* it doesn't exist?

Five-year-old me loved the thought of her toys coming alive at night and mythical creatures flying around outside.

It's not such a fun thought anymore. Not since I know what is lurking in the dark.

I'm currently sitting around a campfire listening to a conversation about football. I like football as much as the next non-obsessive American, but I don't want to spend hours talking about it.

I tap my fingers against my soda can and wish everyone else would get up and do something else. When we break off and go our own ways, I can get away. The radio is in my pocket already and Kayla has one too.

While Andy was briefing everyone, I swiped two radios from the staff cabin. It was embarrassingly easy to do. I can see how Lillian managed to get keys.

Olly watches me from the other side of the fire.

I don't know what he's thinking, but we're still in a fight. Usually, he would be sitting next to me. Tonight, however, he sat as far away from me as he could.

His little tantrum over my simple question hasn't been forgotten. I still have a lot of questions and he clearly doesn't want to answer any of them. There has to be a reason for that.

"Why is he staring?" Kayla asks, looking anywhere but at the boys across from us.

I shrug, not really in the mood to talk to her about it. "I don't know, but it's starting to freak me out. He's going to have to find something else to look at if I want to get away."

"You remember at school when you needed to call your cousin about Bieber concert tickets, so I told the teacher you were about to hurl? She let you go to the bathroom."

"Please don't tell everyone I'm about to hurl."

She laughs. "I just mean I've got your back." She takes a breath. "You have to be careful out there, Esme."

Kayla will always be my best friend, and I love her, but she is blowing so hot and cold at the moment. I don't know how much I can rely on her.

"I'll be careful. This could all be over tonight."

Sighing, she looks up at the sky. "I hope so. I hate being scared."

"We're going to be fine."

"I can't die," she whispers, curling her hands into fists.

"You're not going to die." I can practically see her heart rate spike. "Kayla, it's going to be all right, I promise."

She purses her lips, and I know she's thinking of her grandma. It was awful. Kayla watched her nana die in that car and thought she was next.

Taking a deep breath, she gets up and plasters on a big smile. "Okay, let's end this tonight."

We both raise our hands in a little wave at the same time.

A wave of nausea almost makes me double over.

"We're going to bed, guys," I say, rising to my feet.

Olly looks up at me with a slight frown, but he says, "Night," with everyone else.

Kayla and I tiptoe through the main room where the girls are sleeping and into our room.

I pull the door closed and turn to her. "Right, I'll go out of the window. They won't see me from this side of the cabin."

Kayla's eyes dart from the door to the window. "Please, please, please be careful."

"I'll be fine. Rebekah is out there with the rest of them."

"You still think she's involved?"

"Hopefully we'll know soon."

"Should I go back out and make sure she doesn't leave?"

"Nah, I don't think she's going anywhere tonight. She's been yawning for the last hour." I'm still tired from the never-ending deer-and-doll night too.

Let's not think about that.

"I'll keep watch out the window and see if she sneaks off," Kayla says.

If Rebekah does sneak off, Kayla will see her from our bedroom.

"Radio me if she does. Like the *very second*, but use a code word in case any of the girls from the main room hear."

"What code word?"

"Er . . . clover."

Kayla scrunches up her face. "That lucky weed?"

"I need all the luck I can get."

"Okay. I'll say 'clover' if I see Rebekah heading your way."

I open the window, haul myself up and swing my legs out. "I'll be as quick as I can."

"*Careful*, Esme."

"That's my middle name."

"Your middle name is Mallory and it means 'unfortunate one'!"

It's a family middle name. We haven't *all* been unfortunate. Just me, actually.

I wave my hand, dismissing her. "See you soon."

Dropping to the ground, I watch Kayla close the window, and then I creep through bushes to meet the little trail into town.

I walk into the night, the trees my only company. The air is warm and silent. I take light steps and look up when I hear a hoot. Damn owl nearly gave me a heart attack. It takes flight and swoops through the trees.

I've been in the woods for about thirty seconds and I already regret my life choices.

It's dark as hell, the air is cooler than usual, and I'm alone.

The dark and I don't feel like friends anymore.

I put one foot in front of the other, following the trodden man-made path toward town. I dressed in dark colors and left my flashlight on my bed, so I'm walking slowly.

The less noise I make, the less likely Lillian is to find me. I think she and Rebekah have been coming from the other side of the lake, where the fire was.

This was by far my dumbest idea since I was fourteen and thought a perm would look great. The curls were so tight, I looked like a poodle.

The forest feels alive tonight. When I'm too far to hear any sounds from camp, I hear the soft breeze dancing between the trees. Small animals scurry away from me before I see them.

When I reach the end of the forest, I roll my shoulders. I made it. I look around and cross the deserted road.

The trees finally give way to houses—big stone houses with large, manicured lawns—and my shoulders lose tension.

Rebekah's house is right on the edge of town.

I make a right and stop. My eyes flit to my phone screen, where the map is showing a dot for Rebekah's house and another one for me.

Besides a few people out walking, I don't see anyone. No one gives me a second glance, probably because I'm not in camp clothing. I blend in. I'm even pretending that the heat isn't making me want to run for the nearest AC.

It takes me two minutes to walk around the block and come face to face with Rebekah's house.

Rebekah is wealthy.

I walk up the drive, clutching my phone. Wiggling my fingers, I take a breath and press the doorbell.

If Lillian answers now, I'm probably going to pass out.

The lock on the door clicks and my muscles tense.

A little old lady with rollers in her hair and wearing a fluffy pink robe answers the door. Definitely not Lillian.

Rebekah's nana?

"Yes?"

"Hi, um, my name is Chloe." My little Pomeranian's name. "My car broke down a block away. I've called Triple A and they'll be here soon, but"—I hide my face with my hands—"ugh, this is so embarrassing, but I'm kind of desperate for the bathroom."

I drop my hands and smile.

"Oh, sugar," she drawls.

"Would it be at all possible to use yours? Please?"

"Of course. Come on in and I'll show you where it is."

"Thank you."

She points to a dark wood door on the right. "Just there."

"I really appreciate this," I tell her, and disappear into the bathroom.

I lock the door, close my eyes and lean against the wall. Clawing at my suddenly itchy skin, I look around. I don't want to be in this house for a second longer than necessary.

Okay, you can do this. I need to find out as much as I can about Rebekah without making her nana suspicious.

After a minute, I flush the toilet and wash my hands.

When I come out of the bathroom, Rebekah's nana pops around the corner. "Over here."

Okay, she's inviting me deeper into the house.

I walk into her little country kitchen.

"Your house is lovely," I tell her. Old people love it when you compliment their home. My nan goes full-on bashful.

"Thank you, darlin'," she replies. "Can I get you an iced tea?"

"Oh, that would be awesome, if you don't mind?"

She waves her hand. "Of course not. Take a seat over there."

I do as I'm told and sit at the round table in the corner. From here I can see the living room. There are little pink flowers all over the sofas.

On the wall behind me is a massive collage. There must be about fifty photos.

"This all your family?" I ask.

She looks over from the fridge. "Oh yes. I have five children and thirteen grandchildren. My first great-grandchild is due in the fall."

"You all look so happy," I tell her, scouring the collage for pictures of Rebekah.

And, *bingo,* there she is. Smiling in a picture with people I assume are her cousins. Her face steals my breath.

"Do they all live close by?"

"Oh, we're scattered, I'm afraid. Every one of my children chose different colleges across the country. The grandchildren have done the same, but they all come back to visit."

"That's good you get to see them."

She nods. "My granddaughter Rebekah spent some time here

over a few summers, but she's older now, so she's got better things to do."

So that's how Rebekah and Lillian know each other. They must have met when Rebekah came to stay with her grandma. They spent summers together plotting.

"Are your grandkids coming this summer?"

"Some of them might. Rebekah has an internship. Some accounting firm. She's always been good with numbers."

Internship? That's why she told her mom she was needed in the conference room.

Wow, Rebekah's nana doesn't know she's just ten minutes down the road. No wonder Rebekah was acting so shifty at the arcade and hiding in corners. She was afraid she'd be seen by locals.

There are so many more questions I want to ask, but I'm very aware that it's going to seem weird if I keep going. I don't want her to call Rebekah and talk about the stranger whose car broke down and who asked lots of questions about her.

I have what I need for now.

I smile at Rebekah's grandmother. "Thank you so much for letting me into your home. I should get going now. Triple A will be here soon."

"All right. You be careful out there at night, Chloe."

The night isn't my problem. Your granddaughter is.

47

Sneaking out was fine. Well, fine-ish. Except I gave absolutely no thought to the fact that I have to get back.

I've been gone for about an hour. Kayla is on the lookout, and I haven't had any message or a call to say that she's seen something. Our bedroom has a great view of the path toward town. She was in the best place to see Rebekah and Lillian.

You are fine.

It's dark. I'm at the edge of the forest, staring at the trail as if it's going to bite me.

I've always loved adventure. On every vacation with my parents I'm the one who wants to explore the area and go on day trips.

I can now confirm that adventure is highly overrated.

Give me my sofa, snacks and Netflix any day.

Is the forest thicker than it was an hour ago? The damn thing is alive and growing. Maybe the forest doesn't forget either.

One foot. *Just move one foot.*

You can't stand here all night!

I step into the mist.

I want to move that foot backward and head to the bus station. I could be at the airport in a little over an hour. Of course, with no ID, I can't actually get on a plane.

Whatever my next move is, I have to go back to camp and get my stuff. And I can't leave Kayla on her own. I have to stay with her. Bestie solidarity and all that. I can't leave Olly and Jake either. We're all here for a reason.

The hairs on the back of my neck stand as I realize something: why Lillian is doing this now. In one of my first conversations with Olly, he mentioned that he also got a CIT pamphlet. He probably got the same one I did, with the creepy threat on the back. Lillian must have sent one to all of us. Jake had to have seen what happened that night for Lillian to send him a pamphlet.

Which means Lillian knows that Olly and Jake were there the night of the accident.

I have to get back to camp to warn them.

Tapping my fingers against my legs, I take a deep breath, inhaling a lungful of courage and dewy air.

I step forward slowly and take one last look over my shoulder before I walk into the woods.

The air is heavy. I feel like I could choke on it.

I squint to see more clearly as I follow the little trail and try to keep my eyes everywhere. Literally. I swivel my head from left to right constantly, looking for Rebekah or Lillian through a thin screen of mist.

I want to curl up and make myself as small as I can, but I don't want to look like I'm scared. If Lillian is out there, at least she can't hear or feel the thumping of my heart.

Ahead of me, something rustles.

I dash to a tree and plant myself against it. Jagged bark digs into my back. I cower as my heart pulses. It could easily be an animal. It's probably an animal.

Stepping around the tree, I make my way to the next one, almost tripping over my feet.

No falling!

The noise is gone. I'm sure it was a deer. The poor thing is probably in danger too.

Crunch.

I whip my head around. That was behind me.

Gasping, I turn and bolt toward camp.

I dodge trees, steeling myself for the flash of a camera . . . or worse. Nothing comes. I sprint, my sides burning with the exertion.

I break through the trees and sob. I'm back. I'm safe.

Stumbling, I slow and creep toward the cabin, I wipe my tears and keep to the wall, bracing myself against it. When I reach the window, something sitting on the windowsill catches my eye.

A little roll of white paper. I gulp and curl my hand around it and stuff it into my pocket.

Kayla unlocks and opens the window when she spots me. I haul myself up and Kayla grabs my arms to help me in.

"You okay?"

I nod. "Fine. Nothing happened. Rebekah's nana was lovely but said nothing we didn't already know. Rebekah knows the area and must have met Lillian here."

"Sorry you had to do that."

"It's fine. I'm going to get some sleep."

I get ready for bed clumsily but in record time and climb the bunk ladder with the rolled-up paper still in my palm.

With a yawn, I get under the blanket and lie down.

The thick paper is soft between my fingertips as I peel it open.

Squinting, I read the red ink on the paper.

Nothing you do goes unnoticed—LC

The writing is neat and tall, with slashes that spike at the end of each letter. I press my lips together as fear runs ice-cold through my veins.

Not only did she know that I'd snuck out and leave a note on the windowsill, but she probably followed me too.

Lillian or Rebekah must have crawled on the ground close to the wall so Kayla wouldn't see them plant the note.

Did Lillian follow me to Rebekah's nana's house? I was careful to check my surroundings. I didn't get that twitchy feeling like someone was watching me.

I gulp.

She's everywhere.

Maybe she realized I was gone when it was too late for her to follow me, and now she's trying to freak me out. She knew I was up to something. The fact that she hasn't burned the camp to the ground proves that she knows I haven't gone to the cops. I would expect more of a retaliation if she thought I'd spent the evening at the police station.

"Did you see anyone while I was out there?" I whisper in the darkness.

"No one at all," Kayla replies, handing me a bottle of water. She takes a sip from hers. "What was Rebekah's nana like? How did you get in?"

I take a long swig of water. "I pretended that my car broke down and I needed to use her bathroom. Thank the Lord for Southern hospitality. She invited me in and made me iced tea."

"What did you find out?"

"Rebekah stayed with her nana for a few summers."

"So that's how Lillian met Rebekah."

"Yep." I cover my yawn with the back of my hand. "Man, I'm so tired."

"Wait, you can't go to sleep yet. What else did you find out?"

"Not a lot. I wanted to bring up Rebekah's burns, but I didn't know how to without it sounding weird. Her nana thinks that Rebekah is interning at some accounting firm."

"She really doesn't know she's here?"

"Not a clue. I doubt anyone does."

Kayla laughs humorlessly. "God."

I down the last of the water. "I'm really mad. Lillian should just talk to us if she's pissed."

And, of course, we should have said something ten years ago. That doesn't justify what they're doing now, though. They're not just messing with me and Kayla anymore, they're messing with all of us.

"I was thinking . . . I think we should try to leave a note for her." Kayla says.

"That's risky. We can't have any evidence of us contacting her."

"We don't have to write 'Love, Esme and Kayla' at the end."

I scratch an itch on the back of my head. "Right, but wouldn't it be obvious?"

"We can't keep quiet and take all of this for another four weeks, Esme."

God, that's a long time when you're being terrorized.

"I'm with you there. When we talk to her it has to be face to face."

"When? Everyone is so on edge. We play games and roast marshmallows, but we're also constantly looking into the forest."

"I don't know *when*."

Kayla's looking at me for all of the answers when I don't have a single one. How should I know how to handle this situation? This is the first time I've been threatened.

We do need to start beating Lillian at her own game, though. We have to get ahead of her and turn this around.

There's no reason why we can't play too.

What we did is going to come out eventually. Going along with her crazy is only prolonging the inevitable.

Making that leap is scary. I like the people I'm here with, and I'm scared of how they're going to see me and Kayla when they find out the truth.

Lillian left her creepy little note for me. Maybe Kayla and I can get a camera and set it up to catch her? I need to know when she's in our room and what she does here.

I blink heavily, my eyes begging me to close them. My head is swimming. Rubbing my forehead, I groan. I'm getting a headache or I'm getting sick.

Being ill right now is the last thing I need. I have to be on my A game. No, E game, because Esme is going to take Lillian down.

I frown as my muscles turn so heavy, I can barely lift a finger.

My eyes close and I'm gone.

48

Groaning, I rub my foggy head and roll over.

The mattress is cold and damp.

What . . . ?

My eyes flick open and for a second, I see a blur of brown and green and white.

When my vision sharpens, the first thing I see clearly is moss.

Gasping, I jolt and scramble to my feet.

I'm in the forest.

I stumble to a tree, frowning as my brain tries to catch up.

Kayla and I were talking and then we went to sleep. What happened?

My back hits a tree and I glance around. The forest is silent, eerily silent.

I shake my foggy head as my heart races.

Lillian. The crazy bitch *drugged* me.

How? It couldn't have happened at Rebekah's nana's house.

It's been too long. I think. I don't really know how long it takes to drug a person.

My pulse whooshes loudly in my ears.

Stay calm. Stay. Calm.

I have to get back.

Lillian will be watching.

Taking long breaths in and out, I try to ground myself as my stomach flips.

Don't give in.

She's here. How else would I have ended up out here?

All I have to do is show her that I'm not afraid. That I'm not interested in her game and I'm not feeding into whatever sick fantasy she's trying to play out here.

I retch silently.

I want to run and scream and leave.

What do I fear most, Lillian or letting Lillian win? Letting her win. Though the other is a very close second.

Lillian is a hunter, and I'm her prey.

I curl my hands into fists and feel something like dried paint on them.

My body tenses.

No, please *no*.

Slowly, I raise my trembling hands in front of me. They're red. I look down and see dark splatters on my white pajama top.

Blood.

Oh God. Whose blood is it?

I frantically swipe my hands down my top, but it does little to get the dried blood off.

I look up, my head swiveling in every direction.

Where is she?

Clamping my teeth together, I take long breaths so I don't hyperventilate.

Stay calm. Breathe. Think.

Somehow, I need to get back. Lillian put me here, so there must be evidence of the path she used.

You can do this. Focus, Esme.

I crouch down and trace my footprints back to the imprint my body left in the moss. I run my hand over the dip where my head was. This is where she left me.

I look around. Which direction did they carry or drag me from?

There. Two sets of footprints pressed into the mud and moss. They're not deep, so I must have been out here a while. It's still dark; I can only just see in front of me.

You. Can. Do. This.

I have to get back to camp before sunrise.

Crawling on my hands and knees, I find the next set of footprints and the next.

Please let this take me back to camp and not to wherever Lillian is hiding.

I place one palm down and then the other and shuffle forward.

My breath swirls in front of me.

The ground is cool and damp, and my knees are probably covered in mud by now. I sink softly into the ground every time I move. I wish I would sink completely.

A rustling in a tree above me makes me freeze. Shit. My stomach rolls.

Long pine tree branches reach out, some touching the branches of other trees like the whole forest is connected.

It was just a bird.

Move.

I crawl again, following the indentations in the moss.

A cackling that sounds like it's coming from every direction rings through the woods, bouncing off the trees.

I sit up and look around, but I can barely see anything through the mist.

Nope. Screw crawling, I need to go *now*.

Forcing myself to my feet, I take off. My head is clearer, and I don't feel dizzy anymore. I have a better chance of finding camp now. I can do this.

Lillian can go to hell.

I fly between trees, following the footprints.

The cackling sings out again. I whimper, pushing myself even faster.

She's *not* going to get me.

Rounding a tree, I stop dead in my tracks and I dry heave.

I clench my fists. Lillian has killed another deer. I blink hard, hoping the image will disappear. It doesn't. She tied the deer to a tree upside down.

Gagging, I press one wrist to my mouth. The deer has been cut open. A large gash stretches the length of its body and everything that should be inside is outside. The gory red mess of organs lies on the ground beneath it.

Lillian is a psychopath.

And I *have* to get out of here.

I pant, sprinting through the forest as if I know where I'm going. Mist parts as I run through it. My arms swing with every step, sending me flying a little faster. My gym teacher swore by pumping your arms to increase your speed, and I'll try anything.

Images of the deer and the blood on my hands flash through my mind, spurring me on. I might be scared to the core, but I won't give in to her.

Whatever she throws at me, I will fight.

Yes!

I whimper as I come to the edge of the forest. I've made it.

"Esme." Lillian laughs from behind me.

Go.

I race along the lake, never slowing.

Kayla and I need to do something drastic and soon because Lillian is getting *way* worse.

I sob as I run up the stairs to my cabin, and then stop. I just want to get to my friend.

Placing my hand on the doorknob, I take a breath and quietly open the door. I lock the damn thing behind me and tiptoe into my room.

She could have killed me tonight.

Jesus. Lillian *kidnapped* me.

We were wrong. She *does* want to hurt us.

49

In my room, I lean against the door and then sink to the floor. My breath comes out heavy and desperate. She had me and she could have easily killed me.

She's in control and there is nothing we can do.

That *can't* be true.

"Kayla," I rasp as quietly as I can manage, clawing the floor.

I need help.

I blink and burning tears streak down my face. "Kayla, *please.*"

She jumps awake, flicks on the lamp and props herself up on her elbows. "What? *Esme?*"

The room floods with light and I slump against the door.

I'm back and safe.

You are not safe here!

When Kayla's eyes land on me, her mouth pops open.

Slipping out of bed, she pads toward me.

"Oh my God, what happened to you?" she asks. "You're covered in dirt and . . . blood!"

"I woke up in the forest."

"You did *what?*"

I shake my head, trying to make sense of it. "I went to sleep here and woke up in the middle of the forest with blood on me."

"Jesus."

Kayla rushes to close the distance between us and wraps her arms around me.

I fall into her embrace. "I didn't know what was going on. I was so scared," I sob. My chest caves and I almost drop to the floor again.

"It's okay. It's okay," she hushes me, her hands shaking. "Come on."

She helps me walk to the bed and sits me on her bunk. I stare at the window, half expecting Lillian's face to be on the other side.

"How did you get there?"

"I—I don't know," I tell her. "I don't remember anything other than what I told you. I think Lillian drugged me. She must have!"

Kayla stands and grabs a bottle of water off the chair. She opens the lid and takes a towel from a pile in the closet.

I watch as she kneels in front of me and wets the towel.

"You're going to be okay, Esme."

Am I?

It doesn't feel like it. I'm cold and tired and I just want to go home.

What we did that night was bad, but we don't deserve this.

"She must have drugged you as well," I say.

Kayla nods. "Yes, I figured."

Her voice is small and squeaky.

She's scared.

She wipes my hands with the towel and smears some of the blood.

Clenching my teeth, I turn away.

"She did this to me," I say, my vision blurring with tears.

"And you survived." Kayla scrubs a little harder. "Whatever the little psycho is doing, we can beat her."

Can we? She drugged us and hauled me into the woods.

"Esme, where did the blood come from?"

The deer flashes in my mind.

"When I was running, I found it."

"Found what?"

"A deer, a small one. It was tied to a tree."

Kayla scrubs even harder, like she's trying to take off a layer of skin. "Tied?"

I close my eyes. "Upside down, cut all the way down the middle and—"

"Stop! Please don't finish telling me, Esme."

"I'm sorry." I snap my teeth together.

She doesn't want to hear it. I had to *see* it.

"There, all clean."

I look at my hands. "Thank you."

"Take your clothes off. I'll bag them. You can wash in here with the towel and water, and then we'll get you changed."

"Keep the clothes. In case."

"In case of what?"

"In case they're needed for evidence."

"We're not telling anyone what we did, Esme!"

"We might not have a choice. We'll hide them for now."

"Fine. You get yourself washed."

What I really want is a shower, but it's four in the morning.

I stand and strip off my clothes. Kayla stuffs them in a plastic bag, which she hides at the bottom of the cupboard.

She hands me the bottle of water and towel. I manage what's probably the least effective wash of my life, but it's the best I have right now.

"Here, put these on," she says softly, handing me fresh pajamas.

I curl my hands tightly around my heart pajamas and hold them to my chest. "Kayla, what are we going to do?"

We're too calm. I want to freak out properly.

Yeah, because that's going to get us far.

"We figure this out in the morning," she says.

"Are you suggesting we go back to sleep?" I look at the bottle in my hand and my face falls. "Where did you get this water?"

Kayla drops the plastic bag in the trash can. "From the kitchen."

I whip a pile of clothes off our chair. There are two more bottles of water beneath them.

"Oh shit," Kayla says, turning the open bottle around.

"Lillian drugged these and left them in our room."

"How did she know we'd drink them tonight?"

"Because it's summer in Texas . . . and because she's watching us."

"I can't deal with that." Kayla shakes her head and clutches her hair in her fist. "I hate her. We have to do something. We can't live like this, and we can't let her get away with what she's doing to us."

"Can we just get through the night and then we'll come up with a plan."

"When do we call it quits and dial nine-one-one?"

"I don't know," I reply.

"I'm scared of people finding out. Things are going great with Jake. I finally feel more myself after being in therapy for years."

"This won't change that, Kayla."

"It will. Of course it will change that. It changes everything."

"You care too much about what people think."

She snorts. "And you don't?"

"I did. But I'm caring less and less these days."

Kayla turns. "Sleep with me?"

"Oh, I was planning to."

I stuff the spiked bottles of water in the bag with my bloody clothes. Kayla gets into bed and scoots to the wall. I turn off the light and slide in beside her.

"She's worse than I could ever imagine," she whispers.

"I knew there was something wrong with her that night, but I never imagined she would be this sick."

"I need this to be over. I can't take it."

I nod. "Me too. She's crazy and dangerous and threatened the campers if we go to the cops. They're just kids. We need to do this ourselves."

"Do *what* ourselves? What does that mean?" Kayla asks, the fear in her voice ringing through the air.

"It means we take control."

"Like how? That doesn't sound like a very good idea. What do we do precisely?"

"We're going to *her*."

50

Kayla and I are about to do something mighty stupid.

We talked last night—or early this morning, rather—and we know that if we take Lillian on ourselves, she won't have any reason to harm the others.

It was a pretty crappy realization as we're both petrified.

We just barely made it through another day. I didn't get any time alone with Olly to warn him about Lillian, but it doesn't matter now. Kayla and I have a plan to end all of this tonight.

"Night," I say to Cora as we cross paths. She is heading toward the other counselors, who are sitting by the campfire, and I'm going into our cabin.

"Sleep well, Esme."

Not likely.

Kayla jumps as I walk into our room.

"Whoa."

Her eyes are round.

"This isn't a good idea," she says.

"You want this to be over too," I remind her. "We have to make contact. No one else can stop this."

"But now? Like, you want to go outside *now?*"

"All the girls are in bed, but I think I heard some whispering. We'll leave it a little while longer."

Kayla's fingertips dig into the wood. "Esme, we should wait. Come up with a real plan, one we've thought about for longer than three minutes, and then we'll go have a chat with Lillian."

"We'll talk ourselves out of it."

"Maybe we should."

I stare at her. "Really? You're the one who wanted to send her a note."

"A note. Not go out there and find her. I'm not sure if you've realized yet, but she's not exactly a reasonable person. Don't you think she'll have something planned for when we do come face to face?"

"Yeah," I say. "That's why we need to do it on our terms. We can't give her time to plan anymore. We'll be right there, and she'll be the audience in our show."

"You need to sleep, Esme, you're delirious."

I wish I could, but I'm too wired.

"Keep a lookout for the others. When they go to bed, we're out of here."

Kayla sighs, defeated.

Walking to our window, she peeks around the blind. "The

light is still on in the multiuse cabin. Everyone around the camp-fire has either gone to join them or gone to sleep."

"Ugh, they need to go to bed. Are you coming with me?"

Kayla looks over her shoulder. "Yes, you're not doing this alone."

I smile at her even though my stomach does a flip.

What if our going together isn't a good idea? Should we let Lillian have the two people she wants to hurt alone?

We could be feeding her sick fantasy.

We're definitely doing that.

≈≈≈

Two hours later, Kayla and I both watch from the main room windows as the rest of the counselors and CITs filter into their cabins to sleep.

"Go," I whisper as Cora comes toward ours.

We dash into our room and hide behind the door.

I listen, biting my lip as Cora tiptoes into her room and closes the door.

"Now?" Kayla whispers.

"A few more minutes. Wait until she's in bed."

Kayla leans back against the wall and looks up at the ceiling. In the silence, I hear her breathing grow faster.

"Okay, let's do this," I say when the rustling in Cora's room stops.

Kayla follows me as we tiptoe out of the cabin.

The room is louder tonight, a few of the girls snoring.

The very second we step onto the porch, my plan feels weak and really stupid. Really, *really* stupid.

I close the door behind us, wincing as it clicks shut.

Am I going to let that stop me? *Nope.*

"All right," I say, zipping up my hoodie. "Let's go do this thing."

"Wait," Kayla says, gripping my wrist. "What if she turns violent?"

"We are so past that. From what we've seen, Rebekah hasn't left her cabin, so Lillian is alone. Two against one. This time we know what we're walking into and we won't underestimate her."

"What if what she wants is to harm us?"

"How much worse can it get?"

I don't know if I'm getting a fresh dose of adrenaline or of stupidity, but I know we have to do this. Lillian is becoming bolder and it's only a matter of time before one of the campers sees something or gets caught in her crazy games.

This started with Kayla and me, and it has to end with us.

We step onto the grass and quickly duck around the back of the cabin.

"Where now?" Kayla whispers. "The forest is huge."

"We start looking at the site of the fire damage."

Kayla shivers despite it being hot out. "I hate it there."

"Not my favorite place either."

"Can we not go through the woods to get there? Let's walk around the lake."

I narrow my eyes. "That's a great idea, if we want to get busted. Andy probably looks out his window periodically."

We walk along the edge of the forest, just deep enough that we should be hard to spot, especially in the dark with black clothing on.

"I should have texted my parents," Kayla mutters.

Don't bite. Don't respond.

"Really?" I say three seconds later. "We're not going to die. You don't have to say goodbye to anyone."

"Y-you don't know that."

"And if you really thought we were going to *die* tonight you wouldn't have left the cabin."

"Can we not argue, Esme?" she snaps.

"Can you be a little less pessimistic, Kayla?"

"You're arguing with me."

Yep, and while we're arguing, you're not stressing out about Lillian.

I bet she's somewhere watching us. I want to look for her, but, one, I don't want to freak Kayla out, and, two, I think Lillian will want to see where we're going before she reacts.

The feeling of being safe at this particular moment clashes with everything I've felt over the past week.

"How do you think Rebekah has been able to keep up this lie the whole time?" Kayla asks.

I shrug, even though she can't see the movement. "Some people lie as naturally as they breathe. Rebekah thinks she's on some revenge mission with Lillian. They both hate us for what we did."

Kayla looks at me. "But this isn't really Rebekah's fight, right? How far would she go for someone else's revenge?"

"We'll be fine."

I don't want to answer her question, or I'll turn around and hide under my bed.

Kayla whips one arm out. "What was that?"

I look around and bite my lip. "What? I didn't hear anything. What did you hear?"

"Someone walking."

My pulse thuds. "Lillian. That's not surprising. Come on, we're almost there."

"You're not scared?" Kayla asks, her eyes wide.

"Did you really think she wouldn't show? She's probably been behind us the whole time."

Wrong thing to say, Esme.

Kayla gasps.

"Don't freak out yet," I tell her. "We're going to be fine. I promise."

She stumbles beside me. "You can't promise that. I don't want to die." Her voice trembles.

"You won't die."

I can't promise her anything, but I would do anything to protect her.

Kayla grabs my arm, her fingertips digging into my flesh.

We pass a wooden Private Property sign. We're at the camp's edge.

"I hate walking past these," Kayla says, running one hand over the sign.

Another three minutes and we're there. We walk into the circle.

"What now?" Kayla mutters, her eyes large and alert.

"Now we wait. She'll show."

To be honest, I'm sure she's already here, watching.

My stomach lurches.

Where was Olly watching from that night? What tree did he hide behind? Why didn't he help Lillian? She knew he wasn't with us and that he wasn't responsible.

Did Jake really see nothing?

"Olly had nothing to lose by helping Lillian that night," I say.

Kayla turns to me. "Huh?"

"He said Jake called him and he ran, but why? I don't understand why he wouldn't help."

"We didn't help either, Esme."

"We were responsible for the fire and needed to run. But if we stumbled across a fire and saw a person hurt, we would help."

That, at least, I can say with absolute certainty. We didn't know how bad she was hurt.

"Esme," a low musical voice sings.

I whip my head around to where I think it came from.

"What the hell?" Kayla mutters.

"Looks like Lillian is here."

"Rebekah too?" she asks, gasping.

"I don't think so," I whisper. "Remember, she didn't leave her cabin. At least not before us. Maybe she has the night off from villain duty."

"Esme."

Kayla squeezes my hand so hard my fingers grind together.

Okay. Be brave.

"Lillian, we're bored with this," I say.

"What are you doing?" Kayla's voice is low.

"No one is impressed with your stupid juvenile games," I continue. "You're stalking a camp for *children*. Grow up and show yourself so we can deal with this rationally."

Words are coming out of me as if I've summoned every ounce of courage I own.

I wish Kayla would slap her hand over my mouth.

But this has gone on long enough, and I'm so done. I can't spend another day half watching four girls and half watching the woods.

"You're going to get us killed!" Kayla snaps.

"No, I'm going to finish this."

"Perfect Kayla and Esme, loved by everyone at camp."

Kayla and I look up at the same time and see a girl, a couple years older than us, appear from the trees.

She's here.

She's angry.

And she's armed.

51

My dad owns a gun. I've fired guns at the shooting range. I've never been particularly scared of them before.

It's very different when you're staring down the barrel of one as your stalker points it at your face.

Kayla steps closer, her side plastered to mine.

I lift my chin to appear unafraid, but my skin is crawling.

Don't show fear.

"Hello, Lillian," I say.

She steps into view and tilts her head. She's wearing a black hoodie with her dark hair in a ponytail and hanging out from the hood. "I'm honored you remember me."

"It's hard to forget when your initials are carved into my bedroom wall."

Lillian glowers.

I'm being catty.

I'm pissed.

"There is a gun aimed at your head," she says.

"You've put children at risk."

"I would never hurt a child!"

"You've scared plenty of them."

"Collateral."

Nice.

"Why didn't you come talk to us?"

"Why didn't you stop and help me?"

My stomach drops. *Rein it in, Esme!*

I wince, my face heating with shame. "We are so sorry about that night, Lillian. It was . . . the worst night of our lives. I wish I could turn back time and do everything differently. It's a poor excuse, but we were young and petrified."

"It *is* a poor excuse. Half of my body is scarred for life. I spent a month in the hospital. My family ended up bankrupt and we lost our house because we didn't have enough money for medical care. I've been following you two on social media for two years. Your lives are perfect."

That's not true.

"Almost everything on social media is perfect," I say. "It's not reality. My life isn't perfect, and I'm far from it."

Lillian's lips curl viciously. "You definitely aren't perfect, Esme, but no one knows that because you never told anyone what happened."

"I'm sorry. We were *scared.*"

"You ruined so many lives that night and you don't even care."

"We care. We—"

"Shut up!"

I jump back at the acid in her voice.

Her free hand meets the one around the handle of the gun, steadying her aim.

I raise my palms. "Okay, okay. Look, we can talk. Please believe me, Lillian, we never wanted you to get hurt that night."

"Did you see Jake and Olly that night?" Lillian asks.

"No," I tell her. So she did see Jake. What did he and Olly do that night?

And since when did Kayla lose the ability to speak?

"Have you been watching us at home?" I ask, afraid to hear the answer.

"Of course I have. Since Kayla's disastrous cheerleading tryout."

God. That was when we were sophomores. Lillian has spent days, months, *years* coming up with the perfect revenge. She found us in Pennsylvania.

"Your friend mute?"

Kayla pushes harder into me.

"Scared," I say. "You have a gun pointed at us. Why don't you lower it and we can talk? We'll answer any questions you have. I'll find a way to make you believe how sorry we are."

"Let's take a walk," Lillian says.

Kayla shakes her head.

Lillian's cold blue eyes turn black. "No? You're saying no to me?"

"Where do you want us to go?" I ask, to get her mind off Kayla's reluctance.

She wants us on her terms. We decided to confront her and

now she's trying to take back control. Surely the gun gives her enough of that?

"I have a place," Lillian says.

I grit my teeth. "Okay. Where is this place?"

"In the forest. An abandoned cabin that's mine now. You two should be used to cabins in the woods. Let's. Go." She inches her chin to the side.

I take Kayla's hand and pull her along. "No, Esme," she whispers, trying to tug me back toward camp.

"We have no choice. It'll be fine," I tell her.

"You don't know that!"

No, I don't.

"Hurry up, ladies! We haven't got all night."

Why haven't we got all night?

What exactly does Lillian plan to do before sunrise?

52

We slowly walk deeper into the forest with Lillian right behind us. I can't see the gun, but I feel its presence like a dark cloud following us, ready to shoot daggers of lightning.

Beside me, Kayla's body shakes violently, her breath coming in short pants. Her fear is feeding mine.

We can't give up.

I try to make eye contact with her so I can calm her down before she has a panic attack.

What do we do? We could fight Lillian now and speed this whole thing up. Maybe we'll get away. Or do we go along with her and hope a better opportunity to run comes up? Once we reach her destination, she will have full control. That's not a position I want to be in.

I should try to get the gun, to knock it away from her and grab it. We'd be in charge then.

Seems like a semi-decent plan. Unless she's further back than she sounds, and I can't reach the gun.

In that case, Kayla and I are both dead.

Squinting, I see the outline of something big and square in the distance. A building.

I swallow. "Are we going in there?" I ask.

"Keep walking," Lillian barks.

That's a yes.

"Esme," Kayla whispers, her voice trembling.

"It's okay."

The pine trees around us blow in the soft breeze, like they're alive and leading the way. The only audience to whatever Lillian has planned.

Whatever she thinks is going to go down, I have to keep a clear head and fight back. Kayla and I are not going to die tonight. If that's what she even wants. Lillian is understandably angry, but *murderous?*

There's a big leap between wanting to kill someone and actually doing it.

Hunting people isn't like hunting deer.

We approach the building. It's a cabin, about the size of the staff cabin at camp.

"What is this place?" I ask.

"An old ranger's cabin. They built another one closer to town along with the new camping site. No one comes here anymore."

No one comes here anymore.

I take a breath. We're all alone out here. But we're not alone, not really. Kayla and I have each other and we're strong.

"What are you going to do?" I ask.

"Get inside, Esme."

I can hardly refuse, can I? I turn to her and I'm met with the barrel of a gun. Swallowing my nerves, I look past it to meet her eyes. "Lillian, please. You can't take this back. Whatever you do, you'll have to live with it. That's not going to be easy, it eats away at you. Trust me."

"Trust you?" Her hollow eyes round. "After that night, you expect me to trust you?"

"No, I don't, but I'm telling the truth. Living with guilt is hell. I know it's what I deserve."

"You deserve much worse than to live with a little guilt. I have burns over forty percent of my torso. It was *agony*. I'm scarred for life. What do you think living with that is like?"

I want to curl up inside myself.

"Lillian, I'm so—"

"Don't say sorry! Do *not* say sorry. Just get inside!"

Kayla whimpers and grabs hold of my arm. "Esme, we can't."

Lillian tilts her head.

"It's okay, Kayla, follow me." I take her hand. She grips mine so hard it almost crumbles.

I turn back around, and Kayla and I walk side by side, both stiff with fear, toward the door.

Kayla reaches out. I watch her hand shake around the doorknob.

"Inside," Lillian barks.

I don't look at Kayla as we step inside the cabin because I don't want to see her fear. I told her that everything would be okay. I'm not sure it will be.

The room looks warm and inviting. There's a stone fireplace, and a lamp sitting on a table, glowing orange. There's a fluffy white rug on the floor and a small leather sofa with a red blanket draped over the back.

In one corner is a little kitchen with a kettle and a microwave. Two doors are at the back of the cabin. I assume one is a bathroom. The other I don't want to know. It was probably an office before, but who knows what Lillian is using it for.

The cabin looks quaint and comfortable. Not exactly what you'd expect for a villain's lair.

"Sit down," Lillian instructs, pointing with the gun toward the love seat. Kayla and I don't hesitate. We have to be careful.

There will be no silly and disorganized escape plan.

I sink into the soft, worn leather and look up at Lillian. She stands close to the fireplace and faces us. That's when I see what's on the wall behind her. A photo collage. Loads of photos of me and Kayla. Ones from when she was chasing us through the woods, ones of us at camp, and even ones of us sleeping.

I press my lips together so I won't react.

The fire is littered with ashes. She's been lighting it. It's too hot to need a fire, even at night. What has she been burning?

I'm certain I don't want to know.

"What are we doing here, Lillian?" I ask.

"We need to have a conversation."

"We could have had that anywhere. You know where we live. Why all this?"

Kayla nudges me as if she thinks I'm going too far. *Me.* Lillian has been messing with us for weeks. She slaughtered a deer, drugged us and left creepy notes and messages. She scared a camp full of kids and now she's freaking kidnapped us and *I'm* the one who has gone too far?

"Do you really not get it? You ruined my life!" Saliva sprays from her mouth as she bares her teeth at us.

I meet her eyes. "I get that, and I can tell you how sorry we are and how much we regret it, but it seems that's not good enough. You won't accept that we wish that night could have been different. Nothing we say or do will make this better, so why are we really here?"

Her head tilts again like she's unsure. But I know she has absolutely thought this through. She knows what she wants from us. She can exact her revenge, but that will never make things right. Is she just now accepting that?

"Look, whatever you do here tonight isn't going to make up for the fact that a terrible thing happened to you. Hurting us will make you feel better for about two minutes and then you're back where you started. It changes *nothing.*"

She levels the gun at my forehead. "You don't know what you're talking about!"

"Yes, I do, and you know I'm right."

"Shut up, Esme!" Kayla hushes me.

What are we supposed to do if we can't talk to her? Lillian wants something from us; otherwise she would have just shot us in the forest.

"Kayla's very close to getting a bullet in her skull," Lillian says to me.

I feel Kayla shudder. She whimpers, then clamps her mouth shut.

"She's scared and confused," I say. "We don't know what you actually want. Do you just have questions?"

"Do I have questions?" Lillian's manic laughter cuts through my heart. "I have a lot of questions."

"We'll answer anything," I say softly. Maybe I can get her talking about that night and draw some emotion out of her other than rage.

"Why did you sneak out?" she asks.

"There was this group of older kids and they would sneak out. We weren't actually friends with them; they were too cool to be seen with us. But we thought if we snuck out too, they might like us. It was stupid, but we were kids."

Lillian scoffs.

"We're sorry that things got so out of hand . . . but you made mistakes that night too."

I'm dancing on the edge here. Calling her out isn't my finest idea, but Kayla and I aren't taking all the blame.

Lillian's eyes narrow. "You let me burn. You *ran*."

I close my eyes against the image of Kayla throwing Lillian backward. In that second, she was just reacting; we never intended for Lillian to get hurt, but she landed in the fire, knocking the wood onto the ground.

Lillian tilts her head. "Now I'm going to light a fire and do the same to you."

53

My eyes fly open.

"Burn us? No. No, no, no!" Kayla gasps for air.

I squeeze her hand. *Please calm down.*

"Or I could just shoot you."

My mind spins so fast I can barely catch my breath.

Five dolls. Four with their eyes crossed out. She wanted us dead this whole time.

Bile hits the back of my throat.

Lillian's eyes look straight through us. "You think I'm crazy, but you have no idea what that night was like for me. I can still feel the overwhelming pain and smell my burned flesh. I couldn't call for help. My dad is . . . not a nice man. I was scared what would happen."

"What did you do?"

"I couldn't call for help," she repeats. "Everyone would know that I had run away. You don't understand, I couldn't let that happen."

"What did you do?" I ask again.

"I dragged myself to the lake. I tried to soothe my burns in the water, but it only made things worse."

Kayla gasps.

"Someone else must have called the cops, because I eventually heard sirens. I ran with everything left in me. When I got home, I set fire to my bedroom and that's how my parents think I got burned. We all got out, but our house was ashes." She smirks. "My hair straighteners were blamed."

"Jesus."

I press one hand against my rolling stomach.

Lillian was ten. She did all of that before she hit puberty. The hunting, mutilating animals, and burning down her freaking house! She set fire to her home so she wouldn't get into trouble. And she thinks she's better than us?

"Why didn't you tell anyone? The fire in the woods wasn't your fault."

"That wouldn't have mattered to my dad."

"Okay," I say, trying to wrap my head around this. I need to talk to her as if this is all totally normal behavior. "He would have blamed you?"

"He's not a forgiving man. A lot of people respect and look up to him. They think he's an amazing husband and father. No one knows the truth. If he knew I'd snuck out of the house . . ." She shakes her head and I have to fill in the blanks.

Things would've been very bad for her.

"Are you sorry too, Kayla?" Lillian asks. "You pulled Esme away. I saw her turn back to help me."

"Kayla was scared," I say.

"I wasn't asking you!" Lillian snaps. "Kayla can speak for herself."

"Of . . . of course, I'm so sorry," Kayla says, her voice husky. She clears her throat. "W-we never meant for anyone to get hurt. We liked . . . we liked hanging out with you."

Kayla is making it sound like we were all friends that night. It's a good move.

We didn't like it, though. Lillian showed us the head of a deer that she had hunted and killed. It made me nauseous. I was instantly petrified of Lillian. Kayla completely freaked out when she saw the deer's head. She started screaming at Lillian that she was a freak.

Lillian lowers the gun to her side.

I press my arm into Kayla's, willing her to understand what I can't say. *Do not move yet.* That gun can be raised quicker than we can reach her. She's not close enough.

Kayla seems to get it or she's just thinking the same thing, because she sits perfectly still.

"Did you send that CIT pamphlet to everyone there that night?" I ask.

"Yes. I wanted you, Kayla, Jake and Olly here."

"Rebekah?"

"I met her a few years ago at a group for burn victims. She's too easy to manipulate. So desperate for a friend she would do anything."

"Why Jake and Olly?" Kayla asks.

"They watched and did *nothing*. Jake was the worst. I saw him later, when I was on my way home. He and Olly were wandering in the forest again. This time they looked right at me and saw the burns. Jake called me a psycho and pulled Olly away. They both ran. I knew then they were there the whole time. Jake's not sneering now."

Olly hadn't mentioned that.

I steal a glance at Kayla. Her eyes are wide.

"What did you do to Jake?"

Jake might have made mistakes, but he was just a scared kid. How could Lillian not see that?

Lillian's eyes sparkle as she looks at the doors in the back.

Oh God.

"He's in one of those rooms," I whisper.

Slowly, she nods. "He's very quiet."

"What did you do?"

"Go and see, Esme."

My heart stalls.

"What?"

"I'll wait here with Kayla. If you even think about escaping, I'll put a bullet through her head."

I lick my lips. "Lillian, please."

"Get up, Esme!"

With my heart in my throat, I stand up and turn toward the doors. "Which one?"

"Bathroom. Door on the left."

What could she be doing with him in the bathroom?

I wrap my trembling fingers around the doorknob and turn it slowly.

"Go on," Lillian says.

The door creaks as I nudge it open.

There is a bathtub.

Jake looks at me from the tub, eyes wide, pupils dilated.

54

I stumble back and grip the edge of the doorframe. Jake. She's killed him.

Dried blood trails from his mouth to his chin. It looks like it would flake away if you touched it. His face is pale, like a porcelain doll's.

"Find him?" Lillian asks.

My blood burns. I want to scream at the laughter in her voice.

Turning, I look at Kayla first. She shakes her head, her face crumpling.

Then I look at Lillian.

Lips pursed, dead eyes alight with satisfaction.

"Why?" I rasp.

"He doesn't care about anyone but himself. People like that make me sick. Star of the football team thinking he's better than everyone else, worth more."

"He was probably scared that night too."

Lillian scoffs. "Yes of course he was. Little Esme, always

looking for the good in people. Who are you kidding? You're not even good."

"I'm not the same person I was back then. It's been *ten years*. I've grown up, I'm stronger, and I would never make a mistake like that again. No one is the same as they were when they were eight!"

In the back of my head, I can't stop thinking, *She is a murderer.*

I was stupid to ever think we could talk this through. The revenge she wants isn't the kind that Kayla and I are supposed to survive.

Lillian thinks our deaths will make things right.

"You haven't changed that much," she says. "Neither of you told the camp that all of this involved you."

"We never thought you would do something like this," I say, nodding back toward Jake. "He's dead, Lillian. You *killed* him. How long ago?" It couldn't have been longer than a few hours. No one knew Jake was missing.

She waves her free hand. "About an hour before you came to me. He was an asshole."

"He didn't deserve to die. You could have dealt with this another way."

She rolls her eyes. "Don't advocate talking when you've spent ten years hiding your sins. It makes you a hypocrite."

"What does all of this make you?"

"*You* are the ones who hurt *me*! All I'm guilty of is speaking to you that night!"

"You terrified us with that deer's head. You ran at Kayla when she called you out on it. She only pushed you out of self-defense.

She never meant for you to fall into the fire. And now you've *killed* Jake!"

"I didn't have a choice, and he deserved everything he got. I wouldn't harm an innocent person. That's the difference between you and me."

I push away from the door. The smell from the bathroom is making my stomach churn.

"You were scared of your dad and we understand that. We were scared of our parents too. Can't you see, Lillian, we didn't feel like we had a choice either."

Her face freezes.

We all feared something that night.

I've made it sound like our parents were cruel as well. Maybe she'll relent if she thinks we shared a similar childhood.

"Shut up!" she screams. "Shut up, you bitch. You have *no* idea what you're talking about."

I raise my hands, palms facing her. "Okay, I'm sorry. I didn't understand."

Except that I do. I understand fully. Fear can be debilitating.

"Okay," Kayla says. "Here's what we're going to do. Jake was a bully to you, so you did what you had to."

Lillian looks surprised but nods. "He was evil."

"Yes," Kayla replies. "But thanks to you, he will never hurt anyone again. We need to get rid of his body, though. If the cops find him, he can be traced to you. Your DNA will be everywhere."

My jaw drops.

What is she saying?

Kayla shakes her head at me. "Esme, this is the only way. We have a responsibility to help Lillian cover this up after what we did to her. We'll scrub Jake clean and bury him deep in the woods. Then, we'll burn this cabin to the ground."

What the hell? She was madly in love with him five minutes ago.

Lillian watches Kayla as if she's some complicated puzzle.

It's not complicated. Kayla is in full survival mode and it's disturbing. I've never seen her like this.

"You're just adding another secret to the one we've been carrying! We can't do this. It's *Jake*, Kayla!" I say.

I ignore Lillian's smirk as she watches us disagree.

"What she had to do was our fault and this is what we deserve for not doing the right thing all those years ago." Kayla stands and Lillian makes no move to stop her. "Now, let's strip his clothes off and put them in the fire."

"Stop! Do you hear yourself?"

"What's the alternative, Esme?" Kayla snaps.

Lillian kills us. But how do we live with ourselves if we help hide her murder? How do we walk away from this? What is she going to do after we bury Jake? She's never going to let us walk away.

"There has to be some other way."

"You could die with him," Lillian says. "Kayla is the one willing to do what's necessary . . . but would she help me clean up and hide her bestie's body too?"

Kayla eyes widen. She looks at me, pleading.

"Kayla?" I whisper.

THE LAKE • 729

"Don't make me do that, Esme. We made a pact ten years ago to never talk about that night. We can do that again. We'll help Lillian, and we can go home knowing that this is all over."

My head swirls with conflict and confusion.

If we do this, would Lillian really let us walk away? We can't do that to Jake or to his family.

Maybe this was Lillian's plan all along. She could be setting us up for Jake's murder.

"Kayla, this might not be what you think," I say.

"What do you think it is, Esme?" Lillian asks.

Kayla's face is red, like she wants to throw something at me. We are not going along with this blindly.

"I don't know. What happens if we help you?"

Lillian's lips curl, but her smile isn't friendly. "You go home."

"What, and we never hear from you again? Or are you now thinking that with Kayla's offer comes an opportunity?"

Kayla looks at us both.

"I'm not stupid, and neither are you, Lillian. Eventually people will start asking questions, wondering who was terrorizing the camp, why an old cabin is on fire, and where Jake went. . . . The cops will come looking. They might link it to you; after all, your DNA is all over this place. But if we help, our DNA is on his body too."

With wide eyes, Kayla looks from Lillian to me.

She was never going to let us walk away. If we're convicted of a murder she committed . . .

"I tell you what," Lillian says to Kayla. "If we kill Esme too, we'll bury her and Jake, and no one will ever know. If you refuse, you both die here today. Two bodies, three bodies, I don't mind how many I get rid of."

My stomach turns. She can't be serious.

"No," I say.

Kayla is my best friend; she would never do that.

Tell her, Kayla!

Why isn't she telling Lillian to get lost?

"Kayla!" I snap.

Tears well in her eyes. "I'm sorry. I can't die. I can't."

Her words punch the air from my lungs.

"Kayla, you're my best friend," I whisper as fear grips my throat.

She wipes tears from her cheeks. "I'm sorry, Esme, but I choose me."

55

I know I should run. I should shove Kayla into Lillian and make a run for it.

Will my legs move? *No.*

"You can't, Kayla," I say.

Lillian's smile grows. She is loving this.

Fire burns in my veins.

Turning us against each other is a bonus for her.

Kayla wipes her tears again.

"Kayla!"

She doesn't look at me; instead she turns her head toward Lillian.

"How does that feel?" Lillian asks. "To have your best friend in the whole world turn against you so easily. There was barely any hesitation."

Kayla may be petrified of dying, but I *never* expected this.

"That's not my best friend talking," I say.

Kayla cowers.

She's consumed by fear. Lost.

I step closer to the sofa.

Lillian aims the gun steadily at my head but makes no move to pull the trigger. Instead she watches what I'm about to do with Kayla. . . .

Kayla doesn't meet my eyes, but she turns her head, showing me that she knows I'm there.

"Don't, Esme," she whispers. "I hate this."

Lillian is a few feet from Kayla, and the fireplace is a step or two behind her.

I shove Kayla with every ounce of strength I have. She flies backward with a scream and into Lillian.

Get out.

I take off without looking back. Something slams against the wall. The thud sounded like a head, but I can't be sure.

I yank the door open and sprint outside.

My legs burn as I try to get away as fast as possible.

Behind me, I hear Lillian shout.

Then I hear two sets of footsteps.

I look back, but the thick forest is dark. I can't see them, but I know they're coming. I take a path similar to the one I remember, but now I'm deeper in the woods.

I have not been out here nearly enough to know where I'm going without a map and compass.

I can figure this out. I can get away from Lillian—and *Kayla*—and get help.

Stay calm. Don't overthink.

Stepping around a tree, I run to the next one and plaster myself against it.

I take a breath and listen carefully, willing that sense to take over. Lillian has a gun and Kayla is broken beyond recognition.

She's scared right now. The thought of imminent death has made her lose herself. When she stops and thinks, even for a second, she will see what a monumental mistake she has made and beg for my forgiveness.

Above me, the sky rumbles. I raise my eyes and see a fork of lightning through the leaves.

A thunderstorm. That's going to make it harder to hear them, but it will also make it harder for them to hear me.

I peer around the trunk in the direction I need to go. No one is around; the forest is dead quiet.

They could be hiding and watching me. Lillian has been watching in the shadows for weeks. For *years*. Kayla doesn't know how to sneak around, though; she will be tripping and falling all over the place.

She's a liability to Lillian. What happens when Lillian realizes that?

I press my hand to my stomach and breathe through the wave of nausea. What if she kills Kayla?

The sky rumbles again, and the thunder is followed by a quick flash of lightning.

Forget Kayla.

I look around again. Nobody. Pushing off the tree, I sprint to the next one, planting my feet on the ground quickly and quietly like a deer escaping a predator. My heart thuds faster with every step.

I'm not supposed to be the prey out here.

The sky lights up again and thunder rolls.

I still don't know exactly where I am, but I think I'm close to camp.

Trees whiz past in a blur of brown and green.

I pant harder, trying to get enough oxygen.

You need to hurry up.

Lillian could be anywhere.

If I don't get out of here, I'm going to die.

Go, Esme! Now!

With my stomach tied in knots, I push myself to go even faster. My feet hit the ground harder and my pulse thuds so fast I can't hear anything else.

I dodge trees, bouncing off each leg to get around each obstacle as quickly as I can. The sky lights up. I push harder.

A slicing pain in my side makes me double over, but I don't stop. I can't stop.

Thunder cracks through the air.

Breaking through the trees, I fall to my knees. Camp.

I raise my head and gasp.

"What is going on?" I whisper, vision blurred.

With my last ounce of strength, I haul myself to my feet and grab a branch so I don't fall.

Four cop cars. Red and blue lights flash across the camp, bouncing off trees.

What happened here while we were in that little cabin with Lillian?

We were gone for only two hours.

Turning, I lose my footing and slam right into Rebekah.

56

I leap backward and she shows her palms. "I'm not goin' to hurt ya."

"You were working with Lillian!"

"Yes, but I never expected . . . *this.* She was so broken when I met her at a support group a few years ago. I thought she just wanted to frighten y'all, to make you think about what you did and to be sorry. She said she wanted you to be as scared as she was that night. I got that, so I agreed to come here as a CIT and help her."

I back up, my eyes scanning the forest. I haven't heard Lillian or Kayla for a while. That's both reassuring and unnerving.

"What changed your mind?"

Rebekah takes a breath. "When I went to the cabin to find her a little while ago, I saw . . ."

"Jake."

She nods, wide-eyed. "I knew she saw him that night too, but I never thought . . . This is crazy, Esme. We need to get away from her. Where's Kayla?"

I swallow the urge to throw up. "She's with Lillian."

Rebekah gasps, one hand flying to her heart. "She killed her, too?"

"No," I say. "Kayla's on her side. We were in the cabin and Lillian said either we both die or just me. Kayla chose herself."

Rebekah's jaw drops. "What? How could she?"

I don't know, but she did. Somehow I need to get Kayla back.

"What's happening here?" I ask, looking around.

"It's been evacuated. The cops got an anonymous call about an hour ago about someone stalking the camp. The cops took all the kids to the police station until their parents can pick them up. I came back to find you and Kayla. I'm sorry, Esme. I didn't know how out of hand this would get. Lillian never made it sound like she wanted to hurt anyone."

"She wanted revenge."

"I swear I didn't know that she was so dangerous."

"Is anyone still here?"

"Andy. He's talking with the cops."

"Who would call the cops? We all agreed we wouldn't. It doesn't make sense." I lean into the tree I'm holding and try to make the pieces fit together.

"I don't know, Esme, but we need to get away from the forest."

"Esme!"

Rebekah and I jolt at the same time and swing around.

"Olly." My jaw drops. I start to run to him but stop myself. "What really happened the night of the fire? Jake was with you the whole time?"

He looks over my shoulder. I do the same. No one is there.

"I left him out of the retelling, just like you left Kayla out. After the fire started, Jake and I didn't go back to my brother. We stayed and watched the whole thing. Lillian saw us. We ran and eventually bumped into her again a little while later. Jake told her off. I didn't want to admit that we were scared of a girl, but we so were. After that, Jake and I agreed to keep quiet," Olly says.

"You saw her after, when she was burned, and didn't help her or tell me!"

"You're lecturing me on morality?"

"Hey, y'all can't do this now!" Rebekah snaps. "Lillian could be here any freakin' second!"

A shrill siren cuts through the air as another cop car races along the road and into camp. We watch from across the lake as it screams to a halt.

"Let's go," I say, and start running for help.

At least that's what I want to do, but I'm stopped by the bang of a gun.

The hollow sound radiates through me.

I turn. Rebekah and Olly are looking at me with wide eyes.

Was it me? Did Lillian shoot me?

I don't feel pain.

Then I see it. A red circle spreading across Olly's shirt.

"No!" I scream as he falls to his knees.

Lillian walks into view with Kayla right behind her.

I drop to the ground in front of Olly and place my hands over the wound.

His blood is red-hot and seeps between my fingers. "You're going to be okay," I tell him.

His eyes travel behind me and he whispers, "Esme."

Turning slowly, I look over my shoulder. Lillian is close. Kayla cowers behind her, eyes trained on the ground.

"Now you can join your disgusting friend Jake," Lillian says to Olly.

"You're a psycho," he spits.

Her lip curls. "I'd finish the job for that, but you'll bleed out soon and I need the bullets."

"Lillian, what happened?" Rebekah asks.

"Oh my God, stop. Do you know how tragic you are? Quit the poor-me act, Rebekah, it's boring. Get on the ground beside them."

"Lillian, can we talk about—"

Bang.

I blink in horror as blood splatters from Rebekah's forehead and she falls heavily to the ground.

I whimper, pressing my lips together.

Rebekah's eyes lose focus and her jaw drops open.

"You have to get out of here, Esme," Olly croaks, wincing in pain.

How?

"I can't leave you. I can't move my hands. She's right, you'll bleed out."

"Don't worry about me. Try to get back."

I shake my head, my eyes welling with tears until Olly is a blur. "Please hold on."

"Esme," Lillian sings.

My body ripples in disgust at the excited tone in her voice.

"Hold your hand over the wound and press hard," I tell Olly.

Olly replaces my hands with his hand and winces.

I rise to my feet and face Lillian. "You're sick."

I'm done trying to play nicely with her.

Lillian smirks. "Do you think I care what you think of me?"

"You were burned, something terrible happened to you, but everything that's happened since then has been on you. No one else is at fault here but you. Stop pretending what you're doing is justified. It's not. You're a *murderer*."

"Shut up!" she screams.

"Wait," Kayla says.

Lillian stills and glances to her side.

Kayla opens her mouth and her eyes widen when she realizes she has nothing to say.

"Go ahead, Kayla," Lillian instructs.

"Um . . . I was thinking . . ."

Lillian turns her head.

I take the chance. Screaming, I launch forward and knock into her.

Lillian falls back, shouting out.

I spot a rock. *Do it.*

Without hesitation, I pick the rock up and smash it against the side of her face.

"Run, Esme!" Olly shouts.

I leap to my feet and turn to him. "I'll help you up."

"She's not dead. Go and get help!" he shouts, still pressing his hand against his wound.

Olly . . .

"Go!" he rasps, spluttering. Dying.

I take off, my eyes stinging with tears. Maybe I should have killed her. But I don't want to have to live with that.

I sprint toward the lake, but a third gunshot brings me crashing down. I freeze.

Gasping, I see Kayla stagger toward me holding her side. I run to her.

"Kayla, no!"

Her legs give way as I reach her.

"Go, Esme," she croaks.

I fall to the ground and cradle her. "Oh my God, Kayla. I'm so sorry. I'm so, so sorry."

"No, I'm so sorry, Esme. I was scared and I didn't think."

"Why did she shoot you?"

"She told me to shoot you, and I refused. I was trying to run away with you."

"Kayla," I whisper as tears stream down my cheeks. "You're not going to die, you know that, right?"

"I—I feel cold," she murmurs. "It's okay, though, because I just realized I would do anything to protect you."

When it came down to it, she chose me.

Curling around her, I sob. "Please don't leave me."

Her breathing rattles and my eyes widen. "Kayla!"

Something lands beside me.

I look down. *What?*

Squinting, I reach down and pick up something black from the grass.

My breath is knocked from my lungs when I realize it's the gun.

Suddenly, I know who called the cops.

Kayla's body relaxes, her full weight laying in my arms, and she takes one final, ragged breath.

No. I sob, my heart splintering into pieces.

"Police! Freeze!"

My heart stills. I look up and see Lillian smiling from between the trees. She turns and silently disappears into the forest.

Then, with wide eyes, I turn to find five gun barrels pointing at me.

Kayla, Rebekah, Olly and Jake are dead, Lillian is gone . . . and I'm holding the gun.

ACKNOWLEDGMENTS

As always, I would first like to say thank you to my husband and sons. I love you guys.

Sam and Vic. What would I do without you and our "Ungodly Hour" morning sprints? Though recently we've been spending more time drinking coffee and sending each other GIFs than writing!

Kim, thank you for keeping me organized and taking care of my Facebook reader group. Tasha's Tribe is an awesome place for my readers because of you.

Ariella and Molly, thanks for being part of this journey with me. You are the best team.

Wendy, Alison, Colleen and Heather. Thank you for working with me on this book. You guys are my rock stars!

And to my readers, THANK YOU SO MUCH.

DON'T BE AFRAID.
BE TERRIFIED.

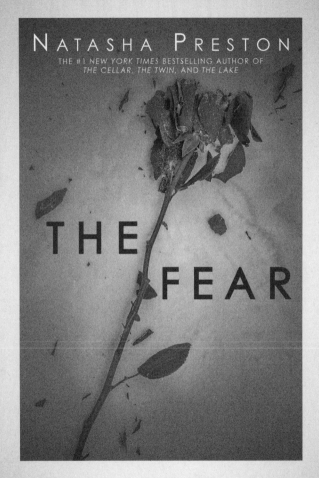

It's just a stupid meme—people reposting and sharing their biggest fear. But when her classmates start turning up dead—dying in the way that they said scared them the most—Izzy knows it's no joke.

With each death hitting closer to home, Izzy sets out to try to stop the killer. Soon she's on a path that will lead her right to the killer . . . and her own worst nightmare.